# Praise for the historical fantasies of Judith Tarr

## Kingdom of the Grail

"Eloquently penned mythical history. . . . Drawn with depth and precision, Tarr's array of characters are as engaging as her narrative is enchanting." —*Publishers Weekly*

"Enchanting. . . . Ms. Tarr weaves fresh magic into the strands of one of our most beloved legends, crafting a mesmerizing tale guaranteed to hold lucky readers absolutely spellbound." —*Romantic Times*

"A master of historical fantasy . . . Tarr makes the blending of medieval legends, often attempted by lesser writers with indifferent success, into a worthwhile addition for most fantasy collections." —*Booklist*

"Combines remnants of Camelot with the *Song of Roland* into an exciting story. The key to the plot is Ms. Tarr's uncanny ability to make her primary and secondary players seem so real that both the fantasy elements and the historical perspective appear genuine. The novel will charm fans of the Arthurian and Roland legends and medieval epic adventures." —Harriet Klausner

"With her customary artistry and feel for period detail, the author of *The Shepherd Kings* weaves together the legends of Camelot and the *Song of Roland*, creating a tapestry rich with love and loyalty, sorcery, and sacrifice. Tarr's ability to give equal weight to both history and myth provides her historical fantasies with both realism and wonder. Highly recommended." —*Library Journal*

*continued . . .*

## The Shepherd Kings

"Never one to gracefully deposit the reader at the beginning of a new story, [Judith Tarr] starts this one with a bang. Tarr has once again created a powerful female character . . . with the brains to match her beauty. [She] brings all her research skills to the fore as she dramatically describes the final battle. . . . *The Shepherd Kings* has more excitement, color and spectacle, undiluted sex, intrigue and adventure than one ordinarily finds in several novels by less talented storytellers."
—*The Washington Post*

## Throne of Isis

"In this carefully researched, well-crafted novel about Antony and Cleopatra, Tarr weaves . . . a marvelously entertaining tapestry."
—*Booklist*

"Tarr's historical outline is unexceptionable, her wealth of cultural detail impeccable."
—*Kirkus Reviews*

## Pillar of Fire

"A book that can be savored and enjoyed on many levels—perfect for beach reading, what with its lively portrait of enduring love between two who can never publicly acknowledge their commitment, and for such higher pleasures as those afforded by finely wrought characterizations and insights into the minds and hearts of the mighty."
—*Booklist*

"With her usual skill, Tarr combines fact and fiction to create yet another remarkably solid historical novel. This is a highly entertaining blend of romance, drama and historical detail."
—*Publishers Weekly*

## King and Goddess

"A dramatic tale."                                    —*Publishers Weekly*

"Pleasingly written . . . provides fascinating insights into Egyptian history and daily life. Readers lured by history in general and Egypt in particular will enjoy it."     —*The Washington Post*

"This historic fiction brings the turbulent era alive."
                                          —*St. Louis Post-Dispatch*

## The White Mare's Daughter

"Culture clashes, war and goddess worship set the stage for Tarr's well-rounded and lively prehistoric epic. Tarr's skillful juxtaposition of two vastly different yet spiritually similar societies gives a sharp edge to this feminist epic. [Her] fully fleshed-out characters and solid, intricate plotting add depth to an entertaining saga."                      —*Publishers Weekly*

## Queen of Swords: The Life of Melisende, Crusader Queen of Jerusalem

"Tarr vividly portrays the contrast between the self-righteous, primitive Crusaders and the cosmopolitan, sophisticated residents of the sun-blasted land the Franks call Outremer."
                                          —*Publishers Weekly*

## Lord of the Two Lands

"Her prose is lean and powerful, and she exerts admirable control over an impressive cast of characters, some imaginary, others not."                               —*The Washington Post*

# PRIDE OF KINGS

## JUDITH TARR

A ROC BOOK

ROC
Published by New American Library, a division of
Penguin Putnam Inc., 375 Hudson Street,
New York, New York 10014, U.S.A.
Penguin Books Ltd, 27 Wrights Lane,
London W8 5TZ, England
Penguin Books Australia Ltd, Ringwood,
Victoria, Australia
Penguin Books Canada Ltd, 10 Alcorn Avenue,
Toronto, Ontario, Canada M4V 3B2
Penguin Books (N.Z.) Ltd, 182–190 Wairau Road,
Auckland 10, New Zealand

Penguin Books Ltd, Registered Offices:
Harmondsworth, Middlesex, England

First published by Roc, an imprint of New American Library,
a division of Penguin Putnam Inc.

First Printing, September 2001
10  9  8  7  6  5  4  3  2  1

 REGISTERED TRADEMARK—MARCA REGISTRADA

LIBRARY OF CONGRESS CATALOGING-IN-PUBLICATION DATA:

Tarr, Judith
Pride of kings / Judith Tarr.
p.   cm.
ISBN 0-451-45847-8 (alk. paper)
1. Great Britain—History—Richard I, 1189–1199—Fiction. 2. Richard I, King of
England, 1157–1199—Fiction. 3. Crusades—First, 1096–1099—Fiction.   I. Title.
PS3570.A655 P75 2001
813'.54—dc21      2001019596

Printed in the United States of America
Set in Galliard
Designed by Leonard Telesca

PUBLISHER'S NOTE

*This one is for Marty
with many, many thanks*

# PRIDE OF KINGS

# PRELUDE

Summer clung that year with breathless persistence. The heat of it had killed King Henry. Now Henry's son came to his throne on a day so hot, so lifeless and still, that not even the dogs deigned to stir out of their patches of shade.

"This is a soft spring day in Jerusalem," said William the Marshal. The sun was just coming up over the walls of the Tower of London, casting long rays across the roofs of the city and drowning in light the slow curve of the river. The east was lost in haze, the west still dim with twilight. The world between was a golden shimmer.

Richard came to lean on the parapet. Any other man about to be crowned king would have been either quivering with excitement or pale with exhaustion from the long night's vigil over holy relics and sacred signs of the realm. But Richard was as fresh as if he had slept the night through, and as calm as if this were any other day in the tale of the world.

"Jerusalem's a furnace," he said, "from everything I've heard tell."

"A foretaste of hell," William said. His skin remembered the burning of that sun through the weight of armor, the sharp catch at the throat of air as dry as the dust underfoot. In this green and misty country it seemed impossibly remote.

Richard stared into the rising sun. His eyes were full of its light. "Jerusalem," he said. "My city. Mine. God blast that Saracen who tramples it under his heel!"

William held his tongue. Richard's hands were fists, his cheeks flushed with the swift flare of anger. He did not see London at all, nor this realm of Britain, though he stood in the heart of it, waiting to be crowned its king.

William's eye caught movement beyond him, figures walking

toward them from the stair to the court below. They seemed to rise up out of the light, through the veil of morning haze that dimmed even the nearer corner of the Tower. There were three of them. One was tall. The others were smaller but no less potent to the sight that was William's gift. He nodded slightly to each of them: recognition, respect, acknowledgment that the time had come on which they had all agreed.

At their coming, Richard came out of his dream of Jerusalem into the trained affability of the prince. "Neville! Ready to lose another hundred marks with the dice? And Father Hugh. And . . . my lady." He bowed over the slim white hand.

Lady Eschiva smiled at him. Richard's charm was difficult to resist—or for that matter his ruddy good looks. Whatever else the lady was, she was young and a woman, and Richard was a fine figure of a man.

Ah, thought William wryly. He was jealous. She never smiled so warmly at him.

In the dance of greeting, the four of them had taken places in a circle round the uncrowned king. Father Hugh, bishop that he was but dressed as always in the simplicity of a monk's habit, took the gate of the east, and Neville, the king's forester and gaming companion, took that of the west. Eschiva's place was the south. Which left William the north, and a clear view past Eschiva's shoulder of the morning light on the river. Boats and barges were beginning to fill it, bright with banners, celebrating the crowning of the new king.

But here they were enclosed in a globe of light, with Richard in its center. It was not complete—not until the king was consecrated. Soon. Moments now. If—

Richard looked from one to the other, frowning. "Oh, no," he said. "Not your pagan rites again. I've told you before, and I tell you yet again—"

"My lord," said Eschiva. "Lord king. The crowning in the abbey today, that makes you King of the English. But this rite will bind all Britain to you."

"Will all Britain speed me on Crusade? Will it pour out its silver for my armies? Will it arm them, horse them, help them to destroy the Infidel?"

They were silent. William's head was full of words, but none of them was either wise or useful. He knew Richard best of all of them; he had known what Richard would do, what he would say. Still he had ventured to hope that after all Richard would consent to be king in heart as well as name.

Richard laid a heavy hand on his shoulder. "Here, man. Buck up. I'm taking the crown like a good Christian king. Then I'll take Jerusalem."

"But not Britain." Eschiva's voice was almost too soft to be heard. "We guard it; we defend it. We protect it from evil. But without a consecrated king, our powers are immeasurably weaker. Would you have an England to come back to, or English from whom to reap your harvest of silver?"

"Lady," said Richard with more forbearance than he would have granted a man, "I am not a pagan. These mummeries mean nothing to me. I cry your pardon for it, but I can't do this. My whole heart is against it."

"Your heart will not be whole," Father Hugh said, "until you do it."

"No," said Richard—politely, because this was a priest of the Church and a famously holy man. But there was no shaking him.

He bowed to them all. "And now, lady, Father, my lords, I have a crowning to get to, and servants that must be beside themselves with looking for me. May the Lord Christ keep you."

That was pointed enough, and abrupt enough, too. Richard escaped before any of them could move to stop him.

With his departure, the light about them died. They were three very mortal men and a very young woman, standing on the Tower of London in the rising heat of morning.

"Well," said Neville with a kind of desperate lightness, perching on the parapet. "That's that."

"That will never be that," Father Hugh said sharply. For as saintly a man as he was, he had a remarkably quick temper. "If we don't shake some sense into that one's head before he sets the crown on it, all our labor will be for naught. We'll be four guardians without a liege lord—and Britain will be without a king."

"I do wonder," Eschiva said with relentless clarity of sight, "whether this is, after all, the true king of Britain. He chose this day, though it's marked as a day of ill omen. He refuses the fullness of the rite. He takes no thought for the realm—only for his crown, his silver, his war."

"They're all like that, these Angevins," Neville said. "It's the devil in them. They'll defy God Himself if it suits them."

"Or they'll use Him to defy the guardians of their own realm," said Father Hugh. He flung up his hands. "Ah. Well. What's done is done, and what's not done, we can't compel. We'll do what we can, and pray he comes round; or else pray that our enemies are occupied elsewhere this eon."

"Hush!" said William quickly. "Don't name them."

Father Hugh was hardly repentant, but he shut his mouth tight and crossed himself for good measure. "Gods and saints defend us," he said.

"And may they defend Britain," said Eschiva, "for surely this king will not."

The Bishop of Ely had found a miracle: a place in the city of London that was not bursting at the seams with people. It was a corner of the cloister in Westminster, of all places. The Minster itself was already full, though it was hours yet until the king came in procession to be crowned. But here was silence, a scent of incense and old stone overlaid with the sweetness of roses that grew in the garden.

He had come to pray and to meditate, and to steady his mind. A great charge was laid on him, to be justiciar of England while Richard sailed away on Crusade. He felt the weight of it bowing down his narrow shoulders. His crooked leg ached; he made an offering of the pain.

There was no wind in the world this morning, only the heavy, suffocating heat. Yet the air about him was alive. The hum of voices from the Minster, the rumble of the organ in the choir as it touched the deep notes, found resonance in his bones.

When the voice spoke, it seemed perfectly a part of that place and that moment. "William," it said. "William of Ely Isle."

He raised his head that had been bent in prayer. An angel of light stood before him, floating on wide and gleaming wings.

He fell on his face. "William," said the angel in its voice like far trumpets crying, "William the Norman."

He stiffened at that. He was a foreigner here; even the angels, it seemed, were determined to remind him of it.

"William Longchamp," the angel said, "king's servant. Do you love this realm at all?"

"I am loyal to my king," he said, choking out the words.

"But do you love the realm?"

"I am not—" he said. "I don't understand—"

"Your spirit is weak," said the angel. "Come, I give you a prayer, words spoken in the tongue of heaven. Say these words thrice, O man, and you will be strong—stronger than any mortal in Britain."

"Strong enough to serve my king?"

"Just so," said the angel.

But still the bishop would not give way. "Why? Why the likes of me?"

The angel's smile was terribly, monstrously sweet. " 'Like an earthen vessel,' " it sang, " 'more precious than gold.' You are a cup that craves to be filled. Emptiness that cries for completion. O most mortal of men, most loyal of servants, will you not serve the true king of Britain?"

Ely gasped like a runner in a race. "I live to serve my king."

"Indeed," said the angel, "you do." It bent low to the earth, where Ely was lying, and whispered in his ear, a swift flow of words that crept through the barriers of his understanding and set firm in memory.

The angel rose above him, mantling its vast white wings. "Speak!" it commanded him in ringing tones. "Speak the words!"

Obediently Ely spoke them. They rolled out of him through no will or power of his own. They shook the earth underfoot; they rent the veil of light that lay over the cloister. The scent of roses grew so strong, so supernally potent, that he came near to fainting with it.

The angel laughed. Its wings scattered in a drift of white rose petals. It danced, spinning like a whirlwind, trailing a comet's tail of silver fire. "Now," it cried. "Now it can begin!"

Ely lay in morning light that seemed as dim as dawn, abandoned, empty. With the words had gone all strength that was in him. The angel—if angel it had been—was gone. What he had done, he could not be sure of, except that he had done something: raised a power, taken down a wall, opened a gate. As to what would come in, now that gate was open . . .

He crossed himself with all the fervor that was left in him. God had blessed him, he told himself, and sent an angel, and granted him the power to speak for all of England, to ward and defend it against the Evil One. And so it was done, and well done. The king could be crowned. The kingdom could go on. And Ely—Ely had wrought it.

He allowed himself the smallest flicker of pride. It was a sin; he would do penance for it. But it was a lovely indulgence.

*   *   *

John Lackland, no longer so lacking in land now that his brother was king, had been too restless to linger with the rest of the procession. Much as he loved the pomp of ceremony and as eager as he was to stand near his brother at the crowning, nonetheless he found himself in the Minster while the morning was still young, pressed in among the crowd. There were hawkers moving through the throng of common folk outside, peddling holy relics, images of the king, sweets and pasties and sour brown ale.

Those within were a lordlier gathering. Unless they had brought food and drink of their own, they suffered the long hours in hunger and thirst, fasting like monks in the king's name. But unlike monks, they kept no vow of silence. They amused themselves with gossip and backbiting and the occasional feud, which never quite came to blows under the vault of this roof, but there was ample time later for that.

No one seemed to recognize him in plain clothes, with a hat shading his eyes. It was miserable in the heat, but too useful to cast aside. He was greatly interested to hear what people said of his brother, his family, and even, here and there, of him.

"Well, he's got land enough now," said someone nearby. "Count of Mortain, and that's just the jewel in a substantial crown."

"Will you lay a wager on how soon he tries for the king's own crown, once the king is off on Crusade?" asked someone else.

"I would, but the king's too clever: he's got the boy sworn to three years' exile before he comes to claim what's his. The Crusade will be over then; the king will be back to take him in hand."

"God grant," the second man said piously.

John's lips stretched in a mirthless smile. He had marked the two men's faces, and their garments, too. They were barons with some pretensions to wealth: one wore a heavy collar of gold that would have looked well on a prince, and the other's cotte was of silk so rich and heavy that the man's broad red face was streaming with sweat. Maybe he would have an apoplexy as the heat of the day rose. That would be a pleasant diversion.

John slipped between the two men, greatly amused as one cursed and the other aimed a cuff at him. "Insolent puppy!" one growled to the other.

He went on past a gathering of men that had the look and sound of a dogfight about to begin, and a cluster of ladies fanning themselves and passing round vials of gaggingly potent perfume. They would have done better to begin with a bath.

Past these ladies, round a circle of stout personages who must have bought their places here, since they neither looked nor dressed like nobles, he paused. The heat was no worse; there was even a breath of air where he stood. Yet he felt suddenly, terribly light-headed, as if the floor had dropped from beneath him, and he was falling free through infinite space.

He staggered but kept his feet, borne up by the press of people. Another was not so fortunate. He might not even have seen her if he had not leaned against a pillar; she was in the arch of the colonnade, under the jeweled brilliance of a window. As he straightened, gathering his whirling wits, she crumpled in the arms of a second woman.

He caught a blur of dark hair, dark eyes, but his sight was full of cream and red-gold. It was an extraordinarily beautiful lady who fainted almost at his feet. His hands were quicker than his mind; they braced the sinking weight, lowering it to the cool stone of the floor.

The lady was not unconscious as he had thought; not quite. Her lips moved. "The walls," she said in Latin, which rather startled him. "The walls are broken. I must—mend—"

"Hush," said the lady's companion in that same learned language. "Hush, lady. Be still. Rest."

"No," the lady said. She began to struggle against their hands. "No! The walls are broken. We have to mend the walls!"

John's eyes met those of the lady's companion. They were dark indeed and very fine, in a face that was not beautiful, but comely—yes, it was that. Now he had seen it, he would not forget it. "Help me," the dark woman said.

John nodded briskly. His dizziness was mostly past, leaving a sensation of remarkable if somewhat frenetic well-being. He grunted a little as he lifted the lady: she was no delicate wisp of a thing. But he was strong enough, and he had not so very far to carry her: just to a small door that opened on the cloister.

It was quiet there, and to his surprise it was deserted. He thought he caught the passage of a shadow, a dark-clad figure slipping away toward the garden, but as soon as it was gone, he put it out of mind.

He laid the lady on tended grass in the shade of a rose arbor. She had stopped her babbling; as he drew back, she caught his hand in a fierce grip. Her eyes fixed on his face. They were wonderful eyes, neither grey nor green but somewhat of both, like mist over the moors of Britain. "You must mend the walls," she said distinctly.

"Certainly, lady," John said, "if you will but tell me where—"

"Swear," she said. "My lord, swear—you will mend the walls."

"I will mend the walls," John said.

That seemed to satisfy her. She sank back on the grass, loosing a long sigh.

John looked up again into her companion's eyes. They were wary. It struck John, studying that plump and pleasant face, that the lady was a beauty, but this was a woman of both wit and sense.

"You go, messire," the woman said. "I'll look after her. She takes these fits; now it's over, she'll sleep a while, and be none the worse when she wakes."

That was not exactly the truth, John thought as he met that steady dark stare, but it was all she would give him. Still, because he was curious, he tried for a little more. "The wall she asked me to repair—if it's anywhere in reach, I'll be pleased to oblige her."

"It's nowhere within your reach, messire," the woman said without a shadow of doubt. "Don't trouble yourself; she'll be tended and kept safe. I thank you for your help, and for your kindness to my lady."

That was a dismissal. John almost disdained it, except that her eyes were so clear and so very firm. He had done all that he could do, they said, and indeed more than he should.

He let himself be dismissed, in the end, not because she wished it, but because the sun was climbing toward a brazen noon, and he had still to prepare for his brother's coronation. He paused only once, to wonder: was the lady mad? Or had she spoken prophecy? If somewhere there was a wall, and he was oathbound to mend it, then what did it enclose? Hell or heaven or somewhere between?

He shivered as he made his way back through the steaming throng. Foolishness—it was only a poor weak woman gone daft with the heat. And yet his heart persisted in beating harder, his skin in prickling as if something had passed just now which would echo down through the years.

He shook off that flight of fancy. Richard was waiting, and the crown, too, which Richard had inherited. That, John had determined long ago, would be his one day, when his time came. That was more than prophecy. That, in his mind, was certainty.

# PART ONE

# THE LION'S CUB

Christmas and the New Year, 1190–1191

# CHAPTER 1

Snow fell on the eve of Christmas, drifting deep across the holding of La Forêt in the County of Anjou. It buried the vineyard on the hill and weighted the boughs of the wood that gave the demesne its name, and softened the stern lines of the castle that the old lord had built, he who had come to this place from the lands across the sea.

Arslan was not a complete stranger to snow. He had seen it on the summit of Mount Hermon, and once he had been hunting in the heights of Syria when a storm blew out of the distant north. But this came well up his thighs, and though he was young, he was tall; his two servants, turbaned Seljuk devils that they were, waded in it to their waists.

Yusuf's lips were blue, but he was laughing, stalking his brother through the wilderness of white that had, the morning before, been the jousting field. He was as glad as Arslan to have escaped the castle with its suffocating crowd of people, all more or less appalled by the infidels in their midst.

One would think, thought Arslan, that none of them had ever seen a Turk before, or a man of Outremer—and never mind that anyone past the age of twenty would have known Arslan's father. Memories were short in this country. Arslan, born last and late and not of lawful wife, was as preposterous here as a phoenix in a flock of starlings.

He could have wished for feathers of flame like the living phoenix. Wool and leather and fur barely sufficed to warm his blood, born as he had been in the fierce sun of the east. His teeth were chattering; his feet were numb.

Yusuf caught Karim and pitched him into a bank of snow. Karim's turban flew off. His three long plaits were black against the endless white, his scarlet coat like a stain of blood. He screeched and turned on his brother. They rolled and thrashed in glorious battle.

"Charming savages."

Arslan refrained from whipping about to confront the owner of the voice. His nephew Rogier, heir of La Forêt, was the least hostile of the family. He treated his uncle with an odd mingling of hero-worship and friendly exasperation, as if Arslan had been a large and imperfectly housebroken lion cub. Arslan almost preferred the open enmity of his brothers, all of whom took deep offense at his existence.

Inevitably, Rogier's hand descended toward his shoulder—he was tall enough to escape the ignominy of being patted on the head. Arslan managed not to be there when the hand found its target. He sprang into the midst of the battle of Seljuks, plucked the two of them apart, and held them till Karim stopped snarling and Yusuf stopped cursing in gutter Turkish. Arslan spat a phrase at him, brief and horrifically profane. Yusuf stared in awe.

Arslan turned to face his eldest brother's eldest son. Rogier seemed as impressed as Yusuf. "Was that a paynim spell?" he asked.

"Yes," said Arslan, straight-faced.

"Will you teach it to me?"

"It's very dangerous," Arslan said. "If you speak it in the souks of Outremer, you could be killed."

"Truly?" Rogier's eyes were wide. "But won't it kill my enemies first?"

"It might," said Arslan blandly.

Karim took pity on the innocent. "Messire," he said in his sweet husky voice, with his accent that was no less pure than Arslan's, "if you would learn Turkish, there are many better and safer words to learn. I will teach you, messire, if he will not."

Rogier blinked. It always shocked these people to hear an infidel speak good French.

Then he blinked again, because Karim was smiling at him, and Karim's smile was dazzling. Karim was a beauty in the Turkish mode, all smooth brown skin and bright black eyes and white, white teeth. Arslan watched Rogier thinking: if this had been a woman, and if it had not been an infidel . . . or even if it were . . .

There were things aside from gutter curses that Rogier was best left ignorant of. Arslan retrieved Karim's turban and tossed it at him. "Here, dog of a Turk. Make yourself decent."

Karim's eyes lowered in a fair semblance of contrition, but Arslan caught the sidelong flash of a glance. That hellion was in no way repentant. Arslan's scowl promised retribution—later. For the moment there was Rogier to dispose of, and that was never easy. Rogier was determined to ride away on the king's Crusade, and equally determined to learn every possible thing before he went, from his uncle who had been born and raised across the sea.

"Tell me again," Rogier said. "Tell me how the kingdom fell."

Arslan stopped clenching his teeth and let them chatter as they would. "Perhaps," he said through spasms of shivering, "if we were warmer—if there were a fire to sit beside . . . ?"

"Ah!" said Rogier. "God's bones, this cold must be chilling you through. Come, come in, we'll call for hot wine, we'll build up the fire. Then you can tell me—"

"How the kingdom fell." But Arslan said it under his breath, with more than a hint of a snarl. The memory was still raw, though three years and more had passed since the debacle of Hattin: the terrible heat, the smoke and fire, the dry and deadly rain of infidel arrows on the gathered chivalry of Jerusalem.

He had forgotten to move. He had even, for a moment, forgotten the cold. Karim tugged at him. "My lord. My lord, come. You'll freeze if you stand."

He let himself be drawn back through the snow to the castle, within the walls that his father had built, and into the keep that was eerily like the keep of Beausoleil in which Arslan had been born. It had the same airy elegance, the same processional of arches, but the floor here was paved with stone—grey and red and cream and white— in place of the mosaic from Byzantium that was the pride of Beausoleil.

The hangings that warmed the walls had been woven by the old lord's baroness and her ladies, a great work of years: in the center behind the dais and the baron's high seat, a tapestry of lions, and flanking it, the pageant of the Crusade. But Arslan loved best the one that hung from the gallery: the unicorn in the wood, with a crown of gold about its neck, and a lion's cub fawning at its feet.

Lions were his father's emblem: for that lord of Anjou and Outremer had also been called Arslan, which was "Lion" in Turkish. Arslan the elder had been christened Olivier, but no one remembered it. Arslan the younger very occasionally recalled that his name was Baldwin. That was not his true name, nor the essence of what he was.

The baroness who had woven these hangings had died years before the younger Arslan was born. Her successor was given more to adorning her person than her castle. Arslan had won what heart she had with bolts of Byzantine silk, one of which, nearly in entirety, had gone to make the gown in which she held the Christmas court of La Forêt. She outshone every lady near her, and every lord or squire or page in the hall.

She was, he had to admit, very beautiful, in the icy manner of the north: hair as pale as sunrise in winter, eyes like sky over snow. She bathed that perfect skin in milk, for which her lord kept a herd of asses and a pair of maids to milk them. Arslan beside her always felt large, clumsy, and excessively burned by the sun.

Today he was simply glad to be warm. He had not known how cold he was until he felt the heat of the fire on his cheeks. They burned with cold, if that could be believed.

A mob of servants surrounded him, extricating him from his mantle. They brought a heated stone for his feet, chafed agonizing life into his hands, and poured hot spiced wine into him until his head spun. He tried to convince them to flutter about Yusuf and Karim, but nobody would listen.

He managed, amid the flurry, to evade any telling of tales, particularly the one Rogier had demanded. Rogier's father had him in hand, besetting him with some duty of the demesne to which the young lord responded hotly, "I don't need to do that! I'll be gone on Crusade."

"Will you now?"

Arslan's brother Olivier was the true son of his late mother: a sturdy, stocky, thickset man without a grain of humor in him. His eyes were bright blue, his curling brown hair thinned to nothing on the crown. He had a choleric temper, which his children justly feared, but at the moment he seemed more sardonic than angry.

This was an old wrangle, the lines of it worn as smooth as the responses of the Mass. "I *am* going," Rogier said. "You can't leave me behind."

"There should be a man at home to look after the demesne," said Olivier.

"Well, what of *him*?" Rogier's finger jabbed toward Arslan. "He's done all the Crusading he needs to do. He was at Hattin. He was there when Jerusalem fell. He—"

"He might wish to win it back," said Olivier.

Arslan's head had begun to ache. To leave this icy country, to feel the sun on his face again, to be among his own people, his own kin, his own kind . . .

These were his blood kin. His brothers, his brothers' children were all here, gathered in La Forêt before they rode on the Crusade. They had all taken the cross, every one.

And yet although he shared their blood, he could see nothing of his father in them. They were all their mother's children. Only he, the bastard born in Outremer, was their father's image; and he was more truly kin to the Seljuks than to these his brothers. *Them* he understood. They had been born in the same country, raised in the same world.

Looking at his brothers, listening to them, he understood how his father could have left them. Once the baroness was dead, once his eldest son was of age to take the barony, he had set himself free. He had given the title and the holding to Olivier the younger, and taken ship and sailed away—sailed home.

Arslan could have wept with longing to be home again, and to see his father's face. But there was no home to return to. Jerusalem was fallen. Its lords and knights were dead or taken captive. Arslan the elder was dead in the debacle of Hattin, killed in the last hopeless charge. Beausoleil was taken; a Saracen emir sat in the high seat. If Arslan would take it back, he must take it in the Crusade.

All of that was in his heart, words tumbling over one another until they were one long cry of grief and rage and loss. But he could not say any of them. His head was a pounding agony.

He felt hands on him, lifting him. He wanted to struggle, but his body was not his own. He slipped free of it as if it had been an outworn garment, and stood watching as servants carried it out of the hall.

People shook their heads, clucked their tongues. "He's weak in the head," one of the nephews said. "All that sun, it boiled his brains away."

"It's the cold," said his niece Lisette. "He's not used to it."

"And *I* say it's the devil in him," declared his second brother's wife. "After all, we all know what his mother was. Don't we?"

"What, a dockside whore in Acre?" Arslan's brother Gerard spat in the fire. "All that dizzy claptrap about mysterious ladies and secret sorceries and how she could never marry a mere mortal man—that's a pretty tale for a winter's night. She was as mortal as any of us, and not half as respectable, either."

"Ah now," said Olivier. "Let's not insult our father's memory. If there was ever anything he had, it was taste in women. Maybe she was no better than she should be, but I doubt she plied her trade on the docks. Higher up is my guess, and trained to please princes."

"Like his own mother?" Rogier asked. "She was a courtesan, wasn't she? And a foreigner, too. Which means that Grandfather wasn't any more legitimate than—"

His father knocked him flat with a backhanded blow. "That's enough, puppy. Go on, see what's keeping the servants. I want my dinner."

Rogier slunk off with his hands clapped over his bleeding nose. The conversation turned to other things. Arslan drifted back toward his body.

He had a room to himself, even as crowded as the castle was with guests and kin, though not for the honor of his rank—as the youngest of several sons, and bastard-born into the bargain, he had none. By rights he should have lodged in the hall with the rest of the hangers-on and the poor relations. But the servants would not share room or bed with infidels. It was simpler to tuck their master away in a corner, and his tame devils with him.

This had been a chaplain's cell: it lay just beyond the chapel, and it was small and bare. It had a hard narrow bed and a mat of rushes on the floor, but it had one signal virtue: it was set above the kitchens, and the heat from below came up in blessed waves. In summer it would be a steaming misery, but in winter it was wonderful.

He hovered above the body on the cot. It was a slack and uninteresting thing, long and awkward and much too brown for this country. There was nothing about it to mark it a devil's get.

He let himself be drawn back into it, into the darkness of closed eyes and the sea-swell of breath. He rode the tide of blood out of the darkness into a golden light.

He stood in a strange far country, in a field of green grass, under a sky the color of fallow gold. A river flowed through the heart of it, full of fish like living jewels. On the river's bank grew a grove of trees. They were thick with blossom and laden with golden fruit. The mingled scent of flower and fruit was almost more than mortal spirit could bear.

This country he had seen before. He had walked in it since long before the battle that broke his world. It was always the same: the grass, the river, the grove.

Yet on this eve of the most Christian of feasts, which fell just after the old gods' solstice, he saw a new thing. A track ran through the trees, a straight track, leading up the hill and away from the river. When he set foot on it, he caught his breath. The world was clearer, the sunlight brighter, than it had been before.

The track ascended the slope of the hill to a high level. There rose a castle. It was a squat, dark, ancient-seeming thing, with a round tower and a gate carved above the lintel with intertwined images of men and beasts, flowers, vines, and birds, in dizzying profusion.

The gate hung shattered from twisted hinges. The wall beyond it was cracked, crumbling into rubble.

It looked as if lightning had struck both gate and wall. Even as Arslan stared, the castle seemed to sink deeper into ruin. The moat was stagnant, choked with weeds. The grass beyond showed signs of blight, spreading slowly, dimming the everlasting green.

The straight track ended at the edge of the moat. There had been a bridge: shards of it floated in the murky water. Arslan could see nothing through the gate, only a blur of pallid light.

Above the broken gate, the carved figures writhed and twined. That which sat highest, which seemed both man and stag—man's face, stag's crown of antlers—raised its head from the stone and gazed down at Arslan. The eyes were dark and whiteless like a stag's, the face long and keenly carved.

The voice seemed a man's, but was no more truly human than the face. "Child of fire," it said, "you are late. What kept you?"

Arslan discovered that his mouth was gaping open. He shut it. "Was I summoned, lord?"

"Long since," said the horned king. "See, the gate is broken. Had you come sooner, that might have been prevented."

"Lord," said Arslan, "I did not know."

"You did not choose to know." The horned king came down from the lintel, standing in the ruin of the gate. He was very tall, taller than Arslan, towering even across the expanse of the moat. He was clad all in green, and although his body was a man's, he stood on cloven hooves.

Arslan had never been one to gibber in fear, even before the face of death. That as much as pity for his youth had preserved his life after Hattin, but he might not be so fortunate now.

"Child of fire," said the horned king, "your human blood may excuse you, but the time for excuses is past. Listen now and remember the words I give you. And when it is time to speak them, mind that you speak, and be not silent."

"Am I a servant?" Arslan inquired.

"You are a messenger."

"And no more?"

"For now, that is enough," said the horned king. "The eagle's nestling shall be brought to you. See that you tell him: The walls of air have fallen; the gate of the worlds is broken. Another was crowned on a day of ill omen; a dark spirit cursed his kingship, and condemned him to long wandering and bitter captivity. Only the true king may mend what is broken, and undo what has been done. If he delays, or if he refuses the charge, the kingdom will fall."

"The kingdom? France? Jerusalem?"

"Those are not in my care," said the horned king, "although they labor powerfully against me. I am bound to the isle of Britain, and Britain's king is in my charge."

"Britain's king sails to Jerusalem," Arslan said.

"The King of the English sails on Crusade," said the horned king. "The king of all Britain comes to you on the wings of storm. Wait for him; be ready. When he comes, you must speak."

"But there is no—" Arslan stopped. What, after all, did he know of Britain, except that it lay at the edge of the world? The Count of Anjou was king of it—that was Richard, called the Lionheart, who had taken the cross and was already, God willing, well on his way to the Holy City. Arslan's brothers, his nephews, their relations and hangers-on, would follow him in the new year. Arslan would go with them. He was going home to win back all that the infidel had taken away.

"What have I to do with Britain?" he asked the horned king, "or Britain with me?"

"Britain calls you," the horned king said. "It has need of you."

"Jerusalem needs me more."

"Jerusalem has the full might of Crusade. Britain has only you, and the few who guard it, and the one who must come to make it whole again."

"But why—"

"Child of fire," said the horned king.

It was, Arslan realized, an answer. Ifritah's child: child whose mother had been a spirit of fire.

"Remember," said the horned king. "Remember the words that I have given you. Be sure to speak them when the time has come."

# CHAPTER 2

Once on a time in the Kingdom of Jerusalem lived a lord whose heart was a sad and empty thing. He had had the love of friends and brothers; kings had embraced him, and queens had granted him their favor. Even the glorious lady of Aquitaine knew him and found him delightful, and he fancied that he loved her. But that was no more than a shadow of the truth.

After King Louis' Crusade, the lord, who had been born in the eastern kingdom, sailed to his father's castle in the land of Anjou and took it as lord and heir. There, as a good lord did, he took a wife for the sake of the demesne, and begot sons, and daughters to trade in fine marriages. But when the lady died bearing yet another daughter, who died soon after her mother, he yearned again to see his own country. His eldest son had come to man's years and was already a father, for he had married young, as lordly folk might.

The lord laid aside his lordship, passed the mantle and the coronet to his son, and sailed away, back to Jerusalem. He was then a man of full years, rich in sons, famous in battle. But his heart was a cold, small thing.

One evening in the fall of the year, after the season's wars were ended but before the brief sharp winter had come, a traveler came to seek lodging in the lord's castle. It was a woman, riding alone and fearless in this land of perpetual war. Her dress might have passed for a pilgrim's, as dark and voluminous as it was, save that she wore no cross, nor emblem of any shrine. Her only jewel was a stone as red as blood, hanging on a golden chain.

She was beautiful. On that, everyone agreed, though each told a different tale of it: some that she was tall and fair as a white lily, others that she was dark and small and sweet as a Damascene plum. Or perhaps she was both, for she was not of mortal blood.

She made no secret of it. She walked in other worlds than the one men knew; she spoke with spirits of air and earth and fire. She saw things, knew things that were hidden from mortals. She was herself a spirit of fire. She had come to this place for love of a man, of the lord whose heart had never known such love as she had to give him.

"Love is fire," she said to him. "Love is the heart's blood. I saw you as I swam the currents of air. I saw the emptiness in the heart of you, and yet I saw how great that heart was. I loved you then, bodiless spirit though I was, shaped of essential fire."

"And now?" he asked her. They were lying together, for she had come to him that first night and every night thereafter, and delighted him with arts and pleasures such as he had never known could be.

"And now," she answered him, "I love you to the depths of the earth and the height of the sky."

He drew back from her, resting his eyes on her changeless and ever-changeful beauty, which tonight was dark, as he loved it best. "Why? Tell me true. I'm mortal; I'm no longer young. I—"

"Only mortals care for youth," she said. "I was old when the stars were made."

After a speechless moment, he said, "Then to you I'm the work of a moment—here and gone in the blink of an eye. How can you love so brief a flicker as I am?"

"The body passes in a moment," she said, "but the spirit is everlasting. From before time I have known you. When all the worlds have passed away, I shall know you still."

"That," he said after a long moment, "is a remarkable span of immortality."

She smiled, though without mirth: her eyes, now dark, now green, now blue as a summer sky, were somber. "What our spirits have is of eternity. This of the body . . . it passes swiftly. Love me while we both can, my lord. Love me with all your heart."

He was an obedient knight: he did as his lady bade. And in the passage of time she bore him a child, a son who was the very image and likeness of his father. It would seem that there was nothing in him of his mother at all, but for the light in his eyes, which was not quite mortal, and the golden bronze of his skin, so that even newborn he seemed dyed by the sun. Yet as he grew, it became clear to his father and to those who knew him well that he had inherited more from his mother than his face might have promised. He too could walk between worlds and speak with spirits, and when he dreamed, he dreamed true.

The lady had nursed her child as ladies never did, cherishing him at her breast and, it was said, teaching him all she knew. But when he was old enough to be weaned, she laid him in the bed beside the lord as he slept, set her blood-red jewel about the child's neck, wrapped shadows about her, and vanished away.

The lord never spoke of her again. He raised his son as a lord's son should be raised, and taught him all that a baron of Jerusalem should know. The boy was fostered in his father's house, with no indulgence granted him for that he was the lord's own son, and rose from page to squire in his father's service. So did he come to the great battle in which the Kingdom of Jerusalem fell, and lived; but his father died in his arms.

It was said by those who might have had eyes to see that when the lord died, an angel of light came to take his soul; and when it came, his soul rose singing, unfurling wings of light, and soared upward into the spirit's arms. They twined about one another, till there was no telling which was the man and which the immortal spirit; and the song that they sang was pure and supernal joy.

So ended the tale of the lord who loved a spirit of fire.

Arslan remembered his mother perfectly clearly, though like his father he did not speak of her. She never wore the same face for two days running, and yet he always knew her. Because of her, he dreamed this dream of the horned king and the ruined castle, the gate that must be shut and the walls that must be built anew.

If he looked inside himself, he could see the walls. Walls of air—walls of magic and of light. They warded the kingdom and protected it from harm. While they stood, no ill thing could enter the realm. Yet they had fallen, because Britain had no king, and the walls were built and sustained by the king's strength. Britain stood in sore need of a king; and while it waited, its defenses lay open to any hostile power that might rise against it.

Arslan had come in the west of the world with the cry for Crusade, sailing with the Archbishop of Tyre after the fall of Jerusalem. That was his purpose and his duty: to win back the Christian kingdom and drive out the infidels—not to play messenger on behalf of a country he had never seen, because of a mother who had abandoned him before he could walk.

He left the golden country with no little bitterness. And yet as he passed through the orchard, he paused. A shadow shifted among the trees. It seemed to be attached to a human shape, a tall form dressed in white, which passed almost too quickly to catch. He had only a glimpse: a turn of milk-white cheek, a fall of red-gold hair. A faint chiming accompanied it, like the ringing of tiny bells.

As soon as he had seen it, it was gone. But when he came to the place where it had been, something gleamed in the unfading grass: an apple of gold, no larger than the tip of his smallest finger. It chimed as he lifted it, soft and eerily sweet.

The golden bell was solid in his hand, cool and smooth. It carried in it a memory of the lady who had worn it on her girdle. He might have paused to taste that memory, but the dream was losing substance about him, the golden land fading to mist, slipping away before the grey chill of mortal earth.

Arslan started awake. As often after a true dream, he knew exactly where he was and who he was and how he had come there. His cell of a room in La Forêt was surprisingly warm: the kitchen was in full fly, preparing the Christmas feast.

He had been undressed and wrapped in blankets and furs. He struggled out of them. One hand was clenched about something small and round. He opened his fingers and stared. It was a golden bell in the shape of an apple, no larger than the end of his smallest finger. It chimed as his hand shook, too sweet for mortal earth.

He wrapped it in a bit of silk and laid it with care in the bag of his belongings, next to the ruby on its golden chain that had been his mother's.

Clothes were set out for him, fit for a prince: shirt of finely woven linen, cotte and cap of crimson silk, hose and shoes made to his measure. The collar of gold had been his father's; the links were heavier than iron, but he put it on regardless. He would not shame the old lord's memory.

He did not mean to make an entrance. The banquet had just begun. His brothers were seated at the high table with their wives and a gathering of high ones from the lands round about: lords and ladies mostly, and a prelate or two. His nephews and younger kin laid claim to tables down below, with much raucous hilarity.

It all stopped as he paused in the entrance to the hall. He had seen before how the last of the daylight was gathered in that place, long beams slanting through louvers in the roof, falling full upon whoever entered. He must have blazed like a torch.

Properly he should have shared the high table with his brothers, but bastard blood was not granted that much honor here. Rogier and a gathering of young rakehells from the demesnes nearby made a place for him among them, with such noise and hilarity that it had sucked him in before he could resist it. He was a figure of glory and splendor: he had fought in real wars, been wounded with scars to show for it, and they were sure that he had killed armies of infidels. Nothing that he said could convince them otherwise.

Today it was a distraction. He threw himself into it, with laughter and jesting and enough bawdry to draw frowns from the high table. Anything indeed to forget the dream of the golden bell and the horned king.

The maids were always after Arslan. He was strange, he was exotic, and they had all heard the rumor that he had brought with him some gift or art out of the east. When he refused them, they merely thought him charmingly shy. When once or twice he had allowed himself to be importuned, he found the others more insistent than ever, as if he had been a bowl of sweets and they all must have a share.

Even on this night, after the feast and the revelry and the solemn Mass at midnight, Arslan found plump Jeannette lying in wait near the door of his cell. She was shivering, and not only to invoke his pity: under the woolen mantle she was bare. She leaped into his arms, pressing hard against him, as eager for his warmth as for what else she had in mind.

Karim came to his rescue, somewhat belated but to excellent effect, with white teeth and gleaming blade and eyes full of the very devil. He pried Jeannette loose, wrapped her tightly in her cloak, and sent her on her way with a spate of evil-sounding Turkish. She fled with gratifying speed.

"Now she'll tell everybody you put a curse on her," Arslan observed.

"Good," said Karim. "I hope she gets boils where the sun never shines."

"You're jealous."

The Turk's glare was as sulfurous as his reputation. Arslan laughed at it, which did nothing to mollify him. "I would never trouble myself with *you*," he said. "I'll have a prince of the Jinn or a king of men—and nothing between."

"Alas that I am neither," Arslan sighed.

"Well," said Karim as if he had decided after all to be magnanimous. "You can't help it. Are you going to sleep, or will you keep vigil through the night?"

"I had hoped to sleep," said Arslan, "unless I find another eager maid in my bed."

"Not if my brother stayed awake at his post," Karim said in a tone that promised dire things if Yusuf had failed of his duty.

Arslan grinned. He was as close to home as he could be, here, with this child of the Prophet. When they had found Yusuf drowsy but awake, and no one in Arslan's bed, Arslan was truly content. He would sleep; please God, he would not dream, not for the rest of this night.

# CHAPTER 3

Karim watched the lion's cub sleep, with Yusuf snoring at his feet. The night was deep and cold, but the room was warm. The things that whispered about Arslan were still for once; the shimmer that was on him was muted almost to nothing.

Men could not see what Karim saw, or else did not understand it. Women sensed it; they would have pursued him even if he had not been good to look at. Karim was not a man, and had chosen not to be a woman. That maybe was why he—or she, as she was born—was permitted to see clearly.

When she shut her eyes, she did not see this room of stone in cold and distant Anjou. She saw the dusty heat of summer in Acre, the throngs of people about the quays and the ships, and the one ship, the ship on which she had hidden herself, widening the gap of water between itself and the shore.

It was a Frankish ship. The Archbishop of Tyre sailed in it with an embassy of lords and prelates. They all grieved for the loss of Jerusalem to the infidel, but no few of them were eager to set sail into the west, either to return home or to see for the first time the places where their fathers had been born.

Karim, who was then Kalila, had come to Acre with Yusuf, fleeing the fall of Beausoleil. The rest of the old lord's servants were dead or fled, but Yusuf had been young Arslan's friend from the cradle, and Yusuf's twin Kalila had been their constant shadow. Yusuf never doubted where he would go. Nor, though her brother might think otherwise, did Kalila.

Both of them tried to leave her in Acre—as if she could live in a Christian convent, she who had grown up as wild as a boy, and was faithful to the Prophet besides. She let them think that she was safe in the abbess' care, but as soon as they were gone, she abandoned the skirts the nuns had imposed on her and put on trousers, plaited her hair like a man's and wound a turban about it and went after them.

She slipped onto the ship in a company of squires and servants. Once aboard, she had no difficulty finding a place to hide. The ship was laden with baggage and cargo, and full of people. One more, even a seeming boy in Turkish dress, was barely noticed.

Arslan found her on the third day out from Acre. She was sure that she had not been careless, but Arslan was what he was. She had been sleeping in the hold, curled atop a bale. She woke to find him standing over her.

She could make herself see him as men did: tall and slight now but promising to be a big man when he was grown, with fair brown hair streaked with gold, and steady grey eyes. But she had always been able to see the other half of him, the half that was his mother. That part of him gleamed in the dimness.

He could see her as clearly as she saw him. He simply said, "You had better come with me."

Yusuf was livid, of course. He would have whipped her—if Arslan had let him, and if she had been inclined to let him try. He had to settle for cursing her in three languages.

When he had cursed himself out, he said with surprising coherence, "The first ship we meet that's headed eastward, we set you on it. You will go back to Acre, and you will stay where I bid you stay."

"No."

Yusuf stared. Arslan had been lounging on the bunk in the tiny cabin, listening in silence to Yusuf's tirade. He did not sit up, nor did he raise his voice, but once he had spoken, Yusuf could find no more words to say.

"She's not safe in Acre," Arslan said. "Not an infidel woman, even with Abbess Constance to protect her. Better she stay with us. Or are you afraid you can't look after her?"

Yusuf gaped like a fish. Kalila had to bite her lip to keep from laughing.

"Your name is Karim," Arslan said to Kalila. "You live, ride, fight, in all ways as a man, as long as we travel this road."

She nodded. It was hard to keep the grin from her face. Yusuf's glare told her that there was no keeping it from her eyes. She had won, and he knew it.

*   *   *

Yusuf had learned to endure the ruse. Sometimes she even thought that he forgot and looked on her as his brother. She had taken to thinking of herself as a man, because it was simpler. As little place as there was in this country for a Turkish soldier-servant, there was no place at all for a Turkish woman.

And yet tonight she remembered it. Her breasts ached in their bindings. Her courses had come; they were the most vivid reminder of the truth. After all a eunuch might grow breasts, and might be cut to the shape of a woman, too, but he did not know the tides of blood that a woman knew.

When she plotted this deception, she had not thought past the voyage from Acre. What she would do in France, how she would carry on, she had never paused to consider. They were going back to Outremer, that she knew; then, she supposed, she would be Kalila again, and live once more in Beausoleil—or anywhere else that Arslan chose to live.

She regarded him in a kind of despair. He did not know, and she would never tell him, the true reason why she had followed him. Fear was reason enough, dread of being alone in a world of enemies—for who would understand or forgive a Muslim woman who willingly served a Frankish master?

Arslan would never understand, and perhaps never forgive, that Kalila loved him, and had since they were children. She had never been fool enough to hope for love in return. He was as easy with her as with her brother. Even when she took sick on the voyage and he had to nurse her because Yusuf was ill, too, even more than she, Arslan tended them both alike, with utter lack of shyness. She was his sister, the companion of his childhood. She would never be more than that, if never less.

The spirits were troubling him again. Even in sleep his brows were knit. His gaiety in the hall had been too hectic; he had laughed too loudly, drunk too much. He always flung his humanity in the spirits' faces, as if he could drown them in mortal flesh.

She guarded him as best she could. She was as mortal as he longed to be, but she had grown up within the circle of his magic. Touched by the devil, the Franks had said of Beausoleil's Turks, the Seljuks who had been in service to the old lord since his mother's day. That was truer than ever once the strange lady came to the castle, bore the lord a son, and vanished into the air from which she came.

Kalila could see far enough to be of use, nor had she any fear of the things that came as often as not and danced about Arslan while he slept. Small things, wild things, sometimes monstrous, always strange. They loved to hover above him, staring with eyes that bulged from misshapen faces or quivered on stalks or glowed like lamps in formless gloom. They were drawn to him like moths to a flame.

The greater things, the spirits of air and fire, came on him more rarely, and most often under the sky. Their curiosity was less benign, their interest more dangerous. The small things had little wit and few words, but the great ones were clever and often wicked. They could speak to him, and sometimes did. He knew their languages, not even truly aware that that was anything to marvel at. Some, he said, were his kin. But he never saw his mother. She did not come to him as the others did, not even when he slept, when he might not be aware of her.

Kalila would have something to say to her of that, if she ever did come back. Arslan pretended that he did not care, that a spirit of fire should never be constrained, nor was it wise to expect such a thing of her; but his heart was human. It ached with the loss of her.

The morning dawned bright and bitterly clear, but by midday the snow was falling fast. The guests settled in for a long winter's revel, in the warmth of wine and dancing, feasting and laughter and singing of songs.

Many of those were songs of Crusade. All the men of fighting age had taken the cross. By spring, they declared, they would be in Jerusalem.

Arslan's wild mood of the night before had given way to an almost supernatural calm. He did not join in the singing, nor would he tell tales of Outremer. He sat by the fire, wrapped in robe and mantle, and the more uproarious the revels became, the quieter he was.

He looked like a bird on a branch, feathers ruffled against the cold. Karim the Turk came and sat at his feet, snarling at the dogs that would have claimed the honor.

It had not been wise to come here just now, as the young men sang of the evil Saracen; but Arslan was too quiet. His eyes were full of the dancing of flames. Deep in the fire's heart a salamander coiled: supple fiery body, hiss and snap of words that Arslan could understand.

Whatever the creature said, Arslan did not respond to it. He had gone deep inside himself. Kalila had not seen him so withdrawn from the world since his father died.

The singing ended. All the young folk had leaped up to dance, beating out the swift rhythms of an estampie. The sound of it was like the battle music of the Saracens: rattle of drums, clatter of nakers, pealing of pipes.

Arslan shivered violently. His eyes cleared. The salamander vanished in a shower of sparks.

He leaped up so suddenly that he came near to bowling Kalila over, and whirled into the dance. The dancers greeted him with a whoop and a cheer.

When he lounged about he was as awkward as a yearling colt, all legs and arms and angles. But in the dance he was pure grace. There he was his mother's child, all air and leaping fire.

Kalila sighed to watch him. It was the wild mood again, that made him flare up like a torch. He was troubled, worse than she had ever seen him, and it made him strange. Perilously so.

The ladies were vying to dance with him. He warmed to none of them, though one bold black-eyed creature won a smile that dazzled even the watcher by the fire.

There was nothing a Turk could do but watch and pray Allah that he would remember to be prudent. He had never been one to flaunt himself, but that habit stretched thin tonight.

It struck Kalila with a kind of shock, that he was wearing not his father's golden collar but the blood-red ruby that had been his mother's. He had never worn it before; it had always lived in his belongings, hidden and apparently forgotten. It was a defiance of sorts, though of what, she could not tell.

The dance ended with a thunderous flourish. The dancers dropped to benches and stools, flushed and breathing hard. In the sudden and almost deafening quiet, some of the elders persuaded the third brother, Amaury, to sing. He had a surprisingly sweet voice for so plain and foursquare a man.

Arslan's voice joined it, consenting to sing after all. It was an old song of this country, that his father had loved. The brothers' voices wove smoothly together, Amaury's lighter, Arslan's darker, but subtly alike.

It was as close to amity as he had come with any of his brothers. Amaury even smiled as they wove a skein of melismas, rippling up and down, first one and then the other, then both together. They finished with Amaury on the low note and Arslan on the high, a shift that made the musically inclined laugh and applaud.

As the applause died away, Arslan won the loan of a lute with a bow and a smile. He tuned it carefully but quickly, to a scale that was not common in this country, and sitting cross-legged as near the fire as was safe for the lute, he began a new song. He sang in French, but the words and the melody had been born in the east.

It was a love-lament, a woman's cry of pain for her lover who was gone to the holy war, and he sang it high, as he had learned to do from singers in the markets of Outremer. But when he sang the lover's response, he sang it in his own voice, that had broken late but settled deep.

Kalila watched faces as he sang. Some of them had begun to realize that it was not a Christian song, even before it sang of the perfidy of the Franks, the breaking of oaths and the profaning of holy places. Expressions of pleasure gave way to frowns, and here and there to scowls. Arslan seemed oblivious, but Kalila had learned how deceptive that could be.

When he shifted to Arabic, indignation mounted to outrage. He was provoking it—daring them to rise up and thunder denunciations. Some of his brothers were close to it, but Olivier held them down with the force of his will.

He waited for a pause in the song before he rose from his high seat. Arslan smiled sweetly up at him, fingers wandering over the lutestrings, playing a softer variation on the melody. "Enough," said Olivier. "Enough of your heathen spells. We're Christians here; we've taken the cross. We'll hear no more of this mummery."

"You'll hear a great deal of it in Outremer," Arslan said, "if by God's will you come there. The land was theirs before we came to take it. We live in the world they made, surrounded by them, forced more often than not to make alliance with factions of them against greater or more deadly factions. Your world is a simple thing, my brother, a matter of light and dark, good and evil, Christian and infidel. But in Outremer, in the land beyond the sea, there is no simplicity. Nothing is as it seems here. The only truth is the truth of the land under your feet and the sky overhead." Arslan shook his head. He must see what Kalila saw: no understanding; no will to understand. "The land kills you, or it changes you. No man comes back unaltered from across the sea."

"I and mine will come back Christians," said Olivier, "and not apostate, or I will take their lives with my own hand."

"No doubt you will," Arslan said. He laid the lute down gently and rose, making it one fluid movement from floor to feet, as it was done in the east. "Good night, brothers, my lords, my ladies. May the Lord Christ be merciful to you, and grant you the gift of understanding."

He might have made his escape while they all stood in shock, but Henry, the youngest but for Arslan, was blindingly fast on his feet. He had knocked Arslan down and set to pummeling him before anyone, even Kalila, could move.

Kalila sprang. Henry was like a man of stone, oblivious to blows, hammering at his brother. Arslan made no move to fight back, only to protect his face and his more tender parts. Kalila went for the dagger that was all the weapon anyone could wear in hall. It was sharp, and of better steel than they had here: Indian steel, with a shimmer on it like water.

The blade flew from her hand. She tumbled backward, sprawling in the rushes amid the dogs, staring as Arslan stood up stiffly. His brother lay gasping at his feet. No hand had touched either Kalila or Henry. Arslan's lip was split; his eye was already blackening. "I did deserve that," he said mildly.

This time, when he left, no one stopped him.

Kalila scrambled after him. Once he was out of sight of the hall, he let himself limp in earnest. She slid in under his arm and held him up. He said no word to thank her, but he did not drive her off, either—with word or hand, or in the other way that was granted him by his mother's blood.

"Why?" Kalila demanded as she tended his wounds. Yusuf had been idling about, tooling leather for a bridle, when she brought Arslan back. He had not even argued when she sent him for water and cloths and herbs from the castle's store.

Now he crouched at Arslan's feet as if he could be of any more use than Kalila in stopping whatever that fool had in mind to do. But Arslan seemed to have subsided into apathy again, submitting docilely to Kalila's ministrations.

At Kalila's sharp word, he shivered a little—or maybe it was the sting of the ointment she was spreading on his lesser cuts and bruises.

"This is not my country," he said. "These are not my people. They know nothing, they understand nothing. They blunder about like bulls, bellowing and tossing their horns. Ah, God, to be home again, and away from this alien place!"

It was all Kalila could do not to take him in her arms and rock him like a child. But that would have made him furious.

Yusuf tried to comfort him with words. "We can go," he said, "as soon as this storm of Iblis stops. The Count of Anjou is in Messina— we can go there. Or we can go to Genoa and find a ship that sails straight to Acre."

Arslan shuddered more deeply than before. "The Count—he's King of Britain, too."

"And Duke of Normandy," said Yusuf, who prided himself in his erudition. "It's not really Britain. It's England. He's King of the English. Britain's the Welsh, too, and the Scots. They're not exactly—"

Arslan was barely listening. "King of Britain. King of—" He flung himself free of them both. "I was *not* brought here for this!"

Kalila's glance crossed Yusuf's. He was as baffled as she. But she thought she understood a little. "He had another dream," she said. "Maybe as bad as before—"

Before his father died, when he saw how the battle would end, but could do nothing to stop it. But she could not say it.

"What," said Yusuf, "that his brothers will die in the Crusade? That's little enough loss."

She kicked him till he yelped. "Hush! They're his kin, as little as they like to recall it."

"They're God's fools," Arslan said clearly. "They'll live to see this place again." He looked into both their faces. "I may be mad, but I'm not deaf. This has nothing to do with my brothers."

"Well," said Kalila with a flash of temper. "What is it, then? You're just short of spreading batwings and flying shrieking through the hall. If it's not your brothers, then is it—Allah." Her wits, at last, caught up with her tongue. "O Allah. Not you. It can't be—"

He gripped her shoulders and shook her till she fell silent. "I do not foresee my death," he said.

His fingers were tight enough to bruise. She welcomed the pain: it kept her focused on him. "Swear," she said. "Swear that that's the truth."

"By my father's spirit," he said.

She sagged in his hands. But she had not taken leave of her senses, even in fear for him. "What, then? What has you in such a state that you're not fit for man or beast?"

He could be incorrigibly stubborn, but she had known him since they all shared a cradle. Under the weight of her stare, he gave way. He let her go and sank down, an untidy tangle of limbs on the radiating warmth of the floor. "My mother's kin have summoned me as if I have a debt to them. This isle of Britain, this place I know nothing of, has need of me. It's managed somehow to misplace or mischoose its king—and I, it seems, am expected to find the remedy for that."

He was making little enough sense, but she was accustomed to finding intelligence in his babblings. "Britain needs your magic. And that means—"

"No Crusade," Arslan said. "No return home. I am to go away from it, as far away as man can go. For a country I don't know, for a king to whom I never swore fealty, for kin to whom I owe nothing. Not one thing."

"They must need you badly," Kalila said. "Maybe because you're your father's child as well as your mother's? There can't be many who walk in both worlds."

"I don't want to be needed," Arslan said. "I want to go home."

She fixed him with her most quelling glare. "Why, you great baby," she said. "You're whining."

"Wouldn't you?" he shot back.

She laughed more in startlement than in mirth. She had expected rampant indignation, not this bitter clarity. "Not I," she answered him. "I'd pitch a shrieking fit."

"I did that, too," he said. "What I said to my brothers about things being simple . . . I was talking to myself. They're going to a place they can't begin to understand—and so am I. What do I know of this Britain? Nothing! And yet it's calling me."

"Maybe," said Yusuf, "you're being called to its king. He's going on Crusade. Maybe he needs you, to understand what he's going to?"

Arslan sighed heavily. "Would to God that were so. But the summons was clear. I'm called to Britain, not to the king."

"All I know of it is that it's on the edge of the world," Yusuf said. "And it's wet. I've heard it never stops raining."

"Then we'll grow gills and learn to swim," Kalila said.

Arslan's brows rose. " 'We'?"

"You think we'd let you go alone? Who would protect you from yourself then?"

"*You* could go home," Arslan said.

She shook her head. "Not without you." It was as close as she would come to telling him the truth, and it was all she intended to say. He could argue all he liked, but her mind was made up.

He must have seen it in her face. He glanced at Yusuf, but found no different answer there. He shook his head. "You'll regret it," he said.

"Probably," she granted him. "But not before you do."

"I regret it already," he said. He lay back, wincing as the movement jarred his bruises.

"There is this," Kalila said. "You won't be traveling with your brothers."

His smile was crooked, but it was genuine. "There is that," he said.

# CHAPTER 4

❧

John Lackland left the castle of Chinon against the advice of anyone with any pretense to weather-wisdom. Truly, he admitted to himself, they had the right of it. But he was unbearably, unlivably restless, and he had had a message from Richard in Messina, where he wintered on his way to the Crusade. Richard had revoked John's oath of exile from England. John was free to go, to take the lands he had been given when his brother was crowned.

He knew perfectly well why Richard had slipped his leash. It was his curse to know why men did what they did. Richard did not want John running off to plot sedition with the King of France. John in England, Richard would be thinking, would be too preoccupied to make trouble in Normandy or Anjou.

To think, John reflected, that when Richard was crowned, he had feared so much for the security of his crown that he had forbidden John to set foot on his lands in England for three years—until the Crusade was over and Jerusalem was won and Richard had come back. Richard was a simple soul, taking all in all, and not remarkably quick-witted except when he had a battle to fight.

John had endured the feast of Christmas in Chinon, but all his dreams, waking and sleeping, were of England. Why he should be so smitten with it, though he had been born in the heart of it, he did not understand: his blood and kin were bred in France, in Normandy, Anjou, Poitou. And yet he loved the land of England more dearly than he had ever loved a woman: a love that he confessed to no one, not even those he most trusted. His sentence of exile had both grieved and infuriated him, but he had come to reckon it worth the price. The exile would end, and he would go home again to the land where he was born.

He rode out from Chinon on the feast of Stephen, with a small company of men-at-arms and a squire and a knight or two. The rest of his household would follow when it pleased, which might not be until spring, from the sound of his seneschal's fulminations.

His brother William, whom everyone called Longsword, had been apt as always for mischief. He rode at John's side as they left Chinon behind. The snow that had fallen on Christmas Day had, by God's grace, blown and drifted from the road, so that the party could settle to a good, fast pace.

William's big bay snorted and sidled, snaking his head at John's smaller, lighter chestnut. William brought him in hand with rein and spur, easily, hardly aware that he had done it. His eyes were on the sky. "Snow again by nightfall," he said.

John shrugged. "We'll find shelter."

"Anywhere but Chinon, eh?" William rolled his wide shoulders and yawned till his jaw cracked. "God's feet, it was dull. Almost made me miss your mother. Whatever else you can say of her, she does know how to hold a revel."

"My lady mother," John said through the sour taste that always filled his mouth at the thought of her, "is safe, thank God and His saints, with my dear brother in Messina. And may she stay with him until his Crusade is long over—even if she does have a gift for making festivals."

William snorted, precisely like his horse, but had the sense to let be. John set his mind to riding as far as he could before night and the storm drove him back within walls.

It caught him midway between noon and nightfall. He had passed an abbey an hour before; his sergeant had been minded to stop there, but John would not hear of it. And now the snow had begun to fall, and the light was fading fast. The road straightened as it descended through a narrow valley and into the shadow of a wood.

He did not remember this road or this valley or this wood, not within a day's ride of Chinon. It was the early twilight, he told himself, and the thickening snow. It confused the senses. He could hardly lose his way: the road was perfectly straight, the trees marching on either side of it. The snow whitened the track, but although it must be falling thick beyond the wood, here the branches caught and thinned it. It barely rose to the horses' fetlocks, swirling as brightly as if lit by moonlight.

The men-at-arms rode in silence. Even William seemed subdued. The pale light limned their faces in silver and shadow, framed by the grey steel of mail and helmet. The only sound was the thudding of hooves, the creaking of leather and the jungle of harness, and the occasional soft snort of a horse or a sumpter mule.

Sometimes in England, John had felt as if the track he was on had taken him briefly out of the world. He had never felt such a thing in Anjou before, though elsewhere in France, in Brittany and in the wood near Chartres, he had known the same strangeness. The air for the moment was keener, the snow more luminous; the trees darker, taller, their branches more densely woven.

He was not afraid. The road was straight, his way clear. If need be, they could camp under the trees. He would prefer a castle or an abbey, or at least an inn, but a tent would do. Surely morning would find them in country he recognized.

The snow was falling thick enough now that even the trees could not keep it wholly at bay. John began to resign himself to a camp in the forest. Maybe God would send a deer for their dinner, or a coney or two—though he had seen no living thing, now he reflected on it, since his horse set foot on this track.

In spite of himself he shivered. It was only the cold, he told himself. His feet were numb. He worked his toes in the fur-lined boots.

Just as he gathered himself to call a halt, the trees thinned. A blast of wind smote him, driving stinging needles of snow into his face. Through the blinding gale he saw how the road had begun to bend and curve, winding down a hill to the black arc of a river. A castle rose on the steep hill above the river, a shadow in the early dusk, blurred by the swirling snow.

As John rode out of the wood, the world closed about him once more. The light was mortal, and fading fast. The snow was no more luminous than it should be, nor did it shimmer as his red gelding plodded through it.

The castle too was quite mortal, if rather more elegant than was the wont in Anjou. It had a faintly foreign look: the high clean-cut walls, the round towers, the gate with its crest of rampant lions. The device carved between them he recognized: it was the triple cross of Jerusalem.

Here it seemed was a lord who had gone on Crusade—perhaps with John's own mother when she was Queen of France, before she parted company with saintly Louis and ran off with the Devil's get.

John could appreciate the irony. Here was he, twice forbidden the journey to Jerusalem, begging for lodging from a lord who had not only gone to defend the Holy Sepulcher, but come back to tell of it.

William hailed the castle with his hunting horn, its high sweet note ringing upward to the lowering sky. The snow had lightened for a bit, but now it came back heavier than ever, so that they could barely see the carving over the gate.

Light sprang up in the tower. The drawbridge lowered over the moat; the portcullis rose. A figure stood in the gate, torch in hand, guiding them in. There were others beyond, a crowd of people in festival dress, whom curiosity had brought out of the hall.

But John's eyes were on the man with the torch. Boy, in truth, as John rode closer and could see: tall and beginning to broaden across the shoulders, but still no more than sixteen summers, if he had so many. In that light he seemed made of metal, gold and bronze, and his eyes were grey steel. That skin was burned deep by a hotter sun than Anjou had ever known, and those eyes had a look of far distances, of a bleaker land and a wider sky.

And yet it was not the mark of Outremer on this child that held John fast. It was another thing, a thing he had never seen before. The boy's flesh was as fine as parchment, and light shone through, bright and warm as the fire in a king's hall.

The boy greeted him with grave courtesy, his accent good Angevin but with a slight strangeness beneath. "Be welcome in La Forêt, my lord," he said. And to the rest: "And you, my lord, messires."

John bowed. William was too startled for such formality. "La Forêt Sauvage? But that's three days' ride from Chinon! We can't be—"

John kicked him into silence. "It's an ill night to be traveling," he said. "We're glad of your hospitality, my lord."

The boy waved aside the title with a gesture too graceful for France. It must, like the faint oddity in his accent, have been born in Outremer. "No lord, I," he said. "The baron my brother is in the hall, with a proper welcome, and food and drink and dry clothes, too."

John bowed again, somewhat piqued by his own error. Of course this child could not have built the castle. He was much too young.

As the boy turned, John stopped him with a word. "Wait. Do you have a name?"

"My name is Baldwin de Beausoleil," said the boy, "but everyone calls me Arslan."

"Arslan," said John. He liked the roll of it on his tongue. "Arabic?"

"Turkish."

"And I am plain John," said John.

Did the boy know how dazzling his smile was? He did not add anything to it except to say, "Come, messire. The lord is waiting."

Not "*my* lord," John noticed. And if this boy was no lord or baron, then the gaggle of gawping youths behind him were all the more impressive, because they were flat in awe of him.

Richard had that gift of making people love him. John, who did not, had learned that envy served no purpose. This boy had even more charm than Richard, and more intelligence, too—though that was hardly difficult. He led them all from the gate through a snow-swept court to the inner keep, and thence to a singularly handsome hall.

The lord of La Forêt was a surprise and a disappointment. He was ordinary: a plain dark man without either looks or distinction. John had seen a hundred like him in this land of France. Nor, from the look of him, had he yet seen Outremer. He wore the cross of Crusade on his shoulder, as did every other man in the hall—all but Arslan. That, John found interesting.

This lord Olivier did not recognize John. John remembered him now, vaguely, from this court or that in Anjou: a minor baron, not excessively rich in lands, but possessed of a small renown for the quality of his wine. He took John for William's squire, an impression that John did not choose to correct. The men-at-arms, safe and warm by now in the guardroom, were not there to betray him, and William would not, once John had caught his eye.

William, the lord did know: he was so obvious a Plantagenet, big ruddy man that he was, like his brother Richard. That he was a bastard seemed to matter little to this provincial notable; the man fell over himself to make old King Henry's son welcome, blustering and preening and making a proper fool of himself.

William could well appreciate the jest. He allowed the lord to set him in the place of honor and to relegate John to the place proper to a squire or hanger-on, well below the high table. When his glance crossed John's, it was full of wickedness. He would take as much pleasure as John would, when the baron woke to the truth.

For the moment John was content to play the game. It left him free to do as he pleased, which was to capture the boy Arslan and say to him, "I don't suppose one can bathe and change one's clothes and rest in a warm room."

"One can," said Arslan with a flicker of that astonishing smile. "One can even find a meal that's better, and fresher, than the high ones are partaking of. I don't suppose yonder lord would wish for the same?"

"If he does," John said, "he'll not get it before I will."

Arslan laughed. "Poor man! He'll curse you later, I'm sure."

"That," said John with relish, "he most certainly will."

It was a fine conspiracy, slipping out of the hall through a door behind one of the tapestries and following the young Frank with the Turkish name to a wonder and a marvel: a bath built in the Roman style, but much newer than Rome.

"It's a *hammam*," Arslan said when John exclaimed at it: "a Saracen bath, but much smaller, of course; baths in the eastern cities are built for hundreds."

The hot pool was blessedly hot, the cold pool breathtakingly cold, and the room in which John sat basking in steam was such bliss that he could not bear to leave it. Almost as delightful was the servant who attended him: a Turk of the true blood, a boy no older than Arslan, with a dark smooth face and bright dark eyes and a turban over long black plaits. He spoke French as well as Arslan did; his name, he said, was Yusuf, and he too was born in Outremer, in the castle of Beausoleil.

Truly John pitied William, condemned to be honored as a lord while John, ignored and no doubt forgotten, knew the delights of an earthly paradise. When he was cleaner than he had ever been in his life, clean to his fingertips, with his hair cut and his face shaved and his body clothed in a rich warm robe, he sat by the hearth in the cavernous kitchen. The cooks fed him choice cuts from the roast, bread and cakes fresh from the baking, fruits dried and stored in honey and spices, green herbs grown in the shelter of the kitchen garden, and wine mulled with cinnamon and cardamom and cloves. "No king ever dined more royally," he said to the cook, who took the praise as his due.

Arslan and the Turk shared his dinner, and a second Turk who was, they said, Yusuf's brother Karim: somewhat smaller, somewhat fairer-skinned, and much prettier than Yusuf. John would have taken him for a girl, and at first was sure of it. But then, he thought, these eastern youths were famous for their beauty; looking at this one, he could well see why.

It was a convivial gathering, there in the corner of the kitchens, while the cooks labored mightily to feed the high ones in the hall above. John, born a prince, had not done such a thing before, nor imagined that he could do it. Nor could he remember laughing as much as he laughed here, or being so perfectly at ease with anyone, still less such strangers—and two of them were not even Christian.

As for the one who was, John did not need to wonder for long why this of all the brothers of La Forêt was playing the servant in the kitchens. Bastard seed of a king might have the baron groveling at his feet, but bastard seed of the baron's own father won little honor and less courtesy.

Arslan seemed unperturbed by it. He was not born in this world, nor could it touch him or hold him. He was as free as a man could be.

And so, for this one evening, was John. Soon enough he would be a prince again. Tonight he played the squire with rare glee, amid much merriment from the cooks and the servants.

He was sorry when it ended. The cooks sent the last of the feast up to the hall, the tower of marzipan and spiced fruits and elaborate cakes that was meant for an image of the Tower of David in Jerusalem. Even as they did that, servants and scullions brought down the platters and bowls and cups and scoured them, and others brought the remnants to be dispensed to the poor, and began to close up the kitchens for the night.

Arslan led John out to a chorus of farewells, guiding him to a room that was both warm and handsomely appointed, with John's own bodyservant waiting and John's belongings in it. Arslan left him at the door, bowing low and smiling. "Rest well, my lord," the boy said.

He was gone before John could stop him. The way in which he had granted John the title, and the clear and slightly wicked glance that had gone with it, told John quite enough. Arslan at least had recognized King Henry's youngest and thoroughly legitimate son.

John was not accustomed to such feelings of gratitude as he felt then. Whether the boy knew it or no, John owed him a debt; and he would pay it. He swore that to himself, as Petit the bodyservant prepared him for bed.

# CHAPTER 5

The horned king waited on the other side of sleep. Arslan had gone to his bed smiling, light of heart as he had seldom been since the slaughter of Hattin. Odd too, he had thought, to be consoled by that of all travelers who might have come to the gate of La Forêt. John Lackland, Count of Mortain, youngest of the Devil's brood of Anjou, by all accounts was a difficult man. Arslan could see that; charm was not John's greatest gift, nor was he particularly sweet of disposition. And yet Arslan had taken to him.

He had been thinking of that as he fell asleep. He greeted without surprise the tall strange figure that stood in the nothingness between waking and dream. It was even less manlike than before, its crown of antlers broader, its eyes darker and deeper. "Good evening, lord," he said civilly. "I trust I find you well."

Spirits had no patience with human pleasantries; nor, it seemed, did old gods. "Time is short," the horned king said. "He is here, the one I told you of. We brought him to you by the straight track. The straight track will bring you to the sea. There a ship will be waiting. See that you sail on it, you and he both. There will be fair weather for the voyage, but not if you delay. Tarry too long, and the magic will escape our hold; then may the elder gods defend you."

"For you will not?"

"We cannot."

Arslan sighed in his dream. "And if he refuses this burden?"

"He must not," said the horned king.

The snow fell heavy through the night. Morning came late, pale light struggling through clouds and snow. Guests and travelers would go nowhere this day.

The revelry in hall had an edge of strain. There were too many of them, forced together for too long, and no escape to the freedom of the hunt or the tilting yard. The ladies, far more accustomed to tedium than the men, had retreated to Lady Mathilda's bower, there to do whatever ladies did when they had got rid of the menfolk.

Some of the younger men had got up a joust in the gallery, tilting at one another with blunted spears. Their laughter was loud, their jesting coarse; it did not sound particularly amicable from below. They tried to lure Arslan up among them when he ventured into the hall, but he was not as bored as that.

He was looking for John. King Henry's son was not in his chamber, nor was he in the hall, although his brother was. Olivier was holding William captive, regaling him with a lengthy dissertation upon the proper way to tread grapes for wine. William's eyes were glazed, his expression fixed in an expression of lordly benevolence. Arslan had no doubt that William would take revenge on his brother, come the time.

Arslan considered a rescue, but William was a man grown. He could fend for himself. Arslan slipped out more quietly than he had come, eluding a baying pack of young men with mayhem in mind.

In the end he found John in a place that, in retrospect, he should have thought of long since. It was in a neglected corner of the castle, quite near the room in which Arslan slept. There were the books that the old lord had gathered, such as he had not taken back with him to Beausoleil, kept carefully in locked chests. The room was small but furnished like a scriptorium, with a lectern and a reading table; it had a window, large and paned with precious glass, and a bank of lamps.

When Arslan first came to La Forêt, he had found the library shut and locked, full of dust and spiders, and shamefully neglected. He had had it cleaned and aired, its lamps filled, the chests unlocked and the books brought out. They were better preserved than he might have expected—and they were treasures, books of history and philosophy, of songs and tales. They would have been too frivolous for the dour man who served as Olivier's chaplain, but he had had the sense, at least, not to cast them out.

John had built himself a nest in the window embrasure, banked in cushions and coverlets and fur-lined mantle. He was a small enough man, and the embrasure was large enough, that he could coil in comfort, with a book propped on his knees and the cold light of the snowfall shining clear on the pages. He looked wonderfully content.

Arslan watched him for a while. He was the runt of King Henry's litter, people said, youngest and smallest of the lot. He was not ill-favored; for all his lack of height, he was well made, and his face was pleasing enough. He had inherited his mother's dark eyes, striking against the ruddy coloring of the Plantagenets, and her fineness of feature. When he was at rest, when his face was not set in lines of wariness and ingrained suspicion, he was good to look at. Surprisingly so, from all the tales that Arslan had heard.

He wore masks, Arslan thought. He sheathed himself in layer after layer of armor, until the spirit was hidden beyond threat of discovery. This maybe was as close to the truth of him as he would let himself come.

Would any of his masks or semblances hear what Arslan had come to say?

Arslan drew a breath, squared his shoulders, and made an audible point of entering the library. John looked up with an arch of brow. The drawbridge was up, the portcullis down. He was walled against the world. Even so, he smiled faintly, with a glimmer of honest warmth. "Good day, messire," he said.

"It's crashingly dull, if you ask the poor prisoners in the hall," Arslan said. "Your brother is going to come after you with an axe if my brother torments him much longer."

"He'll take the axe to your brother first," said John. "We'll escape in the uproar."

Arslan grinned at him. "We could run now. No one would come after us."

"In this storm," said John, "no one would ever find us again."

"Would that be a tragedy?"

"Sometimes I think not." John closed the book carefully, yawned and stretched. "I suppose it would be charitable of me to set poor William free."

"It might also be charitable of you to let my brother continue in his ignorance. He'll be mortified when he realizes that he treated the bastard like a prince, and let the prince be treated like a servant."

"I'm not a saint," John said. "Haven't you heard? I'm the Devil's get."

"And I'm her firstborn son."

"What, you?" said John. "You're a blushing innocent. I'll wager you have to invent sins to confess—you've none of your own."

"She let them baptize me," Arslan said, "and I didn't fly shrieking out the chapel window. But then, she said, it was only water, however holy mortal men might think it. She had a terrible turn for blasphemy, did my mother, but she called it the simple truth."

"Your mother was a Saracen?"

"My mother was an ifritah."

"Is that a sect of Islam?" John asked him.

"It's a sect of devils." Arslan looked into eyes that did not believe him, not at all. "Not, mind, that the jinn are all or even mostly evil. Many profess the faith of the Prophet. I know of no Christian jinn, but maybe there are a few among the worlds. In the old days they were gods, but with the coming of the Messiah and the Prophet, that went rather out of fashion."

"And I had taken you for a sane man," John said with a touch of regret.

"The half of me that is mortal is sane enough. The rest vexes me more often than not, but it has its uses."

"Do you know," said John, "I must have fallen asleep in the middle of Boethius. I'm dreaming you and your wild tales. I'll wake and it will be evening, and if God is kind, the snow will have stopped, so that at the stroke of sunrise we can be away from this place."

"Where will you be going?"

"To England," John said as if there were nowhere else a man should wish to be.

"Then there was no need—" Arslan bit his tongue.

John's ears were quick, as quick as his wits. "No need for what?"

"To bid you go to England."

"I am going," said John, "whether I am bidden or no. And truly, messire, unless he is a king, I will do no man's bidding."

"It is a king," Arslan said, "who made me his messenger, but as to his being a man, I fear he's even less of one than I am. Do you know the horned king?"

"The lord of wood and water," John said. Clearly he had decided that, since this was a dream, he could speak as he pleased. "He rules in the heart of Britain. *He* has taken an interest in me?"

"He says," said Arslan, "that the gate is open between the worlds, and the walls of air have fallen. The true king must mend them both, or the land is lost."

"I," said John with exquisite bitterness, "am no king. I am the least of my blood, the last, the afterthought. A child of three summers is named heir of Anjou, not I. You've come into the wrong dream, spirit. Go and beset Arthur of Brittany; that is the king you look for. He was bred for it. I was an accident."

"I don't know this Arthur," Arslan said. "I was sent to you."

"To me? Lackland they call me, because when I was a child there was no inheritance left for me. My father tried to carve me one, and all my brothers revolted. Now Henry the Young King is dead, and Geoffrey the Duke, the master of intrigue, is dead, and Richard the perfect knight is gone away on Crusade. And maybe there is a throne and a crown for me, but not now. Not till there is no other choice."

"You are chosen," said Arslan. "The way is open for you; a ship is waiting. Britain has great need of you."

"Why?"

This was a difficult man in truth, Arslan thought. He gave the only answer he could think of. "Because there is no other choice."

John laughed. "Ah, truth! You'd make a wretched courtier, boy."

"Are you any better?" Arslan asked him.

"Not in the slightest," said John. "But then I'm a king's son. I can say whatever I please, and no one dares to be offended."

"In many places," Arslan said, "a demon's son shares that distinction."

"But not here."

"Ah well," said Arslan. "My brothers never did forgive our father for leaving them. When he proceeded almost at once to console himself for the loss of their mother, that added insult to the injury."

"Men do that," John said. "I'll wager they do it themselves."

"But not with spirits of fire."

"You do believe that," John said.

"I know it." Arslan met the narrowed dark eyes. "Will you come to Britain by the swift way? There is a track laid for us and a ship waiting, and fair sailing promised, if we go quickly."

" 'Us'? You go, too?"

"I also am summoned," Arslan said, and shut his mouth on what more he might have said.

John said it for him. "Whether you will or no. What, would you prefer to follow the Crusade?"

"Yes," said Arslan, biting off the word.

"Then go. I free you. If I'm the chosen one, whatever I've been chosen for, I'm given that power, yes?"

"No," said Arslan.

"Why? You owe Britain nothing."

Arslan shrugged. "I'm needed."

John's lip twitched. "Jerusalem has Richard. Britain has—what? A whole man and a good part of a demon between the two of us?"

"And a pair of Seljuk Turks, a king's bastard, and a company of men-at-arms. And," said Arslan, "an old god with the head of a stag."

"A mighty army," John said dryly.

"Perhaps the enemy, whoever and whatever it is, will underestimate us."

"We can pray for that," said John.

"Then you will come?" said Arslan.

"I want—need—to be in England. For the rest of it, let's strike a bargain. I'll go with you, and take your way. If you prove false, your life is forfeit."

"I won't prove false," Arslan said.

"Let us hope that you do not," said John.

# CHAPTER 6

~⌘~

It was not John's charity that betrayed him to Olivier; it was William. John's brother had had enough of the baron's too-eager hospitality. As John came down with Arslan, braving the hall and hoping to be fed, William sprang up with a grand show of delight. "John! My lord of Mortain! Come, sit, warm yourself with wine."

Olivier's expression was altogether satisfactory. The color had drained from his face. He stared at John as if the prince had sprouted a devil's horns.

John smiled and took the chair William had vacated, which in fact was the lord's own. It had been made for Arslan's father. John was dwarfed in it, but no more so than Olivier.

John did not carry himself like a small man, unless it suited his purpose. Today he was as royal as he needed to be; he made that high carved seat seem no more than adequate for his rank and station. He was gracious to the lords and lords' sons who waited on him like servants, and royally condescending to the baron.

He expected that Arslan would be seated beside him, waited on as he was, given every honor that they judged worthy of the trueborn son of Henry Plantagenet and the Duchess of Aquitaine. Arslan would have been more than happy to efface himself, but John was taking revenge with remarkable thoroughness. He could not be content until Olivier himself served as cupbearer to them both, and brought them meat and bread and sweets, and served them with his own hands.

John had not made a friend this day. Nor, if he knew it, did he care. He had taken the lordship with the lord's seat. It was his feast, his revel, his entertainment. He called for singers and dancers. He demanded mountebanks and jugglers. He breathed life into the revel, shifted and focused it, until they forgot boredom and the tedium of the storm.

He ended it as he had begun it, by royal fiat. It was not particularly late, but night had fallen some time since. He sent the revelers to their beds, Olivier among them, dismissed as if he had been one of the squires. "See that my men are made ready to ride," John said to him. "We leave at sunrise."

He did not tarry to hear whether Olivier replied. Arm in arm with Arslan, he swept toward the room that he had been given.

At the door, Arslan dug in his heels. It was open, and the bed was occupied. He recognized both of the young women there. Jeannette and her sister Marguerite lay side by side amid the coverlets. He had an eyeful of rosy breasts, broad swelling hips, mingled tumble of curls, before he turned and tried to bolt.

John was there, barring his way. "Won't you tarry?" he asked.

Arslan's cheeks were burning. Even John's laughter could not keep him in that place. He fled as if he had never seen a woman in his life.

"Ah, innocence," he heard John say behind him.

He did a thing he should never have done, that he had never done before where anyone could see. He whirled and flung the fire that was in him. He did not strike to harm; he was not as far gone as that. John stood gaping in a shower of sparks, cool and pale as the snow that swirled about the castle's walls. Arslan shook the remnants from his hands, turned, and left with something resembling dignity.

Not until he was well gone did it dawn on him that not only John had seen. The sisters had been watching, too, as blankly astonished as John.

Now he had to leave La Forêt. Even if John had not won Olivier's lasting enmity, this would make the castle unlivable. Arslan the old lord's bastard was difficult enough to bear. Arslan the devil's child would be more than anyone could endure.

He took refuge for the night in his familiar cell. No one vexed him there, and no sound but the wailing of the wind and the soft rasp of Yusuf's snore. Their baggage was packed and laid by the door: surprisingly little for as long as the three of them had been on this side of the sea.

Now they would cross another sea, into a country he did not know at all. The Turks seemed unperturbed. The whole west was alien to them; it mattered little how far they went or how many seas they crossed.

He could learn from their example. It distracted him a little from the memory of the two women in John's bed, and the thought of what they were doing there while he lay alone.

The snow had stopped not long after nightfall. By morning the sky was clear, the sun rising over a world of stainless white. The air was surprisingly warm after the bitter cold of past days; already drops were falling from the castle's roof and sliding down from the battlements.

John's party was mounted and ready to ride by full light, but it was much nearer noon before their lord emerged from the warmth of the castle. He offered no apology. He simply bade a princely farewell to the castle and its fuming, shivering lord, mounted his horse, and rode out the gate.

Arslan's farewell had taken them all by surprise. It interested him to see who was honestly regretful and who was simply startled, and who was openly glad. Rogier spoke for them all: "You're going with *him*? Why?"

Arslan shrugged. He had no answer that would satisfy any of them.

"It should be obvious," his brother Amaury said. "This is a king's son. He'll be a king himself in time, it's said, and he's openhanded with his father's bastards. There's hope of advancement, isn't there, little brother? Better than you'll have here, with a small demesne and four older brothers."

Four older, legitimate brothers. That went without saying. Arslan had not thought of that at all. Patrons were never lacking for a man trained in the wars against the infidel, though he be landless and fatherless and bastard-born. This was another thing, a thing of his mother's world, which these sons of a mortal woman would never have understood.

He let them think what they would, and bade farewell to them without regret. He would miss the castle more, because it was so much like Beausoleil, but even that had slipped from his mind almost before the road had taken him out of sight.

He had come to this place in such hope, eager to meet his brothers, full of dreams and foolishness about his kin and his lineage and the land that had been his father's. He had found a cold welcome and acceptance that came grudgingly if at all. There was no place for him here.

Outremer was overrun with Saracens. La Forêt did not want him.

Britain was demanding that he come to it. It was a simple choice in the end. Maybe the gods and powers had made it so. It was very like them to have done such a thing.

He rode from La Forêt without a backward glance. They had escort for quite some time: lords and squires and guests of the castle, delighted to be freed from the confinement of the hall. His brothers did not ride with them, nor did most of the nephews. Arslan was glad of that. It was a lively, bawdy riding, with John in the thick of it, and his brother the Longsword telling tales that made Arslan's ears burn.

Just short of the town of Miremont, the escort turned back. John's company rode round the town, rather than slow their pace by passing through it.

Arslan had been riding in the rear, away from the boisterous good cheer of his brothers' friends and relations. Past Miremont he found himself in the van beside John. The road was changing, shifting underfoot. It had not yet straightened as his heart told him it would, but they were not entirely in the world any longer, either.

John looked well rested and rather pleased with himself. "They think I've stolen you," he observed.

"They're glad to be rid of me," Arslan said.

"I suppose they are. They're so very respectable. Is it true that your father had a whole retinue of Seljuks, which he kept right there in the castle?"

"He had a dozen, and their wives and children."

"All infidels?"

"To the youngest babe in arms."

John contemplated that, narrow-eyed. Then he laughed. He laughed softly, but it went on for quite a long time. One would have thought that it was the most wonderful jest he had heard in a score of lifetimes. "Oh! Oh, by God's sweet Mother. What a horror of a life your brothers must have led!"

Arslan had never thought of it so. And yet, when he remembered the way of things in France, and not only in La Forêt, he began to see how perfectly, appallingly strange the old lord and his servants must have been. His brothers would have striven to forget all of that—until Arslan came to remind them.

He did not find it a grand jest as John did, but it roused him to a little more charity toward his brothers. He would serve a day or two less in purgatory for it.

The sun sank with wintry swiftness, casting long shadows across the snow. The road now was almost perfectly straight. They were entering a wood of ancient trees, dark and deep except for the faint ruddy glimmer of sunset on the track.

"I've seen this wood before," John said beside him.

"Yes," said Arslan. "This is the Worldwood. It runs between the worlds, and guards the straight tracks. It brought you from Chinon to La Forêt. It will bring us to the sea."

"Will that be the sea of the world I know?"

John was not frightened, exactly, but he was not at ease, either. Arslan tried to reassure him with the truth. "We'll come back to mortal earth, and mortal water, too."

"Soon?"

"As soon as may be."

Arslan rode in silence while John brooded on that. It was clear, this change in worlds. That there were other tracks, other worlds, he felt keenly; if he allowed himself to drift half into a dream, he could even see them like shadows upon shadows, laid one over another on this single track.

Shapes moved about and through him, travelers as he was. Some might have been aware of him. Others were oblivious. All moved with purpose, and the track bore them straight to their certain end.

The track was warded with great bonds of magic, strong powers that thrummed in his bones. Beyond it was a swirl of darkness and confusion.

Wild Magic, he thought. It seemed greatly agitated. Sometimes as they passed through the wood, he saw foregatherings of spirits, tumbled masses of living will. The Wild Magic was wilder there, mounting to a whirlwind. The spirits struggled against it, clinging to what strength and form they had. Not all were strong enough. Those melted and shredded and vanished into the storm.

He felt it as a dart of icy cold through the fire of his spirit. It had no care for him at all, for good or evil. It simply wanted to scatter and roil and confuse, because that was its nature: to undo order.

The straight track was a great frustration to it, and a great force against it. It had laid siege to the track in places, but the wards held.

Their passage both drew the Wild Magic and repelled it. Spirits had always followed Arslan, curious to see an ifrit housed in human flesh, and some of them had been odd and rather wild. But these who gathered about the track were drawn to John as well.

Arslan looked at him with the inner eye, the eye he kept shut in the mortal world. Devil's get indeed: spirit of air and swift water, shot with a strange dark fire. The Demon Countess' blood was strong in him. It was Wild Magic, but different, as if it had been mingled with a jinni or an ifrit or a spirit of like semblance—as if John's foremother had been, like Arslan, a halfblood, but of spirit and Wild Magic rather than spirit and man.

That was why, Arslan thought, John must be king, and not Richard, not simply because Richard had refused the burden. John had inherited the full measure of his foremother's magic. Richard had not. Richard was altogether human, completely of earth.

The Crusade would have been the safer choice. Better the Saracen than the things that waited beyond the straight track.

And yet, as Arslan recognized this, he came closer to acceptance than he had before. Here was death or worse. It was a worthy fight, worthier than that vexed conflict between God and Allah—although Arslan would have been most ill advised to say so. His heart had never truly been in the Crusade, only in winning back what was his. But this, which threatened the cords that bound the world: this was a war worth waging.

# CHAPTER 7

John had been half hopeful, half afraid that they would camp beside this strange track or lodge in an inn or posthouse that belonged to Faerie. But as night fell, the track brought them to the gate of an abbey that was a great deal more than half a day's ride from La Forêt. As with the ride from Chinon, the track had shortened the way, and brought him where, just then, he needed to go.

That tonight it was an abbey struck him with fine irony. There was nothing Christian about the road that had taken him here, but evidently there was nothing in it that either feared or despised the Lord Christ. The monks welcomed them with Christian goodwill, fed them rough bread and coarse cheese and refectory ale, and made them part of the offices of the evening and the night.

John noticed that Arslan's Seljuks did not shun the chapel, though they refrained from participation in the offices. He also noticed that the monks exchanged glances but did not cast them out. That was miraculous tolerance in this year of Crusade.

After Vespers, when the others went to rest before the Night Office at midnight, John remained in the chapel. The candles flickered about the altar. The air was full of whispers. Wind blew without, and a sound like the sighing of waves, though this place was two days' hard ride from the sea.

He prayed for a while, not to ask for anything, not really, but only to remind the Lord God that he existed. God in his reckoning was a great deal like King Henry: powerful, choleric, and inclined to forget that he had sons, except when he had a use for one or more of them.

John had been the favorite, all the others insisted: Henry coddled him and cherished him and scraped together bits of land for him. But if that had been coddling and cherishing, then God help the rest. To

John it had seemed that he was for the most part ignored unless there was a holiday or an occasion to be trotted out and flaunted as proof, yet again, that the king was as manly a man with his queen as with any other woman he set eyes on.

And to think, thought John, that when he was born he had been intended for the Church. Henry never had explained why, when John was still very young, he had had his son brought out of the abbey of Fontevrault and sent into lordly fosterage. It was a fortunate decree; John had no calling to the priesthood. But it was done as only Henry would do it, abrupt, headlong, and high-handed; nor had he ever thought to ask his son for an opinion in the matter.

There was a kind of blessedness in the chapel tonight, a deep familiarity. John's earliest memories were of candles, incense, and sacred chanting. When his soul was vexed and his temper uncertain, his surest refuge was in chapel or abbey: asylum for the spirit, however brief.

His prayer slipped from words into silence. He knelt in as much peace as his restless heart could know, without need of sleep, for here he had heart's ease.

Out of that peace, a figure took shape. John regarded it without fear. It seemed to be a man, long and lean and lantern-jawed, with sparse fair hair and clear blue eyes: a Saxon of the old blood, dressed in miter and cope over a monk's habit.

As the apparition came to stand over him, only his nose told him that it was not a man. There was nothing about it of human scent, either rank or sweet. He was reminded vividly of wild roses in the hedges of England, and the delicate fragrance of the wood-violet in the copses in the spring. And yet in every other way, this seemed to be a man. He breathed; his bones creaked as he sat on the altar step. His eyes on John were bright, but he squinted a little, nearsighted. His voice was resonant, a deep warm rumble of a voice. "Good evening, John of Oxford."

No one had ever called John that, though he was born there. John Plantagenet, John Lackland, John of Mortain, of Ireland, of Cornwall, of Gloucester—but never of the place where he was born. Oxford had simply happened to be where his mother was when she came to her time. She would have preferred France; Aquitaine for choice. But queens were not always given choices.

He was born in the heart of England, at the dark of the year, on the eve of Christmas. None of that had been of any great moment, not to his parents or his kin. But it would matter greatly in this world of shadows and apparitions and straight tracks.

"Good evening," he said, "my lord bishop."

The apparition smiled. "Yes, I was a bishop once—of Worcester, as God blessed me."

John's eyes widened. "Wulfstan? You are Wulfstan of Worcester?"

The shadowy bishop bowed. "At your service, my lord."

"That is a great honor," John said. "I've heard you called a saint, round about your old see. Have you come to bless my undertaking?"

"You will do it, then?" Wulfstan asked.

"I'm not entirely sure what I can or will do," said John, "but I am going to England, now that my exile is ended."

"No one has spoken to you, then?" said Wulfstan.

"Only the boy who looks mortal enough until he's aggravated. Then," said John, "he sends off sparks."

Wulfstan smiled. "Ah yes, the ifritah's child. His mother's kin are allies of ours."

"But," said John, "are you not a Christian saint?"

"Christian certainly," Wulfstan said, "and rather more a good soul than a bad one. But do you know, when the flesh sloughs away, certain matters shrink in significance. These wars of yours, these jihads and Crusades—such folly. What should it matter which face of God a man worships? It's God still, no matter the name."

"I think that's heresy," John said slowly.

Wulfstan laughed, deep and joyful. "Surely! Surely it is. So then, young prince: you know what need we have of you."

"I know something of walls and Wild Magic, and a little of urgency. But no more than that," John said. But then he added, "I know that something about me is useful to you and yours. What? That I was born in England?"

"And that you are a descendent of a certain unearthly countess," said Wulfstan, "and trueborn son of Britain's king."

"My brother is king," John said as he had to Arslan.

"Your brother refused this charge," Wulfstan said.

"So it's left to me?" John found the taste of that bitter, but not unfamiliar.

"He was not suited," Wulfstan said, "nor truly chosen. He knows nothing of Britain, nor cares for it. His heart is in Jerusalem, or failing that, in France. Whereas you . . ."

"Britain is dear to me," John granted him.

"And that," said Wulfstan, "we need. That love of the land, that knowledge of it, its people, the language they speak, the lives they live on the green earth—so few kings have it."

"I am not a king."

"So you are given to saying," Wulfstan said. "What if I told you that you are in error? That you can take the power and the strength of the title, and do what must be done? What would you say to that?"

"I would say," said John, " 'Get thee behind me, Satan.' "

"'And all the kingdoms of the world shall be thine,' " Wulfstan said from the same Scripture, but with a smile that took the mockery out of the words. "One kingdom, in truth; and there is a price."

"Of course there is a price," said John. "What is it? My immortal soul?"

"That is safe from us," Wulfstan said. "Our prices are more immediate, and more obviously difficult."

John raised his brows.

"If you do this," said Wulfstan, "you must do this as true king of all Britain. You will be crowned by our rite, consecrated to the task before you, endowed with rights and powers beyond the reach of mere mortal kings."

John found that he could not breathe. All the kingdoms of earth, indeed. All he had dreamed of but never honestly expected to win, not freely, not without the taint of treason.

As if his thoughts had bred the words, Wulfstan said, "The price is this. You will be king in heart and spirit, but in the world of men there will be no knowledge of this. They will see you as a traitor, a betrayer of your brother's trust. They will declare that you have seized what was never yours to take, and they will hate you for it—hate you long and hate you well, and curse your memory long after your body is dead. You gain the truth, John of Oxford, but the mortal world will never know it."

"What, never at all?"

"Not in this age of the world," said Wulfstan. "All the worlds and the powers in them will bow before you, but mortal men will scorn and despise you."

John considered that, not long, but carefully enough. "I will be king? With the powers of a king?"

Wulfstan nodded, bowing his head in its antique miter.

"Will I rule? Will that be contested?"

"Men will contest it," said Wulfstan, "and when your task is done, if it can be done, you will be forced to submit. You will bow before your brother as if he and not you were true king."

"Why? What makes it so vital to conceal the truth from mortal men?"

"The illusion of free will," said the dead bishop of Worcester, "and the laws of the high magic. No power without price. No strength without weakness. No glory without humiliation."

"How like the Church," John said.

Wulfstan smiled. "Yes. Very like."

"I was never fit for that life," said John. "What makes you think I'm fit for this?"

"You may not be," Wulfstan said. "The choice is yours."

John regarded him with arched brow. "The illusion of free will?"

"Just so," said Wulfstan.

"Must I choose now?"

"No," Wulfstan said. "You are given the right to refuse, until the moment the kingdom is sealed to your spirit. Thereafter you are bound. While Britain stands, you stand. If Britain falls, you fall with it. Your heart will be given to it, and your strength will be bound in it."

"All my strength?"

"All of it," said Wulfstan. "Nor can that kingship ever be taken from you. Whatever men say, whatever they remember, you have the truth."

Truth, thought John, or the shadow of it that glimmered in men's eyes. To know within himself that he was king, but to be forbidden the image of it in the world he had lived in until now. Forbidden forever, it seemed; condemned perpetually to an ill name, because he had chosen, or been forced to choose, this thing of mist and magic.

The Devil's brood he and his brothers might be, but their feet were planted firmly in earth. They lived to rule this world, fought one another viciously for it, plotted and schemed and intrigued endlessly on its behalf.

This vision of a man a hundred years dead was bidding him cast it all away in the name of—what? High magic? Spells and gramaries? What was truth, after all, and what was shadow?

"I know what I would be giving up," he said. "Tell me what I would gain. The title of king is a pleasant prospect, but what use is it if I can't hold it in this world as well as the rest?"

"You will be king of men in your time," said Wulfstan. "Now we need a king who is more. What do you gain in your impatient youth? Magic. Powers over the land, over wind and water. The authority to command spirits and the armies of the air. A little power, too, over men: to heal, to bring comfort."

"And no more?"

"What would you wish? Wealth? Women? Flocks of eager flatterers?"

John came near to spitting at that. "Give me men who are loyal, and will stay loyal. Give me as much power as I need, when I need it, and the knowledge to use it. Promise me that in the fullness of time I will wear England's crown in this world as well as the other. Do all of that, and I will consider this."

"All of that is yours by right of your kingship," Wulfstan said.

"If I choose to take it."

Wulfstan inclined his head. Even as he completed the gesture, he faded like an image reflected in water, shimmering and shattering into nothingness.

John was still kneeling on the chapel floor. His knees ached; his body shook with cold. He rose stiffly. The peace he had found in that place was long gone. He would sleep, if he could, and let the thinking spin itself out on the other side of the dark. Then, with God's grace, he would know what to do.

# CHAPTER 8

❧

"Tell me why I should do this."

Arslan had the soldier's gift of waking at once and completely, but even with that, he lay blinking at John. The Count of Mortain must have been sleeping: his thick ginger hair stood on end, and his face had a rumpled look. Yet there was no sleep in him at all. He was fiercely awake, every sense alert.

"Tell me why," he said again.

"Because you have no choice," Arslan's tongue said for him.

John laughed. While he indulged in his paroxysm of mirth, Arslan sat up, wrapping cloak and blankets about himself, and rubbed sleep out of his eyes. It was not quite dawn: his skin knew the feel of it, how the earth turned between night and morning. In a little while the bell would ring for the morning office, but the silence now was deep, the monks taking what sleep they were permitted before the call to devotion.

At last John stopped laughing. He grinned at Arslan like a fox in a hedgerow, all sharp teeth and wild eyes. "I knew I could trust you for an honest answer."

"I always say what I think," Arslan said.

John sat at the end of the bed, tucking up his feet. "It's a grudging offer they make me. I can be king—but the price is ghastly high. I don't recall my brother suffering any such thing. Our father died, which was more a relief than not, and he was king. Simple. Straightforward. Uncomplicated. Then off he went on his Crusade, leaving the mopping-up to me."

"Did he know what he was doing?"

John shrugged. "Who knows, with Richard? Sometimes I think his skull is solid bone. Other times I suspect he has a certain low cunning that could, in some lights, pass for intelligence."

Arslan carefully kept his thoughts to himself. He had seen Richard Coeur-de-Lion, and his formidable mother, too. John was more like Eleanor than he would ever have wanted to know.

"They promised me loyal men," said John. "How loyal can you be?"

"How loyal do you need me to be?"

"Would you die for me?"

Arslan had to ponder that. "For you, no," he said. "But for what you will be, if you choose to take it, and if I choose to serve you, yes, I will be loyal to the death."

"Even if they call you John's yellow dog?"

Arslan shivered. The man had prescience—or wit that passed for it. "I don't care for what men say. My heart is given where it is given. When my father died I took no new liege lord."

"Not even Richard?"

"Men love him," Arslan said. "I can see why. But he's not my lord."

"What, did he proposition you?"

"Never to my face," Arslan said levelly.

"Strange," John said. "He's fond of the big fair ones. You're better than passable to look at. I suppose you can fight, or you'd not have survived Hattin."

"That was luck," said Arslan, "and my father taking the blow that was meant for me."

"Really? He died for you?"

Arslan wanted to strike that brightly interested face, those cold intent eyes. He thought maybe John wanted that; he mastered his temper and kept his voice steady. "We're a loyal family," he said.

"Even to one another?"

"Peculiar as that may be," Arslan said, "yes."

"It's odd," John said. "I should take this thing the Powers offer me, which may cost more than I ever gain from it, if only to know what it is to have a loyal servant."

"It's an oddity of your reputation," said Arslan, "that although you have no gift for making men love you, you keep certain servants and close retainers about you for years on end. If they're not loyal, then what do you call them?"

"Competent," John said. "I have no patience for fools. Flatterers I loathe. Serve me well and I'm the best of masters. Serve me poorly and I have no mercy. I will not be deceived by smiles or pretty words.

Service is *service*: do your work, do it well and in timely fashion, never shirk or dally. I do not hear excuses. When I command, that command is to be executed."

"And if the command is folly?"

"Tell me so. Convince me. If you succeed, you have your will. If you fail, I cast you out."

Arslan bowed to that.

"Then I will do it," John said. "I'll take this thing that's thrust on me."

"Because of me?"

"Is that too great a burden to bear?"

"It's no more than I can carry," said Arslan. He hoped that that was the truth, for if it was not, then he was bound to it regardless.

From St. Gervasius' abbey to the sea, by the straight track, was a short day's ride. They began in fair weather, warm for winter, like a foretaste of spring. Even the Worldwood seemed almost bright, with sunlight slipping through the branches to dapple the forest floor.

Arslan should have been glad to be so close to the end of the journey, but he had roused from his interrupted sleep to a sense of jangling uneasiness. It had only grown worse as they rode into the Worldwood. The others were less cowed by the strangeness than they had been before; they laughed, chattered, sang. None seemed aware that their voices had no resonance: the sound sank as soon as it rose, swallowed in the shadows under the trees.

These were men of war, and yet they had posted no guard, sent out no scouts. That was wise, maybe; mortal men should not wander too far afield here. But that left them with no certainty that the way would be clear. They were riding into a kind of war. Might not the enemy have discovered their riding, and mounted an ambush?

Arslan brought in his Seljuks with a glance to either side of him. They had a wary look, too, he noticed.

"We'll ride ahead," he said to John. "It might be wise to bid your men string their bows."

"Danger?" John asked, quick as always.

"Maybe," said Arslan. He did not wait for John's leave, though once he was gone, he wondered if he should have.

If truly John wanted competence above all things, then he would understand. And if not, then not.

Arslan took the lead, with the others behind. Their short Turkish bows were strung. He freed his own from its case as he rode, uncoiled the string, bent the strong recurved arms and settled the string in place. His grey mare, bred and trained in Outremer, snorted softly. She knew the smell of danger in the air.

And yet this might be nothing that mortal arrows could pierce. Bow and lance and sword were a comfort, even so.

All his senses unfolded. Beneath the scent of melting snow and winter bark and deep leafmold was something strange, sweet yet dark, like the smell of death. The silence was too deep, too still. The shadows were full of eyes.

The wards on the road were clear now to his perception, as if he rode through a colonnade of light with arching roof and glimmering floor. He had expected to find it under siege, but nothing stirred beyond it, not even a fugitive shadow.

That did not comfort him. He called the Seljuks in closer. "Be alert," he said in their language, as if spirits of air could not understand any speech of men that they pleased. "Karim, if we're attacked, go back to John; tell him they should all sing psalms as loudly and devoutly as they can. Don't rest until they do it. It may protect them."

"We could chant holy Koran," Kalila said.

"By all means," said Arslan, "but not as you ride back to those faithful Franks, or they'll take you for the devil you're fleeing."

The flash of her smile reassured him. She was unafraid; her heart was strong. "Will it be worse if I come at them singing the *Te Deum laudamus*?"

"Notably worse," Arslan said, "coming from the likes of you."

She sighed with vast regret. "And I sing it so well, too."

Levity eased the weight of foreboding. It strengthened the wards, made their bindings glow brighter. Still there was something ahead, waiting, like an army in ambush.

As easily as Arslan had moved among the worlds of men and spirits as a child, he had never learned the art or craft of it, any more than he had learned to breathe. It was born in him, native to him. Likewise with such other gifts as his mother had left him; they were there, but he had no tutelage in them.

Now truly he felt the lack. Like a child who had spent his life galloping about on an aged and evil pony, now he came face to face with a knight's destrier, armored and accoutered and ready for battle. Whatever he had thought he knew, none of it was enough.

He would have to do what he could. Once he had opened his senses, he could feel the men riding behind, and John in the midst of them, a spirit shot with darkness and light. When he thought of what was ahead, he struck what felt for all the world like a castle wall, high and cold and impregnable. Walls of air? Did France have them, too?

A castle could be taken by siege or by treachery. There was no wall that truly could not be broken.

Not, at least, in the mortal world. That was poor comfort here, where mortals seldom went.

The track went on, as straight as ever. Arslan felt the temptation to relax his guard, but not as a natural human weariness. Maybe it was the other blood in him, but it seemed to him that it came from elsewhere—from outside the wards and the track. He willed himself to be more alert than ever.

It was hard. That other will was softly relentless. There was nothing to fear. Nothing threatened the track. Nothing waited in ambush. Nothing, nothing, nothing.

He beat it back, lashing by pure blind instinct. Fire roared out of him. The track itself trembled; the wards burst into flame. He felt the walls go down—there was a strangeness in it, as if they would have fallen whether he broke them or no. For an instant he caught the glimmer of another power, and another presence or gathering of presences. Then they were gone, and he saw before him the thing that waited.

It had coiled itself just past the track's end, on an open windswept moor beside the northern sea. A stone circle stood between, crumbling and moss-grown but still intact. The track ran straight into its center and there vanished. Beyond the circle, gleaming darkly in the winter evening, lay the child of old night.

It was a serpent, but the coils of it were taller than a tall man, and the head that rested atop those coils was as long and broad and deep as the horse Arslan sat on. Its flat unblinking eyes fixed on the track's end.

There was nothing in those eyes that Arslan could touch. They were absolutely, unreachably alien. This thing existed to eat. That was all its being, and all its purpose. It was set like a snake at a rathole, simply and coldly to devour whatever came out of the stone circle.

It was pure insult. To regard the chosen king of Britain as nothing more than vermin—whoever, whatever had done this, had found the one certain way to assure that John would take the kingship that was offered him. John would do it for revenge, no more and no less.

If, of course, he survived this journey. Knights with long lances would have served better here than men-at-arms with pikes, or even Turkish archers.

Arslan brought his horse to a halt at the edge of the Worldwood. A thought had come into his mind. It was a wicked thought, a thought perhaps unworthy.

This was a test: of John's pride, of his servants' strength. If he failed now, Britain would know that he was not the king it needed. If he passed the guardian, he would meet other tests, maybe, but none so simple or so purely contemptuous.

The Wild Magic was nowhere within reach of his perception. This was not high magic, either. It was—

He peered closer. It was illusion. The walls that he had sensed, the foreboding, were part of it. He rode forward. His grey mare jibbed a little, but she was obedient to his will.

He did not know how to banish illusion, except by refusing to see it: by wishing it away. This was a strong deception, a thing of power in its own right.

Just within the circle of stones, he halted again. His bow was in his hand. He set an arrow to the string, an arrow made of olivewood from Outremer, fletched with the feathers of the desert falcon. It was made to fly straight and true, and pierce the heart of whatever it struck.

He aimed for the center of the coil. The serpent was stirring, rousing to his presence. He drew the string back as far as his strength and the bow's curve would allow, and loosed.

The serpent lifted its head. Its eyes glittered. It hissed, flicking a forked tongue as long as a man's body.

The arrow vanished into the blued steel of scales. Arslan held his breath.

The illusion collapsed upon itself. Where it had been, a human shape lay on the ground. Arslan's arrow had pierced its shoulder.

He advanced warily, alert for ambushes. Things were fluttering beyond the stone circle, faint flickers of strangeness, beings that were not quite coherent enough to be spirits, but were more than winds or wafts of mist.

He paused between two massive stones, under the weight of the lintel. The world's wind blew about him, pungent with sea-salt. Waves crashed beyond the headland; once or twice he saw a fan of spume.

The sorcerer who had wrought the serpent's spell had gone still. He was alive: he breathed in gasps. He was clothed in a monk's habit, and the head was tonsured, with a ring of greying dark hair clipped above the ears.

It was a man indeed, and mortal enough to Arslan's senses; he was past middle years but still hale, sturdy and stocky, and bearing the pain of the wound in teeth-gritted silence. Arslan knelt and got a grip on the monk's shoulder, and worked the arrow deftly through the joining of bones. The monk wheezed with the pain of it but did not cry out.

When the arrow was free, Arslan stanched the blood with his shirt, and brushed the wound with a little of his fiery self. As he bound it up, he saw that the monk's eyes were on him, steady and dark, and somewhat puzzled.

"You were supposed to be a fighting man," the monk said.

"Every fighting man knows plain field surgery," Arslan said. And after a pause: "So. It was a test."

"You weren't supposed to know that," said the monk.

"What was I supposed to be? Mindless muscle?"

The monk laughed, startled; then he blanched and gasped as his wound protested.

"Karim," said Arslan over his shoulder, "bring John here. It is safe?" he demanded of the monk.

"For the moment," the monk said.

Arslan helped him to sit against the sun-warmed face of a stone, and fed him spiced wine from the bottle that had come from La Forêt. His eyes widened at the quality, but he did not try to drink more than Arslan would give him.

"That was a very foolish thing I did," the monk said as they waited for John. "There was a cold-drake waiting here for you. We disposed of it, but I reckoned that you should have a warning." He peered at Arslan. "How did you know?"

Arslan shrugged. "I felt it." He peered in his turn. " 'We'? There are more of you?"

"Waiting with the ship," the monk said.

"I felt the cold-drake, too," said Arslan, "but I didn't feel you vanquish it. I didn't feel your presence, either, nor the others, whoever they are. I only felt that I should know more—feel more. I'm too untutored."

That, for him, was a great outburst. If this too was an illusion, and the monk's face concealed a demon's snarling mask, then he might be in actual danger. But he sensed no such thing.

"We sent the cold-drake back whence it came," the monk said. "It was simple enough, as such things go."

"Not simple for us."

"You will have teaching," said the monk firmly, more to himself than to Arslan. "You as well as John. Yes, we did see you as brawn to his brain. But now I have you in front of me . . . brawn in plenty, and more coming, certainly, but there is a great deal more to you than we thought."

"I'm glad to hear it," Arslan said dryly.

He was watching the monk while they spoke, measuring the pallor of the skin and the tautness of pain in the lips and nostrils. There was no immediate danger, but the man should rest soon; and the sun was sinking low.

"How far is it to the ship?" Arslan asked.

"Just over the hill," said the monk rather more faintly than he had before, "in the harbor under the headland."

Arslan measured the distance in the long golden light. "Yusuf," he said. "Wait here. Bring the others when they come."

Yusuf frowned, but he held his tongue. Wise man. Arslan helped the monk onto the grey mare's back. She suffered a stranger's presence for Arslan's sake, carrying him carefully, setting down each foot with delicate precision. Arslan walked beside her, ready to catch the monk if he lost his grip, but the man seemed able to ride.

It was not far to the edge of the headland. A path wound down the slope, steep but not impossibly so. Down below was a white curve of sand and a little harbor, sheltered from the wind, and a ship floating at anchor. It was a lovely ship, not large but substantial enough, with a high prow carved like a dragon's head, and a single tall mast.

A smaller boat was drawn up on the shore. A handful of armed mariners stood about it, surrounding three who must be of higher rank: two tall men with a look of war about them, and a woman who made Arslan think of a bright spring morning in the hills of Outremer.

She was as splendid as sunlight in this cold place, with her crown of fiery braids and the spray of sun-kisses across her cheeks. She was tall, and more robust than slender; no delicate flower, she. Something about her was familiar, but his memory would not, just then, tell him what it was.

It was she who came forward through the circle of guards, striding swiftly, with such an expression that Arslan felt as if a blast of fiery wind had swept across him. She had the monk in her arms and was lowering him from the saddle before Arslan could move; when he reached to help, her glance was like a slap.

He ignored it. Between them they carried the wounded man to the boat, where the two men waited. They took him there and settled him in the boat, wrapping him in cloaks.

The taller and fairer of the two men boarded with him, and all of the mariners. Arslan found his way barred by the darker, broader man and the woman.

He elected to stand where he was. John was coming; the boat would come back, surely, once it had taken the wounded man to safety.

It seemed he had chosen rightly. The woman's temper cooled a perceptible fraction. The man smiled at him.

He started a little. This man had come to Outremer on pilgrimage, and ridden for a season with the armies of the Kingdom of Jerusalem. He had changed little in the years since, save that he was a little broader, a little thicker, and there was a thread or two of grey in his dark beard. The scar of the sword cut that he had taken in a skirmish near Nablus was old now and faded, but still visible, cleaving his brow and just missing his eye.

"My lord William," Arslan said.

"So you remember me," said the Marshal of England.

"Very well, messire," said Arslan. "You're one of the guardians, then. I should have expected it."

"It's my fault you're here," the Marshal admitted. "I did warn Father Hugh not to underestimate you."

Arslan lowered his eyes. He could not honestly confess that he was sorry he had shot the man. He said instead, "I hope I didn't hurt him too badly."

"He'll live, I think," the Marshal said.

While they spoke, Arslan had been aware of the woman watching them. She was not as old as he had thought; the fierceness of her expression aged her. He suspected she might not be so very much older than he was himself.

She was terribly angry with him. The Marshal's pleasure in his presence irked her beyond measure. He began to wonder if she was even as old as he was. Her temper was more a child's than a woman's.

He kept his thoughts to himself. John was coming: he felt as much as heard the thudding of hooves above. In a little while the first rider came down the path: Kalila leading them, John's party behind, Yusuf bringing up the rear. The knot in Arslan's belly eased. They were all safe, unharmed, no wounds of body or spirit. It seemed they were to escape France unscathed.

# CHAPTER 9

The ship's name was *Mathonwy*, and she was a magical ship. Arslan came to that conclusion as she drew up close to the shore, sent out a ramp, and loaded all the horses into her hold, every one, and their riders and the baggage and the sumpter mules, too. For the high ones there was a cabin above, no smaller than a sleeping cell in a castle, furnished well and handsomely. She was a tidy ship, perfectly in order, with bright paint on her rails, and a glorious purple sail that went up in the last of the light.

The sun as it touched the horizon sent a shaft of living gold across the water. It was a straight track, lingering long after the sun had set, paling slowly from red-gold to the blued silver of moonlight and starlight.

As they set sail upon it, Arslan, gazing back, both saw and felt the wall that rose, a veil of light between the ship and the land of France. Walls of air, he thought: defenses of the kingdom. Faintly he felt the power behind them, the web of magic that had wrought them, and a glimmer of awareness that someone, some power, had breached them. But it did not turn outward toward the invaders. The straight track protected them.

The ship's captain was a mortal man, a wiry dark person with a face tanned to leather by years of wind and salt, but not all of his crew were of Adam's blood. Arslan saw the sheen of scales here and there, and a ripple of gills.

Father Hugh, whom he had wounded, was resting below. The others played host above to John and his brother William, to Arslan and the Seljuks. William the Marshal Arslan knew. The other man, taller and leaner, was Hugh the Forester. The woman's name was Eschiva, and she was Father Hugh's kin, which made clear to Arslan why she was so terribly put out with him.

John knew all of these people, and was at ease with them. For him this was a gathering of kin and friends. For Arslan it was strangeness heaping on strangeness. Strangest of all was the sense that even as they sat at ease and spoke of trifles, they worked magic, sustaining a net of power so strong and yet so simple that it needed a bare fraction of their awareness.

He settled in a corner and listened in silence to gossip of people he did not know, names he had not heard before, tales of deeds and places that were all new. Most of those tales were like enough to those that he had heard in Outremer: marriages and alliances, feuds, wars, petty squabbles and reconciliations. He let the names pass over and through him, preserving them in memory for when he might need them.

Out of all their chatter, one name in particular caught his attention. It was yet another William, this one surnamed Longchamp, Bishop of Ely. He was the king's justiciar in England, and it seemed he was promising to be difficult.

"He's loyal to a fault," Neville said. "To the point of blindness, even. If it's in defense of Richard, it's justified, no matter what it is or how it's done."

"Richard?" John inquired. "Or himself?"

"Is there a man alive who has no thought of his own betterment?" the Marshal asked.

"Saints," said Neville promptly.

"Saints are the most selfish of all," John said. "They do all that they do for their souls' salvation. All that self-sacrifice, self-denial, prayer and good works—all for a throne in heaven and eternity in paradise."

"What a bitter man you are," Neville said.

"Not bitter," said John. "Clearheaded. So: Ely will be trouble. How bad?"

"We aren't certain," said Eschiva, "but he was in Westminster before the coronation. I felt his presence when the walls fell."

John barked laughter. "William Longchamp, a sorcerer? He's a great many things, few of them particularly appealing, but that, surely—"

"Not all magic needs real power," Eschiva said. "Only a willing vessel. If he were seduced, persuaded to do it for his king's sake, he well might succumb."

"You'd make him out to be a holy fool?" John shook his head.

"Sorcerer or idiot, I can't believe either one. That is a perfect monster of politics, but when it comes to affairs of the spirit, the man is a cipher. It must have been someone else."

"Ciphers are the most fitting vessels for the Wild Magic," Eschiva said, but she did not press the argument further.

The men went on to speak of other things. She resorted to silence.

Arslan knew better than to address her, but he could not help himself. "I do think you may have the right of it," he said.

She started, as if she had forgotten his presence. His words were no visible comfort. "You know the man, that you can judge?"

"Maybe I saw him in a dream," Arslan said.

"Ah," she said. "A dreamer. We have an army of those."

"I should hate to be alone in the world," Arslan said.

"It seems you failed to dream my uncle," she said with a touch of acid.

"I could have shot to kill."

That took her aback. "You would not have—"

"Such a soft world you live in," he said. "It must be all the mist and green. Where I come from, the bones of the earth are bare."

"And all the men who walk on it are savages."

Arslan laughed. Even if it offended her, he could not help it. "My lady, if you could see the newcomers fresh off the boat from France or Germany or your green England, unwashed since the midwife caught them from their mothers' wombs, riddled with lice and sores, dressed in clothes we wouldn't shame a slave with, and convinced that they are the height of culture in the world . . . Lady, we are hard people, dwelling in a hard country, but when it comes to savagery, your people put us all to shame." He bowed to her with elegance that he had learned in the court of Saladin after the battle of Hattin, before he was ransomed from his captivity.

She did not respond as he had expected. Her look of utter affront burst into a ripple of mirth so light and joyous that he stood with his mouth open, gaping like an idiot.

His father had told him of Eleanor, twice a queen and forever the Duchess of Aquitaine: how splendid the world was when she was in it. Her beauty was not perfect; her wits were too sharp for mortal comfort; she was spoiled, selfish, headstrong, and haughty. And yet she was Eleanor. The elder Arslan had loved her till he died, even knowing what she was.

So was it with this lady of Britain. It must be a curse of the blood: to see clearly, and still to love immeasurably.

It happened all in a moment, between one swift-caught breath and the next. He had to struggle for that second breath. His hands were cold; his sight was dimming. It was just as the songs said: love was a sickness, and he was like to die of it.

The corner held him upright. Her laughter had faded; for the first time she seemed to see him, not simply as an annoyance, but as himself. A moment ago it would not have mattered. Now he would have preferred she not see him at all.

That was the way of the world. He scraped himself together somehow and managed a level stare, while she took him in feature by feature.

At length she said, "You're seasick."

He dared not laugh; his stomach would let go. He let her fuss over him, taking a kind of black pleasure in it, sipping the posset she ordered, lying where she insisted he be put, wrapped in furs and coverlets against the cold of night on the sea.

The men were amused, and John most of all. "Dear maiden knight," he said. "I think the lady likes you."

Arslan pretended that he was too far gone to hear. John was not deceived: his laughter was brief but full of merriment. "Rest well, messire," he said.

Arslan did not rest well. They were all in the cabin, all but the lady, who slept elsewhere on the ship. Even without her it was not a restful gathering. The Marshal snored. William Longsword talked in his sleep. John made no sound, but he was a restless sleeper; he tossed all night.

The sickness passed. Arslan still could not think of her without a rush of fire over his skin, but that he could bear. It was the shock of it; the sheer astonishing force of knowing that here, in this woman, was all he wanted or needed. Even if she did not love him in return, it did not matter. Nothing mattered but that she was there to be loved.

He rose softly and slipped out of the cabin. The ship was sailing on its track of starlight, breasting the slow swell. It was a quieter sea than he had ever heard of between France and Britain, a sea of stars and darkness.

He leaned on the rail. Huge shadowy shapes glided below, matching the ship's pace. They were singing a song as strange as he had ever heard, even among the spirits: a song of notes so deep they throbbed in his bones or so shrill they mounted to pain, to harmonies that had nothing human in them. They were the ship's guides and its guardian spirits, and there was such beauty in them that it came near to breaking his heart.

His heart was a fragile thing tonight. He was glad of the sharp chill in the air; it gave him something to think of besides the shock that he had suffered.

"So," said a man beside him. "You hear the singers."

He glanced at the monk whom he had thought deep in drugged sleep. The man—Father Hugh, that was his name—was awake and brightly so, carrying himself erect, without pain.

Arslan was startled enough to touch him without his leave. "Your wound is gone!"

"We dwell in the high magic here," said Father Hugh. "It heals all ills."

"Not all," Arslan murmured, very low, but that was not for anyone else to hear. Aloud he said, "I'm glad to see you well."

"It was a salutary lesson," Father Hugh said.

"For me also," said Arslan. "Will you teach me, Father? I know so little, and need to know so much."

The monk smiled. "I would be honored."

"Even though I did you harm?"

"That was no one's fault but my own."

Arslan left that to silence. After a moment he said, "Teach me my first lesson, Father. Who are the great ones below? What song are they singing? Are there words in it?"

"Words in a language no man knows," said Father Hugh, "but it's said that they sing of things beyond the comprehension of those who walk on land. They are perfectly of water as men are of earth, born of it, wrought for it. And yet they breathe air. If they stay too deep, linger too long, they drown."

"Creatures of the sea can drown in the sea?"

Father Hugh nodded.

"It's like magic," Arslan said. "All marvels have their price. The very water that surrounds them can be their death."

"It's quite like magic," said Father Hugh. "You understand a great deal."

Arslan shrugged off the compliment. "It's in the blood," he said. "Some things I just know. But far too many are strange to me."

"I'll teach you what I can," Father Hugh said, "but not tonight. Tonight, we both rest. Come morning we'll reach harbor. There on the shores of Britain I'll begin your lessoning."

Arslan bowed, swallowing a yawn. He did not know if it was some magic of Father Hugh's, or the simple relief of knowing himself both forgiven and endowed with a teacher, but he felt, at last, that he could sleep.

The great singers' song had softened. It carried him into the cabin and onto his cot, and lulled him into a dreamless peace. If the ship met any enemy, or ran afoul of the Wild Magic, he never knew. He only woke to the lookout's cry: "Land! Land ho!"

# CHAPTER 10

~

They came to harbor in the brisk morning, with a fair wind blowing and a clear sky overhead. It would rain by evening, the captain said, weather-wise to this changeable country, but for this little while the sun shone.

The place to which they came was not the great port of Southampton, where royal landings most often were, but a village to the westward that would not look askance at a magical ship or its odd crew. Arslan never heard its name, if indeed it had one. John was to be given a day or two before unmagical England knew of his presence; then he would appear where he was expected to appear, and be the king's brother, the exile returned, the Count of Mortain.

Here he was something rather different. They disembarked on a stretch of wave-washed shingle, walked the stiffness out of their horses' legs, then mounted and rode through the village of round huts and silent people. They looked like the ship's captain, wiry dark people with a faintly foreign look to them. To Arslan they were very like the people of Sidon and Tyre, the old sea-people who had roamed the world since it was young. Most of these were women. The men would be out with the boats, fishing on this fine morning.

Just at the edge of the village, a very old woman sat by the track, mending a net. It was a large net and finely woven, heaping in billows about her knees. Her face was a mass of wrinkles, her chin sparsely scattered with white hairs, but the hair of her head was thick and long and white as foam.

The eyes in that shriveled apple of a face were bright and piercingly keen, their color difficult to reckon: now grey, now green, now blue, like the sea itself. They rested for a while on Arslan, but fixed on John. "A fair day to you," she said as he rode past.

John drew rein. The four guardians were watching closely, and trying not to look as if they did it.

"Good day to you, beldame," John said. "We thank you for the use of your harbor."

The ancient's smile was broad and toothless. "You are welcome," she said civilly. "It's an honor to be of service to the king of all Britain."

"I'm not king yet," John said, "though it does have a lovely ring to it."

The old woman cackled at his wit, even as feeble as it was. "I gave you a gift, O king hereafter. Just as you raise the walls of air, so shall you bring them down again. Beware the enemy who wears the face of a friend, and choose carefully the one to whom you swear fealty. Take care that you see the truth when it is to be seen."

John raised a brow. "Riddles, beldame? Are they a requirement of my office?"

"They do keep your wits sharp," she said. "Go with the gods, king hereafter, and may the Wild Ones bow to your will."

John bowed to her without excessive mockery, and rode on. Arslan paused a moment. Her eyes had returned to him, and they were bright indeed. For a moment the shriveled crone vanished; in her place he saw a lady both tall and fair, with hair like seafoam and eyes as changeful as the sea, and beauty to break the heart.

She drew up the net that she had been mending, spreading it across her knees. There were patterns in it, images, shapes of things that were and had been and were yet to come. He caught but a glimpse before it was a net of knotted cords again, and she was an ancient fisherwoman, mending her net in the winter sunlight.

He bowed lower than John had, to his mare's neck, and sweeping down, kissed her hand. That startled her, but not to her displeasure. Her smile sent him on his way, its brightness a blessing, and a warm welcome to this country that had called him to itself.

The rain set in after noon of the brief winter day, a true rain of Britain, more mist than downpour. It softened the landscape through which they rode, turned the low rolling hills to silver, and sank through layers of fur and leather and linen to set a chill in Arslan's thin eastern blood. They had come away from the sea onto a broad green plain, and a straight track on it, aiming like an arrow into the mist.

The four guardians had taken places at the four points of heaven, casually, without making a great show of it. It meant that none of them led, for they were riding north and west. Neville and the Marshal rode on either side of John, in the places of west and north. Hugh and Eschiva rode behind, east and south.

Arslan happened to be riding between the latter two. It was like riding in the midst of a shieldwall, but the shields were wrought of mist and magic.

"Show me how," he said to Father Hugh.

"Watch," the monk said, "and open your heart."

That would have been simpler if he had not been so keenly aware of Eschiva's disapproval. Her lightness with him the night before was gone; she had returned to her wonted distance. He had to struggle to put her out of his mind, and out of his body's awareness. Then he could begin to see what Hugh did, how he wrought mist into defense, and united his will with those of his fellows.

This was the wall and shield that Arslan had yearned for on the track from La Forêt. It concealed them from the sight of the spirits of air, and protected them from the Wild Magic. There was a great deal of that abroad, swirls of mist, eerie hoots and howlings, shapes that passed half-seen. They made Arslan think of curdled cream and faery gold, and murrain on the cattle.

He was tempted strongly to leave the circle of protection; to ride away from the track on the open plain, and stand face to face with the things that drifted and floated and flew beyond the wards. It must be the blood that was in him: he was vulnerable to the temptations of magic as the others were not, even those who were mages.

He did not resist the temptation so much as fail to submit. The wards held him, and the presence of the two on either side of him.

As evening drew in about them, they came to a low swell of hill. A single stone crowned it, now seeming no taller than a man, now looming like a high crenelated tower.

There was a door in the hill, a hollow and a spring and a lintel of stone that topped a simple wooden panel. Father Hugh approached it with a complete lack of ceremony, as if it had been the door of his own house. The others followed slowly, the men-at-arms in the rear, narrow-eyed and wary. To them the straight tracks had been but roads, and the ship had been a simple ship, but all too clearly this was no plain earthly hill.

The door opened like the postern of a castle. There was light within, no brighter than the rainy evening. They entered into a broad high passage, the walls of which seemed made of mist or grey glass, through which shone the pale light.

Father Hugh left them there. The other guardians bade farewell without objection. To John he said, "I've preparations to make, my lord, and duties I can't shirk. I'll meet you in Southampton when you come out from under hill."

He had no words for Arslan, but blessed him with a smile and an embrace. He sat on his mule while the rest of them rode through the gate. His sturdy figure diminished quickly, lost in dark and rain.

The passage descended slowly but perceptibly. The light, rather than dimming as they went deeper, grew brighter little by little. The passage grew broader and higher. Tall gates rose before them, wrought of silver and gold in an intricate twining of beasts and birds, flowers and vines, and golden apples suspended from silver branches.

Arslan's hand went to his purse, where he still carried the golden bell that he had brought back from the horned king's country. Memory niggled at him, teased him, and fled.

The guardians who remained joined hand in hand to open those lofty gates. A flood of light poured out. It was as bright as sunlight in high summer, dazzling, blinding. Arslan felt himself drawn inward, and the others about him, men and horses and sumpter mules.

When his sight cleared, he saw that they were in a court like that of a castle. Walls of stone surrounded them, and a colonnade, and an inner gate that lay open on a golden hall. Servants waited to take their horses, seeming human enough save that they were all so tall and fair. Others led them into the hall, into light and warmth and the sounds of music and merriment.

There was a great gathering here, but their faces were a blur, lost in mist and light. Only those who sat at the high table were clear to see. Arslan was somewhat surprised not to find the horned king. These were all human shapes, human faces, although as with the servants, they were just a little too tall, a little too fair to be mortal.

He who sat in the high seat, crowned with gold, was a golden man, and all his garments were amber and topaz and ruddy gold. Only his eyes were dark. Arslan met them as he was brought into the hall. They were full of starlight.

He was the last to come in, but for the men-at-arms, who were taken away, walking like men in a dream. John walked in the circle of guardians. His brother followed. Even Arslan's Seljuks were ahead of him, and not separated as John's men had been. That was interesting, but Arslan could not fix his mind upon the thought.

The golden king welcomed them with words that slipped from Arslan's memory as soon as they were spoken. The others seemed alert enough, returning the welcome with studied courtesy. Their words did not slip away so easily. The golden king's name was Gwyn, and this was his kingdom, this land under the hill.

Arslan found that if he slipped aside somewhat, his sight grew clearer and the revelers stranger; their hall shifted from mortal grandeur to a shimmering and nearly incomprehensible vision. They were wearing earthly forms out of respect for their guests. The shapes they wore among themselves were far more fantastical.

They drifted toward him as he stood apart from the rest, intrigued as spirits always had been by the oddity of him: a spirit of fire inextricably bound in human flesh. These had wit and volition, and thoughts that ran almost as humans' did. They were very like his kin, the jinn and the afarit.

"You should eat only what is at the king's table," said a creature like a tall white candle, whose human semblance was that of a very slender, very pale, perfectly sexless child with eyes as old as mountains. "That is mortal sustenance, that we gathered in mortal countries. All else that is here, if you partake of it, it binds you in this place."

"Truly," said the creature's companions, who were now a flock of butterflies and now a circle of ladies in cloaks as jeweled bright as butterflies' wings. They tempted him with bowls and platters of dainties, and cups full of enchanting sweetness. "Eat; drink. Stay with us. How strange you are! How interesting. Why, you might keep the tedium away for a whole fraction of an eon."

"Is it as dull as that here?" Arslan asked them.

"Worse than dull!" they cried. "Excruciating. Feasting and reveling, reveling and feasting. Even when the Wild Magic comes and scatters some of us into the devouring air—even that is but a moment's diversion."

"You do nothing but feast and revel?"

"And hunt," they said with a gleam of faery eyes. "And dance. And sometimes, if we are fortunate, we find a mortal to play with."

"I'm only half mortal," Arslan said.

"Better and better," they declared. "Here, eat. These are the apples of the sun. They'll turn your blood to living fire."

They were golden, and they shone. Arslan reached simply to touch one, but a hand slapped him away.

He had not seen the Lady Eschiva move, but she was here, and not with the high ones before the dais. She raked the revelers with her glare. "For shame!" she said. "Teasing this child who deserves better. Beg his pardon, all of you, and swear to let him be."

She had power in this place: they did as she bade them, though with a wicked gleam of eyes and a flicker of laughter. Before Arslan could speak again to them, she had dragged him away.

He was too fascinated by her to resist. "You're no more mortal than I am," he said.

He thought she might slap him again with hand or voice, but she had remarkable control of her temper. "No more and no less," she said, "but notably better schooled. What was your mother thinking, to let you live in such ignorance?"

"She had no say in the matter," he said stiffly. "She was long gone."

Eschiva pulled him up to the dais and all but flung him into a chair at the end of the table. There was food, drink, all mortal, scattered in careless profusion by servants who were imperfectly apprised of the order or appropriateness of human sustenance. Closest to him he saw a loaf of sugar beside a wheel of cheese atop a haunch of venison that had been snatched from its spit rather before it was done; a basket of green herbs and one of roots fresh plucked from the earth, and what had the Seljuks clapping their hands with delight: a vast and steaming pilaf in a copper basin, studded with dates and currants and bits of what proved, on examination, to be goat's meat spiced with pepper.

That and a tall jar of sherbet cooled with snow made a feast for an eastern prince. Arslan ate at first because his stomach demanded it, and then because it was as good a meal as he had had since he left Outremer.

Eschiva followed his lead, warily. The rest were picking their way through the jumbled bounty, but none seemed as well content as Arslan was. John's expression was distinctly sour, though he covered it with an attempt at a smile.

"You must pardon us," the golden king said. "It's been some little while since we played host to mortals whom we would not keep in our kingdom. We understand that you sleep, and that you bathe in water, yes? Both things will be given you, after this gathering is ended."

"You are most kind," John said. He even sounded as if he meant it.

"It is kindness with a purpose," the golden king said. "You were chosen to be king of all Britain, in the seat of Bran and the seat of Arthur. This night is given you as a gift, to feed your strength and to teach you the beginnings of what you must know. You may ask me anything, and if it is in my power, I will answer."

"Anything at all? Without restriction?"

The golden king smiled. "Within the limits of the time you are given here, and the knowledge that is granted me."

"How much time am I given here?"

"One of our nights," the king answered him.

Arslan waited, but John did not ask the question that he should have asked. Instead he said, "And in the morning, where will we be?"

"You will be where a mortal prince should be," said the golden king, "and the world you walk in will be the world of men. This night is your respite. It is our hope that you will use it well."

"My respite?" John asked. "From what?"

"From all that awaits you."

"And that is?"

"You must earn the crown that waits for you. Powers will oppose you: some to test you, some to destroy you. There will never be time to determine which. You must do as your heart bids, always, and never falter."

"Then it's likely I'm not your man," John said dryly. "That's more the province of my brother, who also has the advantage of being crowned King of England."

"He is not king of all Britain," said the golden king.

"Nor, it seems, am I," John pointed out. "I was given to understand that when I set foot on this shore I would move at once to take the power and the crown. Now I discover that instead I'm to be subject to some sort of heroic testing, in which I can fail far more easily than succeed. May I ask where is the profit in that? I can wait my brother out and be king when he succumbs, sooner or later, to one of his bull-brained battles—and that will be a kingship without any of the costs that your magics demand. Why should I trouble myself with any of this?"

"Because if you do not," said the golden king, "if you prove weak or unfit, there will be no England to be king of."

"Show me," said John.

"Come," said the golden king.

When they went, no one followed but Arslan. Either the others knew already, or they were not permitted to share in this.

They walked through the halls of a castle, and at the same time they traversed the tracks of a wood and the windings of a deep cavern—all at once, all together, in this world outside of the world. Arslan schooled himself to see as John would see: halls of stone, marvelously figured tapestries, long gleaming colonnades and marble stairs. One such brought them into a garden of stone, a courtyard full of images both human and fey.

It dawned on Arslan that these might not be the work of hands; they might be men and women, beasts both mundane and magical, and creatures of faery blood, all enchanted, all turned to stone in the garden of Gwyn, king under hill. In the center of them was a wide basin, likewise of stone, and clear water in it, gleaming in the sourceless brilliance that illuminated this country.

John stood by the basin. He was more real than anything here, a sturdy man, not tall, with hair the color of rust on cold iron. Beside him the golden king shimmered and flickered, insubstantial as a flame. "Look in the water," said Gwyn. "See what you wish to see."

John bent over the water. Arslan, somewhat apart from them both, did the same. At first he saw only the shimmer of light, then the shadow of his own face. But as he stood staring, the water rippled. Shapes came clear in it.

Blight on the corn. A murrain on the cattle. Milk soured in the pail, and dogs running mad. Small mischiefs united into greater ones, and those into outright ills: plague in the villages, war in the fields. Brother rose up and slew brother, driven on by the pricking and goading of small devils and creatures of the darker magics. Rents opened in the soul and the soil of Britain. Miasma poured out. The earth sickened; the sky dulled. Rain fell unceasing, rotting the corn in the ear; then it ceased to fall at all, and the land withered to dust. Nor even then could it be at peace; armies rampaged across it, rending what little was left to rend, and destroying all that remained to be destroyed.

Every land had its king, and every magic its match. A land without a king was a land open to dissolution. That had already begun, was gnawing at the edges of this island.

John swept his hand across the water. Visions shattered. He whirled on the golden king in a flare of sudden rage. "Stop this! *Stop it!* Either give me the means to do what you want me to do, or leave off tormenting me. I'm your king or I'm not. There's nothing between. Crown me here or let me go—or if it suits you better, drown me in this basin and put an end to the whole cursed game."

The king under hill was hardly dismayed by John's outburst. "Your temper is a weapon," he said. "It can win the war, or it can turn upon you and cut your throat. Have a care as to which you choose."

John snarled and stalked away from him. The king watched dispassionately, as an immortal could, who had seen and heard and done everything long before. The garden was enchanted: no matter which edge John stalked to, he found himself back by the basin, glaring sulfurously at the golden king.

After the third fruitless departure, he planted his feet on the stones and his fists on his hips. "Very well. I take your point. I pray you also take mine. Give me what I need, or let me go."

Gwyn smiled as if at a clever child, reached into the water, and drew out a thing that, Arslan could swear, had shaped itself even as he reached for it. It was a rod as long as John's forearm, made of pale wood inlaid with silver in intricate patterns such as Arslan had seen on the gate of this castle. Its summit was a stone, round like the moon, and clear as water. In it Arslan saw the shimmer of visions, too small or too swift to make sense of, except for one: a field of lilies, and a leopard trapped in them, tangled in their crowding stems.

"This is the scepter of Alba," said the golden king, "which lay in the hand of Bran the Blessed. No mortal may bear it who is not the chosen of Britain. He who dares will be blasted with fire, and struck down for everlasting." He held it up, flat on his palms. "Will you take it?"

It gleamed in his white hands. John eyed it narrowly. It seemed a harmless pretty thing, but he could not doubt the death that slept in it.

He was no coward, whatever people said of him. He reached for it with a steady hand. His fingers closed about it. No lightnings woke. It was heavy: his hand dipped, and he caught his breath at the weight of it. But it was not too heavy for him, not once he had taken it in the crook of his arm. It nestled as if it belonged there, a thing of silver beauty, cool and clean as water.

John ran his finger down the length of it. "So," he said. "You weren't lying. I am the one."

"You doubted it?"

He shrugged. "Mortals always doubt. Youngest sons of many brothers—we trust nothing, believe nothing, expect nothing but the worst."

"You know the worst," Gwyn said. "What can happen to this kingdom, and once it falls, to other kingdoms within its compass, as the rent in the world grows wider. You know what can become of you if you fail. What's left but courage and a certain compulsion to do what must be done?"

"Why," said John with a crooked smile, "nothing."

This time when he walked away from the basin, the garden let him go. Arslan followed. As he walked through the stone images, he felt their eyes on him, and even more strongly on John, as if the scepter had roused them. Their awareness was a shiver in his spine. The world had changed, however subtly. Whether John succeeded or failed, Britain would not be the same again.

# PART TWO

# THE SCEPTER OF ALBA

## Candlemas through Advent, 1191

# CHAPTER 11

T hey rode out from under hill in much the same weather in which they had ridden in: mist and rain, and a penetrating chill that was the cold kiss of Britain. It was the tall boy from Outremer who first seemed to notice that something was different; who marked the golden flowers that starred the winter grass.

"How long," he asked Eschiva, "is a night under hill?"

She kept her eyes on the track, as if she needed them to sustain her part of the wards. He need not know how the sight of him could shake her. "As long as it needs to be," she answered him.

"How long was the need this night?"

He was not going to let it go; not that one. She chose to answer directly, partly out of temper, and partly to stop his questions. "A month," she said, "and a little more."

"What, not a hundred years?"

"That would hardly be useful," she said.

He fell silent. He was biting back a smile, she could tell. He was not as dour as he might wish people to think. That was his defense, because he was so young, and had seen so much. He schooled his face to stillness, and relied on his size, his big bones and wide shoulders, to convince the world that he was older and stronger than he was.

Only with his wild Turks did he let his mask slip. She had caught glimpses of it, flashes of brilliance that came near to stopping her heart. Temper then was her defense, as stillness was his.

He was the most beautiful human thing that she had seen in all her years. When she was thinking clearly, which in his vicinity was not often, she granted that he had a pleasing but not excessively pretty face, with that firm chin and those grey eyes and that old-gold hair cut short for the wearing of a helmet. But it was not his face or even his strong young body that captivated her. It was everything about him, within and without. The turn of his head when he was startled; the dart of his glance under level brows; the voice that though young was promising to be rich and deep. He was all promise, and wonderful in it. And the spirit that was in him . . .

She was old enough to know better. The office to which she was bound had never forbidden her the pleasures of the body, but she had taken no time for them. Nor had she been subjected to the yoke as so many young noblewomen were, married off in childhood for the sake of her inheritance. She could be a nun of the strictest order, for all she knew of the ways of men and women.

John called this boy the maiden knight, but she knew he was not yet knighted; she suspected he was not the other, either. Surely there had been maids and servants enough, maybe even a lady or two, who had found him as irresistible as Eschiva did.

She had duties, great ones. She was a guardian of the isle of Britain. She protected the king who would be, and guided him on the ways that were laid for him. She had no time or space to spare for this obsession.

No, she thought. The truth: she was afraid. He woke sensations in her that she had never known before. She made her feel all strange to herself. That strangeness tangled her tongue, and frayed the edges of her temper; it struck her dumb when she would have said what was in her heart. What, after all, if he did not yearn after her as she yearned after him? Or more frightening still—what if he did?

John appeared at Southampton on the eve of Candlemas. Where he had been since Christmas, or how he had come there, was never quite made clear. Eschiva, with the rest of the guardians, saw to it that no one pressed the question. It was enough that he had come, and was openly in England.

The Bishop of Lincoln, in his capacity as a prince of the Church, received Prince John for the world to see, attended by a fair few barons, and such prelates as were minded to travel in this mild winter. Their welcome was effusive and their complaints loud and long, most on the subject of the Bishop of Ely. Arrogant, they called him; high-handed, with no regard for the rights or privileges of their various ranks. He issued decrees as if he were the king and the Lord God rolled into one, and when they taxed him with it, he reminded them haughtily that he was the Pope's own legate.

"He's drunk with power," one of them declared of a morning, not long after John had come to Southampton. Eschiva happened to be in the hall then, strengthening the wards about John. The baron's voice was strident, and pitched to carry; it was thick with grievance. "He's robbing us of what is ours, and conducting himself like a king."

"Ah," said John, "but he is the king's justiciar. The king gave him leave to rule for the duration of the Crusade."

"To rule!" the baron cried. "Not to make himself a tyrant. He's brought in his pack of brothers, given them rich offices and richer heiresses, trampled on the rights and prerogatives of those who already held those offices and were betrothed to those heiresses, sneered at the barons and the commons of England, and to add insult to all these injuries, banned the Lord Chancellor from the Exchequer when the duty of his office brought him there. The very clerks of chancery cannot abide him—and as for the lords and the prelates, they utterly loathe and despise him. Will you tolerate this? Will you submit to it?"

"I will take it under advisement," John said.

This was his world and his element. He had friends here, and allies, and people who, thanks to Longchamp's clumsiness, were disposed to favor him. They rested their hopes in him because he was the king's brother, and because he was newly come and therefore a fresh face, but also because he knew England. He spoke the language, not only the French of the barons and the Latin of the Church, but the old Saxon tongue that was transmuting and changing in this new age of the world. He could walk into any inn or market or cottage and make himself understood; and that was a rare thing in a lord of this realm.

Neville and the Marshal stayed close by him as their offices allowed, and Father Hugh when he was not occupied with his bishopric. Eschiva's place was less easily explained. She was Father Hugh's ward and therefore could be expected to travel about with him, but this was a men's court and a men's world. Ladies played no notable part in it.

While John spent his night under hill, his household had come over from France, and lodged itself in Southampton Castle. He had added to it with the revenues of his many rich demesnes here in England—his royal brother's generosity, as he liked to say, and a great aid to his personal comfort.

That at least Eschiva found useful. There were so many of them that yet another hanger-on, however respectably female, was hardly worthy of notice. The flocks of people and the constant coming and going made guarding him immeasurably more difficult, but it also made it possible to watch over him without attracting attention, either human or otherwise.

John did not linger long in Southampton. Within the week, having gathered a train fit for a king, he set off on the long road through the heart of England. His passing had the look and sense of a royal progress, with banners and trumpets, gatherings of nobles and companies of knights, men-at-arms both mounted and afoot, guards, soldiers, and servants innumerable. They filled the road and overflowed it, driving pilgrims and passersby to the verge, and stopping short any noble company that might be thinking to travel abroad.

It drove away the Wild Magic, too, with its relentless humanity. John was surrounded by it, inundated with it. If he even remembered what else he was and was called to do, he did not betray it to Eschiva.

In Winchester he paused for long enough that Eschiva made free to lodge near the cathedral, in a house that had been known to her kindred for time out of mind. All the walls there were warded, and in the garden roses bloomed even in the heart of winter. The keepers of the house were both quiet and discreet; they let her be, as she wished, and waited on her without intrusion.

It was restful to sit in the garden, a handful of days after John's train arrived in the city, and feel the sun on her face, and know that she had no duties pressing upon her. It had been a long while since that was so.

She had fallen into a doze: her needlework was slipping from her lap, and someone was standing near her, watching her. "What heaven!" said a familiar voice, half mocking, half envious. "Sun and solitude, and not a care in the world."

Eschiva started fully awake. "Susanna! What are you doing here? I thought you were immovably fixed at Aunt Bertrada's."

Her friend and cousin came gladly into her embrace and kiss of welcome, then sat on the stone bench beside her, smoothing skirts that had seen their fair share of muddy roads. She was altogether her wonted self: a little round dumpling of a woman with dark curls escaping the modesty of her veil, and cheeks flushed to rose with sun and wind and the pleasure of Eschiva's company.

"All's been well?" Eschiva asked her, just as Susanna asked the same.

They laughed, parried, settled: Susanna said, "All's as well as can be expected. Aunt Bertrada is her usual self, of course, and the rest of the household, too."

Eschiva rolled her eyes at that; their aunt's house was a famously uproarious place. "So then—what brings you here?"

"Aside from a craving for a few days' peace? You, of course," said Susanna, "and a certain restlessness of disposition. In a word—I wanted a change."

"Did you also find yourself wanting a certain personage of royal blood?"

Susanna flushed.

Eschiva bit back a grin. "He's here, of course—alive, and as sane as any of that brood can be."

"He has the scepter?"

Eschiva nodded.

Susanna drew a breath, then let it go. "That's well," she said.

"Have you seen him yet?" Eschiva asked her.

She shook her head. Her cheeks had flushed just a little more than before.

"I'll take you to him," said Eschiva. "He'll want to know—"

"No." Susanna's voice was perfectly flat. It was also perfectly unlike her.

"He should know," Eschiva said.

Susanna's face and heart were closed against her. Some things even Eschiva could not touch, and this was one.

Eschiva bit her lip and was silent. She well could remember when it had happened. After Richard was crowned, he had given out lands and titles to his brothers both legitimate and not, and informed John that he was to marry a great heiress: Isabella, Countess of Gloucester. Through that marriage John gained the envy of every baron and knight and fortune-hunter from the north of England to Provence. It was the richest prize in England, and it came bound inextricably with a woman whom John had despised since they were children.

Richard had no humor, and no appreciation of irony; Eschiva doubted that he had taken thought for anything but the splendid extravagance of the gift. Their mother Eleanor had known exactly what she was doing in advising Richard to so enrich his brother—as she had known that, however much he loathed the woman, John would take her for the sake of the lands and dower that came with her.

Isabella's protestations had been loud and prolonged, but she had had no choice but to submit. She came heavily veiled to the wedding, though whether it concealed bruises or the marks of weeping or both, no one there could be certain. John had done his duty that night, but thereafter he was not known to attend his wife again.

Susanna had been in Gloucester then, attending the countess. It was not her first encounter with John. That had been pure accident, just before Richard's crowning, when the walls of air were broken. She had been there, and Eschiva, and John. She had drawn his eye then. When he found her again in the sour dregs of his wedding, the spark between them flared to a flame. He had gone to her, and she had comforted him. When the terms of John's exile were pronounced and he left England for France, she had remained behind in Isabella's service, with what conscience Eschiva could not tell; the old gods knew, she was far from the first woman to lie with the lord while attending the lady.

She came to their aunt's manor near Gloucester in the spring of the next year, while Eschiva was there as well, with a child in her belly and no word of what had passed between herself and her lady. Eschiva had had to hear it elsewhere: how Isabella had called Susanna to her and said coldly, "Whatever else I am, madam, I am no fool. You kept that man's hands off me, and for that I thank you. But you will understand why I cannot have you here."

Susanna had understood. She had come to her kin knowing that she would find sanctuary, and borne a son at midsummer. The son, whom she had named Geoffrey, had lived and grown strong. He was in that house still, well out of the countess' sight; John knew nothing of him.

"Do you know," Susanna said now, "people are whispering that he is Richard's? He's growing tall, and he has that red hair, and he's bold. He loves horses and armor and weapons."

"Does her grace of Gloucester believe that she might have been mistaken as to your child's parentage?" Eschiva asked.

"Her grace of Gloucester knows both Richard and John too well," Susanna said.

"Pity," said Eschiva.

"You think so?" Susanna rubbed at a mud stain on her skirt, succeeding only in making it larger. She desisted with a little sigh of frustration. "If ever a woman is going to draw the Lionheart's eye, it will not be a little brown dumpling like me. The whole world knows he gives his heart to tall and brawny and fair. Like," she added, "my lord John's new squire. Now there's a face to set Richard's heart a-beating."

Eschiva stared at her. "You've seen him? But you said you hadn't seen John."

"I haven't," Susanna said. "I met the squire in Father Hugh's lodging—I went to pay my respects before I came here. He escorted me to your door."

"He didn't come in? He didn't—" Eschiva stopped abruptly. She was babbling. She was angry—because a boy who barely knew she existed had done no more than courtesy demanded.

Susanna's brow arched. "Lovely, isn't he? As he must be, for you to notice him."

Eschiva gathered the rags of her aplomb and put them on. "He's difficult to miss," she said.

Susanna laughed. She was as delighted to have shifted the conversation away from John as to have found occasion to discomfit her cousin. "Oh, he is a beauty! And those devils in turbans who follow him everywhere—they're as exotic as leopards. Are they as dangerous, too?"

"I'm sure they must be," Eschiva said.

"Oh, stop that," said Susanna. "You can't stop blushing no matter what you do. He's beautiful, and I'm sorry now I didn't bring him in."

"I am glad you didn't," said Eschiva. She was sure she meant it. "Now tell me the news from Gloucester. Are you waiting on Isabella again? Is Geoffrey well? How is Aunt Bertrada?"

"I'd rather gossip about that golden boy," Susanna said, but she said it in jest. She consented to shy away from Arslan, knowing that as long as she did, Eschiva would not press her to tell John that he had a son.

# CHAPTER 12

From Winchester, by somewhat roundabout ways, John led his entourage toward Gloucester. He had duties there, matters of the great estate, and a gathering of barons from the west of England and the marches of Wales, all waiting impatiently for him to find his way to them. The fact that his wife was also there could not have escaped his remembrance, though he had been doing his best to keep his bed occupied by women other than the ineffable Isabella.

He called her that with such a twist of scorn that people had been known to cross themselves when they heard it. Arslan often wondered which of the two he should pity.

"Probably both," Susanna said.

They were within a day's ride of Gloucester, even at the snail's pace of a large retinue led by a reluctant lord. She had settled into the position of Eschiva's maid, which she had held before, and seemed comfortable in. Although she had not parted from John's lady on the best of terms, she spoke of Isabella without any of John's rancor.

"Childhood enmity can be the worst of all," she said, "and those two were raised together. They know everything there is to dislike about each other, and have long forgotten any liking they might have had."

"And still the king commanded the marriage?" Arslan asked.

"They were betrothed as children," said Susanna, "by the old king, who was thinking of lands for John, as he always did. When he died, Richard saw no reason not to go on with it—it was a princely gift, and Richard loves to be thought generous. There was a great to-do over it, as it happens; they're cousins, and well within the bounds of consanguinity. The Church was properly horrified. There was even an Interdict. In all that, I don't think Richard would have noticed what they thought of each other, and Queen Eleanor wouldn't care."

"She should have," Arslan said.

"Indeed," said Susanna. "John loves women, any and all of them, but he won't ever take one who is unwilling. It's one of his least acknowledged virtues."

Arslan's cheeks were warm, but that was an accustomed state when he rode with Susanna. She was splendidly forthright, and she seemed, for whatever reason, to have adopted him as a friend. He had taken to riding with her whenever John did not require his services, which was most of the time: now that the prince had his household back, he had half a dozen squires and pages innumerable, and no immediate and pressing need for an ifritah's son from Outremer.

But Susanna was always glad to see him, and she always had something for him to do, if only to keep her company on this large and boisterous riding. She knew magic, too, in the quiet and almost casual way that Father Hugh knew it, so that sometimes he wondered if the good bishop, preoccupied with affairs of state, had passed on Arslan's teaching to this learned lady.

She always knew when Arslan's mind began to wander. Woolgathering, she called it. "Wasn't there another heiress," he asked before she could tax him with it now, "who would have been more suitable?"

"Princess Alais." Eschiva had deigned to join the conversation, which was a rarity. "Sister to the King of France, and some say old Henry's leman. She carries a great dower in Normandy, and alliance with the crown of France."

"That wouldn't have done," Susanna said. "Not for John, and still less for Eleanor. John and Philip together would be too dangerous a threat to her Richard. She wanted John bound to England, even if he had to be kept out of it till Richard's Crusade was over, and well separated from any real power in France. Gloucester is rich enough, she reckoned, to keep him quiet. If he loathes his wife too much to get heirs on her, well, so much the better: no rivals for her Richard's eventual children."

"Very eventual," Eschiva murmured.

"Richard's not a man for women," Susanna agreed dryly. She sighed, stretched, turned her face toward the sun. "Poor John! If they need him, they'll need him badly, but it would suit them all much better to fold him and lay him away in a box until there's no one else left to claim the inheritance."

"They need a golem," Arslan said. And when they stared at him:

"It's a magic of the Jews. They make a man of clay and give him life with a sacred word, and he does their bidding."

Susanna laughed, a joyous whoop, more like a boy than a lady of dignity and breeding. "Don't tell the queen that! She'll make herself one, and then she won't need to vex herself with sons."

"Best not tell the sons," Eschiva said, "or they'll be horribly offended. After all, if women didn't need sons, why would they trouble with them? Or with husbands? Or with men at all?"

"For pretty?" Arslan ventured.

He never discovered what she would have said to that, or if she would have had any words to say: John drew to a halt beside them and said, "So this is where you've been getting to. Ladies, has he been telling you lies about me?"

"Splendid ones," Eschiva said.

She had brightened measurably at his coming, as if it were a rescue. Susanna, to Arslan's surprise, had closed in upon herself. He could hardly see her face: she had shrunk down and hidden it with her veil.

"Good," John said to Eschiva. "Lies are never worth anything unless they're suitably egregious."

She smiled. Her eyes were warm and full of laughter. "You ran away," she said.

He grinned at her. "Just a little way, and just for a little while. My courtiers don't even know I'm gone." He spread his arms for her to see what he had done: he had taken off the crimson mantle and the cotte of sky-blue silk in which he had been riding gloriously ahead of them all. The tunic and the cloak he wore in their place must have been borrowed from a man-at-arms.

Her eyes widened. "You didn't."

"I did," he said with visible glee. "Andres is a fox-faced man, too, and apt for a game. We've a wager on how long it takes the lot of them to see that it's not John Lackland riding in front of them and looking princely."

"Not as long, we can hope, as it took my brother to learn that you weren't a squire," Arslan said. "Have you drunk the ale in an English guardroom? It's ghastly."

"So speaks a man whose family makes the best wine in Anjou," John said. "You never learned to appreciate the coarser things in life. English ale, now—the true nut-brown ale—is as glorious a creation as any fruit of the vine."

"It tastes like horse piss," Arslan said.

"Why, messire!" cried John. "I'll set you a challenge. Drink a tankard of the best ale in Britain, drink it to the bottom, then tell me it's vile."

"I can do that without drinking a drop."

"Then it's not a challenge," John pointed out. "Well?"

Arslan sighed. "Where is this best of the worst, then?"

"Why, that's the beauty of it," said John. "It's in Gloucester, in an inn called the Green Man. It's said Robin Goodfellow himself blessed the innkeeper's brew, many a year ago, and to this day there is no better in the world."

"Very well," said Arslan, "but if I do this, you have to promise me a cask of wine from La Forêt, to take the taste away."

"And if you discover that it's not as bad as you feared," John said, "*you* must buy me a barrel of old Hobden's ale, and broach it with me in the hall of Gloucester Castle."

"Done," said Arslan, and they clasped hands on it, under the eyes of the two women.

Eschiva was amused. Susanna was watching John with a kind of queasy fascination. Arslan would never have marked her for a woman who feared any man alive, even the youngest of the Devil's brood. Yet she seemed to see something terrible in his face, from which she could not turn away.

The veil slipped, baring her face. John turned, caught by the flutter of fabric. His first glance was quick but deeply appreciative. The second lingered. Recognition grew and blossomed. "Lady," he said. "Susanna."

"My lord," she said. She sounded stiff, even cold, but her eyes were burning. "You look well."

"And you," he said.

"I'm surprised you remember me," said Susanna.

Anger flashed across his face, too quick almost to catch. "Why, because I have so many women? Some I do forget. But some I remember."

"How am I memorable, my lord?"

"How are you not?"

"I have a sharp tongue," she said, "and no beauty to speak of, but a certain buxom handsomeness that is, I'm told, more appealing than not."

He shook her words out of his head, impatiently. "I see you don't remember me at all."

"I remember every moment," she said. "Every word. Every touch."

"I can't claim the same," he said, "but you—the spirit of you—I could never forget that."

She bent her head. Arslan had seen queens who were less regal than she was then.

Their horses moved together, walking side by side. Arslan and Eschiva were left to their own devices. He eyed the pack of squires, but even Eschiva was preferable to that. She might understand him little and like him less, but she was not vocal about it. And she had never yet offered to dip his head in the privy by way of welcoming him to the prince's service.

He caught himself smiling at that, just as her glance crossed his. For an instant he saw the warmth again, and more than warmth. He did not pursue it, any more than he would have run shouting after a bird that he had in mind to capture. He let it slide away instead, and kept his smile for a little longer, until it faded of its own accord.

Gloucester was waiting for them in festival dress, bright with banners and bunting. The countess was not at the gate to receive them, but the bishop was, with an impressive train, and the Lord Mayor with his council, and a flock of notables craning and peering to see how John would present himself.

Fortunately for his standing with the west of the kingdom, he had reclaimed his royal mantle and sent Andres back to his company of men-at-arms. He had also, without explanation, summoned Arslan to ride in the squire's place at his right hand, closer even than his brother Longsword. That did not endear Arslan to his fellows, or his rivals, as they seemed to reckon themselves.

Arslan shrugged off their glares. John wore high rank well, when it suited him. He had a regal carriage, an air of one who had been born the son of a king and a queen. He wore it in this cool bright evening, and for a little while he even exercised himself to be charming.

It was well after dark before he came to the castle, where his wife had been waiting with her ladies. He had feasted with the mayor and the bishop, and tarried with a gathering of the barons. He had not drunk so much as to be unsteady on his feet, but his cheeks were flushed and his eyes were just a little too bright.

The Countess Isabella was not precisely as Arslan had expected. He looked to find a formidable woman, a sort of mother abbess, thin and cold and severe. The lady who waited in the lamplit hall was lovely, with a cloud of dark hair beneath a drift of veil, and skin like milk and roses. He could see that as she aged she would grow plump and lose that fragile beauty, but tonight, in the flower of her youth, she was exquisite.

The only flaw in her was the eye she turned on John. She did not hate him, nothing so grand or so noble. She disliked him intensely; his face, his body roused in her no desire at all, only weary disgust.

He greeted her with chilly politeness and kissed her hand, barely brushing the milky skin with his lips. She drew away just a little more quickly than she might have done. "My lord," she said. Her voice was husky and sweet.

"My lady countess," John said.

She grimaced slightly at the scent of wine that hung about him, but forbore to remark on it. "Your chambers are ready, my lord," she said. "You may repair to them whenever—"

"I don't think so," John said, measuring each word distinctly. "Arslan! Lion of the infidels. We had a challenge, yes? A tankard of ale at the Green Man. Let's put on our walking clothes and conclude our wager."

"Tomorrow," Arslan said in all courtesy, but without any yielding in it. "Tonight, my lord, we rest."

John gaped. Nor was he alone in that, at all. The countess was staring as if she had never seen his like before.

"Good night, my lord," Arslan said. "Will you require my services to prepare you for bed?"

John's face was thunderous. Arslan held his breath. Suddenly John laughed. "Go to bed, boy. I've a castleful of servants; I'll manage. But tomorrow, remember: we have an appointment to keep."

"I won't forget, my lord," Arslan said a little breathlessly.

# CHAPTER 13

❦

Eschiva and Susanna lodged outside of Gloucester with their aunt Bertrada and their aunt's brown mouse of a husband and a throng of offspring and fosterlings. They had a dozen children alive and well and at least that number taken in fosterage, and every one of them was possessed of magic in one degree or another. It made for a lively household, and not only on the human side of it.

The milk had curdled again that morning, and the butter turned to beer in the churn. "It's getting worse," Aunt Bertrada said to Eschiva as they contemplated the rather decent beer. "Even with all the wards up, between the boys' pranks and half the girls calling down the moon at once, there's enough Wild Magic in this place to turn it on its ear. Did you know we had a plague of frogs yesterday? Every time one of the servants spoke, out hopped a frog. We thought it was Edwy making trouble again, but he'd spent the night in a spider's larder, wrapped in spidersilk and screaming for his mother."

"And that was Wild Magic, too?" Eschiva asked with raised brows.

"That was an alliance of Edwy's most recent victims, giving him his just deserts." Bertrada sighed gustily. "Ah well. We have beer, if not butter, and so far the bread is baking as it should. Would you mind touching up the wards if you've a moment? You always did have the best hand with those."

Eschiva smiled, not at the flattery—Bertrada never flattered anyone; she simply told the truth—but with the pleasure of being among kin. The wards were weak almost to vanishing. She secured them from the four corners, taking her time about it, as if this were a lesson such as she had learned in this very house.

As she came to the fourth quarter, which happened to be near the gate, she saw a horse she recognized, standing in the courtyard, and one of the fosterlings beside it, contemplating mischief. Eschiva rebuked her heart for beating harder, then decided to call it anxiety for the grey mare's safety.

She need not have worried. The redheaded imp stopped short in the middle of his spell, screeched, and bolted, trailing smoke from a singed posterior.

Arslan's mare continued to doze, hipshot, in the fitful sun. The protection on her glowed for a little while longer, then faded.

Eschiva bit back her grin before she entered the manor hall. Bertrada was there, and most of the children. Those were as quiet as Eschiva had ever seen them, standing in a circle, wide-eyed, staring speechless at the ifritah's son.

He did look splendid. He was wearing John's livery, and not the seam-straining makeshifts he had had before, either. This was new and made to fit him. But that was not why they stared.

Even with wards, the hall was full of spirits, drawn there by the magic of the place. They had all, to the last cobwebby sprite, gathered above him and joined and begun to spin, so that he was crowned with a wheel of fire.

He raised his hands and spoke a word. The wheel slowed and frayed and became a ring of spirits again, floating over his head, as fascinated as the human children. "I cry your pardon," he said to Bertrada, who looked somewhat astonished herself. "They're not usually so exuberant."

"It's the fire in you," Bertrada said with creditable aplomb. "It makes them giddy. You must be the count's new squire: the lion's cub from Jerusalem."

He bowed. "At your service, my lady," he said.

Sturdy, practical Bertrada, who had never blinked at anything in hell or heaven, blushed and dimpled and simpered like a girl. At least, thought Eschiva, there was someone else in the world who could not keep her head in his vicinity, either.

Arslan straightened and put on a more dutiful face. "I've come with a message for the Lady Susanna," he said. "Is she in this house?"

"She's in the herb-garden," Bertrada answered before Eschiva could say a word. "Come, I'll take you there."

She had no need to do that at all, with two dozen eager young things clamoring for the honor. She disposed of them in much the same way that Arslan had calmed the spirits, but with rather more noise.

She could not dispose of Eschiva, nor did she try. The three of them, stalked by a gaggle of children and spirits, sought out the green and scented space that was the herb-garden. Susanna was there with her son, holding his hands as he proved to her that he could walk.

There was no mistaking the lineage of that sturdy infant with his coppery curls. He already had the imperious manner—and the temper, too, as his balance failed and he sat down abruptly. His roar would have done justice to old Henry himself.

He had decided the night before that Eschiva was worthy of his notice, but at the sight of Arslan he rose unaided and ran bellowing toward him. Arslan caught the child before he careened onto his face, swung him up, and stood in sudden, deafening silence.

After a long moment Bertrada said, "I hope he doesn't think he's yours."

Arslan's cheeks turned a darker shade of bronze. Susanna retrieved her son, ignoring his squawk of protest. "You may tell my lord John," she said pleasantly, "that I will not be flaunted in front of his wife."

"My lord John bade me tell you that he understands perfectly," Arslan said, "and he'll be calling on you after he settles a certain wager."

Her brow arched at that. "He may call on me," she said, "but I may not receive him if he comes too numerously attended."

"I'll tell him, lady," Arslan said.

"You will not tell him of this," Susanna said, as her son craned toward Arslan.

He bowed. His expression was carefully constrained. Geoffrey bellowed to see his new passion walk away without him. He would not stop until Arslan had come back, taken him in hand, and said lightly but firmly, "That will be enough, sir. I'll come and play with you, but I have to attend my lord first."

Geoffrey did not like it: his brow puckered and his eyes clouded dangerously. But under Arslan's steady stare, he submitted.

For a long while after Arslan had gone, escorted by the crowd of children, the three women said nothing at all. Bertrada stirred first. "Ah," she said, a long sigh. "Now that is a wonder and a marvel."

"Isn't he?" said Susanna. "Father Hugh has been teaching him magic. I've helped as I can. Do you think . . . ?"

"As long as he's in Gloucester," Bertrada said promptly, "I'll be delighted."

They had made no mention of his opinion in the matter. Eschiva elected not to remind them. Geoffrey was their lure, and they well knew it. They would be thinking to learn as much from him as he learned from them—and all for the good of Britain. Always. Of course. That he was such a delight to the eyes was simply coincidence.

John came in the evening, and his attendance was certainly small enough: Arslan and his Turks, and no one else. The daymeal was almost done. The youngest children had been sent off to bed; their elders were nodding over their cups of well-watered wine.

John was dressed in a plain dark cotte, without excess of princely finery, and Arslan wore his own clothes instead of the squire's livery. Even the Turks were as unobtrusive as they could be. It was almost ostentatious, that lack of ostentation, and John knew it. His eyes as they met Susanna's were glinting, and his bow was low, as if he had been a plain knight and she a queen.

She received him likewise, invited him up to the high table, and poured him wine in the best cup, which was made of Roman glass and ornamented with gold. It was very polite, very cool, but there was enough magic in that hall that even the children could not have failed to sense the fire that leaped between them.

Bertrada had laid claim to Arslan, and the Turks stood against the wall as good servants should, which left Eschiva to share silence with her uncle Godfrey. He had brought a book to dinner again, unperturbed by his wife's disapproval of the habit, and was happily immersed in it. Eschiva was not altogether certain that he knew John was there.

After a polite interval, she made her excuses to her oblivious uncle, who after all was lord of the manor, and slipped away. Her mood was odd. What was between Susanna and John was so strong that she felt it in her own body, made sharper by the magic of this house. She did not want to feel it; she had hoped to escape it, but her chamber was no refuge. The bed was too clear a reminder.

She thought she might seek out the chapel, but when she stopped wandering, it was the garden she stood in, the same herb-garden in which Susanna had been playing with Geoffrey. It was deserted in the long light of evening, pungent with the scents of rosemary and bay, marjoram and sage and thyme.

Eschiva plucked a sprig of rosemary, rubbing it between her fingers as she passed through the herb-garden and the kitchen garden to the fishpond. There she sat on the stone bench, watching the fish dart and dance below the water, and the dragonflies above it, threading the loom of the evening.

He came so softly, so quietly, and was so much a part of the luminous silence, that she hardly woke to his presence. When she did, she knew that he had been there for a good while, sitting on the pond's rim. Her eyes came to rest on his profile. There they stayed, as if the sight of him were heart's ease.

*Enough,* she thought. Bertrada's influence, no doubt, and the fragrant warmth of the summer evening, and the magic that glimmered about them. She slid down beside him, meaning only to sit there, close enough to touch, but just as she lowered herself to the ground, a pebble turned under her foot. She could swear she heard a burble of faery laughter; or was it only one of the fish, leaping to catch its dinner?

Whether it was magic or her own clumsiness, she slipped and overbalanced, falling headlong into his lap. He caught her as he had caught Geoffrey—was it only that morning? She had to close the embrace, or send them both tumbling into the pond.

The world stilled. They sat face to face, arms about one another, staring, hardly breathing.

"Your eyes," she said. "They're the color of rain."

"Leaves," he said in the same dreamlike tone. "Leaves in mist."

"Rain," she murmured, "on leaves." She moved as inevitably, as easily as the rain falls, and touched her lips to his. He was as warm as a fire. She could feel it in him, burning under the skin.

It leaped at her touch, so that she gasped in delight. No maiden, no; but no jaded man of the world, either. His skill had no arrogance in it, no vaunting self-assurance. He asked, he did not simply take.

She had never kissed a man before who was not father or brother or kin—and certainly not in such a way, deep and immeasurably sweet. She would have drowned in him and been content. It was he who drew back, gently, and let her remember how to breathe again.

She brushed her fingers over his face, along the level brow, down the cheek where smooth skin gave way to the prick of young fair beard. He shivered lightly under her hand. She had to kiss him again, to make him stop, and then again, because the taste of him was so dizzyingly sweet. Then she laid her head on his shoulder and sighed. She had completely lost her wits—and yet she had found what she had, after all, been looking for since before she could remember.

"I thought you hated me," he said.

"I thought you were profoundly indifferent to me," she said.

His breath hissed, loud as wind in her ear. "Oh, no! Never. But you were so . . . oblivious."

"Haven't you ever seen a wall before?"

"We don't build in ice, where I come from."

A gust of laughter escaped her. She raised her head, needing to see his face, the steady grey eyes, the faintest hint of a smile in the corner of his mouth. "No, you build in fire, and house it in stone. Do you know what an imposing man you are going to be?"

He shrugged at that, uncomfortable, reminding her that he was still no more than a boy. "They say I'm the image of my father."

"Was he an ifritah's son, too?"

"Oh, no," said Arslan. "His father was the heir to a holding in Anjou. His mother was a courtesan, born among the Byzantines, but she had kin in Damascus, too. He never married, because she would never marry him. I'm bastard blood twice over."

He said it without bitterness, which was remarkable; but then what about him was not?

Oh, indeed, she was in love, and besotted, and she knew it. She was as dizzy as if she had drunk a whole jar of wine. "My mother never married my father," she said. "Spirits don't. It's even in Scripture. Neither marrying nor giving in marriage. That's the way of their kind."

"Your mother—"

"My father was a god long ago, a lord of living water. My mother . . ." Her voice chilled in spite of itself. "My mother went to him on the night of Midsummer, and consummated the ancient rite, and so continued our lineage."

"How lofty," he said. "How dutiful."

"Wasn't it?" She smoothed her hands along his shoulders. Such lovely wide shoulders, such beautiful strong bones. She was a tall woman, but beside him she was small.

"Are you gold all over?" she asked him.

He could blush all over: his breast was as hot as his cheeks. She unlaced his cotte and the shirt beneath, and slid her hands over his skin. The shirt was softer than linen, but his skin was softer than that. She loved the feel of it. And yes, it was gold, all the way down, smooth and unvarying.

His eyes were on her, drinking her as if she had been wine. The whole of his heart was in them. Such a great heart, so warm, and so utterly, perfectly hers. What she saw there, the love that he had for her, was almost too much to bear. It was the most wonderful, the most terrible thing she could have imagined.

"I never knew," she said. "I never even guessed—" She pulled away in sudden temper. "Why didn't you let me see?"

"And be rent with your scorn?"

"I would never—how could you—"

"How could I have known?"

She wanted to hit him. She kissed him instead, because she had to do something. This time she ended it, glaring at him, more furious rather than less, the longer she looked into those clear eyes. They refused to hate her; they would not judge her. They simply loved her.

That must be the ifrit in him, that he was so pure a spirit. The river-god in her was a roiling, tumbling thing, headlong and turbulent and never very wise.

"I'm going to ask John to knight you," she said.

She had startled him. Good: she never wanted to be dull. "Knight me? But lady, why?"

"Because you'll be better served with land of your own here, and I'll ask for that, too. And," she said, "because I can love a squire, but a knight suits me better. If I'm going to be scandalous, and I do fully intend to be, I want to be a scandal with a man in the world's eyes, and not a boy vexed by other boys' gibes and jealousies."

"But I am a—" He broke off. "How do you know about—"

"I am what I am," she said, "and I have eyes in my head. Everyone loves you—except the rest of John's squires."

"They don't hate me," he said. "I'm the new one, that's all, and I'm a foreigner. I'm fighting my way through; no one's killed me yet. I'll earn the place I deserve, and in the proper time, too."

"Not if you're knighted."

"I don't want to be knighted," he said. "Not till I'm ready. I do thank you, lady, it's a kind thought, but if you ask, I'll ask my lord to refuse."

"You are stubborn," she said.

"So I've always been told," he said. "I'm sorry, lady. I'm sure, if it's a knight you're wanting, any one of the men in my lord's train would—"

"I don't want any one of them. I want you."

That silenced him, if only for a moment. "Then you'll get a squire," he said, "but I'll be a knight in time."

"Don't let it take too long," she said.

"Why not? If it's a scandal you want, just think: Bishop Hugh's ward carrying on with one of Prince John's squires, and he a foreigner and a bastard into the bargain. And those devils that follow him about—shocking! Could she not at least have attached herself to a proper English libertine?"

She sat speechless in his lap, and no thought in her at all, only the bubbling up of laughter. A third time she kissed him, and that was the seal on it. They exchanged no more words, and no vows. Not that evening, as the long light faded slowly into dark, and the stars came out one by one.

When the page came looking for them, he found them decorously apart, fully clothed and saying nothing. They had said all that needed to be said.

# CHAPTER 14

John returned to Gloucester Castle in the dawn, with a look about him of deep contentment. Arslan knew well how John must be feeling, although he had had no more of his lady than kisses. He had not wanted more, not tonight. More would have been too much.

She did love him. She, the enchantress, the guardian of Britain, loved the ifritah's son from Beausoleil. It was improbable; impossible. Wonderful.

He was not worthy of her. But he could learn to be. He would not always be a gangling child. He would be a knight, as he had promised her. He would learn magic. He would do whatever the horned king had brought him here to do, and be all that she could wish for in a man.

That resolve carried him through a long day without her. He was dimly aware of duties and obligations, arms-practice, an hour of Latin with the tutor to the squires—John did insist on that; no one in his service would be unlettered, though he might remain forever a fool.

John went in the evening again, as soon as he could in courtesy leave the hall, and again he took Arslan with him. Eschiva was waiting, as was Susanna, and the red-haired imperious child whose parentage no one could mistake. They all said he looked like Richard, but Arslan saw in him a certain resemblance to Susanna's redheaded and imperious cousin.

John truly had not known. He stopped in front of the lord's table, taking it in: the mother, the child, their kin about them. His lip twisted. His brow went up. "Tell me that's my brother's," he said, "and you'll make our mother more than happy."

"You know whose he is," Susanna said.

"His?" said John dryly, for Geoffrey had crawled purposefully across the table and launched himself at Arslan.

"My lord," Arslan said, "I didn't mean—"

No one was listening to him, even Eschiva. John said, "You hid him yesterday."

"That wasn't wise of me," she admitted.

"You've been hiding him since before he was born. Why?"

"You were in exile," she said. "What could you have done but fret?"

"Know that he existed. Send you such help as I could. Give him my name. I do well by my bastards, madam. It's the one habit of my father's that I happen to approve of."

Her cheeks flushed. She raised her chin; her eyes glittered. "I never wanted or needed your charity."

"Surely, madam," John said in the dryest of tones, "but life in this world is never easy for those born outside the marriage bed. Won't you let me smooth his way for him? What is his name?"

"Geoffrey," she said, stiff with temper.

"Ah!" he said. "Another Geoffrey Plantagenet. My brother of that name will be pleased. He's coming, did you know? Since my exile was revoked, he's claiming the same privilege for himself. He'll be taking the see of York, as soon as he finds passage from Normandy. No faery ship for him, alack, and no straight track, either."

"You're babbling," Susanna said.

"So I am," he said. He held out his hands. "Give him to me."

Arslan passed the child into his father's arms. Geoffrey was dubious, but the golden chain that John was wearing proved fascinating. John inspected the sturdy body, the plump baby face with its firm chin already coming clear, the riot of coppery curls. "Handsome," he said. "Really, you should claim he's Richard's; the likeness is remarkable."

"No one who matters would believe it," Susanna said, "and I don't lie for sport. Are you going to flaunt him in your wife's face?"

"Are you telling me she doesn't know?"

"She knew I was bearing. I can presume she knows it was male. I haven't attended her since I began to swell with him."

"No," John mused. "She wouldn't have liked that. Did she harm you?"

"Not at all," said Susanna. "She thanked me for relieving her of the burden of your attentions, and dismissed me. I came here; no one went after me or troubled me. I've been treated very honorably, as husbands' lemans go."

"That is fortunate for her," John said.

"You should be kinder," said Susanna. "The nuns succeeded too well with her. That's no fault of hers, any more than it is of yours."

"Are we quarreling over my wife?" John inquired.

"Are we, my lord?"

"I should hope not," he said. He returned the now blessedly sleepy Geoffrey to Arslan and held out his hand. "Come, madam. This were best finished elsewhere."

She looked as if she might have refused, but in the end she consented. Arslan did not think, somehow, that they would part over this.

Bertrada carried Geoffrey off to bed, taking the rest of the children with her. As Arslan turned toward the room in which he had been lodged before, Eschiva stopped him. "Come with me," she said.

He bowed to her with beating heart, but he hoped his face was calm. She led him through a door behind the lord's table and up a stair that should have been pitch-black, but she made a cold blue light that drifted in the air ahead of them.

Her chamber was high in a corner. She had it to herself, although Arslan thought she might have begun by sharing it with Susanna. Certainly the bed was big enough for two.

She was trembling. So was he, but not so hard, not with such white and exhilarating terror.

"Lady," he said. "You don't have to—"

"I want to." She pulled off her gown with shaking hands and let fall her shift, to stand shivering in front of him. Her hands crept up to cover her breasts, her loins, but she pushed them down. Her face was scarlet.

"Oh, lady," he said. "Lady, you are beautiful."

It was no less than the truth. Her skin was like milk, touched with faint golden flecks from the sun. Her neck was long, her shoulders wide, her arms round and strong. Her breasts were full but firm and high, her waist narrow above the broad swell of hips. She was a strong woman, tall, long-legged, more robust than delicate—no fear here that he would crush her, as big as he was, and awkward in it.

"Now you," she said, her voice shaking only a little. Now that she had begun, she seemed calmer. The dice were cast, the battle begun. Her fear had faded.

He was glad. He did not want her to be afraid. This was not battle, however new she might be to it. He stripped quickly, neatly, as he had learned to do on campaign, folding his garments and laying them out of the way.

When he was done, he stood in front of her. She was watching him, darting glances, but sliding away before they held too long. Her cheeks were still stained with scarlet.

He caught himself flushing in sympathy. He had been born years after her, but he was the elder here; however new to him the love of the heart might be, this love of the body he knew rather well.

It was like riding or dancing or swordsmanship: an art, with its own laws, its own cadences. He moved closer to her, carefully, lest he startle her. She was as skittish as a young mare, shying from the sight of him. He gave her time to calm herself, to grow accustomed to his nearness. She must know how a man was made; she was no sheltered nun. Yet it was not the same to see villeins laboring in the fields or criminals stripped naked for flogging. Those were not meant for her, to touch her, hold her, love her.

He took her hands in his and kissed them. They were cold. "Touch me," he said. "All over. Everywhere. Don't be shy. There's no shame here. No fear."

"There . . . is . . . fear." Her teeth chattered as she spoke. But she did as he bade, steadying as she went on. He saw the effort that cost her, the force of will.

"Softly," he said. "It's the easiest thing in the world, and the simplest."

"It's hard!"

"Because you want to make it difficult."

She glared at him. "What, are you some ancient master?"

"Surely you've heard of the eastern arts."

"You don't—you can't—you left when you were a child!"

"Not quite," he said. She had recoiled as he spoke. He brought her hands back, settling them where they had been, resting on his hips. "In India it's like a sacrament. They make great magic with it, and great blessing. They turn it into a sacred dance, a rite of their gods."

"Show me."

He smiled. "It's never a dance for one. Always two." And often more, but he did not want to appall her with that. He set his hands on her hips, as hers were on his. "See. It's simple. Think of a river, how the reeds sway, undulating in the water. They all dance together, bound by the current. Do you feel it in you?"

She nodded. A little of the white fixity had left her face. She was not quite so stiff; she remembered her native suppleness. Of her own accord she drew nearer to him, almost touching. Her hands ran up his back, then down, waking shivers of pleasure. She smiled at that, quickly, as if unaware she did it. She began to play the chords of him, tentatively at first, then more strongly, until with tremendous daring she closed her fingers about the rampant thing between them. He gasped.

She pulled back, but he closed the space between them, trapping her hands. He traced the shape of her face in kisses. She tilted her head back, eyes shut. She was breathing hard.

He lifted her in his arms. She clung tightly, loosing her grip only when he had laid her on the bed. Her heart beat as swift as a bird's.

He gentled her with lips and hands, smoothing away her fears, teaching her the subtleties of pleasure. Her body arched. She began to purr like a great beautiful cat.

She opened to him at last, with no art or trained skill, only the deep knowledge of the body. She cried out in pain, sharp but short. He reeled in shock and nearly fled. But she held him, arms about his neck, legs about his middle, strong and imperious. The thrust of her hips drove him deep. A groan escaped her, but still she would not let him go. He had no choice then; his body overwhelmed his will.

It was not the long slow dance he had intended. It hurt her, but she would not let him stop. He could feel the pain, throbbing through his skin, touching the fire beneath it. He knew nothing to do but wish it gone, washed over by a wave of pure bodily delight.

His gasp was the echo of hers. For an instant he was within her, looking out through her eyes at his startled face. Then he was himself again, and their awkward struggle had smoothed, their bodies found the rhythm of the dance. She smiled at him, the sweetest smile in the world.

His heart melted at that smile. A moment later, it broke in astonishment. Her body convulsed. She clutched him so tightly he could barely breathe; then that failed to matter.

They lay tangled in one another, breathing hard. She moved first, shaking all over, sitting up and scraping hair out of her face. Her eyes on him were greedy, no longer shy, no longer afraid to look at anything below his face. "Oh," she said. "By the old gods. Now I know why the priests call this a sin."

He reached with no will at all, and laid his hand over the curve of her breast. She arched into it with a little gasp of delight. "I feel," she said, "as if every scrap of me has come alive. As if—"

He pulled her down and kissed her to stop her chatter. She would gladly have had more, but in that he was all too mortal. She had to settle for kisses, and for exploring his body in minute and exacting detail. She paused for his every scar, and lingered over the mark on his shoulder, the small red stain in the shape of a flame, that he had always thought of as his mother's kiss.

There was one other thing that his mother had left him, that had won him sorrow enough in Christian company. She examined it from all angles, frowning. "This doesn't look—is it—because you are—"

"My mother said that my father could raise me as Christian as he pleased, but when the Judgment comes, she would prefer that I be numbered among the circumcised," Arslan said. "Mind you she said it after the fact, when the imam had come and gone. He had no choice but to accept the inevitable—and have me baptized at the earliest opportunity. I'm well secured on all sides of that war."

"What of women?"

He blinked at her.

"What do women do? If they're in Islam, how does the Angel know who is a believer and who is not?"

He gathered his scattered wits. "How does he know if any Christian is a believer?"

"Then he can tell a Christian woman from a Muslim? How? Is there a baptism? A rite?"

"There isn't—"

"I would hate to be a Muslim," Eschiva said.

"I'm not a—"

"Good," she said. She lay beside him, stretching along the length of him, discovering that her head fit comfortably in the hollow of his shoulder. She sighed. Her hand wandered for a little while, but then stilled.

She was asleep. He was loose in every limb, his mind emptying of thought, but he was content to lie awake. Her warmth, the memory of what they had done together, filled him with a profound happiness. He folded his arms about her and kissed the crown of her head, breathing in the rich sweet scent of her, and smiled long and slow.

# CHAPTER 15

That night began a spring and summer of dizzy joy. John tarried in Gloucester, having much to do there; if he left the town, he did so only briefly, always coming back. That could not last, Arslan knew: both worlds were pressing on him, and the time would come when he had to continue his round of the kingdom, both that which men knew and the secret realm of which he was king. But for this little while he paused, and gave his weary household a much-needed respite. It was a gift, a gathering of forces, a hoarding of strength for all that would come.

Arslan's days, like John's, were full of lordly duties. The nights he spent as John did, in Bertrada's manor outside the walls. Sometimes, and more often as spring ripened into summer, he spent part of the day there, too. Father Hugh commanded it, saying that Bertrada was the teacher he needed just then.

She was a mistress of the lore of wood and water, and the powers of earth were secure in her hands. "Fire is your gift and your essence," she said, "but earth and water and air are in you, too. We'll teach you to master them all."

But first, she taught him of earth, which was most unlike his native fire. The secrets of stones, the growing of green things, the power of the wood and the spirits that were in it, those things she taught him in that golden spring. And when night came, he mastered another magic, the magic of his beloved's body.

The quiet broke a little before Midsummer. John came riding back with Arslan late one morning, having lingered much longer than usual in his lady's arms, and found the castle in a mild uproar. There had been excitement now and then, messengers coming in, disputes that needed resolving, petitioners and embassies in ample number. This was a dispute, as it happened, but one that struck the barons to the heart. The Bishop of Ely had gone too far.

The man who waited for John was named Gerard; he was or had been sheriff of Lincoln. "He's seized my possessions," he said from his knees, where he put on a great show of grief and righteous rage. "He demands that I surrender Lincoln Castle. I'll do that—but only to you, my lord. Never to him."

There were barons about, disporting themselves in John's castle and draining his cellars of wine and the ale that, more than ever, Arslan called vile. They waxed wroth at Gerard's tale. Arslan, watching him, reckoned that maybe Ely had the right in this dispute—the man had the look of a bully and a noble thief. But that would not matter to these lords of the realm, or indeed to John, who had been waiting like a cat at a rathole for Ely to overstep his bounds.

John was not the warrior that his brother Richard was, but he did, on occasion, love a good fight. He indulged in none of his usual dallying and lagging about. By evening he was armed, mounted, and riding to the rescue of Lincoln.

He swept Arslan with him, along with the rest of his squires and young knights. There was no time to send word to the ladies in the manor. John did not even think of it. Arslan, who did, had no opportunity. John kept him too busy, until they were riding away from Gloucester in the endless summer evening.

This was not the leisurely amble of a royal progress. They were in armor, and they rode at speed. Arslan's blood quickened even as he yearned after his lady. It had been a long while since he rode to a fight.

He paused once while the walls of the castle were still in sight. "Karim," he said. "Go to her. Tell her where I am. Stay with her until I come back."

The Turk favored him with a long and completely unreadable look, then bowed to her horse's neck, turned and galloped back toward Gloucester. Arslan rode on with a lighter heart.

"You think that was wise?" Yusuf asked him.

"You think it's not?" Arslan countered.

Yusuf shrugged. "It's one way to protect them both."

"And?"

"Kalila is . . . Kalila," Yusuf said. And that was all he would say, for anything Arslan could do.

*     *     *

Kalila rode to the manor in great confusion of mind. Ever since she came to this strange cold country, she had felt odd, remote, separated from the world and the people in it. In France she had been profoundly a foreigner, but it had been a lark: a grand game, to learn the ways of these people across the sea. Here in Britain, the game palled.

It was Arslan. No, she thought as she rode between green hedges in the long golden light. It was the witch who had snared him. From the moment he saw her, he had been under her spell. She had led him on and on, playing the haughty lady of a troubadour's song; then when she tired of that, she had seduced him into her bed. He had eyes, ears, thought for nothing but her. Kalila had seen how, when John rent him away, he had struggled to find his spirit again, to remember who and what he was.

What an irony that he had sent her to look after the witch. She knew perfectly well what he had been thinking. Set the two women together, and let the one in man's clothing imagine that she played guardsman, while she was kept safe from the men's wars.

She could refuse. She could circle round, hide in the rear, appear when it was too late to send her back. Why she obeyed instead, she did not know. She was a fool, she supposed. She loved a man who would never love her in return—she was too clear-sighted to dream that that could change. He was a man for one woman, and one alone; that woman had never been Karim, born Kalila, daughter of Dildirim the mamluk of Beausoleil.

It was a fine black mood for a summer evening, wonderfully darkened by the gaggle of pilgrims who, seeing her riding toward them on the road, shrieked and crossed themselves and pelted her with fistfuls of dung. From what little she knew of their language, she gathered that they took her for a devil. She obliged them with a ferocious snarl and a gesture that would be reckoned horrendously rude in the streets of Damascus. They fled in horror of the demon's spell.

Grinning to herself, she turned off the road toward Bertrada's manor. It sat on a low rise of land surrounded by fields, bordered by tightly woven hedges. There was nothing bright or beautiful about that long stone house with its cluster of outbuildings; not even a bit of carving to make it interesting. Its beauty was transitory: a rose-arbor by the door, and gardens behind, blooming profusely in this brief northern season.

They knew her here, and did not find her particularly appalling, either, not compared to the spirits and creatures of the lesser world who crowded about the place. When she rode through the gate, past the fragrance of the roses, a redheaded imp came to take her horse. It was one of the lady's sons; he was pleased to tell her where to find Eschiva. She was waiting, of course, for her lover, sitting in the garden, dressed all in white. She would not know that that in Islam was the color of death. Or would she?

Kalila must have been a great disappointment, though Eschiva she concealed it with a smile of greeting and a courteous word. "Sir Saracen," she said.

"My name is Karim, lady," said Kalila. "My lord has sent me to tell you, he rides to Lincoln with the prince John. He sent me to watch over you until he comes back."

Eschiva's brows went up. "That was kind of him," she said.

"Good, then you'll dispense with my services. Lady, if you don't mind, now my message is delivered, I—"

"I haven't dismissed you," she said. "He sent you as a gift. I'd be ungracious to refuse it."

"I'm of no use to you, lady," Kalila said.

"Aren't you?" Eschiva's eye was keen, widening slightly as she saw what was there to see. All of it—every small and unworthy thought, and every reason for thinking it.

"Send me away, lady," Kalila said, too proud to beg, but too desperate to keep silent.

"You will stay," Eschiva said, "as he asked. It seems we're to keep one another safe."

"Don't you find that aggravating?" Kalila demanded.

"Very," said Eschiva. "I also find it rather charming. He trusts us, you'll notice, or he'd never have brought us together."

"He hasn't the faintest conception of what he's done."

"Maybe not," Eschiva said, "but his heart is wiser than his head, by far, and he follows it more often than not. His heart knows."

"So well you know him," Kalila said, with a sneer in it.

"Don't you?"

Kalila flung herself down in the clipped grass, with a jangling of armor and weapons and a creaking of leather. "I wish I didn't!"

"Sometimes," Eschiva said, "so do I. I'd be free again, then. I remember when I was free."

"So go back to it. Cast him off. He'll ache for a while, but the wound will heal. He'll be the safer for it."

"No," said Eschiva. "No. I won't do that, even for you, Saracen woman. Is your name really Karim?"

"Kalila."

"That is lovely."

"He renamed me. He commanded all this—the pretense, the armor. I do know how to use the weapons."

"Yes, I've seen you. You're a fine archer. Those who know call you a very good swordsman."

"I am good. I'm better than most men. That doesn't—help—" Kalila pulled of her turban and cast it spinning across the garden. "Don't make me stay here."

"I think you must. He'll come back, Kalila, or we'll go to him. He'll not be lost in this battle, though he may think for a while that he is."

"What do you mean by that?"

Eschiva raised her hands, turned them palm up. "I don't know. Sometimes the words speak themselves."

"If he is hurt," Kalila gritted, "even a scratch, I swear to Allah—"

"We'll kill each other then," Eschiva said.

It was easy to hate her, but difficult to stay angry at her. Which she knew, no doubt, witch that she was, and turned to her advantage.

The Turk would not sleep in a bed. She insisted on spreading a pallet across Eschiva's door, and sleeping there fully clothed, with her sword at her side. She was doing it out of temper, and to prove to both Arslan and Eschiva that she was a dutiful servant.

Eschiva wondered if she had been unwise to force the girl to stay. She had no fear of a knife in the back or poison in the cup—as fierce as the child was, she was not that kind of murderer. But she clearly wanted to be with Arslan, riding and fighting beside him as it seemed she had done before. It was Eschiva's fault that she had been sent away, and she would not fail to blame Eschiva for it.

Still, Arslan had wanted it. Eschiva trusted that heart of his. He had reason for this, that would become apparent in time.

It was lonely without him. Her arms were empty, her bed cold. She hoped he was dreaming of her tonight.

There was a way to be sure, but she refused to make use of it. No magic tonight. No messengers on the tides of sleep. Let him yearn as she yearned, and know the lack of her.

Yes, she was angry with him; quite unreasonably, for he only did his duty to his liege lord. But he was gone and she had stayed, and his absence was more bitter than she could have imagined. She who had never been lonely, who had been sufficient unto herself, had become a wan and drooping thing, all because of a night without her lover in her bed.

Susanna too was alone, but Eschiva did not go to her. Eschiva was hardly fool enough to hope that anyone in this house was ignorant as to where the prince's squire had been spending his nights, but no word had ever been said of it. Eschiva was not in the mood, just then, to break that silence.

She tossed all night long, growing ever angrier at Arslan, but even more so at herself. It was well that he was far away from her. If he had come back then, she would have flayed him alive for abandoning her, and sending no more than a sullen Turkish girlchild in boy's guise to make up for the loss.

# CHAPTER 16

The Bishop of Ely had laid siege to Lincoln. John, in retaliation, took the castle of Nottingham, which stood guard over the road to Lincoln, with such speed and fury that he barely met resistance. The castle's defenders, seeing the prince's army drawn up before the gate, and seeing the force of the wrath that was on him, surrendered without bloodshed.

He was in the castle on the eve of Midsummer, being feasted and feted by the notables of the town. He had already joined with a league of barons to plan the rescue of Lincoln; they were mightily pleased with themselves, and boasting of the great deeds they would do against Ely's armies.

Arslan had gone out somewhere between the first round of wine and the ninth round of bragging. He was perpetually astonished by the length of these summer days, which went on and on through shades of gold into a blue twilight. Tonight was the shortest night of the year. Farther north, some of the Scots in John's train had told him, the sun hardly set at all. Here it did pause for a few hours' rest, but that was far away still.

This town sat amid green fields on the bank of a broad slow river, but beyond it loomed the eaves of an ancient forest. "Sherwood," Hugh Neville said, standing beside him on the city wall, looking out toward the shadow on the horizon. "It's one of my great charges: royal land from end to end, and woe to him who sets foot there without the king's leave."

"Truly?" Arslan folded his arms on the parapet. "I've heard of the king's forests, how they all belong to him, and how the deer are his and only his, and no one else may hunt them. There's nothing like that in Outremer."

"No forests?"

"No lands where the king alone may hunt. Farther east, the lords of Islam have gardens that they hunt in, but it's not the same."

"It's a great prerogative of the king here," Neville said, "and a sore grievance to those who would hunt his deer. Their ancestors were free of the wood, they say, and it irks them endlessly that they don't share the same privilege."

"Why is that?"

Neville shrugged. "It's the law. The king is the king, and these are his deer. It's death to kill one, unless you are the king or have his favor."

It was no more capricious, Arslan supposed, than many another royal indulgence. And yet, thinking on it, he felt a certain crawling in his skin, an uneasiness that seemed to come from the wood itself. "Which king?" he asked. "Which do the deer acknowledge? The one crowned in London, or the one who carries a scepter in his saddlebag?"

"Now that's a clever question," Neville said, but he did not answer it.

He left after a while, walking with his light hunter's tread, and happening, just by the way, to secure wards that Arslan had been barely aware of. There were always wards where John was, enclosing him in their protection, and keeping out the Wild Magic.

The forest was full of it. Arslan could feel it even through Neville's wards.

When Arslan went down from the wall, he did not go back to the castle, but sought out an inn that he had passed on his way through the city. It was full in this long evening, its usual custom much enlarged by a crowd of John's men-at-arms.

Arslan was not in livery; he had taken it off when he left the hall. Yusuf, padding behind him as always, attracted considerably more attention. The Turk was dressed much as Arslan was, in plain wool tunic and undistinguished hose, but his turban and his waist-long plaits and his inescapably foreign face drew stares wherever he went.

He slipped ahead of Arslan, cut through the throng with the dagger of his smile, and stared down a handful of young bloods who had laid claim to a corner. They suddenly remembered obligations elsewhere. He bowed Arslan to a stool that gave him a clear view of the whole common room of the inn, and established himself between Arslan and the rest. "Wine for him," he said to the girl who hastened past, "and barley water for me."

She stopped short as they always did, transfixed by a quite different smile than that which had put her fellow townsmen to flight. Yusuf was not as pretty as his sister, but he was a strikingly handsome young man, and he knew it.

She was back almost before she left, with cups and bowls and pitchers, and a loaf of barley bread and a wedge of cheese. "With my father's compliments," she said.

Her father the publican did not look like a generous man, but she was a different matter. Her eye slid over Arslan, finding him pleasing enough, but came to rest on Yusuf. Half a dozen voices called her away, some waxing imperious, but she lingered yet a while, running one of his plaits through her fingers.

When she finally consented to return to her duties, Yusuf settled with his bread and barley water, visibly pleased with himself, even under Arslan's ironic eye. "You're just jealous," he said, "because she wasn't all over you."

"I don't need to be jealous," Arslan said. He sipped the wine, which was middling horrible, but not as horrible as English ale. The flow of conversation had resumed: the usual babble of gossip, bravado, and contentiousness that filled any inn, anywhere that he had been.

They were talking of John and the Bishop of Ely, and the war that they reckoned was brewing. That was nothing new to Arslan. He yawned and contemplated a return to the castle. But just as he gathered himself to rise, someone said, ". . . in Sherwood."

Arslan paused.

"Yes, it's true," the voice said. It belonged to a stout man in a tunic of good wool, drinking ale with a handful of men of similar attire and girth. "We were coming down from Lincoln by the forest road, not long before his grace of Ely laid siege to it, bringing a wagonload of wool, and they stopped us past the old oak: a whole company of them, dressed in green. I swear to you, they weren't human men. One had ears like a horse, and one had a mouth so wide it split his face, and another of them stood on goat-feet. They left us our wagon and our wool but took our horses and their trappings. It was a long walk back to Nottingham, with us taking turns on the wagon, and the oxen plodding slower, the farther we traveled."

One of the man's companions laughed and wagged a finger. "And what were you drinking on the road, Master Roger? A horse's ears! A horse's arse, more like."

Master Roger glowered at him. One of the others with them set down his tankard with a thump that made them all start. "Damn those outlaws! They've been poaching the king's deer, that's no secret, but if they've taken to robbing passersby, then none of us is safe."

"He called himself Robin, the one who led them," Master Roger said. "Robin o' the Wood. He looked like a man, more or less, crowned with oak-leaves and carrying a great bow. His horse had cloven hooves."

Some of them crossed themselves, but the skeptic scoffed. "Next time go lighter on the ale, and tell your guards to stay awake. Those forest tracks are made for an ambush, and with armies running hither and yon, it's no surprise the bandits have come in for what they can get hold of. Robin, was it? There's been a Robin or a Hob or some-such up Barnsdale way, waylaying travelers and stripping them of their silver and gold."

"This was Robin," Master Roger said grimly, "and he left us our silver. He wanted our horses, and our horses he took, every one."

"Were they shod with iron?"

The fourth man had not spoken until then. He had a clerkly look, though he was not tonsured; his tankard was full, nor had he been drinking from it.

"They were shod," Master Roger said. "But what does that have to do with—"

"Probably nothing," the clerkly man said. "Iron shoes and iron bits, yes? And iron buckles on the bridles. Cold iron is death to *those* folk."

"Not this one," said Master Roger. "He took my own mare, my sweet Rouncey, and rode her merrily away into the greenwood. I valued that mare, I'll have you know. She was worth more to me than a knight's destrier."

"She'll turn up," the skeptic said. "Send men round to the horse-fairs, and tell them to look for a fat black mare with a star."

"A moon," Master Roger said. "A crescent moon. That's why he wanted her—they're moonlight people, those. If he rides her on the wild hunt, she'll burst her heart."

"You're daft," his companion said. "Here, have another stoup of ale. Drown your sorrows."

Master Roger had sorrows in plenty to drown. Arslan sat with his wine while Yusuf courted the innkeeper's daughter, and pondered what he had heard. Green men and not-quite-men, waylaying travelers in the wood. His spine prickled.

There were others round about, too, telling bits of tales such as he had been hearing through all of Britain, but this was different. This was not a matter of curdled milk or ailing cattle. It was alive, aware, and wickedly intelligent. More than that, it had a name.

Names were power. That was a great law of magic. If one could name a thing, one could master it.

Yusuf was thoroughly preoccupied with his conquest of the innkeeper's daughter. Arslan slipped out past him, soft as a shadow, and ventured alone onto the streets of the town.

The churches were full of people praying and taking refuge against the powers of air and darkness. They remembered the old religion here, so close to the ancient wood, but what had once been worship was turned to fear. The priests fed that fear, naming the old gods devils, and shutting off the people from the rites that had kept the town safe against wickedness and faery mischief.

Neville's wards protected the castle, but not the town. Either he did not care, or his power did not extend so far. Father Hugh was in Lincoln, being besieged. William the Marshal was in London, contending with a roil of brangles there. Eschiva . . . Arslan knew where she was, as he knew the location of his own body, and tonight more than ever he regretted that she was in Gloucester and not here.

He could see the wisdom of the pattern: four guardians in four quarters of Britain. But this was a center, on this brief night before the longest day of the year.

The forest gate was open, people still passing in and out though the hour was late. He saw a handful of monks with their hoods and their chanting, going out to the abbey that he could see in the field beyond the wall, and a troupe of players coming in with their gaudy cart, dancing and playing on pipes and drums.

His hackles stood straight up. He stood in the street just inside the gate, armed with nothing but a dagger and such magic as he was born with.

The cart halted. The oxen that drew it seemed mortal enough, unless one happened to take note of their slitted yellow eyes and the hint of fang beneath the soft lips. Arslan smiled at the person who drove the cart, a very short, thick, brown-skinned creature in a very tall cap. "A good evening to you, sir," he said politely. "I'm thinking you'll find better lodging in the greenwood."

"Why, surely we should," said the foremost of the dancers, who looked like a buxom black-haired woman with eyes as green as a cat's. "We've come to see the king, we have, and dance at his crowning."

"One king was crowned two years agone," Arslan said, "and the other's not crowned yet, but I've seen no sign of crown or crowning for him."

"Ah, but you have mortal blood," the green-eyed woman said. "That blinds your eyes when you wish it so."

"No doubt," said Arslan, "but if he's crowned, it won't be in this too-Christian town."

"Christian prayers and cold iron," the green-eyed woman said, while her companions gibbered and shuddered. "Still, we've come as we've come, and we'll go when we've seen the king."

Arslan considered the wards and the castle, the prayers in the church and the chapels, and the shimmer of magic all about these wandering players. He smiled, and drew a sign in fire in the air. "You may come in," he said, "but if you offer harm to any man or beast within these walls, you will answer to me. I will be most strict in judging what is harm and what is simple mischief."

The green-eyed woman bowed low and low. "My lord," she said with no more than half a world's weight of irony.

Arslan stepped aside. The fey folk danced and piped and drummed their way into Nottingham, bringing their magic and their strangeness. The wards thrummed but held. Neville knew; and because he knew, Arslan had no doubt that the rest of the guardians did as well.

# CHAPTER 17

❧

John was up with the sun, which was not at all like him, and calling out his huntsmen. He was going hunting, he declared, on this glorious Midsummer morning. All the people waiting for judgment, for council, for simple curiosity, could ride with him or cool their heels in the castle.

It was a great riding that went out, with hawks and hounds and horns, banners and beaters and huntsmen innumerable, and if not all of them were human, that was no affair of Arslan's. Hugh Neville the Forester rode at John's back, and Arslan close behind. Yusuf, returned late and smug from the inn by the gate, kept to Arslan's shadow as he always had.

Even without Yusuf's excellent reasons, Arslan had not slept in what night there was. He was not weary: he had never slept as others did. A little rest and time to dream was all he had ever needed. He had dreamed awake in the Midsummer dark, seeing things that lingered in memory as he rode in the morning sun: most particularly Eschiva's face. She was angry. Not at him, not exactly, but he had a great deal to do with it.

He sighed as he passed the gate of Nottingham, and put her out of his mind. The players were just outside the gate, crowded about their lurid wagon, staring hard at the prince and his riding. They said not one word, raised not one flicker of mischief.

John was in one of his gracious moods. He bowed to them and smiled, and flung them a handful of silver pennies. They caught each out of the air with hands as quick as a frog's tongue, and never missed a single one.

He had done something significant. Arslan did not know exactly what. Paid a toll? Won passage?

The road did not transmute into a faery track. The wood before them was an outrider of the Worldwood, right enough, but it was no more or less anchored in the mortal world than it had been before. Its roots were sunk deep in living earth; its branches spread to catch the light of the mortal sun. The trees were clothed in midsummer green, starred with flowers in the glades. Birds sang there, and squirrels chittered, and far away a wolf called to its mate.

The belling of hounds overwhelmed the rest. The huntsmen's horns rang high and sweet. Hooves thundered even in the deep mold of the forest floor.

They started a sow rooting for acorns, and the flock of her piglets; she led them to the boar, deep in the oakwood. He fell to William Longsword's spear. John had not come hunting boar, however a royal a pursuit that might be. He was after the king's deer, and the king's deer he would hunt. With the rest, he could be generous.

They sent the boar back to Nottingham in the care of John's brother Longsword, with such of the hunters as reckoned that enough sport for a morning. It was a smaller party that went on, on fast, fit horses, with John in the lead and Neville and Arslan close behind.

The stag burst out of a covert in the deep wood. He was a royal beast, with a great swell of neck and a crown of branching antlers. They were still young, still in velvet, but noble nonetheless. Come autumn they would be glorious.

He had a harem like an eastern king: slender-legged does and spotted fawns. They scattered before the hunt. Someone aimed an arrow at a doe, but John's fierce cry sent it flying wide. He was hunting the stag, and only the stag.

The great beast outran the wind. The hunt pounded after it. A yelp and a *crack* marked a hunter who had ridden upright beneath a branch. He was down, his horse running riderless. No one could stop or slow for him.

Arslan crouched over his grey mare's neck, reins slack, letting her find her way through the woven trees. Her mane whipped his cheeks. He kept his eyes on John, letting all else fend for itself. Branches lashed him. Tree-boles brushed his knees.

They had been running mostly downhill for some while, along a stream that broadened into a little river. The stag could have leaped it easily, but chose instead to run along it. Foam dappled his flanks. For all the branches that clutched at his hunters, tangling in horses' manes, clubbing down unwary riders, he ran unhindered, head and tail high. The forest that fought the hunters favored him.

They were no longer entirely in the mortal world. The Worldwood deepened about them. The light through the tangled branches was more truly gold, the sun lost in a luminous haze. The baying of hounds faded into silence. The only sound was the thudding of hooves, the jingle of harness, the pounding of blood in Arslan's ears.

The hunt was gone, lost. Neville was still with them, and Yusuf who in his way was part of Arslan. There were other riders, but they had never come from Nottingham: shimmering shapes with hair that streamed like flames. Arslan caught his breath: surely that was the horned king at the head of them. But had his face been a skull, or his body bare bones?

Arslan hid his eyes in his mare's sweat-dampened mane. When he lifted them again, he saw only the trunks of trees speeding past, and his mortal companions, and a pair of hounds running ahead: bone-white hounds, skeletally thin, with blood-red ears.

The trees opened abruptly into blinding brilliance. The stag leaped into space, shredding and thinning and vanishing like mist. The earth dropped beneath the hunters' feet. They fell, horses, hounds, and all, through a golden fog.

The world stilled. Arslan clung with a death grip to his mare's wet neck. She stood heaving in knee-deep grass. John was there, and Hugh Neville, and Yusuf with a look on his face like a startled deer. All the rest were gone, lost in the wild wood.

A man stood in front of them, with the skeletal hounds panting at his feet. He seemed human enough, a sturdy man of middle size, dressed all in green. His face was brown and weathered, his hair the color of the heart of the oak, thick and curling, his beard a little darker. His eyes were the russet brown of oak-leaves in the autumn. He had a long bow slung behind him, and a quiver of green-fletched arrows.

And yet, however earthly he seemed, he was not even as human as Arslan. He was Wild Magic given shape and form, playing at man's semblance for the sheer wicked pleasure of it.

He knew that Arslan could see him for what he was: his glance was keen, his bow and flick of the hand an acknowledgment that, in their distant way, they were kin. When he spoke, it was not to Arslan; there was no need of words between them. "I welcome you to the green-wood, prince of men," he said to John. "I trust your journey here was pleasant?"

"It was . . . unusual," John said. He had caught his breath, and found his wits, too. "Messire Robin, I presume."

The green man swept a bow. "At your service, O king who would be."

"Indeed?" said John. "How far will you serve me?"

"As far as a feast and a gathering, and somewhat else for which you have been waiting."

"A crown?"

Robin grinned. He did not look quite so human then: his mouth was very wide, and his teeth were many and sharp. "Splendid prince! Straight to the point, and no wriggling hither and yon. I do like you, lord of men."

"I had been thinking," said John, "that this choice I've made makes me lord of more than men. Was that false, then?"

"Well," said Robin, "no. But that place is to be earned, and not simply taken."

"Ah," said John as if he understood a great deal. He did not say any more than that, except: "Lead on, then, Master Robin."

They dismounted and led their horses, following the green man under the eaves of the wood. The forest track was smooth and broad, the trees marching in ranks as if they had been planted by hands. They opened into a new clearing, wide and sunlit and carpeted with flowers. Its center was a ring of what looked to Arslan like tiny white stones; but as he peered closer, he saw that they were mushrooms, growing in a broad circle.

John stopped short on the edge of the clearing. "No," he said. "Oh, no. I'm not dallying for another month in the faery kingdom. There's a war brewing, and a kingdom that needs me. Take me out of this place and send me home. And mind you send me back on the same day I left!"

"There, there, lord of men," Robin said. "I give you my solemn word, you'll come from here no later than you left."

"The very hour and minute?" John demanded.

"To the instant," Robin said.

John pondered that, taking his time about it. After a stretching moment, he stepped into the clearing.

There was a sound like a harp string plucked under the sea. The ring in the grass writhed and sprouted and grew into a high hedge of amber and silver, with a single gate in it, and sward of flowers within. In its center lay a white hart. It was the color of new snow, and its eyes were rubies. About its neck was a crown of gold.

"Your crown, O king," Robin said. "Go in, take it. It belongs to you."

John did not move. "As simple as that?"

Robin spread his hands.

John narrowed his eyes. He walked slowly round the enclosure. Its hedge had budded and begun to bloom with pale blossoms. The gate was open, the hart at rest. Coneys played in the grass about it, and birds fluttered among them: common sparrows and small songbirds, and ordinary rabbits, extraordinary in this place so far out of the world.

John unfastened his belt with its sword and dagger, and laid them on the grass. He took off his mantle and his cotte, and with Arslan's help, wriggled out of the mailcoat he wore beneath. Last he put off his spurs and his fine leather boots. In no vestige of steel or cold iron, unarmed, alone, in linen shirt and leather breeches and bare feet, he approached the hedge.

It stirred at his coming, the tendrils of it trembling, leaves rustling. Arslan's fists ached with clenching. John's shoulders were stiff, his back rigidly erect.

He entered the enclosure. The hart did not acknowledge him with glance or motion. The smaller creatures went about their business. He watched them all for a little while, first standing, then squatting a pace or two inside the gate.

The air was perfectly still. The light was pellucid. Arslan felt the swelling of power in earth and air.

John's hand darted out. He caught one of the birds, a brown finch with a ring of yellow about its neck. It struggled wildly in his cupped hands, pecking at his fingers. Arslan saw the bright red of blood, the white shock of pain in John's face, but he did not let the creature go.

The hart rose and stretched and yawned. Fangs gleamed; claws flexed. An ice-white leopard in a golden collar crouched where the hart had been. Its ruby eyes fixed on John; its ears flattened.

Arslan started toward the gate. Neville's hand clamped about his arm. "Don't," the king's forester said.

Arslan stood rooted, not willingly, but in Neville's eyes he saw that this was not his choice to make. It was John's testing, and John's to succeed or fail.

The leopard stalked him across the flower-strewn grass. He ignored it. The bird in his hand had stilled. He breathed on it, whispering words that Arslan could not hear.

The leopard sprang. John scrambled away from it, reeling, but never letting go the bird. Tendrils from the hedge uncoiled, clutching at him. He darted toward the gate. It shut in his face.

He spun on his heel and ran toward the center of the ring, where the hart had been. He dropped there, stumbled and fell, but his hands were still together. He still held the bird.

Gently, carefully, he laid it in the grass. It crouched, ruffled and glaring, as he knelt in front of it. The leopard reared up behind him. Just before it sank claws into his back, the bird lifted its head and began to sing.

The song was enormous for so tiny a creature. The leopard burst into shimmering shards. The hedge shrank and crumbled into a simple faery ring. The bird took wing into a perfectly mortal sky. Behind it, gleaming in the grass, it left a crown of gold.

John lifted it in hands that shook only a little. He rose to his feet and turned. Robin bowed low. Neville was on his knees; so, after a moment, was Arslan.

John held out the crown. "Set it on my head," he said to Robin.

The green man bowed even lower than before. "Wise, O wise king," he said. He stepped into the ring and took the crown from John's hands. They were of a height, the two of them, and surprisingly alike, though one was mostly mortal and one was not mortal at all.

Robin of the Wood crowned John Lackland in the faery ring of Sherwood on the day of Midsummer, and laid in his hand the scepter of Alba, which Hugh Neville the Forester brought to him from his saddlebag. It was nothing like a mortal coronation: no pomp, no choirs hymning his glory. No crowds, either, Arslan would at first have said, but the wood was full of voices and eyes, spirits and creatures both magical and mortal.

As he came out of the ring, they came flocking, all the old folk of Britain, to bow at his feet and offer homage. The players came in their wagon, flaunting their gaudy rags, and danced and sang and played their wild music for him, there in the greenwood far from any human city.

*     *     *

They held a festival in that place, feasting on the king's deer, and no one, least of all John, asked who had shot it. The king's forester was with him, after all, and who could prove that this crowd of people dressed in green was not a gathering of innocent forest folk, mortal and not so mortal?

Robin had crowned John at the height of noon. When the sun had begun its slow descent toward the horizon, a disturbance rippled through the festival. Arslan felt it as a chill on his skin, a sensation like a cloud passing over the sun. He glanced at the sky, but it was as clear as it ever was in misty England.

Someone or something was coming through the wood that edged the clearing: something large, that brought silence with it, and a slow sweep of shadow. The trees whispered as it passed.

At last it came out into the sunlight and stood between forest and glade. It was almost startling in that it was, after all, a shape of the mortal world: a knight on horseback, clad all in mail, with the surcoat that had become the fashion in Outremer, and the tall blank casque of the helm. The surcoat was green, the helm wrapped in a garland of green leaves, and the shield was green, and the horse's trappings, all green. Even the knight's mail had a green cast, and the horse—it too was more green than brown.

The horse was very tall, and the knight towered over the revelers. They fell back before him as he rode slowly toward the dais and the new-crowned king.

He halted a lance length from John and lowered his lance to rest just short of John's heart. John regarded it with a cool and fearless eye, looking from that deadly point to the blank mask of the helm. "Messire," he said. "Welcome to my crowning."

"I have come for the crown," the knight said. His voice was as deep as stone grinding on stone, echoing in his helm.

John's brows rose to the rim of that same antique crown. Robin was grinning, showing all his sharp teeth.

"The crown is mine," John said.

"I issue challenge," said the knight.

"I accept," said John without a moment's hesitation.

"I will fight your champion," the knight said. "Single combat, to the death. And to the victor, the crown."

"Oh, no," John said. "It's my crown. I'll fight my own battle."

"You can't do that," said Robin beside him. "You knew that the sparrow and not the hart held the true crown—surely you know this. It's won with blood sacrifice. The blood can't be your own. It must be either the blood of this green knight, or human blood, blood of one who serves you."

Arslan scrambled to his feet. "I'll do it. I'm human enough for that, surely?"

"No," the green knight said. His lance swung past Arslan, past Hugh Neville who had not moved to rise or speak, and pointed at Yusuf. "That one."

"No," Arslan said. "He has never served your king. He belongs to me."

"You belong to this man who would be king." The knight lowered his lance in salute. "This is his champion."

"My lord," Arslan said, pleading.

John rubbed his chin. "It's true, he's only a boy. He has no armor, his horse is—"

Robin beckoned. One of his men in green emerged from the wood, leading a blood-red destrier. Two more green-clad men followed, bearing coat and chausses and hood of mail, surcoat, shield, helm, lance, and sword—all that the faery knight had, but red to his woodland green.

Yusuf was on his feet. His grin was wide and white and reckless. He clapped his hands together. "Oh, this is splendid! My lord Arslan, my lord king, did you know I prayed for this? To be glorious; to fight for a great cause. It's not the holy war, but it will do. I accept the challenge, since it's laid on me."

"*No,*" Arslan said. "I can't allow it. Look at him! He'll crush you."

Yusuf's face darkened. He spoke carefully, with calm that he must have fought for. "My lord, my brother, I beg you. Don't shame me. I was beside you in every lesson you ever had, riding and fighting and shooting. I'm a better archer. You're a better swordsman. We're neck and neck as horsemen. And I'm all human, and it's human blood this needs, if there's any to be shed. This is my fight—these jinn say so. I'm going to win it."

Arslan bit his lip until it bled. Before he could speak again, John said, "An infidel Turk fighting as champion for the king of a pagan realm—it's fitting. Fight well for me, sir Saracen."

Arslan dropped to the grass. His heart was roiling, his head hammering with a mingling of rage and terror. This should be his fight—his death, if death there must be.

He thrust himself up. Yusuf was already stripped to his shirt and trews and being helped into the heavy padded gambeson. The armor and all its fittings fit him perfectly, as how could they not? This was magic, and fate. It had been destined since before he was born.

Arslan's own magic had known. Kalila at least was safe, and Eschiva with her. He would pray that Yusuf won this battle, and destroyed this servant of the Wild Magic.

# CHAPTER 18

Yusuf was a splendid figure in the blood-red mail. With his long braids wound about his head and the hood drawn up, he did not even look particularly foreign. He was strong and proud and knightly, and he grinned at them all. "Am I not beautiful? Am I not invincible? Allah, what wonderful armor this is!"

Even Arslan could not cling to his scowl in the face of such delight. He offered his linked hands of Yusuf's foot, so that he could spring into the saddle.

Just as Yusuf lifted his foot, John left the high seat and came down. While they both stood staring, he took off his gold-inlaid spurs and fastened them on Yusuf's heels with his own hands. "Now you are ready," he said, "sir Saracen."

Yusuf bowed low. Arslan did not, but no one was watching him. Again he laced his fingers. This time Yusuf mounted unhindered. He reached down for the great red helm, which was in Robin's hands, but when he spoke, it was to Arslan. "Don't envy me too much. You'll have your turn."

"Stop chattering," Arslan said roughly, "and win this. Go with God."

"There is no god but God," Yusuf said. He lifted up the helm and lowered it to his shoulders. Robin set the lance in his hand.

He sat briefly still on the red charger's back, as blank and perfect an image of armed death as the green knight who had been waiting patiently since his arming began. Then he touched spur to the charger's side.

The woodsfolk had cleared a broad swath of green. Green knight and red took places at either end. Yusuf's was the east—fitting, but it gave him the sun in his face.

He lowered his lance. Half a breath later, the green knight did the same. Robin blew the signal on a hunting horn.

The two destriers lumbered into motion. It was always slow at first, with so much weight, so much mass, and such heavy horses. They gathered speed with deadly swiftness, hurtling toward one another down the long green span.

They met with a ringing crash. Both lances splintered. Both knights rocked in the high saddles, but neither fell. They slowed their horses and turned. The knight in red was as erect as ever, no sign of distress.

The green knight drew his sword. Yusuf drew the one that had been belted on him. Its blade was dark, like deep water; its hilt was set with a stone like a living coal. As heavy as it was, great broadsword of the Frankish knights, he whirled it about his head as if it had been one of his light Saracen blades, and rode singing toward his adversary.

Arslan was the better swordsman, but Yusuf was not far behind him. Yusuf fell on the green knight, swept past that larger, heavier blade, and smote the helm from those massive shoulders.

Yusuf's mount carried him on past. The green knight sat headless on his horse. After a stretching moment, he dismounted, groping blindly, and found his helm—and presumably his head within it—and restored it to its place.

There was no telling what Yusuf thought of that: the red helm was as blank as the green. He sprang down lightly for all the weight of his armor, and faced the green knight on the green grass. On horseback he had been tall enough, but on foot he was too clearly a boy half-grown. The green knight towered over him.

That was no new thing to a Saracen from the Kingdom of Jerusalem. Yusuf laughed and began to dance a sword-dance about that looming bulk.

The woodsfolk loved him for it. Robin applauded him—but made no move to end the duel. The dark sword struck and struck and struck again, swift as a serpent's tongue. The green knight did not bleed as a man would, nor slow nor weaken. And yet Arslan thought he saw a slow seeping through the rents in the green armor, like the trunk of a tree bleeding sap under the woodsman's axe.

Yusuf sprang straight up in the air, and once again smote the head from the green knight's shoulders. This time the knight did not go seeking it. While Yusuf stood taken aback, he whirled his sword about and struck the young Turk down.

Yusuf's blood was as red as the faery armor. He was still laughing, still fighting. With the last of his life and strength, he thrust his sword where a heart would have been if the green knight had been a man. He fell against the treetrunk body, dying even as he sank to the ground.

His blood dyed the green armor scarlet, and spread in a pool on the grass. The green knight melted where it touched. His armor dwindled to woven wicker, his sword to a wooden stave. Wings fluttered within the cage of his breast. Jackdaws cackled and chattered. Their beaks tore at the bars that confined them, pulling them asunder. They broke free and leaped for the sky.

There were far more of them than should have been contained in a single enchanted knight, however great a giant he might be. They darkened the sun; they swarmed for the trees.

Arslan shut them out of his mind. Yusuf was still alive, lying in his arms, but his spirit was already on its journey. All his blood had bled out on the grass. His cheeks were grey-white; his eyes stared sightlessly into the long dark.

Gently Arslan closed them. "There is no god but God," he said in the Arabic of Yusuf's Faith, "and Muhammad is the Prophet of God."

Those words in this place made the air hum and sing, and the earth throb beneath him. Even Robin paused in anointing John with the blood of sacrifice.

Arslan rose in sudden fury, still clasping Yusuf's body to his breast, and lashed the remains of the faery knight with cleansing fire. They went up like a torch, searing the wings of the last black birds to flap and peck their way out of it.

The red armor was gone, melted into mist. Yusuf's shirt and trews were dyed with blood. Arslan found his grey mare grazing near the edge of the wood, and Yusuf's delicate-headed Arab beside her. He mounted his mare in a single leap, heedless of the deadweight in his arms, and sent her plunging into the trees, with the Arab running, tail high, in her wake.

Robin kept his word to John. The Count of Mortain left the feast to find it still high noon in Midsummer's Day, and his hunt thundering and baying in pursuit of a second, more earthly stag.

Arslan heard of it later. Yusuf did not come back to life once he was in the mortal world again. He was still dead, still slain as a sacrifice for a king he had never asked to serve. Arslan buried him beneath the roots of a great oak that shaded the forest track, digging the grave with his hands and his dagger. Some part of him reflected that he should take the body back to Nottingham and have it tended by those whose office it was. But those were Christians. They would not know what to do with a good and faithful Muslim.

There were words that could be said, from holy Koran. Arslan said them, and the prayers with them, with the genuflections and prostrations. He did not think that Allah would mind. He had not bound himself to Islam, but he was a circumcised man.

The sun was low when he finished. He had washed himself clean of earth and blood in the spring that bubbled from the roots of the oak, before he said the prayers for Yusuf's soul. Now he washed again and drank the achingly pure water, for the blessing and the strength that were in it.

"You do know what you've done, don't you?"

He looked up, too weary for startlement. Robin grinned down at him from the branches of the oak. He was less human in this light than he had seemed before, his teeth longer and sharper, his eyes gleaming like an animal's. "You've sealed it," the green man said. "What his blood began, you've completed. His bones are part of Britain now. His blood anoints its king. He'll be a guardian of the isle forever, with Bran and Arthur."

"No," Arslan said. "Not he. His soul is gone to Paradise. He cares nothing for his bones."

"Doesn't he?" Robin swung lightly down from his branch, and stood with fists planted on hips. Arslan had not remembered that he was so small. He was no larger than a child: but a most evil, wicked, ancient child. "Britain has a king now, crowned with gold and sealed with blood. Aren't you delighted?"

"I should have been the one," Arslan said. "It should have been my blood."

"Oh, no," said Robin. "It had to be human blood. Remember what he said, boy: your time will come. You'll have your chance to get yourself killed—even have your soul eaten, if you've a mind."

Arslan's teeth ached with grinding together. He made himself speak calmly, coldly. "Tell me," he said, "how this was a sacrifice for John, or you, or anyone but me."

"It was blood," said Robin, licking his lips with a tongue as long and pink as a cat's, "and fine, red, hot blood it was, too. There's a certain tang to the Turk, I notice; a hint of eastern spice. Pity there aren't more in the isle. This was a delight."

*Kalila.* Arslan bit his tongue before he spoke the name. If this creature was not aware of her, then God forbid Arslan betray her. She was safe with Eschiva; and there she would stay, protected from royal sacrifices.

He turned his back on Robin, though the skin prickled between his shoulderblades, and gathered the horse's reins. It wrenched at him to leave Yusuf's grave so soon, but the hour was late, and his lord was waiting.

His lord . . .

He stiffened his spine. He more than half expected to find Robin perched grinning in the Arab's saddle, but that creature of the Wild Magic chose to remain behind. When Arslan glanced back, he was amusing himself by turning acorns into apples. He laughed and tossed one at Arslan. Arslan caught it without thinking. As soon as it touched his hand, it vanished in a cloud of butterflies.

Better that than a cloud of stinging gnats. Arslan kept his eyes fixed forward after that, and his face toward Nottingham. His heart was a cold and empty thing. He had not wept for Yusuf. There were no tears in him.

John had come back somewhat before him, with a pair of stags and a barren doe, and birds and coneys enough to make a feast. He was not wearing the crown, any more than he carried the scepter where mortal men could see. That part of him was hidden, and by the stricture of his oath, must remain so.

Arslan came only to gather his belongings and take the road to Gloucester. He had considered simply taking what was his and vanishing, but he was too good a soldier to desert his commander. He went to John in the hall and waited his turn behind many another. When it came, he bowed with stiff formality and said, "My lord, I beg leave to depart your service."

John regarded him with raised brow. "Do you now?"

Arslan inclined his head.

"You will stay," John said. "You're not given leave."

Arslan stiffened. "My lord—"

"Word will be sent to his brother," said John. "You I need here."

"For what, my lord? You have half a dozen squires, and knights innumerable. What use am I to you?"

John leaned toward him. "Hate me as you please, and dream of your revenge, but don't imagine that I'll let you go. I chose him for that fight because I could afford to lose him. You with your blood and lineage, your knowledge, and yes, your skill with a sword—I need you. There's magic to master and a war to settle. You'll keep your word to me, and serve me to the best of your capacity."

"What if you misjudged? What if I'm not competent?"

"I haven't misjudged," John said levelly. "Go to your place. I relieve you of duties until morning, except to attend me here in the hall. You will not ride out of the castle this night, for any purpose."

Arslan set his teeth and bowed, down to the stone floor in the eastern fashion, and went where his duty bade him. It was a kind of revenge, and a kind of penance. He had known what this man was when he entered his service. He could hardly claim to be surprised that John had done any of it: either Yusuf's sacrifice or his refusal to let Arslan run away. John did what served John best, always. He cared little what his inferiors might think of that, nor altered his mind one fraction, whatever it might cost them.

What Arslan felt was not hate. It was nothing so simple. He was deeply angry; he grieved to the heart of him. But his allegiance was given, and in his pride he would not rescind it. Let John remember whenever he saw Arslan, what price Arslan had paid for John's ambition.

# CHAPTER 19

～

Richard's messenger arrived in Nottingham on the day after Midsummer. He had outstripped or outwitted any who might have gone ahead to bring warning; he simply appeared at the gate: the Bishop of Rouen himself, traveling under the royal leopards. His coming found John still abed, alone for once, and his followers idling about in the hall.

Arslan went up to beard the lion in his den. It was an ordeal no one else had wanted. He was not afraid of John, and it gave him a certain petty pleasure to rouse his liege lord out of what must have been a blissful dream. "My lord," he said to the blinking, scowling, bleary-eyed man in the high bed, "Walter of Coutances has come from your brother the king. He's waiting on your pleasure."

"Walter of—" John sat up, scouring sleep out of his eyes. "If this is a jest, boy, I swear by God's bones—"

"He says," said Arslan, "that both your brother and your mother are not amused to hear of your little war."

"He said *what?*"

"He's not amused, either," Arslan said. "Shall I dress you? Would you like a bath brought in?"

"What, so you can stick a knife in my back? Where's Petit? What did you do, drop him in the moat?"

Arslan stood aside so that John's manservant could tend his master. John did not apologize for his rash words, nor had Arslan expected him to. Arslan went down to assure the king's messenger that the king's brother was up and preparing to give him audience.

John took his time about it. Bishop Walter had been bathed, fed, and given opportunity to rest—which he did not take—before John came down to receive him. He took it in good enough part; he had known John from childhood, and he knew princes.

He was the sort of man that Arslan hoped never to become: worldly, jaded, unperturbed by anything that a lord of the world might do. He had an air about him of a man who kept secrets; who knew more than he told, and told much less than he might. There was no honesty in him, nor any simplicity. He was all twists and turns and dark alleys, like the heart of an eastern city.

He was, for all of that, pleasant company, and he was a treasury of gossip from Richard's court. "Not that it's the latest," he said. "He's in Outremer now, after a long and turbulent journey, but I parted from him in Messina—my own journey has been, in its way, as turbulent as his. Storms, robbers, roads lost or misdirected, even a fever that kept me in a hospice for a good fortnight—you'd think I was old Ulysses, with a god's wrath on me."

He laughed at the jest, and his listeners echoed him. Arslan could not help reflecting that Walter had been detained until John's crown was won. Britain was looking out for its own.

"Mind you, but for that, I'd have been here months ago," Walter went on. "But here I am at last, and if my gossip's stale, some of it's still choice. Did you know Richard's married? There's some debate as to whether he did the consummation himself, but his mother finally got him to the altar, and bound him to the princess from Navarre. Poor thing, she's like a wet kitten."

"But breedable, do you think?" someone asked: Arslan did not care enough to see who it was.

Walter shrugged. "Who's to tell? They say the queen chose her for her biddability—and of course her dowry."

"I heard," said one of the barons, "that she's had a rather remarkable education, which included arts that might rouse any man's ardor, even the king's."

"Why," said Walter without visible shock, "that's scandalous. God knows she's a virtuous lady, and well schooled by the nuns in Navarre. What other schooling she might have had, who knows, except possibly her majesty? The queen has never shrunk from doing the necessary."

"Richard's bride is the queen now," said Guesclin the squire.

"Not," said the baron, "as long as Eleanor has any say in it."

That won another round of laughter—which ended rather abruptly. John was standing in the door behind the dais, robed in crimson silk. His brows were bound with gold, but not with the crown of Arthur. This was a prince's coronet. He looked regal, haughty, and subtly dangerous.

They all bowed to him, even his brother's envoy. "I welcome you to England," John said with edged courtesy, "my lord bishop. I trust you had a safe and pleasant journey."

"In strict truth, my lord, it was neither," Walter said, but pleasantly. "I'm glad to have survived it, and to have come safe where I was sent. I bring you greetings from your brother and your lady mother."

"I'm sure you do," John said, almost a purr. "How was my brother when you left him? Was he well?"

"Well enough, my lord," said Walter, "though they say he's suffered somewhat from fever since he came to the Holy Land. That's a pestilential country for the likes of us."

John crossed himself with every appearance of honest devotion. "God guard him, then, and my lady mother, too."

"Oh, my lord," Walter said, "surely you know: she's in Rome. She decided not to go on this Crusade after all. Once his majesty was safely and securely married, she turned back into the west, where she reckoned to be of more use."

John arched a brow at that, but forbore to comment on it. "And you, I suppose, my lord bishop, have come to rein in my lord of Ely. He's laid siege to Lincoln, did you know? The barons are in uproar. It's a distressing state of affairs."

"Most distressing," Walter said, shaking his head. "Almost as much so as the rumor I heard, that you took this castle by force, and have prepared an assault in several fronts of the north and west. Why, if you'll believe it, I heard that it's war here, and your armies are marching against those of his majesty's justiciar. It's even said—and that's outrageous—that you're calling yourself Richard's heir, and carrying on as if he's not expected to return."

"Indeed," John said. "That is outrageous. He's a young man, and strong as a bull. He'll take Jerusalem and be lauded as the hero of Christendom, and then he'll come home. How not? He's the Lionheart. He can do no other."

Walter smiled. John smiled. It was all terribly amicable. "So there's no war here?" Walter inquired.

"There is a bit of a dispute," John said. "His grace of Ely has been at odds with certain of my brother's subjects, and has judged it best to lay siege to Lincoln. I've come at the barons' request, to make peace as I can."

"Why, so have I," said Walter as if delighted, "at his majesty's request. Shall we join forces, my lord? I've sent a man to his grace— I hope you don't mind; I've asked his grace to meet us outside of Lincoln, and see what can be done to settle this small, this trivial contention."

"Perhaps his grace would meet us here," John suggested, "since we're both here already."

"Perhaps he would," said Walter, "but I've a mind to see this siege of his, and speak to the good people of Lincoln. The Bishop of Lincoln—he's not involved in this, surely?"

"He is in the town," John said, "caught there when the siege-engines came. What he thinks of it, I'm sure I don't know."

"Well, then, my lord," said Walter. "Shall we ride? It's not far to Lincoln, no? Shall we be there before dark, do you think?"

"If the road is open," John said, "and we press the pace, easily. But you just arrived; you must be exhausted. Surely, tomorrow—"

"I've been traveling, I sometimes think, since the day before the Flood," Walter said. "Once this is over, I'll go back to Rouen and not stir for a year." He rose from the chair in which he had been sitting. "Shall we go, my lord, and have done?"

John sighed gustily, but Walter was smiling, turning in his fingers the engraved seal that he carried, which was one of Richard's. The Plantagenet leopards paced on it under the crown of England.

John, crowned king of a realm that mortal men were not to know of, bent his head to his brother's messenger. "Very well. We ride." He chose a company quickly: barons, knights, men-at-arms, and one squire.

Arslan was neither surprised nor pleased to be that squire. The others glowered at him, but then they often did. He had not managed to become one of them. What he was, what he was here for, had nothing to do with the things that concerned them. That he had fought in real wars, in Outremer where war was the life and breath of every able-bodied man, roused their resentment. Nor did it help that in their eyes he had John's favor—though it was a preference he could well have done without.

They were at him again this morning, trailing after him, getting in his way as he gathered such belongings as he reckoned to need. His riding clothes were missing, again; there was a hound bitch with pups in his bed, nesting in what had been his two clean shirts. The pups had teethed on them both, to disastrous effect.

He kept his temper, not because he was wise, but because he was on a thin edge, and if he slipped, he would kill something. He did not want that something to be a young pup of a squire.

They were all older than he was. That was another of their grievances: that he was the youngest and newest, but he was immeasurably older in knightly skill and in knowledge of the world. Children could be children for a long while here, long after boys in Outremer were forced to be men.

He found his hose under Guesclin's bed, and his cotte in Alain's clothes-chest. Alain took umbrage. Arslan fended off the wild blow while he rummaged in a box of oddments for the boots that he knew were hiding there. Belt he had on, and no one ever touched his weapons: he had put a wishing on those.

He dressed quickly and slung his traveling bag over his shoulder, and sighed. The door was blocked, of course. Alain held the center, nursing a bruised hand.

They were not going to let him by without a fight. "That's it," Alain said. "We've had enough. Whatever you've done to get my lord in your power, you'll undo it now."

"Yes, and where's your Saracen devil, too?" demanded little Stephen, who had the quickest temper of them all. "We saw you come home last night with an empty saddle and blood on your clothes. What did you do, kill him and eat him?"

Arslan was going blind. It was rage, that was all it was, and he should not indulge it. There was no time, and no profit in it.

But his heart was wailing Yusuf's name, and his grief was overwhelming his wisdom. "Yes," he said, clear and bitter. "Yusuf is dead. This kingdom killed him. What do you care for that, Norman boy? He was never of your kin or kind. He was worth a hundred of you."

"He was a Saracen," Stephen said, sneering at the word.

"He was a Seljuk from the clan of Alp Arslan," Arslan said, "and a servant of the Prophet, and my heart's brother."

"What, are you an infidel, too? Is that your secret?"

Arslan smiled sweetly. "What if I were? What would you do, Norman boy? Shriek and run away?"

"You can't be an infidel," Alain said. "I saw you at Mass on Sunday. You said all the prayers, and took the Eucharist."

"You know what they say of the devil," said Stephen: "that he can quote Scripture."

"Maybe I'm a devil," said Arslan. "Maybe I'll lay a curse on you all, if you don't clear my way. My lord is waiting."

"If our lord knew what you are—" Stephen began.

"He knows exactly what I am," Arslan said.

"That's a lie," said Alain.

"I never lie," Arslan said.

He began to walk toward the pack of them. There were six of them, and he was only one, but they cared for their skins; he, just then, cared not at all for his. If they killed him now, so be it. If one of them was fool enough to get himself killed—*Inshallah*. God's will be done, as Yusuf would have said.

They growled and glared and muttered dire things, but they drew back before him. Only Alain was fool enough to stand in the door. Arslan kept walking as if he had not been there. He thrust out his chest and laid his hand on the hilt of his dagger. Arslan did not check or slow. Alain scrambled out of the way.

Arslan had made no friends in that place, but they never had been well disposed toward him. He shrugged. It would come to a war later, or it would not. He did not care. John was waiting, and there was a greater war to fight than this squabble of squires.

# Chapter 20

∽

The siege of Lincoln was well advanced. The engines were drawn up along the walls, and the rams had gone a fair way toward splintering the gate. His grace of Ely expected to ride into the city in a day or two, if not sooner.

John and the Bishop of Rouen and their conjoined escort had found the forest road unbarred, and no green-clad bandits on it, to help or hinder. They met a party of Ely's scouts within a league of Lincoln, but those gave way before the royal banner. When they rode on ahead, Bishop Walter made no effort to stop them.

John made camp on the forest's edge, in sight of the siege, and Walter raised Richard's banner over it. As they had fully expected, riders came from the army, a pair of monks and a black-clad priest with an escort of men-at-arms. None of them was William of Ely.

It was Walter who received them. John effaced himself among his knights, watching and keeping silent.

The preliminaries were lengthy. These were men of the Church, long in the service of princes, with many acquaintances in common. Even Arslan, accustomed to the elaborate flourishes of eastern diplomacy, had glazed into near-immobility before they finished their endless circling round the point.

"I suppose," Ely's priest said at last, "that you've come to make peace in the kingdom."

"In the king's name," Walter said, "with her majesty's most emphatic blessing."

"Ah," said the priest. "Well. Of course my lord chancellor is most eager to do his majesty's bidding. But it should be understood that his majesty's brother, conspiring with the barons, has—"

"Yes," Walter said. It was a simple word, mildly spoken, but silenced the priest abruptly. "They'll meet this evening and settle a peace. Will you send a man to fetch your bishop, or shall I?"

"My man, your banner?"

"Excellent," Walter said.

William of Ely came riding to Walter's camp on a white mule, with an escort that would have done justice to a king, and the king's banner over him, too. He was, after all, Richard's right hand in this realm.

He found Walter waiting, and a deputation of barons, and John Lackland in the middle of them. Arslan, behind John, looked with interest on the man who had broken down the walls of the realm and compelled it to go hunting for a king.

He was a singularly unprepossessing figure, even in episcopal finery: a small man with a twisted leg and the pinched face of a sickly child. It was an intelligent face, with dark clever eyes, but those eyes glittered with a great deal more pride and temper than a churchman should lay claim to.

He was, Arslan thought, much more like John than either of them would have been pleased to admit. But there was one signal difference. John had no scruples and knew it. This devout bishop reckoned himself a virtuous man. That made him dangerous—more so than John.

Walter brought them together with ceremony, and saw to it that they clasped hands in forced amity before the greetings were done. Then he sat them down under a canopy, with wine and bread but little else, and said sweetly, "My heart is longing for peace between you. Let it be done this night, and we'll all sleep the better for it."

John's smile had no mirth in it. "You don't waste time, do you?"

"The king wants this matter resolved," Walter said. "So, we shall resolve it. My lord of Ely, is it strictly necessary to wage war over such a cause as this?"

"I speak for the king in England, my lord of Rouen," said Ely. "There are accusations of corruption, misconduct, malfeasance—"

"So there are," John said. "Will you cease and desist from it now that my brother has sent his man to curb you?"

Ely half rose. His face was blotched with crimson. "And what of you, my lord Count? Are you still grasping after his crown?"

"Not at the moment," John said. "The barons are up in arms, lord bishop. They cry out against your arrogance and condemn your high-handedness. You would do well to put on a meeker face, and speak softer before his majesty's liege men."

"*You* speak to *me* of arrogance?"

"Now, now," Walter said in tones meant to soothe them both. "There is the matter of the sheriff of Lincoln—he has misused his office, that can't be denied. If that can be settled, will you both consent to withdraw your forces?"

John shrugged. Ely scowled. Walter took their silence for assent. "Good! I had thought a penalty might be assessed for the miscreant, and he must pay restitution for all that he has taken, under the supervision of the Exchequer. He'll stay in office, since his peers seem so determined to keep him so, but be strictly overseen by the Bishop of Lincoln. Who is, I presume, besieged in his city?"

"He is in Lincoln, yes," Ely said stiffly. "That was an accident. He was there when I came. He declined to be released."

"Understandable," said Walter, "but deplorable nevertheless. You'll open the gates in the morning, I hope, and free him to go about the king's business."

"I never held him captive," Ely said.

"No: only his city and his episcopal see." Walter smiled to take the sting out of his words. "But that's over, isn't it? And you, my lord of Mortain—you'll withdraw your troops, yes? I'm sure you'll be pleased to inform the barons that the king has taken their wishes to heart, and remembers them even across the sea."

"I'm sure he does," John said silkily.

They would go on like this until it was settled. Arslan stopped listening and settled to watching the king's justiciar.

He had no magic. That was a shock, and profound. William of Ely was as mortal as a mortal man could be, and completely without gift or arcane talent. Nor, and that was even more startling, did he seem aware that he was lacking in any such thing.

Arslan cultivated patience. The war was settled with barbed amity, not long after the sun set. In the morning they all rode into Lincoln, where Bishop Hugh received them. There was a Mass of Thanksgiving, and a gathering of notables, and of course a feast; for a town under siege, Lincoln was remarkably well provisioned, and it brought out its best for this celebration of the peace.

It was in the Mass that Arslan saw what he had been looking for.

The bishops of Rouen and Ely and Lincoln sang the rite together, attended by an army of acolytes. Walter was a mortal man, and Hugh was notably more than that; neither of them did anything that Arslan had not expected. But as Ely stood between them, he took on the luster that shone on Hugh. He was like a clay lamp filling with light.

It lingered in him for a while after the Mass, but by the time he came to the castle's hall, he was all clay again, and no vestige of light. Arslan, passing by him in the course of serving John, let slip a little of his own magic. It burned like an ember inside of this peculiar man, until it faded and dwindled and died.

He did not think that anyone had caught him, but he should have known better. When all was done and they had all gone to their rest, Arslan received a summons that he could not mistake. It came as a spark of cold blue light, the witchlight that Eschiva could kindle when she pleased, but this had about it no suggestion of her.

Her uncle waited for Arslan in the chapel of the castle. The candles were unlit; there was no earthly light but the single flame of the vigil-lamp over the altar.

Neither Arslan nor Hugh needed more than that. Arslan knelt to the altar and crossed himself before stooping to kiss the bishop's hand. It was more formal than perhaps he needed to be, but he was in a formal mood tonight, even when Hugh turned obeisance into embrace and said with all appearance of gladness, "Lion cub! It's good to see you again."

"And you, Father," Arslan said.

Hugh held him at arm's length, smiling, taking him in. "Yes, you've grown—you've definitely grown."

"Like a weed," Arslan said a little ruefully. "I keep outgrowing clothes. My lord swears that if I grow any more, he'll make me wear a monk's habit, and keep letting out the hem."

Hugh laughed. "A fair great monk you'd make, with those shoulders of yours."

Arslan hunched them, then stood straight, letting himself tower over the good bishop. It had struck him, rather abruptly, that what he had become to this man's ward might not meet with a churchman's approval—even one who was an enchanter.

Was that what he had been brought here for, after all?

It seemed not. Hugh fixed him with a kindly but implacable eye. "So. You've been investigating our breaker of walls."

Arslan's cheeks warmed a little. "I know I shouldn't have done it, but when I saw what he is—and what he is not—I couldn't help it."

"It is difficult to believe, isn't it?" said Hugh. "He's a rare thing: a man so completely without magic that when he comes near it, he draws it like a lodestone. He's an emptiness craving to be filled, and magic can't help but fill him."

"He would make a terrible weapon," Arslan said.

"Keener than any sword," Hugh agreed.

"How did he break down the walls?"

"We don't know," Hugh said.

Arslan stared at him. "You don't— But you have magic!"

"And he does not, and he's told no one of what he did. We know he did it at Richard's coronation; we know when he did it, and what came of it. But we've never known how."

"If we know how, and what used him, it might be a key to restoring the walls."

"We have thought of that," Hugh said, "but he's singularly disinclined to tell the tale."

"Maybe he doesn't remember it."

"We think he does," Hugh said, "vividly. But he never speaks of it. Although, perhaps, if you were to try . . ."

"I?" said Arslan. "What can I do, that your wisdom can't?"

"He has a weakness for the young and the innocent," said Hugh, "and a particular devotion for the Queen of Angels."

"Oh, no," Arslan said. "I'm not going to pretend to be—"

"Why not? In some theologies, you would be reckoned a son of God."

"That is blasphemous," Arslan said.

Hugh laughed at his shock. "And I a bishop, and this a holy chapel. Child, you said it yourself. We need a key, and this man may have it. Is it so ill a thing to simply show him what you are—all of what you are—and let God move his heart, if it's to be moved?"

It seemed a reasonable thing when he spoke of it so. Arslan still did not like the feel of it, but he was an innocent, and this world of intrigue was strange to him. He did want to know how William Longchamp had broken the walls, and whether he knew how to raise them again.

Corruption was as simple as that. Arslan heard himself consent, to Hugh's visible satisfaction.

*    *    *

The Bishop of Ely lodged in the bishop's residence—Hugh's house, no less, and Hugh had given his erstwhile enemy his own chambers, with all the comforts that a lord of the Church could wish for. Ely was sound asleep in the high carved bed in which, according to rumor, Hugh never slept: his accustomed place was a pallet on the floor, a rush mat without cushion or coverlet. One of Ely's monks snored on that while the good bishop slept the sleep of the justly comfortable.

Arslan entered the chamber like a breath of wind. It had been easier than he ever thought to let go his human scruples: to glide invisible past ranks of guards, to slip the bolts of the doors, to enter this place into which he had never been invited. Although, if he chose to think of it so, the true owner of the chamber had bidden him do this; maybe it was not so much a sin.

The man in the bed seemed no larger than a child, curled in a tight knot, with nothing showing above the heap of coverlets but a shock of grey-black hair and a white circle of tonsure. He was dreaming: he stirred and muttered.

Arslan sat on air above the bed, feet tucked up, watching him. Spirits had come out of curiosity, as they so often did wherever Arslan was; they amused themselves with teasing off the coverlets and sending wafts of icy chill and sudden spits of flame across the small huddled body. It shivered; it twitched. Arslan called off the spirits, not without difficulty, for they were hardly tamed things.

Ely had begun to wake. Arslan let slip the bonds of his flesh, so that the fire within shone out of him, bright as a lamp in the dark. There was a purity in it, a freedom he had never allowed himself, except when he was very small. When he lifted his hand, it was like a shape of glass filled with light.

The bishop opened his eyes and blinked, dazzled, throwing up his arm to shade himself. Arslan damped the light a little. The spirits were whirling in a mad dance, caroling in delight.

Tears were running down Ely's face, though whether they were of joy or pain, Arslan could not tell. "Bright angel," he said. "Spirit of heaven. How long it's been since last you came to me!"

Arslan blinked. This he had not expected.

"Did I do well, then?" Ely asked. "May I be of service again? I still remember—in my dreams I live it. Such glory, such splendor. So beautiful a gift to my lord the king."

"Would you live it again?" Arslan asked him. The voice that came out of the fire was not his human voice. This was purified, stripped of mortal substance.

Ely's face was rapt. "Again and again, O angel of God. Every night in my dream I see you, clothed in light. The words you bade me say—they ring like gongs; they clash like cymbals. They split the world asunder and make it anew." He sat up, eyes gleaming. "Shall I say them again? Shall I sing them in plainsong? The Dorian mode? The Lydian mode? Shall I—"

"Once sufficed," Arslan said. "Did you know what you did when you spoke them?"

"I obeyed the will of God," Ely said, "and served my lord the king."

"You are most obedient," said Arslan, "and will be rewarded according to your deserts."

Ely sighed in bliss. Arslan hovered over him, brushing his brow with a finger of fire. "Sleep," Arslan said. "Sleep in peace."

# CHAPTER 21

A rslan gave Ely's memory to Hugh, whole and entire as he had taken it, globed as if in crystal and shimmering like water. The Bishop of Lincoln cupped it in his hands, smiling at Arslan, well pleased with him.

Arslan was not pleased with himself. Though it was barely dawn, he went down to the river and scoured himself in the cold water, over and over, but it did not make him feel clean. Even the full rite of the *hammam* would not have done that.

It was little enough pleasure to wait on John, for whom Yusuf had died, but this morning Arslan was inclined toward mortification of spirit as well as flesh. He was, in fact, in a splendidly black mood when Hugh sent for him again. Almost he ignored the summons, but like Ely, he was an obedient servant.

Hugh waited for him this time in the bishop's house, in a room that he would wager few ever saw: a chamber thickly warded with magics, enclosing so many intertwined enchantments that at first, when he entered it, he reeled and nearly fell. To the eye it was a priestly library and an alchemist's laboratory and a little bit of a mews and a kennel, for through its high windows owls flew at will, and bats roosted in the beams; in cages below, furred things scrabbled or chittered or slept. Arslan saw a pair of snow-white rats, and a cage full of mice with a fat grey cat asleep on top of it, and a masked ferret curled about a child's ball.

In another mood he would have been delighted with this place. Today he wanted only to do his duty and be gone.

He stood for a long while in the doorway, mastering the dizziness and confusion. As his sight cleared, he nearly reeled again.

Eschiva was there, and Kalila behind her—looking so much like

Yusuf that for a wild instant he thought that Hugh had brought him back from the dead.

But Yusuf was dead and buried, and none knew that better than Arslan. The face under the turban would never grow even the soft down of beard that Yusuf had had. She did not know: she was regarding him with a little sullenness and more than a little gladness, but no grief. No anger. Not yet.

Hugh broke in amid the thrumming silence. "Good, all of us are here that can be here. Come and look."

Arslan moved carefully into the room, threading through currents of magic. He started slightly: Hugh Neville grinned at him from a corner, where he was sitting on a stool with his long legs propped on the corner of a table. The king's forester drew himself together and rose, gathering with the rest of them round Hugh, who was standing at the other end of the table. The thing that Arslan had given him was resting there in a nest of white silk, gleaming like crystal.

"See," said Hugh, passing his hand over the globe. It opened like a flower and bloomed into an image like the jeweled glass in a cathedral window. In a cloister full of roses, a bishop knelt in prayer. A being of light appeared to him, with shining wings and a supernally beautiful face. It gave him words to speak, words that made the guardians lift hands to ward and guard.

When the words were spoken and the gate opened, the memory began to fade. But in the tatters of it, Arslan saw what made him catch his breath. Ely had not wanted to remember the thing that had laughed at him once the deed was done, but there was no mistaking what he had seen.

"Robin," Arslan said. "That's the green man—the spirit of the wood."

"Robber and reiver, too," Neville said, "and deep root of the Wild Magic in Britain. If he did this, there's more to it than anyone thought."

"He crowned the king," said Arslan. "How could he have—"

"To force the true king to come to Britain," Eschiva said. "Richard had refused to accept the burden. We were doing nothing to remedy the matter, nor would we have done anything while the kingdom seemed safe."

"Casting down the walls of air put the kingdom in danger— could even destroy it. How is that better than leaving Britain without a true king?"

"It's not," Father Hugh said, "unless there's other danger, worse danger, waiting for us." He shivered. "The Wild Magic is a treacherous thing, serving neither good nor evil, but only and always itself."

"Then we can't trust it at all," Arslan said.

Hugh Neville shook his head. "Not quite. The Wild Magic *is* Britain. This earth, this air, are born and begotten of it. Whatever it does, it does for Britain. It can as easily kill a king as crown him, but while his life serves the realm, it will guard and preserve him."

"It could turn on him in an instant," said Arslan.

"Certainly," Neville said. "But now we know what it's done, and maybe a little of the way. It needs the true king, with full power, to stand against whatever comes. We're indebted to you for that."

Arslan dipped his head slightly in acknowledgment. It would have been ungracious to do otherwise.

Kalila followed him out of the bishop's house. He had expected that, and did not shrink from it, but at the door he turned. "Didn't I bid you attend the Lady Eschiva?"

"She's as safe as she can be," Kalila said. "Where's Yusuf? What's he doing, letting you go out alone?"

Arslan had thought himself master of his face, but Kalila knew him too well.

"No," Kalila said. "Oh, no. That's why you made me stay. Because—you saw—"

"I didn't see anything," Arslan said roughly. "Stay here with her. My lord John is waiting for me."

"Not until you tell me where my brother is."

"In the greenwood," Arslan said.

"But not alive."

Arslan set his lips together.

"Tell me," she said. She was very composed. Stunned, he thought.

When he did not reply, she got a grip on the front of his cotte and lifted him—all the gangling bulk of him—and thrust him back against the wall. Her eyes were blazing. *"Tell me!"*

He told her, baldly, because he knew no other way. She listened in white silence, stirring only when he told of Yusuf's death. Then her fists clenched.

When he was done, he said, "Now will you stay with her?"

"No," she said. Her voice was husky, caught in her throat. "I won't leave you alone. Damn him for dying on you! Didn't he know better than that?"

"You're supposed to be angry at me," he said.

"I am!" She hammered him to prove it, hard enough to knock the breath out of him. "I'm angrier at him. You couldn't help it."

"Don't kill John," Arslan said. "That's my privilege."

She hissed at him. "Don't you do it, either. He's a lord. That's what he does: he gets his servants killed. This servant should have known better than to submit to it."

"I don't understand you," said Arslan.

"How can you? You're a man." She pulled him away from the wall and thrust him into the street. "Enough. Didn't you say your lord is waiting?"

Kalila lay in the dark, bedded down in the hall with the servants and the squires, listening to Arslan's breathing a bare handspan away. Yusuf should have been on the other side of him, protecting his front as she protected his back.

She gave her brother tears, muffling the sobs in her sleeve. The book of his life was written. Hers . . . What would she do now, alone in this strange world? She still had her lord, and he had imposed his lady on her, but how would she live without the other half of herself? They had shared a womb. She could more easily have let go her right arm.

She shuddered deep inside. That way was the dark, and a pit of self-pity. This was written before the beginning of the world. Allah had willed it, for what reason she did not know, but the essence of Islam was to submit. She would submit. Eventually. When the anger had run its course.

Eschiva was awake as Kalila was, but she was alone in body as in spirit. She was aware of Arslan, where he was, what he did: feigning sleep that he did not need, to seem more truly human. He was all raw, torn by the game that he had been made to play.

Her uncle had not done well in setting him that task, however splendidly it had served the cause. He had neither the heart nor the spirit to make a spy, and deception ran against the very grain of him.

Seeing him after those days apart, even clinging to her temper, she had had to rebuke her heart for beating so hard. He was in pain, and bearing it because he could do nothing else.

She should have bidden him stay. Even if they quarreled, it would have been better than this solitude.

She made a wishing there in the night, a word wrapped in a breath and secured in the petals of a rose. Maybe he would catch a hint of fragrance as he feigned sleep, and be a little comforted.

# CHAPTER 22

They all left Lincoln together in a fine show of amity. John would ride back to Gloucester by the long way, through the towns and castles of the north. The Bishop of Ely would return to his see, and thence to the south of England, as far away from John as he could go.

Eschiva rode with John's escort, under her uncle's protection as she had often done before. She did not press her presence on Arslan, nor did she summon him. She left him to Kalila, to heal undisturbed.

What that might do, she knew well. He was not fully aware that the turbaned person at his side was a woman, with all of a woman's needs and desires, but the woman knew perfectly well that he was a man.

This was Eschiva's gift to them both, this distance. She cared little what it cost her. That cost was high, higher than she had thought when she made the choice. She had to watch him riding by day with John or among the guards, always with the turbaned figure at his back, and by night she slept alone while he slept with the other one, the one in man's dress.

He never came to her. He did not even speak to her. She might still have been in Gloucester, for all the notice he took of her presence.

She endured it for days, weeks. But as the summer lengthened and the days began perceptibly to shorten, she began to lose her taste for sacrifice. The life that she had led before, the long round of ritual and high magic, was no longer enough. Her body wanted its share, too. It wanted him, warm and alive and loving her as only he could do.

They were in York for the feast of the Virgin, celebrating her who was Queen of Heaven—and if some directed their prayers toward an older goddess and queen, then that was not for the Church to know. Eschiva loved this ancient city, loved the bleakness of the moors that surrounded it and the clarity of the sky above it. It was a cold city, a city on the edge of the world, and when she stood on the walls she imagined that she would leap off into infinite space.

John had had letters that day, a heavy packet of them brought over from Normandy. Some of the news was old: Richard had taken the city of Acre, and his Crusade was well on its way at last. Some was new enough to be startling: Philip of France had left the Crusade in disgust at an excess of bickering and dallying, and proposed to return home. He was in fear of his life, John's informants said, and had been heard to lay the blame on the King of England.

"Not," John had said in Eschiva's hearing, "that Richard isn't as capable of treachery as the next Plantagenet, but Philip always was an old woman."

That won a round of laughter, which died as John continued with his correspondence—darkening greatly at a letter from his mother, though there was little in it but the fact that she was still in Rome. "And long may she linger there," he muttered as he tossed the letter aside.

The next much improved his mood. It came from his brother Geoffrey—like Longsword, one of old Henry's bastards, raised with the legitimate sons and given as much of Henry's favor as any of the rest. Geoffrey was the one of them all who had gone into the Church, and willingly, too: "Our white sheep," John liked to say, with honest affection beneath the mockery.

Geoffrey had been given the archbishopric of York at Richard's crowning, but it had come like John's gift of lands and wife, with a decree of exile until Richard's Crusade was over. After John's exile was rescinded, Geoffrey had reckoned it time to claim his see, but he had been delayed in Normandy. Now he was ready to make the crossing.

"He'll be on his way before the month is out," John said. "Then we'll have a proper conspiracy: prince, soldier, and prelate."

John was taking a wicked delight in the prospect. Eschiva could see ample reason there for alarm on Eleanor's part—and Philip's, too. And maybe Ely's?

Ely's claws were drawn. She put aside the flicker of unease, and left the thick air of the hall for the cold clarity of the walls. It had been raining in gusts all morning; now, near noon, the sun had come out for a while, turning the plain grey stones to jewels, and sparkling in the heather.

Arslan was there, as she had known when she went out. He was shivering: he was not wielding his magic against the chill of August on the north moors. His lips were blue.

She kissed warmth into them, to his profound astonishment. For an instant she thought he might fling her off, but the body's instinct was too strong. He returned the kiss with intensity that left them both gasping.

They drew back at the same moment, with the same tearing reluctance. His eyes drank in her face. "I didn't—I thought—"

"You needed to heal," she said.

"I needed you to heal me!"

"I'm here now," she said.

"Maybe it's too late."

His tone was bitter, but his eyes belied it. She smiled. "Maybe it's not," she said.

The wind, which had died down a little, came blasting back. It whipped her veil from her head and sent her mantle billowing out behind her. He caught it and wrapped it about her, and held her, bathing her in his warmth.

For her he would loose the fire inside him. He smoothed her uncovered hair, making what order he could of its rebellious curls. Her veil had flown far away, out over the moor like an ungainly bird.

She tilted her head back. His arms about her, his face above her—this was home, wherever they might be. "I'm sorry that he died," she said.

Grief passed swiftly across his face, but his back stiffened only a little. "The Muslims say that all is written, and everything is fate. *Inshallah,* they say: God's will be done. He was a Muslim; he accepted what was decreed for him. He'd whip me with the flat of his sword if he caught me feeling sorry for myself."

"Aren't you allowed to mourn him?"

"Mourning is for the living," Arslan said. "I honor him; I remember him. I try to recall why he paid the highest price. I . . . even . . . try to forgive the one who demanded it of him."

"Forgiveness is a Christian virtue," she said.

"I'm not a very good Christian." He kissed her brow, and then her lips, but softly, without the passion he had shown before. "My arms have been so empty," he said.

"What, you haven't been fending off legions of eager women?"

He drew himself up in affront. "What do you take me for?"

"A man," she said, "and young, and very good to look at."

"Does this mean you've been consoling yourself elsewhere?"

"Of course not!" She glared; he was laughing, though not entirely in mirth. "I'm not John," she said. "I can't take consolation wherever I find it."

His cheeks flushed, and not only with the whipping of the wind. "Does Susanna know?"

"Susanna knows him as well as anyone living," Eschiva said. "Don't be angry on her behalf. She's taken her portion, and she's well aware of what goes with it."

"I'm not angry," he said. "Not about that. Or no more than about anything else. He is such a difficult man to like."

"You don't have to like him, simply to serve him. He's not a good man or a particularly appealing one, but he's the king we need."

"I know that," Arslan said irritably. "I suppose I'm being unreasonable. He did the one thing that he could profitably do, and chose the one of us who was most fit for the purpose. I'm angry because I wasn't the one. I couldn't be. I'm not human enough."

Ah, she thought: there was his grievance. Her uncle had made it worse in using him against Ely. Poor splendid child, raised between worlds. She had had the easier way by far: she had been born to magic, and had grown up in accord with it. He did not know how to be what he was.

"Human isn't everything," she said to him.

"Sometimes it is." But he had calmed a little. She turned in his arms and faced outward, toward the wind and the moor. "Isn't this glorious? Wouldn't you love to take wing and fly on the breast of it?"

"Can you do that?"

"We both can—if you put your mind to it."

"Not . . . today. I'm not ready."

"But you will be," she said with sublime assurance.

When John left York, Arslan was riding beside Eschiva. It could seem that he rode with the Bishop of Lincoln and his household, but she was closest to him, and Kalila silent behind. Eschiva did not care who saw them, or what anyone thought, but Arslan was more careful of her reputation. After that first reckless hour on the walls of York, he never let them be seen to touch. When he came to her at night, he came invisible, and left before dawn.

She did not have the heart to tell him that a blind man could see what they were to one another. He was content with his sleights and small deceptions, and she did not find them excessively onerous.

John took his royal progress to the northernmost bounds of England, to the Wall that the Romans had built to keep out the painted people. It was a wind-scoured ruin now, stretching long leagues across the grey-green moor amid the purple of the heather. The spirits here were truly wild, and little accustomed to human presence. Some few remembered the Romans, and celebrated the memory with the calling of ghostly trumpets and the marching of phantom legions.

Here humans were few but the power of the land was strong, its magic so potent that even Britain's guardians had to struggle against the force of it. This was not the end of Britain—the whole realm of the Scots ran away into the icy north—but it was the edge of the world as Rome had seen it. That was a power in itself, and a strong enchantment.

For the true king to come to this meeting of the worlds was a seal of his power and an affirmation of his crowning. John rode along the Wall from Newcastle to Carlisle, and the ghostly armies marched with him.

Carlisle was a grim city, the stones of its walls the red-brown of dried blood. After the gusty splendor of the Wall, it was like being shut up in a grave.

Eschiva could not bear it. She retreated to the moor with a small company of her uncle's guards, to camp in the lee of the Wall. There was a certain guilty pleasure in the escape, and the more so that Arslan had come with her, leaving his lord to the care of his other servants.

People in the city would reckon her mad. They barred their doors and windows at night, and hung charms against the spirits of the air. Such fear was foreign to her. There was danger in the otherworld, none knew it better than she, but she had her wards and protections, and her human guards to watch against more mortal dangers. No robber in this country was so desperate as to venture an armed company camped in the ruins of a Roman mile-castle.

Those ruins, and the earth beneath, gave Eschiva strength. She had a premonition as she lay on it that she would need that strength, and soon. Tonight she could bask in it under moonlight and starlight, with her lover in her arms and the old Roman wall looming above them.

He was asleep for once, and she for once was awake without him. She wrapped herself in the first mantle that came to hand, which happened to be his, and went out into the starlight. The wind was blowing hard beyond the broken walls. It buffeted her as she ascended. Clouds were scudding ahead of it, promising rain by morning, but for now there were still more stars than darkness.

The moon was setting. By no will of her own, she turned her back to it and her face to the south and east. The wind hammered at her. If she had spread her arms, she could have flown.

The whole length of Britain was before her, spread out in the darkness, with here and there a tiny glimmer of light. On her left hand was the sea with its flecking of spume. It dashed the coast with ceaseless persistence.

Far away, off the white promontory of Dover, a ship breasted the waves. It was a sturdy ship, with crimson sails. Because she was seeing with eyes other than mortal, it was daylight there, though dimmed with cloud and the threat of a storm.

A man stood on the ship, bareheaded in the gale. His hair was fiery red, clashing wonderfully with the crimson of his mantle. He was laughing.

Eschiva found that she was smiling. Geoffrey Plantagenet had his brother Richard's gift for winning hearts, and his father Henry's keen wits; but with that he had the bright spirit of his mother, who had caught the king's eye one fine spring day, and kept his interest even after the child was born. It would be good, she thought, to have Geoffrey in England. He might even take the edge off John.

Geoffrey's ship bucked in a cross-current. Her eye slipped aside from it to the darkened shore. In the way of magic, it was still night there, but she could still see the men waiting, the gleam of armor, the flicker of firelight on spears and crossbows.

Someone had laid an ambush for the Archbishop of York. She could well guess who that might be. She raised her power to cry warning, but she was in a mile-castle outside of Carlisle, and all this was happening—or would happen—far to the south and east, off the cliffs of Dover. It was too far; and all the space between was full of tumbled magics.

The wind began to howl like a living thing. Eschiva fought her way down to the camp, and staggered into the first tent she came to, which happened to be her own. The rain came soon after that, a blinding sheet of water that had been born, she could have sworn, out of a cloudless sky. She reached for her power, for the magic that would counter this spell, but it was shut away from her. She could feel it beneath her, trapped in the earth, drawn out of her by the force of the storm.

Arslan would not wake. He was enspelled, too, and the rest of the company likewise, as she discovered when she braved the downpour. Even the horses were asleep, huddled together under a scrap of roof. She was the only one conscious, but she was powerless to do anything either magical or mundane.

She lay beside Arslan, warmed by the heat of him, and schooled herself to quivering patience. Without magic, there was nothing else she could do—except think. And those thoughts gave her no comfort.

The guardians of Britain had been guided away from John. He was alone, riding toward the darkness that roiled now at the heart of the realm. It was drawing him inexorably, calling him with a voice so strong and yet so still that only in the deep silence could she be aware of it.

It was almost too late. The walls had fallen at Richard's crowning; in the years between, the guardians had done as best they might to defend the kingdom. Now, almost, it was beyond defending. If John did not move, and move soon, only the gods knew what would come out of the gate between the worlds, or come sailing over the sea from the kingdoms of Europe.

And she could do nothing, this night, but lie awake and pray. She prayed with all that was in her that John would come safe to the gate, and that his strength when he came there would be enough to do what must be done. For if it was not, then there would be no Britain to guard, and no kingdom to preserve.

# CHAPTER 23

❦

It took them three days to cross the few leagues between the mile-castle and Carlisle, which should have taken half a day at most. When they came there, much battered with incessant wind and rain, John was gone. He had had a message, said the castellan, and had taken his personal troops and his brother Longsword, and ridden off in great haste. The rest of his household was following at its usual pace, with the bishops of Lincoln and Rouen in charge of it; they had orders to await him in London.

"It's the Archbishop of York," said the castellan. "The Bishop of Ely's men were waiting for him when he landed at Dover. They attacked him; he fled, but they caught him in St. Martin's priory—dragged him from the altar and clapped him in chains, because he broke his oath of exile."

Eschiva's lips were tight. Arslan was none too delighted himself: she had told him of her vision. They had been held back from warning John of this thing, and from riding with him to his brother's rescue.

"Hugh Neville," Arslan said: "the forester. Was he riding with my lord?"

"Why, no," the castellan said. "He was called away before the message came. Something to do with an outbreak of deer-poaching in the south."

"What did my uncle say to riding with the household and not the count?" Eschiva demanded. Her voice was sharp enough to make the castellan stiffen.

"My lord was riding hard and fast," the castellan said somewhat stiffly. "I heard the good bishop order his horse, but just after that, he was taken ill. My lord left his own physician, and gave orders for the household to travel no faster than the bishop's health allowed. It was a sudden taking, very alarming, but by evening he was recovered. Then there was the storm, of course, that blew out of the east. He couldn't leave the city until this morning."

Arslan met Eschiva's glance. Three guardians separated from John, and the fourth far away in the south—he was in Winchester, the last Arslan had known. He would wager that William the Marshal had been drawn away as well. It seemed her fears were well founded: the Wild Magic, after so long without a king to keep it in check, was turning against them all, and raising the land to oppose them.

Their guards were tired, cold, and hungry, and one or two had a good start on a winter rheum. "Can you spare a dozen men?" Arslan asked the castellan.

"To ride to Dover?" the castellan asked.

"Or wherever my lord has gone," said Arslan. "We'll be riding fast. I'll leave you these men of Lincoln in their stead, until they come back again."

It was a fair enough trade, and the castellan was a reasonable man. He agreed to it. He even supplied the party with provisions, and gave them letters of passage, since John was not there to provide them.

"You'll be rewarded," Eschiva said, with a smile that dazzled the castellan. He was still reeling with it when they rode out of Carlisle.

John could never stop thinking—that was his blessing and his curse. But on that ride from the north, he came as close to it as he had ever come. He could see only one thing: his brother torn from the altar in the priory at Dover, and shut in the dungeon of the castle. A royal Plantagenet, even a bastard one, and an archbishop into the bargain, should never in the world have suffered such indignity. Even the thought of it roiled his belly.

It began to dawn on him, as he passed out of the north and into the Midlands, that he was not thinking as clearly as he was used to. It also struck him that some faces were missing, that had been near or about him from the moment he left France. Bishop Hugh was taken ill, Neville called away, the Lady Eschiva vanished without anyone wondering where she had gone or whether she was safe. He had thought at the time that she was on some sorcerous errand, but what if she was not? And where was the newest of his squires?

That roused him to something resembling clarity. Arslan had been his shadow since the castle of La Forêt. Now the boy was gone. That he had not forgiven John for his Turk's death, John was well aware; but he was the best of servants. He would go nowhere without leave.

Had he asked for it? John searched his memory. The first night in Carlisle, the boy had said something of escaping a cage. John had let him go, but reminded him that he was expected back in the morning. Morning had brought the news of Geoffrey's capture, and John had forgotten everything but that.

John was an excessively suspicious man. He knew that; he took it into account. But all of his sorcerers were missing, and he was riding through a fog that was not entirely of earthly origin.

Geoffrey's capture was real. Word of it had spread through every hamlet. So had the rumor that the Bishop of Ely was denying, with great agitation, that he had ever commanded such a thing. His men were overzealous, he insisted. But he had not given the order to set the prisoner free.

John gathered forces as he rode, barons who were more than glad to take arms once more against the bishop. Sometimes he fancied that he saw more than the human army: shadows, shapes of air and darkness. They were particularly distinct at twilight, or on days when the rain closed in at dawn and lingered long after dusk. They were marching toward the sea.

The walls of Worcester kept the shadow army out. It was a city: crowded, filthy, malodorous. But the spirits or the ghosts or whatever they were, did not enter there. He felt oddly alone.

On another night he would have called for a woman, but tonight he wanted something else. As soon as he could escape, he took a certain bundle that never left his side, called out a guard whom he trusted, and slipped away from the castle.

The cathedral was hushed, its jeweled windows dark. Candles glowed on either side of the high altar. There was no one else there, except a single cowled figure kneeling in one of the side chapels. It did not move when John went past, but stayed where it was, rapt in prayer.

He had left Benno the guard at the door, not because he felt particularly safe here, but because he did not want the man to know why he had come to the cathedral. If Arslan had not been left behind, it would have been different.

A flash of temper checked his advance. The boy should have been here. John needed him. Where in the devil's name was he?

With an effort John quelled the anger that could too easily swell to rage. He genuflected to the high altar, but turned aside from it to one of the chapels. There, beside a tomb with its carven effigy, he knelt. The chill of stone pierced swiftly through his woolen hose. He ignored it, except to let it sharpen his mind.

Carefully he laid the bag on the floor. It was heavy for its size, and oddly shaped. He could feel the things inside it as if they had been in his own body: the silk of the wrappings, the cold weight of gold and silver, the crown and the scepter that had been given him to keep but not, it seemed, to wield. Neither made him feel any more a king.

"My lord bishop," he said as if the effigy were a living man, "I crave a moment of your eternity."

The effigy lay as it had for the past hundred years. The candles flickered unchanged. Someone had laid a wilted garland on the stone breast. Roses and heather—a strange mingling. Heather did not grow here. Even dry, it kept its sweetness.

"My lord bishop," John said again, "I have need of counsel."

The roses were the color of blood. Their fragrance was potent even in their death.

"My lord," said John, "my defenders are taken away. My brother is shut in a dungeon. The one who did that will be seen to; he's no great concern. But, my lord, something else is happening, and it's making my bones ache—but I don't know what it is or why it is or how to stop it."

Petals fell over his clasped hands, red as blood, white as snow. He looked up into the face of the effigy. It was sitting on the stone slab, looking down at him, frowning slightly as if newly roused from sleep. "Say my name," it said.

"Lord bishop—" John began.

"My name!" the effigy said.

"Wulfstan," John said. And because it seemed that he should, he said it twice again.

With each repetition, the effigy seemed less like stone and more like living flesh. As the third faded, Wulfstan yawned and stretched and took off his miter, laying it on the stone beside him. It had dented his forehead; he rubbed it as he peered at John, looking as human as a man could be. "Lost your guardians, have you? That's not so bad: they can do what they need to do wherever they are. But the ifritah's son—him, you shouldn't have misplaced. You need him."

"I know that!" John said testily. "I want to know why. What's happened? Who's playing us like a handful of knucklebones?"

"And I'm to answer you?"

"Don't the dead know everything?"

"They may, but they're enjoined from telling it."

John knotted his fingers together before they locked about Wulfstan's throat. "I do need help," he said, not humbly, but less haughtily than before. "If I'm going into an ambush, I should try to protect myself."

"Wait here," the dead man said. "The ifritah's son is coming."

"Does he know what I need to know?"

"You both do," said Wulfstan.

"But I don't—"

The long Saxon face was paling to stone again, the tall body stiffening. He signed the cross over John's head, put the miter on his own, and lay down in a creaking of stony joints.

John regarded the effigy in a kind of wry despair. His lips twisted. That was always the way with magic: riddles here, enigmas there. "*What* do I know that I don't know I know?" he demanded.

He did not expect an answer, nor did he receive one. The image was stone, stiff and lifeless.

The ifritah's son came to Worcester the day after John, leading a company of spent men on spent horses. He had the Lady Eschiva with him, riding a grey Arab mare, and the one of his Turks who yet lived. From the look of them, they had had a brutal ride, through weather like the wrath of God.

John was waiting for him. His men staggered straight to the guardroom and fell over in a dead sleep, but he came to the hall with the lady and the Turk, walking as steadily as if he had been idling about with the rest of the squires. He did obeisance with exquisite correctness and said, "My lord, I regret—whatever punishment is due me—"

"You'll pay," John said tersely. "I'll speak with you in the morning. Go on, wash off the mud. Eat. Sleep."

Arslan bowed again. John beckoned to his bodyservant. "Look after them," he said.

He was interested to see the smile that Petit was quick to hide. So: Petit liked the boy, did he? That was a rarity. In Petit's opinion, a squire was good for nothing whatsoever.

# CHAPTER 24

John's bodyservant did as he was bidden, calling in one of the maids to attend Eschiva, and devoting himself to Arslan's comfort. It seemed Arslan was to have the lord's own bed, with all the rest that went with it. Petit turned a deaf ear to protests, even to struggles. It was John's command; therefore he would do it.

After a while Arslan surrendered. There was a sinful pleasure in pretending for this one evening that he was a prince. Eschiva, he knew, was enjoying the same indulgence in the lady's bower, sleeping in the bed that was given to Eleanor herself when she was in Worcester. This in which he lay would be the king's, when the king was in residence.

John walked a thin line there, but tonight Arslan would not concern himself with it. He even surprised himself with sleep, buried deep in the featherbed, wrapped in the warmth of silk and furs.

When he woke, John was standing over him, and he was stripped of all his coverlets. Even in his sleep he had remembered how to keep himself warm. He lay blinking at John, who scowled back. "I'm embarrassed to admit," John said, "how long it took me to understand where you were. Do you intend to marry her?"

Arslan scrambled up, clutching the blankets. It was one thing to be stark naked and facing a lord he had deserted. This was something else altogether. "I asked her. She wouldn't have a landless squire. It's a knight or nothing, she said."

"Did you ask her guardian?"

Arslan shook his head.

"Well," said John, "no doubt he'd laugh in your face, if he didn't blast you to a cinder. She's royalty in that other Britain, of a line so old it goes back before the Druids. Her father was a god in his day.

And of course in this world she's an heiress, with a sizable inheritance in Somerset—the Summer Country, they used to call it. Do you honestly think she's for the likes of you?"

"No," said Arslan, "but when I'm older, if I'm knighted, I'll begin to be less unworthy of her."

"You do aim high," John said.

"No higher than I can reach," Arslan said.

"God's teeth, you're arrogant." John sat on the bed, propping himself with cushions. "What if I order the marriage?"

Arslan's teeth clicked together. "My lord, don't do that."

"Why not? I can remedy her objections, knight you, give you lands—that's easily in my power. You gain her lands and income, which are considerable. You both continue to serve me, without this need to slip away and be licentious."

"I don't want—she doesn't want—"

"Do you think that matters, with noble marriages?" John clapped his hands together. "It's decided. I'll inform her guardian, and find a suitable demesne for you."

"She's going to be furious," Arslan said.

"She's still going to marry you," said John. "Now, up. We're leaving today. Petit will see that you're ready."

Eschiva was not furious when he told her, in the morning before they rode out of Worcester. She laughed so long that Arslan passed from astonishment into indignation. "It's not a joke! He means it."

"I know he means it," she said, hiccoughing and with tears running down her face. "Oh, please! Don't scowl. My uncle won't be too appalled. He thinks highly of you."

"Highly enough for this?"

"Maybe." She wiped her face, still grinning at him. She looked like a hoyden child; she was so beautiful she stopped his heart.

"I know you don't want this," he said. "Even if John commands it, I'll refuse."

"What if I command it?"

He sucked a breath. "You told me—"

"Minds change," she said. "John is right, you know. We'll serve him better if we're less likely to disappear when he needs us most."

"That wasn't—" He stopped before she could stop him. The memory of that ride would not fade quickly. Even with the wards she raised, that his strength sustained, they had had to fight for their passage. The land itself strove to drive them away from John. It was like a beast that had turned against its master, and ran wild where it would.

It was still grumbling, threatening them with rain. John's troops were gathered in the court of the castle, wrapped against the wet. Arslan lifted Eschiva onto the back of Yusuf's mare and turned to take his own mare's reins from Kalila. She was hollow-eyed but steady on her feet; he opened his mouth to command her to stay, but shut it without saying the words. She would never forgive him if he left her behind again—even if it killed her.

Arslan clung as close to John as he could. Eschiva was doing the same. Her face was blank and a little bored, as if she cared for nothing in the world but finishing the day's journey and getting out of the rain. Behind that mask she was sustaining wards of a strength that made his ears buzz. Whatever was waiting at the end of John's road, it wanted him alone and defenseless.

Now John had his defenses, and they were potent, but they had a disadvantage: while the wards were up, no word could go out to the rest of the guardians, wherever they were.

Arslan rode as if this were a road through disputed country in Outremer, quietly but keenly alert. His weapons were close to hand, well oiled and sharpened. He watched the men about John, too; Ely might not be the only magicless man who served as a vessel for the Wild Magic.

Except for the ceaseless, drenching rain, the ride that day was uneventful. It was also slow, much impeded by mud. They rode only as far as Evesham before the early dark drew in, stopping at the abbey there.

Evesham was an old place, a place that had been holy since long before the Christians came to Britain. Its well went down to the deeps of the earth, and brought up pure cold water, blessed with the oldest of old magic.

The abbey was dry, warmer than the air without, and offered simple but plain fare, which warmed their bellies amply. To drink they were given either refectory ale or, for those who wished a blessing, water from the well.

Arslan chose the water, and not only because he had no taste for English ale. It came in a wooden cup, and was perfectly clean, as if it had just fallen from the sky. The young monk who served it was watching Arslan, clutching the pitcher to his thin breast.

Arslan drank in a long slow swallow. The water was cold, but in a strange way it warmed him. He was keenly aware of the half of him that was fire, enclosed in the half of him that was mortal clay. Was that the well's magic, to make the obvious even more so, and sharpen the world to a piercing clarity?

He took that clarity with him to a hard narrow bed. Eschiva was not in it. She had been taken away to a separate guesthouse, with a pilgrim or two and a lady traveling down to Gloucester.

They were not going to Gloucester. John had no desire to be trapped in the cares and necessities of that city, even if Susanna was among them. His eyes and mind were set on Windsor, where the Bishop of Ely was.

All the men, even John, slept in this single dormitory, as stark in its simplicity as the monks' own. Arslan had made certain that John was surrounded by his most trustworthy men, with Arslan beside him, and Kalila on his other side.

Arslan lay awake while the others slept: a familiar thing, and tonight almost comforting. The water of the well soothed the heat in him, and let him see and hear far beyond these walls.

He slipped free of the mortal world, leaving the earth of his body behind. Eschiva's wards did not trap him; rather they surrounded him like a bubble and floated with him out over the green land of England.

She had told him of her vision, how she had seen Geoffrey's ship coming over the sea, and Ely's men waiting for him, to seize him. That was past. He saw the white cliffs and the sea dashing against them, and the stark towers of the castle, with the glimmer in them that was the prisoner. He, like John, had inherited the spark of the Demon Countess' magic, and it burned in him with the anger of his captivity.

Arslan thought to pause, but the same force that had drawn him here drew him onward over the sea. He saw the straight track of the otherworld that had brought him to Britain, gleaming in the grey surge of the waves, and the low dark swell in starlight that was the coast of France.

It was strange to see it from this side of the water, and stranger to feel that it was a foreign country, and that he was in a land that he knew, that—to his astonishment—belonged to him. In the long year's progress through the land of England, John had made it his own; but

Arslan, in traveling with him, had come to belong to it. He could not say that he loved it; it was still colder, wetter, greener than his bones could endure without the protection of magic. Yet it had worked its way under his skin.

The land was alive. He had known that, but he had not seen until now the spirit that lived in the earth of Britain, how it lived in and through the people of the island, and most of all in the body and soul of the king.

The same was true of France. It lay like a great beast, deep in sleep. Its king was a true king, bound to it, consecrated to it—and that rather startled Arslan. Philip, by all reports, was a thoroughly Christian monarch. He had gone on Crusade with Richard, but that was not a happy union. Two men more unlike one another, one could not imagine: the warrior king and the lord of the council chamber, often forced into alliance but never bound in amity. Philip was no friend to Richard or any of his kin, yet he was also, by the laws of his land, their liege lord, overlord of their great domains of Normandy and Maine and Anjou. Moreover he bore great animosity to their mother the Duchess of Aquitaine, for that she had once been Queen of France, but had divorced his father and run off with a boy who became King of England. Some said he had truly hated old Henry for betrothing his sister Alais to first one and then another of his sons, while keeping her for himself; then when he died, she was cast off, outworn and unwanted.

If Henry's queen and his sons had any single devoted enemy, it was Philip. And Philip, true King of France, was the living soul of the land he ruled. Its power was in his hands. Its strength was his strength.

He had left the Crusade because he was ill, it was said, and because there was a rebellion in Flanders. What, thought Arslan, if his illness had risen from his removal from the land? What if he had gone back because he was summoned, and not simply by a mortal rebellion? And what if, once he had returned, he saw England without a known king, Normandy and Maine and Anjou bereft of their lord, and no clear succession to hold against him?

John was crowned; he had the scepter. He was sealed to the king-dom in the blood of a servant. Yet his kingship was not complete. The gate of the otherworld was still open. Until it was shut, the walls of air could not hold. An enemy could invade, and conquer the land of Britain.

William the Bastard had done it by seizing the true kingship, leaving Saxon Harold to be crowned King of England only—just as Richard had been. His invasion had been the claiming of a realm that was his already in the eyes of the otherworld. Would Philip have the desire or the strength to do such a thing?

Arslan thought he might, if only to destroy Eleanor and her sons. He would care little what became of the realm once he had captured it, except to cast it down so low that it could never be a threat to France.

John must move, and move soon: to secure his power, and to protect Britain against this threat from without. Once John sealed the gate, he was sealed to Britain. Then the walls of air would rise again; then he would have the strength to face what came across the sea.

As Arslan drifted above the turbulent shore, a blast of otherworldly wind howled across the stars. It buffeted Arslan, battering him, striving to rend him in tatters. He had nothing to cling to, no anchor, no safety but the frail bubble of Eschiva's wards.

There was nothing in him that the wind could seize on, no cord to bind him, no chink in his armor through which to destroy him. Yet it could drive him back when he sought his earthly form again. It could do what it had done since that night on the Wall: it could sunder him from his lord, and keep him wandering forever, no more than a voice and a pair of eyes.

He flung himself against it. It drove him reeling back. He drew in the wards that protected him, till they were as close as his lost skin. They were not impervious to his unshielded self as his shell of flesh was: they caught fire.

He spun downward toward the darkened earth, trailing flame. He was beyond shock, and well beyond fear. He was close to dissolution.

But he was human enough to say in the depths of his heart, *No.* He would not submit. He would not go meekly into death. In desperation, without coherent thought, he clutched at the only part of earth that was his claim.

He gasped. Breath roared into mortal lungs. He was naked, defenseless, and falling through a storm of icy rain.

Thank whatever gods or saints watched over fools and madmen, he did not fall far; a thicket of branches broke the worst of it. He lay wet, muddy, and stinging with a myriad scratches, on thoroughly solid and mortal earth.

He was warm, at least. That much of his magic remained to him. He had no faintest conception of where he was, except that it must be Britain: nowhere else was so wet or so overgrown with brush and brambles.

He rose gingerly. No bones were broken; the bruises were not quite crippling. A sudden sheet of rain washed off most of the mud. He stood in it, letting it scour him. When he was clean, he began to walk. He chose the direction which seemed most beset with wind and rain, as he had done since he left the Wall. By now, it was a habit.

# CHAPTER 25

A rslan walked the rest of the night in the rain. In the morning, as sun broke through the clouds, he found a farmwife who would give him a tunic that almost fit and a pair of hose that were only a little too short, in return for chopping a stack of wood for her fire. She would have taken another trade, but he smiled vapidly and pretended to be simple, and she gave up the effort.

She told him what he needed to know. He was less than a day's walk from Windsor, where the Bishop of Ely was. Whether it was fate or chance, the wind had cast him where John must go.

He would take it as fate. He came into the town by the castle on a farmer's wagon, perched on a load of cabbages, which he helped to arrange in the market-stall. He was still being taken for a simpleton, with his halting Saxon: he looked like enough to the people here, with his height and his fair hair. They seemed not to notice the deep gold of his skin; some of them were ruddy enough still from working the fields all summer long.

His strong back was useful here. He earned a clipped bit of silver, which bought him a napkin of meat pasties and a bag of apples. With the apples in his tunic and a pasty in his hand, he wandered through the gate of the castle.

It rather surprised him by being open. It was guarded, of course, but not against an army. People were passing in and out. He, in his yeoman's clothes, attracted no more than a glance. He angled toward the direction in which, according to his nose, he would find the stables.

They were full. He took a count of destriers in the stalls, and mules and palfreys beyond them. Either the bishop had called a council of knights, barons, and churchmen, or he had elected to surround himself with a retinue that rivaled John's.

"You!"

Arslan spun. A knight was standing there, an elegant person in golden spurs and supercilious expression. "Boy. Saddle my palfrey. Be quick about it!"

Arslan ducked his head as he had seen servants do. The knight obviously expected him to know which of the long line of light riding horses to bring out, and which of the many saddles and bridles to set on it. He cast a wishing as Bertrada had taught him, bound it to the knight's arrogant presence, and sent it unreeling down the line to a mettlesome chestnut and an elaborately tooled and chased saddle and a bridle inlaid with gold. This man was wealthy, and showy, too.

He aimed a cuff at Arslan for taking too long, which Arslan nimbly avoided, and offered him no thanks for fetching and saddling his horse. The horse pinned ears and snapped at its master, which won it a hard blow to the face.

Arslan was sorely tempted to lay a second wishing on the horse, to rid it quickly of its rider, but it would only suffer the worse for that. He settled for a small curse on the rider, an itch in an embarrassing place, which would torment him until he learned to be a gentler man.

This magic could be a useful thing. He left the stable for the kitchens, which were humming with preparations for the daymeal. There as in the stable, one more Saxon-looking servant was not worth noticing. He had but to see what needed doing, slip in and do it, and look as if he had been there for as long as anyone could remember.

It was harder to get into the hall. That required livery, and a place in the ranks of higher servants. Or, since he was what he was, a cloak of shadows.

He was tiring. He did not remember when last he had slept, and magic, as Father Hugh had warned him, was like any other limb of the body: it needed frequent use to build its strength, and there were limits to it. Still, he reckoned that he could hold for a little while, and he wanted—needed—to see who was with the bishop.

The arrogant knight was there, squirming in his lofty seat. His ride had been brief, and from the look of it, none too comfortable, either. He sat beside another like him: dark and wiry and not tall. These must be Ely's brothers; they were straighter and prettier, but they all had the same narrow face and haughty expression.

Arslan did not know all the knights or barons of England, but it seemed to him that there were far more priests and monks than men of the world, and the knights seemed mostly to belong to Ely's following. The accents were Norman; there were no knights of England here. They had all come with the bishop from Normandy.

England might not support him, but he was strongly defended nonetheless—and not only by mortal steel. The air about him shimmered like the desert of Syria at midday in summer: a hint of the mirage.

Those defenses were a trap, laid and waiting. The touch of Arslan's magic sprang it. He reeled against the wall, stripped of his concealment. Even then he might have slipped away, but the apples in his shirt slipped free as he staggered, and tumbled across the floor. One fetched up against a knight's foot; he cursed and kicked, thinking it was one of the dogs. The man beside him cursed back, and in elaborating on it, caught sight of Arslan.

The outcry sent Arslan to his knees. Hard hands seized him, dragging him down the length of the hall.

He could have wept when the dragging stopped, as much for the pain of bruise on bruise as for the relief of being still again. Fingers knotted roughly in his hair and wrenched his head up. He blinked at the Bishop of Ely.

"Your grace," one of his captors said. "We've caught a spy."

"Ah, that's no spy," said one of Ely's brothers, the one who could not stop wriggling even when he spoke. "That's the simpleton from the stables. What's he doing here?"

"Spying," Arslan's captor said doggedly.

"Probably he wanted to see how his betters live," said a plump prelate.

Ely said nothing. He was frowning, as if he found Arslan's face familiar but could not place it. Arslan prayed that he would not remember; that the commoner's clothes and myriad cuts and bruises were disguise enough.

"Well, now he's seen it," the bishop's brother said, giving up at last and scratching the relentless itch. "Give him half a dozen lashes and toss him out. That will teach him to spy on his masters."

They all glanced at Ely. He waved a hand. "Do it, do it. Get him out of here."

He had obedient servants. Eager, too. They did not wait for an executioner or a whip; two of them held Arslan, and a third stripped off the farmer's tunic and flogged him with a belt.

Arslan had been wounded in battle and in the hunt. He took bruises often enough in knightly exercises. He was battered already by branch and stone and briar. And yet this, which seemed a mild enough punishment when the bishop decreed it, was beyond any pain he had known. The belt's edges were sharp; they cut. Its heavy buckle wrapped around him and smote him like a second, more vicious weapon. He bruised; he bled.

He did not scream. He bit his lip almost through, but he kept silent. They went well past half a dozen lashes, and he went well past the edge of unconsciousness. He rather hoped that the darkness was death, but his heart knew that God was not so merciful.

Sunlight dazzled him. Pain caught his breath in his throat. He was alive, oh, yes, and well able to wish he was not. Something was propping him up, bolstering him around the throbbing in his back.

The rim of a cup thudded against his teeth; icy liquid poured into his mouth. He gasped, choked.

"Hush," said a warm deep voice. "Stop that. Drink it; it's only water."

Water and herbs, sharp and astringent. He had swallowed before he could stop himself.

It cleared his head remarkably. He peered at the man who tended him. It was a sturdy man with a broad blunt face and exceedingly shrewd eyes, in a friar's habit. He stared back without shyness. "Well," he said. "I see you're not the idiot they all said you were— nor the common stableboy, either." He took Arslan's left hand in his, the sword hand, and ran a thumb along the thick ridges of callus. "There's hard work and there's hard work. You never got these swinging a sickle in a field."

Arslan clenched his fist and twisted it out of the monk's grip. "So? This time will they kill me?"

"That depends," the monk said. "Osbert was right, wasn't he? You were spying. But whether for good or ill . . ." He trailed off. "Are you a Jew, sir?"

Arslan hurt too much to laugh. A rib was cracked, or two. Maybe three. He crossed himself with conspicuous devotion. "No, I am not, nor Muslim, either."

"But you were born . . . ?"

"My mother was of Islam." Arslan was not going to tell the rest of it, but if this admission harmed him, he cared little. "I was baptized, Brother. I hope that someone will shrive me before I die. I don't suppose your orders suffice for the sacrament of penance?"

"I'm a simple Austin friar," the monk said, "and occasional physician."

"And magician?"

It was pure bravado, but the monk's stare sharpened. His hand shaped a gesture. Arslan countered it—scraping the power from the bottom, but it was enough, just. Spell and counterspell hovered in the air, their strands interwoven. With the last strength that he had, Arslan transformed them into a butterfly. It fluttered away through the window of that small wood-walled room.

The monk watched it until it was gone. When his eyes returned to Arslan, they were a fraction wider.

Arslan could not fall backward; his nest of bolsters prevented it. Very carefully he slid, turning, till he was lying on his face. He had to pause then just to breathe, and to let the tears of pain finish flowing.

"I think," the monk said, "that my lord bishop wasn't wise to let you go."

"Will you be sending me back?" Arslan asked faintly.

"Should I?"

Arslan did not answer. He turned his head until he could see the monk again. The man was frowning, rubbing his jaw. The rasp of hand on stubble made Arslan clench his teeth.

That this was not the castle, Arslan had long since concluded. But that this was one of Ely's servants, he was not so sure. Nor was he entirely certain that the man was human, even with his habit and his tonsure. Something about him felt odd.

Arslan was helpless, emptied of strength both magical and physical. He had been a fool and worse than a fool. What John must be thinking, after Arslan had given his word not to disappear again—and Eschiva; oh, God, Eschiva.

He buried his face in the darkness of his folded arms. Because he needed first to heal, before anything else, he set all aside but that. It was the same art as clearing his mind for the use of high magic. It was no easier or simpler, either, but it was good discipline. He had not been practicing enough of that, of late.

The monk let him be. He was rather surprised. The man, if man he was, came and went as day faded into night and back into day again. Sometimes he fed Arslan, or gave him something to drink: water with herbs, hot or cold. Once he changed the dressings on Arslan's back, spreading the outraged skin with a pungent salve before he covered it up again. The salve stung like fire, but it was clean; the wounds were healing beneath it.

Some part of Arslan kept count of the days, though his body lay mostly in a half sleep. On the third day, he swam into waking. The pain was much less. He was weak, but only as much as he should have been after three days abed.

The monk was not there. He rose slowly, fighting dizziness, clinging to the wall until the world stopped spinning. The room was not large; the window looked out on a narrow street overhung with windows like it. At the end of the street he could see the tower of a church.

He would wager that he was in Windsor town. It was a misty day, a soft day as they said here; people went about their business wrapped in mantles of the famous English wool. Autumn was well set in, the air raw with a breath of winter.

He found clothes in the chest near the bed, which somewhat surprised him. They fit, which surprised him even more. They were of better quality than those he had had from the farmwife, suitable for a burgher of a town: linen and wool, the linen undyed, the wool dyed russet brown and deep green. Dressing pulled at scars that healed with preternatural speed, but he set his teeth and endured it.

There was a belt of good leather under the rest, and a knife hung from it, fit for little but cutting meat. Last he found a pair of shoes— walking shoes, not the boots of a horseman. For some reason that struck him with amusement.

He had to rest once the clothes were on, but he recovered quickly. There was a considerable pleasure in being clothed again, warmly and well, with mantle and hood to cover it all. He wrapped himself in those and ventured down through deserted rooms, and out into the mist.

It was completely mad, what he was doing. He should find a horse somewhere, mount it and ride away as fast and far as he could go. At the very least he should turn toward the gate of the town and make his escape.

He turned toward the castle. His mind was clear, or so he fancied. He knew what he was going to do, and how. He even reckoned that there would be some use in it, some help to John or to the guardians.

The gate was open today as it had been before, its guards wrapped in mantles as everyone else was. A man of evident means, walking boldly past them, attracted somewhat more attention than a simpleton in homespun. It was not suspicion; they measured him, rather, and reckoned his worth. Shoes, no spurs; knife, no sword: commoner, then, and not a nobleman, but sturdy enough to make a man-at-arms.

It was a day for royal judgment, the king's justiciar speaking for the king in matters of greater or lesser state. There were not many petitioners about; not as there were when John sat in court. If this had been John, Arslan would not have been hard put to push his way into the hall, but here he could simply walk in, ignore the clerk who begged leave to know what brought him here, and wait to be noticed by the man on the dais.

That did not take long. The others all seemed to be known to the chancellor or his clerks. Ely disposed of them rather abruptly, perhaps drawn by curiosity, his glance flicking toward Arslan and then away, over and over.

"You," he said at length. "Come here."

Arslan obliged. He made no effort to seem either simple or humble. He bowed correctly, as a squire should to a royal chancellor; Ely's brothers curled their lips at that. They would reckon that he knew no better.

"Do you wish to enter my service?" the bishop asked.

"I'm already sworn to another lord, your grace," Arslan said, "but I've been separated from him. I would ask your charity, and your indulgence, in finding me a place until I can return to my lord again."

"You speak well," Ely said. "Are you from Normandy?"

"Anjou, your grace," Arslan said.

"Ah," said Ely. "So. Can you read? Do you write?"

"Both, your grace," Arslan said.

"French? Latin? The English tongue?"

"Only a little of the English," Arslan said, "but French and Latin well enough."

"Here, show me." Ely beckoned to one of the clerks. The man brought his writing case and a scrap of parchment.

Arslan sat on the steps of the dais, with the case in his lap and the ink bottle beside him, and wrote the little bit of Latin that the bishop dictated, and the few words of French. He had had teaching: he could write a clear hand. He could read, too, more quickly than some.

"Good," said Ely. "Very good. What with Piers taking ill and Gauthier being called back to his abbey and Brother Benedictus suffering from the shaking palsy, we're in sore need of a clerk."

"I'm not a clerk, your grace," Arslan said. "I don't pretend to—"

"You'll do till we find someone better," Ely said. His expression shifted subtly. Arslan realized that he was smiling. "Courage, lad. I suppose it's the guards you're wanting, and swords and derring-do. Serve me well in this and I'll put in a word for you with the captain. Will that content you?"

Arslan bit down on laughter, ducked his head and lowered his eyes and mumbled, "Yes, your grace."

"You are a godsend," Ely told him. "You'll be in my prayers tonight. And maybe God will be kind and send me the pair of clerks I asked for from Ely Isle, and you'll be free sooner rather than later. In the meantime, look to Thibaut here. He'll instruct you in your duties."

Arslan bowed again, and accepted the dismissal.

Thibaut the clerk regarded the new recruit with a jaundiced eye. He clearly thought little of Arslan's aptitude for his calling. Still, his lord had ordered it, and he was an obedient servant. He showed Arslan the cramped and cluttered space that was the clerks' workroom, and the even more cramped and cluttered room beyond it in which they slept. There was a man sleeping there now, who from the sound and smell of him must be Piers, who was ill. The rest of the clerks were either in the hall or in the workroom, laboring over the endless minutiae of their office.

They greeted Arslan with varying degrees of incredulity, and no more trust in his skill than Thibaut had. "I knew he was desperate," one of them said, "but as desperate as this? What are you when you're at home, boy? Wool merchant? Weaver's son?"

"Why, do I look as if I'm fresh from the sheep?"

"You reek of it," the clerk said amiably. "I suppose you have a name."

"Baldwin," Arslan said, which was not a lie at all.

"Ah! A noble name. Are you a lettered man, messire Baldwin? Are you educated?"

"Probably not," said Arslan, "but I can write well enough for someone else to read, and as you said, he's desperate."

"Well then, get to it," Thibaut said. "You'll scrape the parchment and sharpen the pens, run our errands and keep the place tidy, and when you've done all of that, you can do whatever copying the rest of us lack the time for. There's your bed over there, between Piers and the window, and you'll take meals with the rest of us. You'd best get yourself a gown that won't show the inkstains, though where you'll find one to fit you, you great ox, God knows."

"God," said the clerk who seemed to be the spokesman for the rest, "or Dame Agatha in the laundry. She has a weakness for the mooncalves of the world."

"What woman doesn't?" Thibaut said wearily. "Back to work, all of you. We're behind as it is."

# CHAPTER 26

A rslan had never thought of clerks' labor as hard. Tedious, yes; tiresome, certainly. But beside the sheer brute exertion of knightly exercises or labor in the fields, it shrank to insignificance.

He had not reckoned on its beginning before dawn and going on long after dusk, by the light of lamps and candles. Nor had he thought on the strain of keeping it all in his head, hour after hour, writing each letter without error. Errors were unforgivable. Parchment, as Thibaut never failed to remind them all, was dreadfully expensive, and they could not afford to waste it.

Arslan was glad to be given the servant's work. It let him leave the workroom, see the sun, even walk under the sky. He was not as free to wander as he had hoped, but in the clerk's gown that Dame Agatha had unearthed for him, with his head bent and his shoulders bowed, he discovered that he was as invisible as if he had put on a cloak of shadows.

The mood here was strange. It was determinedly, even desperately ordinary. The bishop knew that John was coming, the whole kingdom knew it, but he seemed impervious to the threat. He held his court, said his daily Mass, occupied himself with the duties of his office. The castle was full of troops, and he had others in reserve, but they were not encouraged to make themselves obvious. Whatever storms raged in the kingdom, here was an eye of calm.

Only once did Arslan see any sign of strain: when a messenger came to the bishop from Dover. No one heard what the man said, but everyone within earshot heard the reply: "Tell him no. No, I won't let him go. No, I won't revoke his exile. No, I *won't* be cowed with threats! Bind him, gag him, I don't care. But stop coming to me with his bluster."

"You could let him go," one of his advisors ventured. "After all, my lord, you've been denying that you ever gave the order to capture him; why not release him? Then even John will have no cause to fall on you with fire and sword."

"John will fall on me no matter what I do," Ely said. "He wants my office, and I'll not give it to him. I certainly won't set that brother of his loose to raise troops and foment rebellion—just as our lord the king feared when he swore them both to exile. He's in prison, and there he stays, unless he agrees to be shipped back to Normandy."

"He'll never do that," Ely's brother Osbert drawled. He was still suffering sorely from Arslan's curse, but he had yet to learn its lesson. He had lost none of his arrogance. "Yes, best he be kept under lock and key. With luck we'll toss Prince John in with him, and so be rid of them both. The king would thank us for that."

"The king released Prince John from his oath," Ely said, though not with any pleasure. "We can't hold him; we have no grounds in the law."

"Oh, the law," Osbert said with a flick of a hand. "That for the law. Can't you just write a new one?"

Ely's expression was thunderous, but his brother—who as the sheriff of two counties should have been slightly more respectful of the law—took no notice. In any event a new messenger had come in with dispatches from London, matters of the chancery that had little to do with men or their quarrels. They all took refuge in that, evading the quarrel that had been brewing.

Arslan could not find the monk who had taken him in and tended him. The house in which he had been kept belonged to a widow of the town, who happened to be visiting her kin in Southwark; it was locked and shuttered when he went by, with not even a servant in residence. No one knew a monk or friar of that particular description, nor remembered that he had been in that place a few days before.

Arslan was unsurprised. He had his suspicions as to who the monk had been. A creature who could be both a robber of the wood and a heavenly angel would think nothing of becoming a holy friar. He was not too poor a healer, either, though Arslan was no more certain than ever of his purpose. Maybe Robin had saved Arslan from his own folly; maybe he had deepened it.

One thing Arslan knew. Messages that he tried to send, birds of the air or spirits on swift wings, either would not go at all, or came back tattered and spent, having come no closer to John than Arslan himself was. A message to William the Marshal had better fortune: he was in London, gathering forces, and his reply was swift, pointed, and brief: "Stay put. Wait. Don't do anything rash."

Rash indeed, Arslan thought. He was here, and that was mad enough. So far he had not been recognized. People seldom looked past the name or the livery; even if they recognized his face, they could never quite remember where. He did his best not to freshen the memory.

He had been a week in Windsor, and was beginning to feel as if he might be there forever, when word came that flung the castle into uproar. John was in Oxford, and that was perilously close, but he was not the cause of the tumult. The Bishop of Rouen, under the king's banner, had gone to London and was waiting there with the Lord Marshal. He summoned all parties in the quarrel to a council, on pain of censure and even excommunication if they refused. But worse than that, because Ely had seized a fellow prince of the Church and held him prisoner, his diocese was to be placed under Interdict.

Ely half rose from his seat. "He will not lay hands on me without reprisal from Rome."

"He's not laying hands on you, your grace," the messenger said. "He simply presents an ultimatum. His grace of York goes free, or Ely goes under the ban. No Mass; no sacraments. No giving in marriage, no baptism, no burial of the dead. No life of the spirit in your see while you deprive an archbishop of his bodily freedom."

"Your master may be a bishop," Ely said with tight-drawn precision, "and the one he protects may be an archbishop, but I am the Holy Father's legate. I have acted according to the commands of my king. If I am to be held at fault, then so must he, for exceeding the bounds of his authority. Let him lay Ely under Interdict; then so shall I do with Rouen, and with York that cries so loudly for its banished archbishop."

The man had fire, Arslan thought in surprise. As he laid the messenger low with that spate of words, he even seemed taller, and he gained a certain regal dignity. The man had little to say to them; Ely dismissed him with sublime contempt.

With that, all that had seemed casual and calm and ordinary transformed into fevered activity. Everyone had his place, and he ran to it.

Arslan's was to fetch and carry for the clerks as they copied out summons after summons, calling in all Ely's vassals and his allies and any who owed fealty to him or to the king whose justiciar he was. Couriers rode out at reckless speed, scattering to the ends of England, and in the scrip of each was a thick sheaf of parchment, the same letter over and over: *Come to London. Stand with the king's justiciar against those who would usurp his office.*

He would go to London in his good time: not so hastily as to seem anxious, nor so late as to seem openly defiant. His men, however, began to ride out in companies, securing the roads and scouring out any who might resist them.

Arslan's sword hand twitched when he saw them mounting to ride. He had not lifted a weapon or ridden a horse since he rode with John. It seemed unnatural to be standing in shadows, dressed in fusty black, with ink on his fingers. He was a nobleman, not a clerk. Why in the world had he let himself be brought down to this?

But that was a passing folly. When the castle woke from its torpor, so did the thing that had been sleeping beneath and about it.

Magic. Power. And more: he had found the gate of the otherworld, the opening of which had broken the walls of air.

It was not in Windsor, but it was close. Once he was aware of it, he could not shut his mind's eye to it. He felt the strength of it, the swirling mass of Wild Magic, high magic, magic of earth and air and water, and above all, magic of fire, since that was his own essence.

Ely was here not only because this was a great royal fortress and stronghold, but because he was bound to the opening of the gate. It was marvelously well hidden. He saw it only because of Ely: the man was a mirror, and in it Arslan found the gate's reflection. No wonder the guardians had been kept from John, if John was coming here.

Arslan's presence in this place was an oddity; he did not know yet what to think of it. He did not feel like a spy. He was learning nothing that John could not already know. Was he here, maybe, to protect John against the strange void that was in Ely, that made him so strong a lure to magic? Or—was he to protect Ely himself?

God knew, the man was no more or less charming than John himself. John's body was straighter and he was notably younger, but his spirit was rather less honest than Ely's.

Ely was an honest man. Arslan had not expected that. Within the limits of his capacity, he was loyal to Richard, and he was devoted to

his brothers. He reckoned himself a good man and a capable servant—none more so, in his mind. No one was better fit than he to
work Richard's will in England.

Once in Arslan's hearing, his father had burst out in a rare fit of
temper. "God save me from honest men!" Arslan had been a child
then; he had not understood. Now he thought he did.

"You! Boy! Where's my inkpot?"

Arslan had been woolgathering there in the hall, and Thibaut had
caught him at it. He hastened to find the wandering pot, made sure
it was filled with ink to the degree that Thibaut preferred, and was
called off promptly to sharpen pens for the rest of the clerks.

It was mindless labor, and let him search out the inner places of his
magic, hunting for ways to lessen the power of the gate. There were
spells of binding, words of power that, combined with certain rites,
could knit it shut. He had not gone far in that study; he was still very
much an apprentice. But the guardians would know all the words and
the bindings, if only they could be brought to the place in which the
gate had opened.

He stumbled over a pair of feet. Osbert cursed and kicked him. He
fell to his knees, still half out of the world, blinking dazedly at the
knight's furious face.

Its fury barely moderated, but the recognition in it raised his hackles even in his confusion. "You! I know you. Guards!"

They were on him before he could gather his wits or get to his feet.
His mind was full of the gate, in a howling like wind and a gibbering
of inhuman voices.

"That's the one!" Osbert was babbling. "That's the idiot who
stumbled into the hall. Strip him—you'll find the marks of my belt on
him. Didn't I tell you he was a spy? God's teeth, the gall of the man!
He turned around and changed his clothes and came back."

"He's only a boy," Ely said. He came down from his seat and stood
over Arslan, looking into his face. "I know you, too. What was your
master thinking, to send you here?"

"He didn't, your grace," Arslan said. "I was brought here by . . .
call it an act of God."

"God?" asked Ely. "Or the Devil?"

"Maybe both," Arslan said, "or neither. You're in great danger,
your grace."

"From you?"

"From what can destroy your soul."

"Are you threatening me?"

Arslan shook his head. "I think I was sent to protect you."

Ely laughed, incredulous. "You? All by yourself?"

"I did reckon it odd," Arslan said, "but who's to question the whim of heaven?"

"Enough of that," Osbert said. "He's a traitor any way you look at it. Will you hang him now, or will you insist on waiting till he has a trial?"

Ely ignored him. "Let him up," he said to the guards.

They obeyed, but they kept a grip on him. Arslan was not inclined to bolt. The gate was still inside him, but he could think around it and see through it. "You can shut me in a cell," he said. "It won't make any difference, though it might fuel a fire here and there. I'm no archbishop, but I'm of some value to the Count of Mortain."

"I hear you're more than that," Ely said. "He favors you. He's to knight you and give you a gift of lands in Somerset, with a noble wife to look after them for you."

Arslan raised his brows. "Your spies are excellent," he said.

"Aren't everyone's? You're not a spy, no. You're too obvious."

"It did amaze me," Arslan said, "how well a change of clothes served as a disguise."

"With maybe a little sorcery to help it." Ely met his stare. "My spies are excellent. You brought more from the east than knightly arts."

Arslan held his tongue. He had brought nothing but knightly arts and an inhuman heritage. All the rest, he had found here. But if Ely did not see it, it was not his place to speak of it.

"I'll hold you hostage," Ely said, "and bind you with your given word. I do believe you'll honor that."

Arslan bent his head. "Insofar as I can," he said, "I will honor it."

Osbert snorted in disgust. "That's no oath."

"Nevertheless I'll take it," Ely said. "Be a little respectful, Osbert. He could be the next king's favorite."

That reduced Osbert to sputtering incoherence. Arslan was rather taken aback himself. Of all things he had expected of this man, humor was not one of them.

Maybe it was not humor. Ely was a practical man. He would have to be, to hold the office he held. "Take him," he said to the guards, "and see that he is suitably dressed and housed and—"

"My lord!"

The voice was quiet, but it had in it a note that drew all eyes. Thibaut was standing among the clerks, glaring impartially at them all.

"My lord," he repeated, "of course it is your right to do with this man as you will, but we are severely shorthanded. He, whatever else he is, is an adequate servant. May we have him back, please, at least until you leave for London?"

"This is a nobleman and a squire," the bishop said. "He's hardly fit for the gentler pursuits."

"He's a fair-to-middling imitation of a clerk, my lord," Thibaut said, "and we need him. He's a hostage; shouldn't he be kept out of mischief? We can do that, and serve the kingdom, too."

"I'll do it," Arslan said, "if the lord bishop will agree."

"Very well," Ely said somewhat dubiously.

"Many thanks, my lord," Thibaut said, and that was heartfelt. To Arslan he said, "Back to work, boy. Or would you rather I called you 'messire'?"

"That would strain you unduly," Arslan said. "I won't ask it of you."

The corner of Thibaut's mouth twitched infinitesimally. "Work," he said. "Now. Messire."

Arslan bit back a grin and obeyed him.

# CHAPTER 27

❧

There was a guard on the door of the room where the clerks slept, who had not been there before. Arslan found that neither surprising nor disconcerting. It did not stop him, either, from waiting till all the others were asleep, putting on his clothes and the mantle that went with them, and slipping like a shadow past the guard. The man stood rigid, spear in hand, oblivious to Arslan's presence. He did not even twitch at the tiny, inevitable shifting of air as Arslan moved. Castles in England were drafty; their inhabitants learned to ignore any but the most authoritative blast.

Arslan glided down the passage. The stair was dangerous if he met anyone in passing: it was steep, narrow, and twisting. He had to hope that no one wandered the castle so late at night, or had a sudden need for that garderobe.

Hope held, or luck if he preferred to call it that. He came down into the courtyard without presenting some unsuspecting man-at-arms with an invisible but unmistakably solid obstacle. A hound or two shivered in a heap, for the air was damp and cold, but they did no more than lift their heads and sniff as he went past them. Dogs never had found him worth barking at, even dogs set on guard.

The outer gate was shut, barred, and secured until morning, but there was always a postern. It let Arslan out into chill starlight. He could taste winter in the wind that shrilled about the walls.

He poised on the shelf of stone and looked out over the moat. Taking a deep breath, he lightened himself almost to air, and walked across the water. He left no footprints amid the ruffling of wind.

When earth was solid under his feet again, he paused. The gate was still inside him, beating like a heart, drawing him away from the castle.

The way that he went, he remembered rather well. He had walked it in farmer's clothes, and before that naked, cast bodily out of the spirit's wandering.

He had come to earth, and into his body, almost on top of the hidden gate. Its strength had brought spirit and flesh together. Now as he approached it, it strove to undo what it had done.

He was prepared for that. All his wards and guards were up. He walked slowly round the place. It was a bit of wood like any in this part of England, a fragment of the king's forest, a thicket of ash and thorn. In its heart lay a clearing, and in the clearing an oak, as ancient as the one in Sherwood beneath which he had laid Yusuf's bones. In this tree as in that, the magic of Britain flowed up from the roots and grew green in the branches. The gate was caught in them.

It was not what he had expected. He had looked for a door, or an opening like the mouth of a cave; even a hollow in the treetrunk. But there was nothing like that here. It was a shimmer in the air, a ripple like a veil of water, only visible from the corner of the eye.

No wonder it was so difficult to close. A door could be shut, a cavemouth blocked, a hollow tree filled up or cut down. One could no more grasp this shimmer than one could touch the mirage.

He was not granted the power to end this thing. How even John would do it, he did not know.

That was for John to do—if he could be brought here. Arslan struggled against the softly clinging force of the gate. It sucked at him, drawing him in, eating away at his wards and protections. It hungered to taste the fire that was in him. But he was not its great concern, nor its purpose, either. It was trap and lure, set to draw a king to his kingdom, and the heart to the realm that for too long had had none.

Arslan stumbled, falling backward, scrambling in the thick mold of the wood. The threefold magic held him in its snare: oak and ash and thorn, the triune power of Britain, enclosing the gate in its heart. He flung himself away from it, mind and body, thrusting back the magic, closing out the siren song of the gate.

He was free, at least enough to walk away, stumbling only occasionally, and falling no more than three or four times. He had a dilemma: to find John on the road from Oxford, to find the Marshal in London—or to walk back toward Windsor and the one who had opened this gate, who even yet did not know what he had done.

On the way back to Windsor in the starlight, Arslan found a spirit that professed itself both willing and able to carry a message to John. Arslan did not dare hope it would succeed, but he had to try. He kept the message brief, and had the spirit repeat it thrice, to be sure it remembered: *I've found the gate. Find me in Windsor.*

When John found Arslan gone, his rage put even his father's legendary eruptions to shame. Even Eschiva was alarmed, and she was afraid of little in this world.

Her fear for Arslan was of another sort altogether. He had not left in the ordinary way. All of his belongings were as he had left them. The bed in which he had been sleeping showed the marks of his presence, but he was gone, vanished, removed from the world.

He was not dead. She would have known. But she could not find him. There was a trace of magic in the empty bedclothes, a lingering scent that told her far too little: only that it had been there, and he was gone.

Everybody fled John's wrath, but she stayed, waiting until he came to himself again. It did not take remarkably long. John was a cold enough man to keep a little sanity in the midst of a towering passion. "He didn't leave of his own will," she said quietly when John's rampage had stopped.

John surged toward her. She stood her ground. He dropped down in an untidy heap, planted elbows on knees and chin on fists, and glared.

One forgot that he was young; not greatly older than Arslan. The youngest of a potent brood, he had learned to match himself with the eldest and the cleverest. He had never been a child, not as other children were.

This morning, with his squire vanished and his escort waiting in varying degrees of patience for him to take the road, he suffered a most childlike fit of the sulks. "He promised me," he said. "He swore he wouldn't do it again."

"He didn't," she said. "I'm sure of that. He was taken. As to where—we'll find him. But not by sitting here, howling at the moon."

"Then how? I can't consume myself with this. There's too much that needs doing in the real world, never mind the world of ghosts and shadows."

"The world of ghosts and shadows is rising to rule the rest," Eschiva said. "I'm afraid it's taken him. If it takes me, you're without defenses. You have weapons—you're armed in ways no one would ever suspect—but I am your shield."

"So, should I keep you in my bed at night, and on the back of my horse by day? Or shall I wear you like an amulet?"

"I'd weigh heavy round your neck," she said.

He grinned, with the lightning change of mood that could be so startling to those who did not know him well. "And then I'd have your Turk hanging beside you, brandishing that fierce sword."

"That is not my—" Eschiva stopped. "Have you seen Karim since Arslan vanished?"

"Why, no," said John. "You don't think—"

"I don't know what I think, except that we'd best be on the road. Wherever either of them is now, we'll all foregather in the end, in Windsor or in London."

"If they're still alive."

"You know they are," she said. She held out her hand as if she had been a queen. He took it as the king he was, though it was in secret, and walked with her down to their waiting escort.

Kalila had not slept well since she was parted from Yusuf, and had hardly slept at all since he died. On the day that Arslan said Yusuf had become a sacrifice to the gods of Britain, she had stiffened in the midst of her archery practice, sent her arrow winging toward the sun, and dropped like a stone. Part of her had died then, and she had known why, though she had not faced it until Arslan told her what had become of her brother.

The night he vanished, she was feigning sleep. What woke her, she did not know. She had been lying in the hall with the rest of them, close by Arslan. When she opened her eyes, he was a huddle of blankets in dim lamplight. He lay utterly still.

She almost rose, almost went to him, struck with sudden fear; then he drew a breath, and she knew he was alive. She watched him even so, with the wariness that one learned in being a guard. This was not simple sleep.

When he vanished, it was as if the mirage of the desert had come to him, flowed over him and swallowed him. His blankets hung for a moment, empty of him, then sighed and collapsed.

She took up the bag of her belongings and rose fully clothed. Her mare was awake in the stable, as uneasy as she. She saddled and bridled the mare and led her out. The porter asked no questions, but opened the gate for her and bade her Godspeed. Whether he saw any irony in laying such a wish on a turbaned infidel, she did not know. She mounted and took up rein and rode where her heart led her.

Maybe Allah did the leading. She went in the direction that John had been riding: south and east. This was easy country to forage in, full of game, rich with fruits of the harvest. She tempted a band of robbers on the fourth day, poor-looking things with only a ribby horse or two among them; they fell on her out of a hedge and thought to pull her down by sheer numbers, but her mare had given her warning. She hacked off the hand of the first man to reach for her, spitted the second on her lance, and shot the third with an arrow aimed backward over her mare's tail, just as the horse broke free with the blinding speed of her kind. They did not go after her. They had been looking for easy prey, not a devil armed to the teeth and mounted on lightning.

The fight got her blood flowing wonderfully. She had been needing to kill something that could talk back to her; rabbits and deer were food, not foes. She rode on with a clearer mind, and a heart as steady as ever, turned toward her master as the lodestone to the north.

She did not know where she was going, or what people here called the towns and castles and villages she avoided in her riding. In another life or another world she would care, but in this one she knew only that he was at the end of her road. She lost count of the days, rode from sun or rain into dark, slept when she or the mare could not go on any farther. The mare was fat in this lush country; a few hours' grazing on rich grass sufficed for her, desert creature that she was.

Kalila found him in the dawn of another damp day, dressed in fusty black, walking down a road toward a town and a castle. Except for the garments that made him look like a none too prosperous priest, he was much as he had always been. His expression when he saw her was beautifully astonished, and then so suddenly, unreservedly glad that she could not regret a moment of that journey.

He mastered himself, of course, as did she. "John?" he asked. "He's here?"

"I doubt it," she said. "I left as soon as you did."

"*Ya Allah*," he said, for they were speaking Arabic, and his wonder was as great as his joy in seeing her. "They always did say a Seljuk could track a thought through thin air, but never till this day did I believe it."

It had not been a thought. It had been love. But she would die before she said such a thing. She held out a hand. He took it and swung up behind her, settling lightly on the crupper. The mare groaned a little, for his weight was considerable, but she was a sturdy thing for all her elegance. She carried them both easily enough.

He would not let Kalila enter Windsor with him. "Go to London," he said, "to the Lord Marshal. Tell him that the gate is found, and tell him I'm Ely's hostage. Serve him as you would me, till I come to London."

This was not a thing he would hear objections to. She had to watch him walk back across the moat, as easy as if it had been dry land, and disappear through the postern gate. As for London, she knew where and what it was, because when he bade her farewell, he gave her the kiss of peace; and in it was a spell.

*Ya Allah,* she thought. He did not love her as a woman, and he would never make her his wife, but she was useful to him as no other mortal could be. That was not a small thing. After she stopped wanting to kill him, she would be glad that she could serve him so well.

# CHAPTER 28

⁓

John would not reach Windsor before the bishop left it. That would hardly trouble him; wherever he found Ely, he would do the necessary. But Arslan was certain now that John needed to come to the gate—and soon. The Wild Magic was growing stronger. Whatever was outside, it must be waking, rising, turning its eyes toward Britain. It was more urgent than ever that Britain bind itself to its king.

Arslan had given his word. He could not in honor break it. He was a hostage until he came to the council.

One learned in war as in council to wait, to bide one's time; but it was never an easy thing. Arslan rode out of Windsor with no clear sense of what he would do. He had knowledge but no power. He could only pray that one of his messengers had succeeded, that the forces that ran wild through the heart and soul of Britain had not prevented them.

When he rode with John, he had ridden with a prince whose people were well disposed toward him. Whatever the high ones might say or think of John's ambitions, the common folk loved him. They loved his name, his lineage; they welcomed his presence and his knowledge of their names and faces, their language, the places they lived in and loved. John loved this land of England, and its people knew it.

Ely despised it. He would not learn even the simplest word of the English tongue; he scorned English efforts to speak French of any sort. *Cattle,* he called the common people; the burghers and the knights were swine. Because he was an honest man, he made no secret of his contempt.

The ride from Windsor to London was tense and silent. No one laughed or sang. When they rode through the villages, people stood by the roadside, watching, saying nothing. Sometimes a stone flew, or a clod of earth. If the guards saw who flung it, he was beaten and left as a lesson to the rest. If they did not see the culprit, they seized the nearest likely prospect and made an example of him instead.

Ely kept his head up and his eyes fixed forward. He wore cope and miter, and flew the banner of a papal legate beside the royal banner of England.

The clerks walked well back in the procession, behind the carts and wagons of the chancery. For Arslan, who had been born a horseman, this was not accustomed exercise. Someone should have noticed that a nobleman was walking with the clerks, but he had been for the most part forgotten once Ely found a suitable place to keep him. He said no word of complaint, nor demanded a horse as was his right.

The others took turns perching on the wagons, but he never did. He could walk; any man could. One foot in front of the other. That was the way of it. Where there was mud, and that was most of the way, he learned to walk without either slipping or miring himself in place. Where there was grass, or forest mold, he strode out as best he could, though that was not so easy once the blisters began.

They were three days on the road to London, between the slowness of foot pace, the muddy state of the roads, and the bishop's long pause to receive a messenger under the papal seal. He had his pavilion raised for that, to confer in privacy. When he came out, his face was ashen.

The Pope was dead. The new Pope had not confirmed him as a papal legate. He had lost the office of which he was most proud. That was a great blow, and he needed the rest of that day to recover, while his escort made camp on a hill in sight of the river that flowed down to London.

Arslan was cravenly glad of the reprieve. When he could escape the labor of putting up tents and building fires and preparing the daymeal, he went down to the river to bathe his feet. They looked worse than they felt; the water stung abominably, but it did wash off the worst of the blood. He dried them gingerly and put on a salve that he had bought from a village woman that morning. It was made with herbs and, from the feel and smell, goose fat; it was soothing, and it might even have helped the wounds heal.

As he was wrapping one of his feet in strips torn from his shirt, a shadow fell across him. "Soft as a girl, aren't you?" Thibaut said, inspecting his other foot, which he had not wrapped yet. It was a rather dismaying object, red and oozing with sores and glistening with salve.

For answer, Arslan held out his hands with their years-thick calluses from bow and lance and sword. "Would you like to see my backside?" he inquired.

"No, nor your ballocks, either." Thibaut squatted beside him, plucked the bandages from his fingers, and set to wrapping them about the outraged foot. He was quick and deft, and much lighter-handed than he looked. "In the morning, requisition yourself a horse. I'll write up the order and put the bishop's seal on it. Your lord will hold us to blame if you come hobbling into London on those feet."

"He won't; I won't let him." Arslan leaned back on his elbows and sighed while Thibaut wrapped his other foot. "They made us walk from Hattin. Most of us were barefoot. I had no skin on my feet at all when the sultan's brother picked me up and put me on his horse. I tried to knock his head off, but I was too weak. I was in a right rage—and he laughed at me. He took me to hunt lions, later on, and taught me a hundred love songs, and all the Surahs of the Koran."

God; he must be coming down with fever, if he was telling this man such things.

"You must have been barely weaned," Thibaut said, "if you were at Hattin."

"That was only four years ago," Arslan said. "I was twelve summers old—I turned thirteen in the sultan's house in Damascus. He offered to adopt me if I would profess Islam, or to make me one of his soldier-slaves if I persisted in clinging to my religion. But in the end he set me free, because, he said, the lion never thrives in a cage. He would be astonished if he knew where I am now." Arslan closed his eyes and sighed. "I wonder what he thinks of your English king."

"They probably appall one another," Thibaut said.

"Or they find each other fascinating." Arslan smiled in the dark behind his eyelids. "I should have liked to see them together."

"What's stopping you? Are you exiled?"

"Yes," Arslan said. "Yes, I am in exile." He said it without great regret. Somewhere between La Forêt and this green hillside, he had accepted the lot that God and the Powers had laid on him.

"You're an odd one," Thibaut said. "If you're going to lie here all the rest of the day, you can make yourself useful. I'll send one of the boys down with a pole and a line." He paused. "You do know how to fish?"

"I could learn," said Arslan.

"Remy will teach you," Thibaut said. "It's not lion-hunting, mind, or Surahs, whatever those are. But fish are good eating."

"Lion isn't," Arslan said, with the memory of that rank meat on his tongue.

"Odd," muttered Thibaut, but more amiably than not, as he went to fetch Remy and the fishing gear.

Arslan rode into London on a sturdy brown cob, with Remy the youngest clerk perched on his saddlebow. They did not throw stones here: they threw overripe fruit, handfuls of ordure, and eggs long past their prime. The words they flung with the redolent missiles were as richly scornful as any that Ely had laid on the people of England.

The bishop paid these people of London no more heed than he had the villagers. They were but offal, dogs that rolled in the mud of this turbulent city. The lords and princes of the Church—those mattered; and they, he was sure, would confirm him in his office. Had not Richard himself chosen him?

It was a noble arrogance. Perhaps it was even justified. Arslan was hardly lofty enough to judge.

The council waited in the palace of Westminster, in the royal house. Walter of Rouen led it; most of the great lords of England were there. But not William the Marshal. He was gone, no one would say where. And John had not yet come.

The Bishop of Ely was given a suite of rooms that had perforce to satisfy him. They were not, of course, the king's. "And I hope," he said sourly, "that the king's brother is not given them, either. He has ambition enough as it is."

That was the rumor everywhere in this place. John wanted to be king, had wanted it since before his brother was crowned. He did not expect that Richard would return from the Crusade; he was preparing himself already, winning over the people, courting the barons' favor, and riding back and forth across the kingdom as a king should do. The fact that he had not been named heir, that Richard had taken a queen, and that the young child Arthur, son of Richard's sister, had been named heir of Normandy and Anjou, did not matter to him, people said. John well knew the advantage of a royal heir of full and suitable age, clearly and visibly present, performing the duties that his brother was too far away and too preoccupied with his wars to perform.

All of that was true, and John was doing nothing to disprove it. He was taking his time in coming, too, causing the council to cool its heels day after day while he lingered on the road.

That was a dangerous game. Kings could play it. Princes might try, but the risks were high. John would know that very well; if there was anything he had a talent for, it was the game of kings.

It was odd, Arslan thought, but since he came to England he had not come into the midst of a great city or a royal court. John had been traveling the edges of the realm, knitting it together.

The center was a grand and tumultuous cesspit of a city, ripe with the reek of too many people crowded too close together with too little concern for cleanliness. Beside the cities of the east it was unspeakably squalid, though no more so than Paris or the half-abandoned ruin of Rome.

It was more than Arslan could bear. The one he had most hoped to see, the Marshal, was gone, and it seemed he had taken Kalila with him, if she had come to London at all.

He went to the bishop, catching him between Mass and the duties of chancery. At first Ely did not even recognize him. He truly had been forgotten, or set aside to be remembered when John appeared. Arslan was almost sorry for his honor that had kept him here; if he had gone, Ely would not even have noticed.

Arslan would have noticed. He offered proper respect, and as the bishop regarded him in bafflement, said, "Your grace, I'm the squire you've taken in safekeeping until the Count of Mortain arrives. I've come to ask for your indulgence."

Ely frowned at him. "You're still here? Why did I think you'd left?"

"I've been with the clerks, your grace," Arslan said, "where you gave me leave to be, since I was needed."

"You're no longer needed?"

"The clerks are up to strength now, your grace," said Arslan, "and my lord will come in his due time. I'm asking your leave to depart from London."

"Why would you be wanting to do that?"

"Three days, your grace," Arslan said. "Then I give you my word I will come back."

"Bring Prince John with you," Ely said, "and we have a bargain."

"I . . . can do that," said Arslan.

"Then go."

"You trust me?"

Ely looked into his face. "Yes," he said. "I do. You're better than he deserves, boy. I hope you know that, because it's highly doubtful he ever will."

"My lord knows himself very well, your grace," Arslan said. He bowed, correct as always. "In three days, your grace—with Prince John beside me."

It was raining, of course. The brown cob plodded resignedly through the mud and wet. Arslan in his clerk's gown, mantled in good English wool, was surprisingly comfortable. He had bought a pair of boots just the day before, with wages that he had been paid for his clerk's duties. They were stiff with newness but they kept his feet dry. He discovered that his heart was light—something that it had not been since Yusuf died.

Yusuf would have whooped and cheered. He had always hated long faces. Arslan caught himself smiling at the memory. That smile, in the end, was his best tribute, better than the grave beneath the oak, and better by far than the grief thereafter.

# CHAPTER 29

John was not riding in the rain. Never mind that it always rained in England, and that he had dragged his household through far worse storms than this one, drawn by whim or necessity. Today he was tenderly solicitous. He kept them in the little market town, which was barely large enough to contain them all, but its houses were warm and dry. Its mayor's house was warmest of all, as large almost as a lord's manor, and remarkably well appointed.

The mayor did not care that the granaries were empty and the storehouses nearly so. John paid well for what was to be had, and made certain that the mayor had a large share of the bounty.

They were still, at their best speed and leaving the bulk of the household behind, well over a day's ride from London. Eschiva had begun to wonder if, like Achilles and the tortoise, John would begin to take smaller and ever smaller steps until he stretched his journey to infinity.

He certainly seemed comfortable here, settled by the fire in a fur-lined gown, playing dice with some of his frequent companions. De Braose was losing, loudly. Brewer was holding his own. William Longsword and John were neck and neck for winner of the match.

Eschiva sat by a window of very good glass, just barely acceptable under the laws that separated nobles from commons, and stitched desultorily at a bit of embroidery. The window overlooked the broadest street of this town, one of several Cheapsfords scattered here and there through the middle of Britain. This Cheapsford was near Windsor and looked to it for lordship, which John knew very well. He had carefully refrained from passing by Windsor and demanding lodging there, although Ely was gone from the castle.

She leaned her cheek against one of the panes. It was cold, blurred as much with rain as with the bubbles and shimmers in the glass. Boredom was not a word she knew the meaning of, not in a world in which there was magic to watch for and nurture and wield, but her sigh had no contentment in it. She was weary of John's dallying; her bed was cold, her arms empty, and Arslan was God knew where.

People were out and about even in such weather, for this was a market town and a busy one at that, overseeing a lively trade up and down the river Thames. Her eye caught a rider, the only passer in the street who was mounted on a horse, a quite ordinary cob in plain and serviceable gear, ridden by a man in a cloak. He was a big man, wide in the shoulders, and he sat the cob with a lightness, even elegance, that better fitted a nobleman in silks than a commoner in plain English wool.

She did not even remember having risen to her feet, still less crossing the hall and running down the stair. Her heart was ruling her body all on its own, with her wits lagging far behind.

Arslan had barely halted in the little courtyard and dismounted from his horse when she came out into the drizzle of rain. The guards had recognized him—wise men; she would have turned them to toads if they had not. They were glad to see him, too, but not as glad as she.

She restrained herself, standing just outside the door, waiting for him to finish greeting the guards and handing his horse to a startled page. "I promised him a hot mash and a bowl of barley," he said to the boy. "I hope you'll keep my word for me."

The page nodded mutely. His eyes were huge.

"Good, then," Arslan said with that quick smile of his. It flattened the page, but he was no more aware of that than he ever was.

He turned and saw her. He was wearing a clerk's gown under the heavy woolen cloak. He was a little thinner, a little finer drawn; he was taller again, as if like a dragon he would grow until the fire of his spirit consumed him.

It was all in his eyes as they came to rest on her. No hearth could warm her as that glance did. She held out her hand. He came to kiss it, sinking to one knee, paying her homage in that damp and dreary place which, just then, was the most beautiful in the world.

Hand in hand they ascended to the hall, where John, having lost a purse of silver to Longsword, had flung the lot of them out and sat in lonely splendor by the fire. He was in a murderous mood, but at sight of Arslan he no longer wanted to kill his brother. He plucked Arslan from Eschiva's grasp, spun him unresisting about, and flung him against the wall. "God damn your eyes! *Where have you been?*"

"London," Arslan answered with some difficulty, for John's hand was clamped about his throat. "None of my messengers reached you?"

"Not a one," John snarled, "if you ever sent any."

Arslan set his lips together. He had an inhumanly equable temper, but that had been worn thin; by what, Eschiva expected to discover, if John would let him live so long.

He did not appear to move, but John cursed and fell back. Arslan straightened, moving away from the wall. "My lord," he said, "I found the gate."

"You what?" John blinked at him, caught between fury and cold clarity. "You found—how did you do that?"

"I fell into it," Arslan said, "as it seems you were about to. It's not far from here at all."

"You had better tell me everything," John said. His voice was flat. "Sit down. Get warm. Are you wet? Petit! Petit, where are you? Bring a warm gown—take Longsword's, he owes me, after what he did to me. God's feet, boy, how much bigger are you going to get?"

Petit found a robe and a servant with hot spiced wine, bread, apples stewed in honey, and a roast fowl. He stood like a fierce small dog, fending off even John, nor would he move until Arslan had eaten and drunk to his satisfaction.

From the way Arslan did both, Eschiva thought he might have been traveling on short commons, or have simply forgotten to eat. Some of the haggard look left him; he sat a little straighter, held himself a little steadier. He more than satisfied Petit's stringent requirements, ate every scrap in front of him and sat nursing his second cup of wine, breathing the fragrance of cloves and cinnamon, nutmeg and pepper.

John had calmed greatly while he ate. After Petit had left, taking the servant and the cups and bowls with him, John sat at Arslan's feet, arm across his knees, and smiled sweetly at him. "Now tell," he said.

Arslan told them everything, from the dream-wandering that had taken his body with it, to his entry into Windsor, to his dismissal from London and the bargain he had made. John heard him in silence, eyes fixed on his face. Sometimes they widened, sometimes narrowed, but he betrayed no other emotion.

By the time Arslan had finished, his cup was empty. John filled it again, absently. His eyes still had not left Arslan's face. "You," he said, "are a very clever creature. Can you tell me, clearly and succinctly, why I shouldn't have you put to death for treason? Entering my enemy's service, conspiring with him to take me captive—did you think I'd laugh and forgive it all, for love of your charming self?"

"No, my lord," Arslan said. "You can finish strangling me if you like, but first let me show you the gate. You should close it soon. Do you see how the fabric of Britain has frayed? Do you feel the gaps in the weaving?"

"I feel them," John said testily, "but surely it can wait until—"

"Until you've dragged your feet to London and played the bishop for a fool?" Arslan shook his head. "You can't leave it that long. It's almost too strong already. It's drawn you to it, and is holding you here. You think this is a game of princes, but think, my lord: Why here? Why not Oxford? Why not a castle that would suit your royal self better than this common house?"

"Maybe I'm in the mood for the common touch," John said, but Arslan's words had given him pause. "How am I supposed to close this thing? Is there a bar? A key?"

"I don't know," Arslan said.

They both turned to stare at Eschiva. She had been wondering if they remembered her. "There is a key," she said. "You'll know it when you come to it."

John scowled at her. "Don't be cryptic. I hate that."

She set her lips together and forbore to answer.

"In the morning," Arslan said, "can you slip away? No escort. Just the three of us?"

"It can be arranged," John said.

Eschiva had a room to herself: her privilege as the only lady in that riding, without even a maid to tend her. The mayor's wife had sent a girl to look after her needs, but the child had gone home before Arslan rode in.

That was a blessing, and pure good fortune. John said nothing when they left the hall hand in hand as they had come in. By the time they reached the door, for this was the mayor's own room, with a door and a lock and a vast featherbed, they were nearly at the run.

There was a fire in the hearth, and the bed was freshly made, strewn with herbs and rose petals. Eschiva barely noticed then; that came later, in the glow of the firelight, as they lay breathless in one another's arms. She could not stop running her fingers down his face, as if she had gone blind and must remember its every line and angle.

He closed his eyes and sighed. She let her hands wander down the length of him, meaning to tease him into rousing again. Instead she paused.

In that first white heat, she had known nothing but that he was there, he was hers, and they had been far too long apart. Now she looked at him—really looked—and made him turn on his face, though he protested.

Her breath hissed between her teeth. "Who? Who did this?"

He shrugged. It did not catch him with pain: the scars were well healed. "It doesn't matter. I brought it on myself."

"I'll kill him," she said.

He rolled onto his back again, wide-eyed. "Don't do that. He's not worth the trouble."

"He *flogged* you." She was almost weeping, but they were tears of rage. "He shamed you. He—"

"If a thing as small as that can shame me," he said, "then I'm much less than I was raised to be."

She blinked through the blur of tears. So often, as much as she loved him, she thought of him as a boy, a beautiful child who happened to belong to her. Then he would speak as he spoke now, and she would understand yet again that he was not a child at all.

"When the walls of air are raised again," she said, "and we've come to London, let's do it. Let's have the banns read, and ask my uncle to say the words. I want to be your lady wife."

"Why? For pity?"

That was a boy's pride, and his temper, too. She kissed it out of him. "For love," she said. "For sheer mortal lust. And because I want it. I want you."

"Isn't it a sin to marry for love?"

"Better to marry than to burn."

"But the fire is so sweet."

His hands cupped her breasts. "Sweeter than honey," she said, breathless. He had risen again—blessed youth, to recover so swiftly. She mounted him, gasping as he drove deep. "Will you?"

"Will I what?" He sounded faint, and rather distracted.

"Will you marry me?"

"Yes." It was a sigh. "Of course. Why would you think—"

"Never mind." She kissed him long and slow, until there was nothing in the world but the two of them, and all else vanished away.

# CHAPTER 30

❦

John was waiting when they came down, carefully refraining from comment at the reluctance with which they moved apart. Horses were saddled in the courtyard, supplied with all the needs for a ride of indefinite duration: water, provisions, a packhorse. The brown cob did that duty; Arslan's own grey mare was waiting for him, in his own gear, and an air of such injured dignity that he took a moment to soothe it as he could. She would forgive him in the end, but not before she had punished him with the lash of her disdain.

She let him ride her, at least, and it was not raining, which was a wonder and a marvel. They rode out in the misty dawn, unseen and unremarked, except by the guard who had been paid well above and beyond his wonted wages to help them on their way, and to keep silence after they were gone.

Autumn was well set in. This green country would barely fade even for the chill of winter, but the leaves in the copses had turned to bronze and gold. They were luminous in the pale sunlight, shimmering in the fading mist.

As the sun rose higher, the air grew warmer, as if for a little while it remembered summer. Arslan kept his cloak, but John and Eschiva took off theirs. She had bound up her hair as was proper, but a wicked gust of wind plucked away the veil and sent the coppery plait tumbling to the Arab mare's rump.

She blushed gloriously, but the veil was long gone. John gallantly lent her his hat. It gave her a look of rakish elegance, and made Arslan ache to seize her then and there, and tumble with her in the grass.

John's presence made certain that the thought remained only a thought. He rode ahead after that, still keeping within reach, but riding as if to a clear destination.

The gate was near. Arslan glanced at Eschiva. She sensed it, too: the blush had left her cheeks, and her laughter had died. Their horses moved together; their hands met and clasped.

He caught his breath. As strong as the gate's call had been while he rode apart from her, now that they were joined, it was like the peal of a trumpet.

She was as startled as he. With tearing reluctance they let go one another's hand. The call faded.

John had widened the distance between them. He was caught in a spell.

Eschiva had seen it. In the same instant they urged their mares to quicken the pace. The horses snorted, tossing their heads, jibbing against a force like a blast of wind.

Desperately Arslan reached across immeasurable space. His fingers brushed hers, slipped, caught hold. The wind buffeted them, but together they were too strong for it.

He tugged, catching her, swinging her onto his saddlebow. She was warm and solid in his arms. The Arab mare, relieved of her weight, ran more lightly at the side of Arslan's taller, heavier, stronger grey. They were closing in on John, but not quickly enough.

The thicket of ash and thorn drew nearer, the oak invisible in its heart, but the gate was thrumming now, shaking the earth. Things were beating against it, tearing at it to make it wider. Huge things, monstrous things, hungry for the earth and the warm rich blood of its creatures.

They would use John, the power that was in him, untutored yet, unfocused. He who had come here to shut the gate and so seal himself to Britain, would burst it wholly asunder, and dissolve forever the barrier between the worlds.

Arslan begged his mare for more speed. She, great heart, flattened her ears and stretched her neck and lengthened her stride. He gave her as much strength as he dared, pouring it out through his hand on her neck.

John was in the wood. The mare was close on his horse's tail, her breeding showing as the heavier English horse began to falter.

A flash of white caught Arslan's eye. The Arab mare sped past him, swerved in toward John. He caught the flying mane and swung onto her back.

She was desert-bred, swift as wind in the grass. But Arslan's cross-bred mare clung close behind, even as John's gelding dropped to a stumbling trot. Arslan forgot him, focused wholly on the chase.

They burst together into the clearing, running nose to tail. The Arab mare dropped her haunches and slid, rearing away from the thing that was no longer an oak tree. The oak was visible in its heart, but the whole of it was a throbbing shimmer.

Arslan's mare veered before she collided with her sister, wheeling, scrambling for balance in the damp grass. Eschiva launched herself from the saddlebow, spun like a tumbler, and came to earth on her feet. Arslan had no time to gape. Only the Arab mare's resistance prevented John from riding headlong into the gate.

Arslan reached blindly inside himself, once, twice, thrice. To his astonishment, nothing hindered him. Every power in this place was fixed upon John.

Three figures appeared in the clearing: Bishop Hugh in full pontificals as if he had been caught in the midst of the Mass, William the Marshal in armor and great helm with his sword in his hands, Hugh Neville in hunting garb with bow and quiver and long knife. Eschiva made a fourth, taking the station of the east, with the morning sun blazing on her uncovered hair.

All four guardians of Britain raised their hands at once. Each spoke a word that rang like a gong. The gate echoed them in a fourfold note.

"Shut it," Arslan said to John, not raising his voice, but putting in it a crack of command. "Shut the gate."

The mare had settled to a quivering, wild-eyed stillness. John looked much the same. "Shut it?" he echoed. "But I don't know—"

"Shut the gate," Arslan said again, merciless.

Deep in the gate, a Thing moved. It was vast and sinuous. It rolled lazily as if in water, blinking a great pallid eye. John flung up both hands, smote them together, and loosed a sharp, wordless cry.

The seams of the world began to tear. Arslan glimpsed what lay beneath: horror; dissolution. He wrenched his eyes and mind away, reached across the space between them, and shook John till his teeth rattled in his head. "*Again!* Shut the gate!"

John's gasp was like a sob. The power beating on him was terrible, overwhelming. Even the guardians could not hold it back. Again he raised his hands. This time he brought them together more slowly, shaking with effort.

The gate surged and writhed against him. Arslan poised quite calmly on the edge of madness. "Again," he said, soft, hardly more than a whisper.

John hissed at him, but yet a third time he gathered his strength, got a grip on the edges of the world, and by sheer force of outraged temper drew them shut. The Things within thrust against him. A talon as large as the oak ripped through the barrier, tore into the earth, and barely missed John's trembling horse. John reared up, and gathered the rage that was in him, and hurled it at the monstrous invader. It seared the talon to ash, and roared through the dwindling gap, and charred the Things within. Their howls of pain split the sky.

John slammed the gate shut, locked and barred it, and sealed it with the fire of his wrath. For a moment longer the gate shimmered in the air, then softly, all but invisibly, it shrank upon itself. A moment longer, and it was gone.

Out of the absence where it had been, after a vast and singing pause, grew and unfurled and blossomed the walls of air. They were like veils of light, yet they rose as high and strong and impregnable as the ramparts of the world.

John was their heart, their center. His presence wrought them; his strength sustained them. His kingship was complete.

The clearing was still. The sun shone. Somewhere in the wood, a bird ventured a tentative note. After a pause, it dared another, and then a third, and thereafter a rippling, soaring scale.

Where the gate had been, the oak stood as it had for a thousand years, spreading its arms to the sun. The world was solid again. Inside Arslan was a memory fading to dream.

The guardians came together from the four quarters. They seemed somewhat dazed. They all, every one, bowed low before John. "My lord king," each of them said. It was true homage, and true crowning—far more so than the taking of scepter or crown. This day, in this place, John was true king of all Britain.

While the king and his guardians held council under the oak, Arslan found John's gelding and the cob grazing together outside the thicket of ash and thorn. He led them in, hobbled them near the mares, and laid out the small feast they had brought. Like any good servant, he made sure he was invisible, until Father Hugh caught him just as he finished pouring wine into cups. He had been going to efface himself, but the gesture drew every eye to him.

The slow heat climbed his cheeks. Although no one had yet spoken, he had a peculiar and pressing desire to run away into the wood.

"This is your doing," Father Hugh said. "Sit and be one of us; I think it's past time you pretended to be anything else."

Arslan sat with a faint sigh. It seemed he was not to be taken to task quite yet for presuming to marry this man's niece.

He had relaxed too soon. Father Hugh smiled at him, rather too sweetly, and said, "What is this I hear? You have designs on something that belongs to me?"

Arslan glanced at Eschiva. Her eyes were lowered; she looked remarkably demure. For some reason that did not comfort him. "I love her," he said. "She asked me to marry her. Should I refuse a lady?"

"She'll not be marrying a landless man," Hugh said, "and I'll not give her to a squire, however nobly bred."

"That will be remedied," said John, "as soon as we come to London."

"I will have him, Uncle," Eschiva said, just as sweet and just as implacable as her kinsman. "I choose him for myself, as is granted me by the blood I bear. Do you oppose me?"

"You know I cannot," Father Hugh said. "But as your guardian I must beg you to consider—"

"I have considered," she said, "that this is the favored servant of a king, soon to be knighted and given lands, and possessed of magic the like of which few of us have seen. But for him, the walls would still be down; Britain would still be without the full power of its king. Is he not owed a debt of gratitude? Am I not sufficient to pay it?"

"You are more than sufficient," Hugh said.

"Good," she said in satisfaction. "It's decided. Will you say the words, Uncle—here, in this place, which is consecrated to the Powers of Britain?"

Hugh knew her too well to be startled. He was not as distressed as he pretended, either: Arslan caught the quick flash of a smile. He was only doing his duty, looking after her as a good uncle should.

Eschiva drew Arslan to his feet—and he was lucky not to trip over them; they felt, of a sudden, vastly too large. Her smile made his heart melt.

"Well," Hugh said dryly, "I don't need to ask what the bride-groom thinks of it all."

Arslan ducked his head, battling a furious blush. They were all laughing at him, but with no malice in it.

They stood under the oak, with the sun dappling them with gold, and the pure spirit of Britain singing all about them. With the gate gone, the air was full of small bright spirits and wild with birds.

John, as king, led them to Father Hugh. He, as priest, joined their hands together. The Marshal bound them with a chain of gold, the Forester with a garland of autumn leaves.

They spoke their vows to one another in the old way, plighting troth in the names of the old gods and the new. Arslan barely re-membered the words even as he spoke them. Her hands in his, her eyes on his face, the deep joy in them, were all that he knew, and all that he cared to know.

He came to himself with a start, to find John face to face with him. "Kneel," John said.

Arslan barely had time to obey before the blow struck him: a right royal buffet and a glorious box on the ear, which rang for an hour after. Through the ringing he felt John bind his heels with John's own spurs, with which that prince was very free, and say to him, "Rise, messire, and live in honor, as a true knight should."

Arslan reeled to his feet. John held him up on one side, Eschiva on the other, until he had steadied. He was grinning like the idiot he sometimes pretended to be.

"Now you're trapped right good and proper," Hugh Neville said: "Husband and knight at once—you'll be lucky if you ever breathe free again."

"It seems to be a willing captivity," the Marshal observed. He laid a heavy arm about Arslan's shoulders. "Now, my young lord. I don't suppose you could send me back to Salisbury? I'll have a great deal of explaining to do as it is—you plucked me right off the tilting field."

"And I," said Father Hugh, "vanished in the midst of the Mass. They'll be calling me a saint now for good and all, and a crashing nui-sance that is, too."

Arslan could find no words to say. He was still dazed by it all, and dizzy from the accolade. But there was still, inside of him, the knowl-edge that had come with the gate but had not gone away with it. It was like a pattern of tiles on a floor, a vision of roads—of straight tracks through the length and breadth of Britain. One had a flavor of the Marshal about it, and one made him think clearly of Father Hugh; a third belonged to Hugh Neville, a green forest track. He opened them as if they had been doors, and let them take each man in his turn.

Then there were only the three of them in the still-warm sunlight. It was not yet even noon, though they had lived lifetimes since they rode here in the dawn.

John was standing by the oak. His expression was odd. There was no suspicion in it, Arslan realized; no lines of calculation. It was as open and clear and simple as any ordinary man's. All through him, as Arslan looked inward, were the bright lines of the leys, the straight tracks. For this moment he was Britain. He was full of her beauty and power, and the purity of her spirit.

He wept as he came back to his flawed and human, but unmistakably royal self. But a part of him remained in Britain, and he in her. That brightness touched him, made him stand a little taller, seem a little more beautiful.

Arslan knelt in the fullness of his heart, set his hands in John's, and said, "My lord, I give you my heart and hand, my honor, my duty, all that is mine to give and to keep, in love and in fealty, as my liege lord, for as long as we both shall live."

John's eyes widened in startlement, but he was nothing if not quick-witted. "Messire, I give you my heart and hand, my honor, my duty, all that is mine to keep and to give, in love and in fealty, as your liege lord, for as long as we both shall live."

Arslan bowed over their joined hands. John kissed his brow; he kissed John's hand.

"I hope you don't regret this bargain," John said as Arslan rose, unfolding up and up, so much taller than he that he laughed even as he spoke.

"I may regret it," Arslan said, "but I'll never betray it."

"No," said John. "Not you. You never will."

"I hope you won't regret me, either," Eschiva said that night.

It had been a splendid wedding night, though no one there knew of it but John. There would be a formal betrothal in London, and a proper reading of banns, and vows spoken at the church door: all the trappings of Christian and noble marriage. But tonight, in secret, they were truly wedded.

"You," said Arslan, "I won't ever regret."

"Nor I you," she said. Her smile was as rich as cream. She was well content with this bargain that she had made.

# CHAPTER 31

A rslan kept his word. On the third day after he left London, he rode back into it at John's right hand, with the whole of John's household in its train behind.

This was a far different entry than that with the Bishop of Ely. The streets were lined with people, shouting and cheering; the missiles that flew were garlands of flowers. Banners unfurled from the rooftops; veils and kerchiefs fluttered from the windows.

By force of his oath, John could not ride crowned, nor carry the scepter where mortals could see, but he caught a garland of blood-red roses wound in leaves of bay, and so crowned himself. The splendor of the gate's shutting was still on him. He was glorious, royal, altogether a king. The farther into the city he rode, the greater was the roar of welcome.

The council waited in Westminster as it had for weeks now, in patience stretched to the breaking point. The extravagance of the people's display did not sit well with Ely and his allies, but the barons seemed pleased. John had cast in his lot with them; his high favor with the people could only help their cause.

He swept in in royal state, and as Ely had predicted, took the king's apartments—though not the king's own chamber. That he left empty, as if to prove false the rumors that he did not expect his brother to return to England.

The Bishop of Ely had retreated to the Tower of London. He was ill, his messengers said. Sick with fear, said the wags in the city, and with good cause. The streets were in uproar. Mobs had begun to gather below the Tower's walls, flinging stones and bits of ordure, and chanting invective that grew more scurrilous the longer it went on.

The Tower was shut against them all, even the messengers from the council, who struggled through at no little cost to life and limb, and found blank walls and barred gates. Night fell on the impasse; the streets were full of torches, and men running, milling in confusion.

All night long the mob surged and ebbed, and the Tower stood silent, grim and impenetrable. In the morning, John led the council to the Tower. He sent a herald ahead to call out in a strong voice: "William Longchamp! You are summoned."

The crowd took up the cry, beating against the walls. After what seemed a long while but was not so long by the angle of the sun, a small crooked figure limped out onto the battlements and stood above the gate. At sight of him, the mob roared like a beast.

He looked down at them, an army ten thousand strong. There was no one with him. He stood alone.

After a long while the crowd quieted. "My lord bishop," John said. "It's a pleasure to see you again at last. Though I'm not sure it's a pleasure my poor brother would share."

The snarl of the mob went on and on, even through Ely's haughty response. "The king gave me power to rule in his name. I carry out my duties as he would wish."

"Why, certainly," John drawled, "and he'd make sure he tossed a meaty bone or two or three or six to his brothers, too. But, my lord, you are not the king, and you are not granted his right of ruling by whim as well as law. How many counties can a man be sheriff of, after all, before he loses track of which is which?"

Ely's glare was pure poison. This was more than dislike, and worse than dissent. This was hate.

John, for his part, obviously cared too little for this man to indulge in anything so strenuous as hatred. He made no effort whatever to hide his contempt. "Let it be, my lord bishop," he said. "Give the lands and revenues back to the Crown, and let the council look after them. Don't you have records to copy? Accounts to render? Go on, don't let us keep you. We know how busy a man you must be."

"Whereas you," Ely said through a throat thick with bile, "can dally about hither and yon, and never a thought or a worry in the world except the procuring of a woman for your night's amusement."

"Women," John said, smiling. "One is seldom enough, unless I'm terribly worn with the day's exertions."

That won laughter from the crowd and a black scowl from the

bishop. "Mock me as you will," he said. "I am still your brother's justiciar in this kingdom. And you, sir, are neither his heir nor his
regent."

John's face darkened at that, but fleetingly. "No, but I am his
brother, and a lord of the realm in my own right. You are only what
his charter makes you. He can unmake you with a word."

Walter of Rouen sighed audibly, drawing all their eyes. He had been
watching and listening with an air of detachment that suddenly became
comprehensible. "I had hoped," he said, "that this would not be necessary. But since there seems to be no help for it . . ."

He nodded to the clerk who stood close behind him. The clerk
bowed and produced a folded sheet of vellum from his scrip. The richness of it, the plethora of pendant seals, marked its importance. He
read from it with grand flourishes, turning the courtly Latin into a
sonorous chant. "We, Richard, King of the English, Duke of Normandy, Count of Maine and Anjou, and so on and so forth, do hereby
declare by this writ that this man, Walter of Coutances, Bishop of
Rouen, is lord justiciar of England, empowered by us to speak in all
ways as if he were our right royal self. We do further declare that
William Longchamp, Bishop of Ely, be removed from that same power
and office, which if he should refuse, we do empower aforesaid Walter
of Coutances to summarily remove and abjure him from that office."

A deep silence had fallen. Ely's face had drained of color. There
was more, in the prolix manner of these things, but the worst of it was
there, in the beginning.

"No," Ely said. He did not say it loudly, yet it was clear in the
breathless stillness. "This is false, a lie. You plotted this," he said to
John. "You did this. I will not succumb to it."

Arslan had been watching Ely, but some prickle of warning drew
his eyes toward John. He was astonished by what he saw there. John
was as profoundly outraged as the bishop was. This served him admirably, and rid the kingdom of a great danger to mortal and fey
alike, and yet he was shaking with fury.

John must have been hoping—even expecting—to be named regent once Ely was disposed of. Why he should think that, knowing
Richard, Arslan could not imagine. Richard in a weak moment might
have revoked John's exile, but even if he would have done more, his
mother would have prevented him. Neither of them trusted the
youngest of Henry's sons.

Either Walter was oblivious, or he chose not to see who else was taken aback by the secret he had been keeping. When his clerk finished reading the king's charter, he smiled at them all. "So, my lords and good people of London. The king has spoken. He does regret it, my lord of Ely, but he believes that this is best for England and for you."

"I do not accept it," Ely said. "I will not step down. This office was given me by the king himself. Only the king himself, in his own person, may take it away."

"This is the king's word," said Walter. "It was given to me in the event that there was no other expedient. My lord, if you will not accept, I have no choice but to declare you apostate and place your see under Interdict. For your people's sake if not for your own, I implore you to reconsider."

"No," said Ely. "I will not. This office is mine. You cannot take it from me."

The mob laughed loud and long. There was little true mirth in it, and a great deal of malice. They had seen what Ely could not yet be aware of: that the gate beneath his feet had begun to open. Ely's men were the king's men—he had chosen them for that, and bound them to it. Now, because of that binding, they were Walter's men. They opened the Tower to him, and captured the bishop and brought him down, and gave him into Walter's hands.

He said not one word. That was the wisest thing he had done since all this began, but as with much else in the world, it was too little and too late.

Ely was not shut in a dungeon; he merited that much consideration still. He was imprisoned in his own chambers, secure under guard. Arslan in a clerk's gown, clutching an armful of books and parchments, was admitted with a cursory glance.

The bishop was praying in his chapel. It was true devotion; the light of it shone in the candlelit space.

He was as much a lodestone for magic as he had ever been. The chapel was full of spirits, drifting in air, watching him as he prayed. Many of them streamed toward Arslan when he paused by the door, whirled in a dance of greeting, but then went back to their contemplation of this man who was, to their eyes, a vast and irresistible emptiness.

There was no one with him. Many of his followers had melted away. Those who remained were huddled in corners, muttering among themselves. More would leave before the day was out. Of the clerks, only a handful were still there; the rest had gone with the chancery to the Bishop of Rouen.

Arslan found Thibaut in the emptied workroom, packing up the books of the Rolls to be handed over to Walter's care. He greeted Arslan with a grunt. "Fetch me that box, will you?"

Arslan fetched the box, then filled it with documents as Thibaut instructed. It mattered to neither of them that he had come up in the world since last they met. Thibaut's world was his work. He would go where the work went, and serve it to the best of his ability. "Lords come and go," he said as he paused between boxes, "but this endures. When the world ends, it's not the princes who will be left standing, but the clerks with their parchment."

"That's some men's vision of hell," Arslan said.

"Yours?"

"No," said Arslan.

Thibaut snorted. "Pass those ink bottles."

When the last box was full and the porters had come to take it all away, Thibaut went with them. There was no farewell. He was going to pretend to be in Walter's service, where the work was, and the everlasting duties of chancery.

The bishop was still in the chapel. His chambers were all but empty now, but something in the air made Arslan's hackles rise.

Ely had come out of the half trance of prayer. As Arslan paused once more in the doorway, he rose painfully to his feet. He had never been a large man, but he had shrunk; his shoulders were bent, his face haggard. More than a simple office had been taken from him.

Still, he was not broken yet. He started as he caught sight of Arslan, and his face stiffened, but not with fear. "Have you come to take me to the executioner?" he demanded.

"I hadn't known there was to be an execution, your grace," Arslan said.

Ely's lips twisted. "Does the mob need a formal judgment?"

"You're safe in this place."

"And when the council ends, when the lords go their various ways? Ely is a long ride from here, and a good part of London to cross before I even begin the journey. Are you a gambling man, messire? What would you lay on my coming alive out of the city?"

Arslan had been thinking this man's arrogance blind, but whatever else it was, it was not that. The mood in the city was dangerous. Celebration could turn ugly if they came upon the one whose defeat they celebrated. Men had died before, rent asunder by the mob, nor was his holy office a protection. Even popes had fallen before the people's rage.

Something was feeding it. The barons' malice, yes, but a spirit of mischief, too. Even without the gate, the Wild Magic was strong in this country. London gave it rich pasturage. The poor, the angry, the mad, all gathered here, and with them the seeds of pestilence in both body and spirit.

"Get me out of here," Ely said. He was shaking. "Get me . . . out."

Arslan could hear the roar outside. They were howling Ely's name. The blind bloodlust was on them, that could turn men into beasts. They needed no sense or reason; they only wanted his blood.

"But you haven't done anything," Arslan said, "except be arrogant where you should have been circumspect."

Ely smiled thinly. "With those stiff-necked cattle, that is more than enough."

"Stay here, your grace," Arslan said with sudden decision. "Pray now for your life's sake. I'll come back as soon as I can."

"Come soon," said Ely, "before someone conveniently forgets to bar a gate."

"My word on it," said Arslan.

Eschiva heard him out without laughing in his face, which was remarkably charitable of her. Rather to his amazement she said, "He is in danger, and more so the longer he stays here. He won't be safe in Ely, either. England hates him too well."

"But how—"

"Leave it to me," she said. "Only promise. Do everything I tell you, exactly, and ask no questions."

He bowed over her hand, taking the opportunity to steal a kiss.

She did not toss him off, but her smile was preoccupied. "Go and fetch him. Bring him here. Be sure no one sees you—even the spirits, if you can do as much."

"I can try," he said.

"Then go," said Eschiva.

# CHAPTER 32

⌯∽

Eschiva would wonder forever after how she came to be in this predicament. The mob was howling at the gates, the object of their detestation was cowering within in guarded rooms, and she looked into Arslan's wide grey eyes and agreed to get the man out of London. She owed the bishop nothing but the most dire recompense for the things he had done in Britain. And this thing that he was, this lure to magic—should it be safe? Was it not better dead?

Arslan did not think so. She grew dizzy when she looked at him; sense began to seem like folly, and reason seemed ridiculous. He saw the man's death in the streets of London, torn apart by a mob that, if anyone had asked it, would have given no coherent answer as to why it had killed him. Gentle soul that he was, Arslan could not bear the thought.

She was not gentle, but she loved him immoderately. She made her preparations, gathered what she needed, and sent messages to certain persons. While she did that, the roar of the crowd sharpened. It had got hold of someone vulnerable, whom it could proclaim to be a toady of the deposed justiciar. He died a little too slowly for mercy.

The lords were doing nothing to quell the riot. John, who could have done it with a word, was indisposed—with a woman or two or three, she had no doubt, and a cask of good wine, and the pack of his familiars. It would suit him very well to dispose of William Longchamp at the hands of the London mob.

Geoffrey Plantagenet was already free, she had heard, and riding from Dover. When he reached London, there would indeed be no mercy. Churchman or not, Geoffrey was old Henry's son, and his memory for an injury was long and bitter.

When she had been waiting long enough to be uneasy, Arslan

slipped through the door of the rooms she had claimed in the Tower, leading a small limping figure by the arm. The cloak of shadows was nearly gone, but she caught a final glimpse of it, reflected in Ely's staring eyes.

They widened even more when he saw where he was, and who was waiting. His poor memory for faces was notorious, but it seemed she was more memorable than most. "You! The witch from Somerset, the count's whore. Then this is not—"

"My lady wife," Arslan said, smooth as glass.

Ely struggled against his grip. "I've been betrayed. Curse you! Damn you to—"

"Be quiet," said Eschiva. She put no particular power in it, but his mouth snapped shut. She looked him up and down. "You're smaller than I remembered. Good. Take him, my lord, and bathe him—the water's drawn, everything's waiting. Be sure you shave him well."

Ely clearly expected to have his throat cut, but he said no further word as Arslan led him into the inner room. When they returned, the bishop several shades lighter and considerably sweeter-scented, with his rough cheeks shaven as smooth as a razor could make them, she had everything ready for him.

Ely did cry out then. "Good God! This is against nature. This is against Scripture. This—"

"This will bring you alive out of London," Arslan said. He had widened his eyes, too, but in amusement rather than horror.

The Bishop of Ely made a strikingly ugly woman, but a surprisingly convincing one. For once his low stature served him well. In veil and wimple, with a woolen cloak and a laden market basket, he was the very image of an elderly nurse or serving maid.

"Now," said Eschiva, surveying her handiwork, "for your life's sake, play this part as I bid you, and keep your curses to yourself."

Ely glowered at her. It galled him sorely to owe her this debt—and that pleased her rather considerably.

Arslan in his clerk's gown once again, Eschiva dressed as a lady's maid, and the Bishop of Ely between them, left the Tower by the most inconspicuous of its posterns. The mob was storming the greater gates, and either did not know or did not care that this small door was there. Eschiva helped a little with that: a word, a wishing, turning minds away from that part of the wall. Arslan sent a gaggle of spirits after them, given free rein to tease and torment as they would. In a little while, the whole mob was baying after a phantom with Ely's face.

They smiled at one another with warmth that could have risen to heat, but for the man between them and the still-significant danger. Not only London was the threat. If any of the lords in the Tower knew what they did—if John learned of it before it was done—they would pay the price of treason.

A boat was waiting in the river, with a boatman who happened to be distant kin to Eschiva. He dared not wait for them close by the Tower; he was some distance downriver. They had to pass through the city, walking openly in the daylight, praying not to be recognized.

Away from the Tower, the celebration had died down. Men of the watch had been out breaking heads, driving the rabble indoors and keeping order everywhere but in the quarter nearest the Tower. That surprised Eschiva not at all. The ordinary commerce of London was going on along the river, a bustle of boats at the quays, and people crowding the streets.

Everyone skirted wide round officers of the watch. They were out in force still, prowling like wolves among the sheep. They were look-ing for signs of suspicion, peering at faces, stopping random passersby. If one troubled them excessively, they beat him and left him as a warn-ing—and that, like the riot around the palace, attracted no notice from the commanders who should have kept them in hand.

Eschiva kept her head down. Arslan diminished himself remark-ably; he would never be small, but he could draw the eye away and cloud the mind until one forgot that he was there. The one between them, the small shriveled figure with the large basket, attracted the least notice of any. There were a hundred like it in these streets.

They breathed a little easier with each step they took away from the Tower. The boat was waiting a Roman mile downriver, hidden among a flock of its kin. Eschiva could see it as they came down the road, and the boatman in it, evidently asleep, with his hat over his face.

A company of the watch dallied about the quay, exchanging in-sults with the boatmen on the river. Their banter was not entirely amiable. Rather than trouble themselves to bring the quarrel onto the water, the men of the watch relieved their tempers among the people on the road.

They were as solid a barrier as an army in a mountain pass, and the boat was on the other side of them. Eschiva alone could have taken to the river, but she doubted that the bishop could swim.

Arslan's glance caught hers. She raised a brow. He nodded infinitesimally. Even she could marvel at how smoothly, how completely he vanished.

Ely loosed a strangled squawk. She caught him before he bolted, and stopped his mouth with her hand. "Quiet! Walk easily. We're innocents; there's no guilt in us. No man of the watch need spare us a glance."

"Certainly I am an innocent!" he spat at her. "God, that I trusted myself to a pair of witches—sweet Mother Mary help my immortal soul."

It would have been remarkably easy to strangle him and pitch his body into the river. But for Arslan's soft heart, she would have done it.

She did close her fingers about his throat, leaning over him, hissing in his ear. "That witch is saving your miserable life, though why he should want to bother, I for one cannot imagine. It's your fault he's in this country at all, and your fault we're all in this danger. Now shut your mouth and play your part, and pray he doesn't get killed creating this diversion—because by God's feet, if he dies, I shall feed you to the fish."

He stared at her as if she had lost her wits, which she supposed she had. She got a grip on his arm, making no effort to be gentle, and cast her glance across the crowd on the bank. The men of the watch had seen something near the bend of the river that drew them in a pack. Eschiva could not see what it was, nor take time to discover. The road was open; people were streaming down it, as relieved as she to escape the notice of those armed and idle men.

She dragged Ely with her into the midst of the crowd. The boatman was awake, moving lazily, edging his boat toward the bank.

Ely stumbled. The basket flew out of his hand, scattering all that had been in it. A howl marked the place where the purse of silver had spilled out on the ground. He lunged toward it. It was all she could do to keep her hold on him and keep him moving toward the river.

They came to it none too soon. She heaved him up unceremoniously and flung him into the boat. Bran the boatman grinned at her. She bared her teeth in response. "You may want to bind and gag him and stow him with the cargo."

"I'll keep him safe," said Bran, whose face showed a sheen of scales when the sun struck it. "I'll sing him the songs of Lir."

This time her smile was real, slow and wicked. "Oh, yes. Do that."

"We'll get him over sea," said her kinsman, "and see that he's delivered safe to Normandy. Look to yourself, cousin, and to that lion's cub of yours."

Bran pushed off from the bank. His passenger had righted himself and huddled in the boat, pressed up against a bale of wool. There was no gratitude in those glittering eyes, but she had expected none. She turned her back on him and forgot him. Her lion's cub, as Bran had called him, was loose in the city; if he had been harmed, even to a hair of his head, she would exact payment.

The watch had left the river; the boatmen had turned their attention to other things. Eschiva tracked Arslan by the memory of him in the air, the kiss of fire, the trail of spirits tasting the richness of this crowded city. He had lured the watch with a flash of weapon, and led them on with taunts and rude gestures. She found the place where they had almost caught him: the market-stalls were still in disarray.

He was sitting on the step of a church, deep in conversation with a ragged young priest. A much less ragged and utterly unpriestly person was taking her time in bandaging his hand. As Eschiva drew near enough to hear, Arslan said, "Oh, no, there's nothing evil about the infidels. They're men like us; they live and love as we do, and worship one God. It's almost our God, and we share the same holy places—and there's the difficulty. We're too close, but not close enough at all."

"That's heresy," the priest said, but without horror.

"I suppose it is," said Arslan, "but it's the truth."

Eschiva watched in fascination as the woman finished bandaging his hand and leaned close. She was spilling out of her very tight bodice, a fact to which both young men seemed oblivious. She hissed in frustration.

"You can't have him," Eschiva said. "He belongs to me."

The woman started like a deer. The other two looked up blinking. Arslan's smile was marvelously warm. "My lady! I caught a spear with my hand, and Father Wilfrid stitched it up; this is his sister Agnes, who bandaged it. Is it done? What we set out to do?"

"All done," said Eschiva.

"Thanks to the saints," Arslan said. He rose, wavering a little; he was pale under the bronze of his skin.

"You're not well," the priest said. "Maybe you should—"

"I'll take him home, and many thanks, Father," Eschiva said. She slipped her arm about his waist and guided him out into the street, protesting mildly but submitting to her will.

He was steadier once he began walking. "You must have bled excessively," she said, "to be this weak."

He shrugged. "I was calling spirits to help me, and too many came. While I fended them off, one of the watch caught me with a spear. I was a fool: I tried to do too much at once."

"Yes, you were a fool," she said fiercely. "You could have been killed."

"But I wasn't," he said with the complacence of the young and the male. He rested his arm about her shoulders and kissed the top of her head. "I don't suppose he thanked you for saving his life."

"You do know him well," she said.

"It was still worth doing," said Arslan. "He's a man of God, and an honest man, whatever else he is."

Eschiva let that be, though she had to bite her tongue to do it. She could only hope that they would not live to regret what they had done.

# PART THREE

# INTERREGNUM
## Advent 1191–Easter 1192

# CHAPTER 33

It was a bleak winter in Britain, even with a true king in the heart of it. The diocese of Ely lay under Interdict. The bishop was gone, vanished—though it was rumored that he had appeared in Normandy, much chastened and subdued, and had shut himself in an abbey to contemplate his sins. His brothers were hostages in the Tower of London, all their bright new possessions stripped away. Geoffrey Plantagenet had the keeping of them; it was to his credit that he did not treat them cruelly, but neither did he set them free.

Arslan had his lady and his knighthood and his Turkish servant, who had returned to him before he left London, but not his lands. John had been preoccupied with much else: completing his royal progress, welcoming his brother Geoffrey and settling him in York, and contending with the imminence of his mother's arrival in England. The old Pope's death had kept her in Rome, but now at last she was on her way through France. John swore that he could feel her coming like a fever in the blood.

France itself had its king back, and that was a different fever, a different fear. The knotted web of alliance and enmity that bound the royal houses of France and England had shifted incontestably toward hostility. Philip's Crusade had not gone well; he had come away even less enamored of Richard than he had been when he began. Now he cast his eye on England, and considered that, as far as he could know, England was without a king.

John was in Gloucester that stormy Christmas, warm in Susanna's arms—for Isabella had managed to be indisposed in one of the manors, as far from John as she could be. Arslan lodged with Eschiva in Bertrada's house, and kept the feast with greater uproar and more magic than he had ever known. Bishop Hugh was there among his kin, and a riding of ladies from the Summer Country, all of whom were kin to Eschiva, and one of whom was her mother.

Eschiva was as surprised by her coming as Arslan. The first he saw of her, she was in the hall, and for a long moment he thought that it was Eschiva, or Eschiva's fetch, for his lady was standing beside him with her hand in his; then he saw the differences, the fine lines in the creamy skin, the thread or two of grey in the bright hair. Her eyes were blue, her expression forbidding, as if she judged him and found him wanting.

They had come in together, he and Eschiva, tousled and wind-blown and laughing from a ride between storms. Eschiva stopped short, nearly pulling him off his feet. "Mother," she said. Her voice was as expressionless as her face. "What a pleasant surprise."

"A surprise, certainly," said the lady. "So this is the foreigner you've taken to your bed. I hadn't realized you'd robbed a cradle."

Eschiva smiled her sweet dangerous smile. "Isn't he beautiful? Don't you envy me? I'll not share him, so don't even ask."

"And here I had thought you might take the veil," the lady said. She rose from her seat by the fire and swept toward them, holding out her hand for Arslan to kiss, and suffering a cool kiss on each cheek from her daughter. "Now sit," she said. "Boy, attend me. Do you sing? Play the lute?"

"A little, my lady," he said.

"You'll entertain me later," she said. "For now, let me look at you. By the gods, you are young! How came such a child to win my daughter? It can't be your looks—those are pleasant enough, but she's seen better."

"Not on this earth," Eschiva said.

Arslan felt as if he had wandered into the midst of a battlefield. He was profoundly grateful when Bertrada appeared, disheveled and dis-tracted, trailing a gaggle of servants and children. "Morgana! Now you've had your sport, come to the stillroom and help me. I simply cannot persuade the athanor to heat properly."

"You have no affinity for fire," Morgana said, "that's your trouble." She rose once more, shaking out her skirts. "Very well, I'll see what I can do. The others are somewhere about—do you need us all?"

"One of you will do, I think," Bertrada said.

It was a rescue, and a clever one. "Quickly," Eschiva said, pulling him up. "Before she comes back."

He was not at all unwilling to run away to the chamber they shared, or to hide there, either. Eschiva stripped off her riding clothes with a fierce show of temper, flinging them against the wall. He sat on the bed and watched her.

When she had calmed a little, he said, "Suppose you tell me how it is that we just ran afoul of your late mother."

"Did I ever say that she was dead?"

"I suppose you let me think it," he said.

She flung herself onto the bed beside him. "She gave birth to me, handed me to Bertrada, and walked away—clear into the Summer Country, and never a glance back. She didn't care then whether I lived or died. I never knew her, never even saw her until I came to my women's courses. Then she came to look at me, and allowed as how I was perhaps worthy to be called her child. I told her that I cared nothing for that, and I would rather have had no mother at all than a mother who had forgotten my existence."

Her anger struck Arslan strangely. His mother had left him, too, but not until he was weaned; and she had never come back. He had not expected her to. He had no such anger as Eschiva did, no such passion of resentment. All that was so old as to be worn smooth.

"Bertrada can't be her sister," he said—rather feebly, but he could think of nothing better to say.

"They're cousins," Eschiva said. "Their mothers were sisters. Bertrada's mother married a quite ordinary man. My grandmother clung closer to tradition: she lay with the horned king, and so conceived her daughter."

"Ah," said Arslan. "No wonder she's so disappointed in you. I'm no god, and I'm half-mortal."

"She's jealous," Eschiva said. "Her river-god lay with her and left her. I get to keep my child of fire."

"Child," said Arslan, "being the most significant word."

"Children grow," Eschiva said. She slid round till her head was in his lap, and contemplated his face from below. "It's the whole of a year since you came out of the Worldwood on the coast of France and shot my sainted uncle."

"Uncle? Or cousin?"

"Cousin," she admitted. "He's Bertrada's brother."

"Yes," said Arslan. "I can see the resemblance. Yet everyone says he's a Burgundian."

"It suits his fancy to let them say it." She sighed gustily. "Bertrada is as much mother as I ever needed. The one who gave birth to me is a stranger. I won't let her tarnish my joy in you."

"Maybe," said Arslan delicately, "she cares more than she lets you know. You can seem so cold, my love, but be burning hot beneath. Might she not be the same?"

"She is cold to the marrow," Eschiva said.

She was determined not to hear any good of her mother. Arslan let it go, for a while. He was hardly the one to sing praises of harmony among kin, who had nothing in common with any of his own.

On the eve of Christmas, the Lady Morgana summoned Arslan into her presence. The morning was dark and raw with sleet. Eschiva was with the children, teaching them the art of casting glamours. Arslan had been in hall with Father Hugh, with Kalila curled like a dog at his feet.

She unfolded herself and padded after him when the lady's maid came with the summons. Father Hugh stayed where he was, warm and comfortable by the fire.

Arslan would far rather have been there than climbing the stair to the ladies' bower. That was a pleasant place on sunlit days, with high glazed windows and a floor of tiles that had been part of this manor since Rome ruled in Britain. In winter, with sleet rattling against the glass and a fire lit in the hearth, it was chill and rather bleak. Even the rugs from the east that covered the floor could not warm it.

As before, he started a little on coming into the room, to see how like Eschiva this lady was. In a score of years, Eschiva would look just as Morgana did now.

But for her maid, Morgana was alone. She had a bit of needlework in her lap, but her hands were folded when he came, her gaze fixed on the flames, watching the dance of spirits within them.

Arslan waited courteously for her to acknowledge his presence. The fire had leaped for him already, knowing him for kin.

It was a long while before she closed her eyes, drew a breath, came back to the world. She stared at him for a moment as if she had forgotten who he was, but recognition came quickly.

As before, she held out her hand for him to kiss, and commanded that he sit. He was glad to be so close to the fire's warmth, even with so cold a companion. When he warmed his hands over the flames, they reached up and curled about his fingers, stroking him with living heat. Down in the heart of them, a salamander crawled through the door between worlds, hissed a greeting, and coiled in comfort.

"Bertrada should have asked you for help with her athanor," Morgana said. "But I suppose that would have interfered with the rescue."

"Do you fault her for it?" Arslan inquired.

"I suppose not," said Morgana. "My daughter has yet to forgive me for forcing her to grow up here, or for giving her a foster mother who knew how to raise a child properly. I have no gift for it. My gift is magic."

"You might have visited her on occasion," Arslan said.

"Yes, I might have," she said. "No doubt I should have. I'll pay for that lifelong."

"My mother weaned me before she left me," said Arslan. "My father raised me. My nurse was a Seljuk Turk; my first words were in Arabic."

"Are you trying to horrify me?"

"Not at all, lady," Arslan said. "You're not a Christian, to be so narrow in your thinking."

Her brow arched. "I, not Christian? What makes you think that?"

He did not mean to smile, but she was so like Eschiva, and he was finding that he liked her. "I'm a he-witch from the east, lady. I know the mark that baptism leaves, and you don't have it. Are you a Druid?"

"My line is very old," she said, "far older than Rome. It bred Bran; it bred Arthur. Boudicca bowed to us, and Caswallon came to us for counsel. We were and are the Ladies of the Lake, the ancient rulers of Avalon. My daughter is my heir, bred to be more than a queen. The blood of gods runs in her veins. Do you still dare think that you deserve her?"

"I know I don't," he said, "but she is rather insistent that I do. And I love her."

"Of course you love her. She was born to be loved. Do you know how long she refused the truth of that? I honestly did expect to hear one day that she had gone into a convent. And that would have been a fine revenge."

"She wouldn't have done that," Arslan said. "She loves the world too much."

"And now she loves you."

Morgana leaned toward him, taking his face in her hands. He sat very still. She looked deep inside him, deep enough to make him shiver, but he did not flinch or pull away.

After a long while she lowered her hands from his cheeks, only to take his own hands in hers, turning them over, tracing the lines and scars with a firm finger. "You'll live long," she said, "unless cold iron kills you. Beware of that, child. Cold iron is enemy to us all; even those of us who can wear and wield it."

"Cold iron and bitter steel," he said. "I was born to war, lady. You might say I was born to die."

"All mortals are born to die," she said. "You were born to magic, child, to power mortals only dream of. I see it blossoming in you. It will become the whole of you in the end. The fire will burn your flesh away, and return you to your mother's people."

He shuddered in his bones. "No," he said. "No, lady. I am a mortal man. I embrace it; I cherish it. I won't vanish among the jinn."

"Not in this age of your life," she said, "nor in the next, either. But in the end, you will. So will my daughter go to her father, and I to mine. It's the way of our blood, child. We don't die. We move from world to world. Sometimes we're reborn, and sometimes not. There is no death among us; no dissolution."

"I'm too young to think of that," he said. "Are you telling me that you've come to take her, and make her your successor?"

"Not in this age of my life," she said, with a glint that reminded him vividly of her daughter. "I came to inspect you."

"Do I pass inspection?"

"Don't get cocky, child. I'm thinking about it."

He bit his lip, but the grin escaped for all that he could do.

"Impudent pup," said Morgana, but without rancor. "Do you see the lute there? Fetch it. Play for me. And no Arab caterwauling!"

Arslan bowed to her will, fetched the lute and tuned it and sang as she bade him. He knew a song or two of her people, and she taught him another and then another. Their voices mingled well; they matched one another's cadences. They said a great deal in that hour, all in music, and all in the words of the songs. It was, he thought as it went on, a meeting of close kin; a thing he had not known since his father died. What a wonder to find it here, in this one who was so like his lady.

# CHAPTER 34

Eschiva heard the singing in the bower. There was such joy in it, and such plain delight, that the bleak day seemed much brighter for it. She smiled as she climbed the stair. Arslan's voice was unmistakable; no other man she knew could sing so deep or so high, sometimes in the same swoop of breath. The other she did not recognize; one of her kinswomen, no doubt.

She stopped short in the doorway. Small wonder she had not known who the woman was; she had never heard her mother sing. Their voices wove in and out, making love to one another with such exquisite passion that she felt the heat in her own belly. And all without their ever touching—all with simple sound. They sat decorously apart, he playing on the lute, she in Bertrada's chair by the fire.

Eschiva's smile was long gone. The greeting she had intended, the bright welcome, died unspoken. She turned blindly and fled down the stair.

It was not reasonable. She knew that. He had sung so with many another woman since she knew him, and many a man, too. He was a sweet singer; he put his heart into his songs. But this was more than she could bear. This amity; this harmony with the woman who had borne her.

She put on a smiling mask. She pretended to be her wonted self. But after the Mass at midnight was done, he tarried for jests and laughter. When he came to bed, she pretended to be asleep.

If he was disappointed, he did not show it. He dropped his clothes and lay beside her. His warmth poured over her, the fire within that he had learned to master. He laid his arm about her to draw her in. She murmured as if in sleep, and rolled away to the far side of the bed.

He did not pursue her. In a little while she heard his breathing slow and deepen. He who slept rarely was deeply asleep.

She who slept as often as any mortal was wide awake. She was remembering how they had all come together after the Mass, and embraced and wished one another joy; and her mother, her cold and regal mother, had not only permitted Arslan to embrace her, she had returned it. Eschiva had won no such concession. Nor had she asked for it, but she should not have had to ask. It should have been given, and freely, as Bertrada had done.

She buried her face in the coverlets and tried to sleep, since being reasonable was beyond her.

The ladies from the Summer Country stayed in the manor until the new year. They left somewhat before John was to pack up his household to go on again to London by way of Salisbury and Windsor. The day of their departure, Eschiva arranged to be elsewhere, but Bertrada sent one of the fosterlings to fetch her. "Your mother is asking for you," the child said. "She says she won't go until you come."

Eschiva gritted her teeth and followed the child to the hall, where they were all gathered. Arslan was there—of course, she thought bitterly. He was kneeling in front of Morgana; his hands were in hers.

"I will not permit my daughter to bind herself to a landless man," she said. "Take therefore this gift, the demesne of Avalon. It is a castle, lands, villages, and in a sheltered corner of it, which may not be precisely in this world at all, a vineyard and an olive grove."

A light dawned in his face. "Olives? In Britain?"

"Maybe not exactly in Britain," she said with warmth that Eschiva had never seen in her, "but it is a part of your demesne. Its seneschal is wise and thrifty and will look after it until you can come there."

"And the price?" Eschiva had not meant to speak, but the words burst out of her. "What is the tribute he must pay?"

"A jar of oil from the olives every Samhain," Morgana said, "and a bag of wool from the sheep."

Eschiva bit her tongue. Arslan was as happy as a man should be who had just been made lord of a rich, if small, domain. It would be a comfortable thing for him, whose father had ruled one small and rich demesne in Outremer and one in Anjou: he had been bred, raised, for just such a thing.

So for that matter had she, but not as a gift from that of all liege

ladies. Still she held her peace past that first outburst, and stood with
Arslan in the gate to watch the ladies ride away. He was alight with
his good fortune, delighted with the gift—but when they turned back
into the manor, he said with honest regret, "I am sorry she had to
leave so soon. Do you think she'll visit us in Avalon, when we settle
there?"

"That won't be soon," Eschiva said. "Have you forgotten that
there's a king in Britain, and he's summoned us?"

"Of course not," he said. "But I should like—"

"You'll be there in summer," said young Brigid, who had the
Sight. "Maybe not next summer. But someday." She skipped past
them, as lighthearted as ever.

And so was he. He caught Eschiva's hand and pulled her after the
child, dancing them both into the hall.

He never even noticed that she was troubled. She hid it well, and
he was full of so much else. His delight in his good fortune lingered
for all of that day. At night, as she had since Christmas, she feigned to
be asleep before him; that ruse would not serve much longer, but for
this little while it sufficed.

She woke abruptly. Her pretense had become truth: a deep and
surprisingly restful sleep, for a heart as sore as hers. Whatever had
roused her, she woke to silence. The nightlamp flickered; the wind
was singing without, promising snow by morning.

Arslan lay on his back, sprawled as if he had fallen there. He was
breathing hard, in gasps, like a runner in a race. His skin was pebbled
with cold: he had flung off the coverlets.

She spread them over him again. At her touch, he started awake.
His eyes were dark, lost; they seized on her face and clung there. "We
have to go," he said.

"Now? This instant?"

"Dawn," he said. "I dreamed—I saw—Philip is back in France.
France is awake. It stalks—it turns against Britain."

Her heart constricted, she hoped not with jealousy, that the dream
should have come to him and not to her. She was a guardian, and she
had felt nothing.

He caught at her hands. She gasped. His dream was in her, sudden, whole, and powerful. Had she been on her feet, she would
have fallen.

All the nations of men and magic were like great beasts resting on the orb of the world. Each had its place, secure within its bounds, like the unicorn shut in bars of silver, or the lion enclosed in gold. The king of each held the key to the cage. He guarded it, tended it. When it yearned to broaden the space that was given it, he unbarred the cage; he set it free.

France was awake. Its king had taken the key. He was turned toward Britain, lusting after it, and the power of his realm had risen in response. It was reaching across the water, a wave of darkness under the stars.

The walls of air protected the island. They were strong and high, sustained by the strength of its guardians and rooted in the earth of Britain. The true king himself had given them substance, and power to hold against the force from without.

It was very strong, fed with the hatred of a king. Whatever Richard had done to Philip on Crusade, Philip had come back an implacable enemy.

Arslan shook her, calling her name. She felt and heard it as if from very far away. Slowly she came back to him, to lamplight and winter's chill and the song of the wind. "Dawn," she said. "We leave at dawn."

He nodded. His eyes were wide, all pupil. Yet he was calm, his voice steady. "I'll wake the servants."

"And Uncle Hugh. And Aunt Bertrada. We have to tell them—"

He nodded. "You do that. Though I think they may already know."

"How could they? *I* didn't."

He blinked a little at her venom, but let it go, rising, wrapping himself in a robe. It happened to be the richest one, the one he wore in hall for banquets. He strode out trailing silk and vair.

Eschiva clutched at the rags of her composure. She had allowed herself to lose sight of her duty, her one great task, the thing that was entrusted her above all others. The wards had remained because they were part of her, but once the threat within was ended, she had done little to keep watch for threats from without.

Hugh had given her no warning. He had been resting here, reading in the library, teaching children the smaller magics. When the ladies came from Avalon, he had spent long hours with them—hours Eschiva had avoided—but none of them had spoken to her of this thing that waited beyond the walls of air.

She found Aunt Bertrada awake in the kitchen, beginning the day's baking, and Uncle Hugh with her. He had the sleeves of his habit pinned up and flour on his nose, as he kneaded a billowing mass of dough. They greeted Eschiva with great good cheer.

"All the packing's done," Bertrada said. "The horses will be ready when it's time. Here, lend a hand. I'm not as young as I used to be."

Eschiva shut her mouth with care. She had been gaping, and ungracefully, too. "Where is Cook?"

"Asleep," said Hugh, "as he well deserves to be, after all the feasts he's labored over."

"You know," she said.

"You thought I didn't?"

He moved aside to let her in. She attacked the heavy dough as if it had been her mother's face, beating it into submission. "How long?" she demanded.

"He dreamed before; he told us of it. We were warned."

"You didn't tell me."

"You had other concerns."

She set her teeth and hammered at the dough. "Maybe you should choose another guardian."

"No."

"I'm not performing my duty. I'm distracted. I am not—"

"You are still the strongest of your line, and the best of us all in setting and sustaining wards. You sustained your part of these through everything, as you sustain the breath in your lungs. No one else can do such a thing."

"Breath is not enough," she said. "This needs mind and soul. I haven't given it either."

"You will."

He had been as sweetly implacable when she was a child learning to master the gifts that were in her. He would not let her escape; she was not to refuse the burden. No matter what grief beset her, what follies and jealousies vexed her, she would go on. She was bred for this. She had no other choice.

She shaped the bread into loaves and laid it aside for its last rising. It was simple work, and soothing. She calmed a little as she did it. She could think, after a fashion.

When Arslan came, she could face him without change of expression. He had recovered from the shock of the dream; he was light on his feet, like a big graceful cat. She suppressed a sigh. Her anger was no less, but she loved him no less, either, nor ceased to want him because he had dared to make a friend of her mother.

They must be allies for Britain's sake. She needed the power that he had, and he needed hers. When the grey dawn came, with spits of snow, she was ready to ride. They had not far to go, only down into Gloucester, but the snow would slow their pace.

The storm would keep John in the castle, too, but not for long, with guardians to guide him to the straight track. The sooner he came to London, the better for the kingdom.

# CHAPTER 35

❧

John was idling abed as any sane man would do on a cold winter's morning, but Susanna was up and doing, as any dutiful woman would be. She met the invasion at the door of his chambers, fended off the guards and squires, and said to Arslan who came in foremost, "You wake him. I don't fancy having my head bitten off."

Arslan laughed and kissed her hands, which made her blush, and ventured into the lion's den.

John was a hummock under the coverlets. Delicately Arslan plucked them away one by one, down to the shivering, glaring, and wide-awake prince. "Good morning, my lord," Arslan said brightly. "I trust I find you well."

John snatched at the nearest of the coverlets and pulled it up about him, and said through chattering teeth, "I hadn't even summoned you yet."

"But you were going to."

"Today," said John. He raked fingers through his hair, ruffling it into startled peaks. "I should have known you'd know."

"France," Arslan said.

"Yes," said John. "That's what I was made king for, isn't it? To hold the key to the defenses."

Arslan nodded.

"Philip has sent me a message," John said after a pause, "in deepest secrecy. He bids me to a council on the marches of Normandy. He has somewhat to offer me, he says. Alliance; power. His sister Alais in marriage, and with her the richest dower in France. And," he said, "all the lands held in fief by my brother Richard, of which Philip is overlord."

Arslan's knees gave way, dropping him to the bed's edge. He scrambled his thoughts together. "Philip wants Britain," he said.

"I know that," said John. "You came all this way in a blizzard to tell me?"

"To tell you that he wants it now. He's laid siege to the walls of air."

"Oh, has he?" John's lips drew back from his teeth. "He doesn't know, then."

"He knows that the crowned king of the English is Crusading across the sea, and the king's ambitious brother is conveniently established in England. Will you be going to France, my lord?"

"Would you be perturbed if I did?"

"I would be perturbed if you let Philip suspect the truth before the last possible instant."

"Thank God," said John. "A man with the wit to understand. I've held him off a bit—we'll see to the defenses first, raise the levies and garrison the coast. I'll leave England secure behind me."

"Should you leave it at all?"

"I may have to," said John. "I'm not going to bring the fight here if I can avoid it. I'll take it to him."

"You'll be stronger on the earth of Britain."

"Ah," said John, "but I'm also bred to the earth of Normandy. I have an advantage, don't you see? When he walks in Normandy, he's no longer in France—but I'm in a land I'm entitled to."

"Not Arthur of Brittany?"

"Arthur is a toddling child," John said tightly, but he kept his temper, which was notable. "I *am* Richard's heir. However long it takes him to discover that, the truth is the truth. I'll confront the King of France on the soil of Normandy. I'll pretend to take the bribes he offers, and turn him back from Britain."

"Even the marriage? You'll take that?"

John's smile had a knife-edge. "Do you see my so beloved wife here? I've sent her away where she'll be happier, and when the time comes I'll persuade the Pope to set me free of her. Philip knows that or he wouldn't be dangling Alais in front of my face."

"Do you want her?"

"Alais' dower is the Vexin—the richest property in Normandy. I want the Vexin, just as my father did before me. She was his mistress, you know, but he'd never marry her. Not as long as Eleanor had Aquitaine. I'll take Alais if I can—why not? She's a little shopworn but she's pretty, and she has a sweet voice. Henry used to say she was a tigress in bed. For that alone she'll be a more pleasant match than the one I'm subjected to now."

Arslan held his tongue. This was the way of noble and royal marriages; it was a cold thing, and grimly practical. Old Henry had married Eleanor in the white heat of passion, but if she had not had Aquitaine, there would have been no marriage. John would cast off Gloucester in an instant if it gave him the Vexin; if it also gave him power over Philip, then so much the better.

It was good, thought Arslan, to be a simple knight without great inheritance, and better yet to be loved by a lady whose family had, by ancient custom, had free choice of their men. He was blessed, and well he knew it.

John's voice broke in on his reflections. "When you're done woolgathering," John said acidly, "you can call the guardians to a council. Have food and drink sent up; post a guard on the door. It wouldn't do for us to be interrupted, now, would it?"

"Probably not, my lord," Arslan said.

"Well then, go. And tell Petit to come in and dress me before I die of cold."

Arslan bowed. John flung a pillow at him; he caught it, tossed it back, and escaped before the next one struck the wall by the door.

It was not the simplest of matters to arm Britain against an invasion that no man without magic could understand. True king John might be, but the levies of England belonged to his brother. Even with the Marshal's help, there were things he could not convincingly explain, and actions he could not lawfully take.

That did not deter John. When it came to law and righteousness, John was a Plantagenet. Law was what he said it was, and right was whatever served him. The crown of Arthur and the scepter of Alba gave him courage even beyond his native arrogance, and gave him also the right to call forth the strength of Britain and send it marching to the sea.

Rumor, of course, ran wild. People saw the troops gathering, saw them strengthening forts and castles along the coast, and concluded not that they defended Britain against an invasion, but that John had roused rebellion against his brother.

John did nothing to quell the rumors. They served too well to deceive Philip, who was waiting in France for John to cross into Normandy. John was dragging it out as long as he could: the longer he delayed, the stronger the realm would be behind him.

Arslan was much on the road that winter, both the mortal ways and the straight tracks. There was no one else who could be trusted for some of the errands he ran, except the Turk whom people knew as Karim; and John was using her as ruthlessly as Arslan. Kalila seemed to be thriving on it. Arslan endured it; it seemed he never saw Eschiva. If they were even in the same town at the same time, they were both so caught up in John's war both open and secret that there was hardly a moment to utter a greeting.

Arslan did not know when he began to suspect that Eschiva was avoiding him. She had been a little cool to him in Gloucester, because of her mother. Then his dream had come, and John had leaped into action.

There came a day when, please God, he was not called out for yet another swift and secret run to some far corner of the kingdom, and when, God be thanked, she was not buried in the duties of her guardianship. Better yet, that day was clear and almost warm, for winter; and they were in Canterbury, which he had decided he loved best of the cities of England. The wolds of Kent were already green with spring, and the old sacred city was warming to it. The walls were made of flints mortared together; their cool grey sheen, this morning, held for him a heart of fire.

Arslan, as John's messenger, had been given sleeping-room in the castle near a corner of the walls. Eschiva happened to be lodging in a convent near the cathedral. It was only wise and proper, for the castle was a rough place, full of armed men and women of questionable virtue. The castellan's wife, like John's, was not friendly with her husband; she was looking after a manor somewhere near Dover. His mistresses, a pair of bright-eyed, buxom, sweet-tempered sisters, would cheerfully have vacated their chamber for a lady of Eschiva's rank and station, but Arslan was not inclined to demand it of them.

There were alternatives. He was considering one or two of them as he rode out of the castle, smiling at the prospect of seeing his lady again after so long—a whole month, God help them; how had the time flown so fast?

It was market-day in the town. He found a bit of frippery for his lady, a ribbon the color of her eyes, and a jar of honey to sweeten the meeting. With those in his bag and a smile on his face, he rode up to the convent's gate.

The portress was slow to answer the bell. He waited as patiently as he could, in a cloud of small curious spirits, mostly creatures of air, and a bird or two. A wren came to perch on his finger, telling him a long and convoluted tale. She took flight when at last the panel slid aside and a dark suspicious eye peered out at him.

He put on his best smile and his most harmless expression. "Good day, Sister," he said. "Would you be so kind as to send a message to my lady wife?"

"And what would you be wanting with a wife?" the nun demanded. Her voice was as sharp as her eye.

"I should like to speak with her, Sister," Arslan said. "She is a guest of your house, the Lady—"

"Eschiva, yes," the nun said. "You must be the husband with the paynim name. She left a message for you. She'll see you in London at Easter."

"Easter! But that's—" Arslan broke off. "Sister, if you'll but let me in and show me to the guesthouse, I'm sure she'll receive me there."

"I'm sure she won't," the nun said. "Our order keeps a strict rule. No man passes the gate."

"Then send her out, Sister, and we'll not vex you further."

"The lady doesn't wish to be sent out," the nun said. "Good day, sir. God keep you." The panel slid shut. The sharp eye vanished.

Arslan stood staring at the blank and heavily barred door. He could perfectly easily have blasted it down, and his retinue of spirits would have been delighted to help him. But he was not a creature of impulse, or of sudden rages, either.

He rang the bell again. "Sister!" he called, pitching his voice to carry through solid oak. "Sister, I've brought gifts for my wife. If you will but—"

There was no response. The door remained shut. The convent was inviolate.

Arslan raised his fists to smite the door, but lowered them slowly. He tied the ribbon about the jar of honey, and found a scrap of parchment in his bag. He had no pen or ink, but a splinter from the door and a swift lash of flame gave him a bit of charcoal with which to write her name and his name and a line of Latin: *For my lady whom I love.* It was all the parchment could hold. He rolled it and slipped it through the knot of the ribbon, and hung jar and parchment from the lintel of the door, pinned there by the dagger he wore at his belt.

He mounted his grey mare, moving slowly as if there were any hope that she could come running out of the gate, calling his name. Of course she did not. He turned the mare and rode away.

His mood was indescribable. Surely she could not still be angry over a thing that had come and gone two months past. And if she could, did she not owe him an explanation?

He paused only long enough to gather his belongings from the castle, to mount and ride away. It was nothing he thought of, not consciously. She wanted him gone, therefore he went. He was an obedient lover.

# CHAPTER 36

Queen Eleanor came across the sea in the teeth of a storm, braving it as she had braved everything else in her long and adventurous life. She landed at Southampton just as John was about to sail out from it. His ship was ready, his men gathered: the forces that would stay and the escort of Flemish mercenaries that would accompany him across the water to Normandy. They were only waiting on the wind to carry them out of the harbor.

He had been hoping to evade her, but the wind that favored her was keeping him ashore. She disembarked with remarkable lack of ceremony, left her servants to deal with the harbormaster, and had herself carried in a litter to the castle.

John had had a little warning: as soon as her sail was sighted, he knew that she was coming. He did not interrupt his game of dice for that, nor command that the hall be set in order to receive a queen. She found him on the floor with a handful of his favorites, casting the bones and roaring when he won the toss.

Arslan was watching the game but not playing in it. His first sight of Eleanor came in the midst of that strained exuberance. She stood in the door, surrounded by women and priests: a tall spare figure in a dark mantle, with wimple and veil. She was so still, her shape so clean in its lines, that she seemed no living woman at all, but a carving in a cathedral.

Her face did nothing to soften the impression. She had been a great beauty in her day; his father had spoken of that, how glorious she had been, with her dark eyes and her fair hair and her skin like new milk. "And, God's truth, she bathed it in asses' milk to keep it white—though when she rode bare-breasted with her Amazons, the sun burned her in places too tender for words."

It was startling to think of that now, and to see this haughty queen in black and white, with her age-carved face and her hooded eyes. The bones were long and elegant, the face still beautiful, like a wood in winter, stripped of all its softness. The hoyden queen of France had become the ice-cold queen of England, and she had no patience to spare for the youngest of her sons.

John looked up in insolence so lazy and so perfectly aware of itself that Arslan marveled at the queen's restraint. Her son was begging for a spanking, provoking her with his every line. She tightened her lips but otherwise refrained from taking the bait.

"Good morning, Mother," he drawled. "I trust you had a pleasant voyage."

"No voyage on water is pleasant," she said. Her voice was both rough and sweet, like harsh wine laced with honey. She entered the hall as if it belonged to her, approached the fire, and when she sat, she expected a chair to be waiting. Arslan was closest and quickest; he drew up the high heavy chair in which John liked to sit, so that it was there beneath her before she fell.

"Pity," said John. "Someday, Mother, you're going to try that game and fall flat on your rump."

Eleanor ignored him, just as she had ignored Arslan. Her maids hastened to relieve her of her cloak and her gloves, and to bank her with cushions. "This climate will be the death of us all," she said. "Get up, boy. The rest of you, leave us.

"Not you," she said as Arslan moved to obey. "You stay. The rest, out."

It did not matter to her that she had dismissed, among others, a brace of archbishops and a pack of barons. Arslan stood stiffly where she had stopped him. She saw more than she let on, that was obvious.

When it was only herself and John and a dozen of her ladies, and Arslan immobile beside her chair, she said, "That's the end of this rebellion. I've paid off the captain of your ship and dismissed your hired swords; I'll be dispersing the rest of your troops. You'll send word to Philip that there will be no bargain this time. I will not have you two plotting against Richard."

John's face was fuller and rounder and much younger than hers, but just then the two of them looked strikingly alike. They had the same stark lines, the same cold black eyes. "Mother, as good as it is of you to come roaring in to protect Richard, you don't understand the first thing of what is happening here."

"Unfortunately I do," she said. "I knew you were a mistake when first you swelled my belly. My courses had been erratic for years; I should have been barren at last, and free of the burden, or by Saint Mary's breasts, I would never have seduced Henry. It was futile, too: I didn't get what I wanted, then or after. The least you could have been was a dutiful son, and not the scheming monster that you are."

"I'm your child," John said sweetly. "When devils mate, they don't breed saints. You of all people should know that."

"So I'm to be faulted for hoping against hope." One of her ladies brought her a cup full of something steaming and pungent. She grimaced, but she sipped it. "Age is hell," she said. "Don't ever grow old."

She was speaking to Arslan. He hoped he did not look too much a fool as he stared at her.

Those eyes fixed on him. He shivered, but it was not an unpleasant sensation. That surprised him. He knew how poorly fire and ice could mingle.

She was staring as if struck by a memory. "By Saint Agnes," she said. "You haven't aged a moment. What, did you find the Fountain of Youth, somewhere in your dusty east?"

Arslan smiled in sudden understanding. "Oh, no, your majesty. I think you're remembering my father. They say I look like him."

"You're his very image and likeness," said the queen. "What a beauty he was! And as stiffly virtuous as any monk in a cloister. I suppose you take after him there, too."

"So I'm told," Arslan said.

She shook her head and sighed. "Such a waste. Why in the world are you here?"

"The winds blew me," said Arslan, "and the waters carried me."

"Your father had no objection?"

"My father died at Hattin."

"Ah," she said without evident emotion. "That's a pity. You're landless, then, and homeless, too, with the Saracen in Jerusalem."

"As it happens, your majesty," Arslan said, "I am lord of the demesne of Ynys Witrin, in the Summer Country. I hold it in fief to my lady's mother."

Eleanor's brows went up. She was not often surprised; she did not like it, either. "Indeed? On whose authority was that done?"

"On that of the Lady Morgana, your majesty," Arslan said.

"The Lady of the Lake?" Eleanor's expression was sour. "Myths and legends, all of that—but there's no denying she has considerable wealth, and considerable freedom to dispose of it as she wills. They say that line breeds no sons. A shame if so; but then you're not the wedded wife's child, are you? As I recall, she was a squat little thing with nothing to commend her but a large dowry. But fertile: she was that—and every one of the offspring as squat and charmless as she. You'd be a changeling, if you were one of hers."

"And a miracle, majesty," said Arslan, "since she was some years dead when I was born."

When Eleanor laughed, for a fleeting moment she was young again: the splendid and headstrong lady who had cast off a whining saint of a king and married for love a youth a dozen years younger than she. Arslan understood then how his father had loved her—as he loved Eschiva, clear-eyed and fully aware of her faults, but bound to her for everlasting.

That was not a thought he wanted to think, not this moment—not so far away and so long removed, with a cold dismissal through a convent gate. He did not even know where she was. Dover, he supposed, or still in Canterbury. He could have discovered her whereabouts if he had seen fit to look, but he refused. He had too much pride after all, and too little stomach for a woman's fits of temper.

Eleanor took his hand in hers. Her fingers were thin and cold, but her grip was strong. "You, I like. Don't tell me you're serving this mooncalf for love—but I can't imagine your father's son serving him for gain."

"Some things surpass human understanding," Arslan said.

"You are astonishing," John said. Eleanor had relieved them of her presence at last, and taken the best suite in the castle—the one which John had just vacated in expectation of spending the night on shipboard or even, the sea willing, in Normandy.

Arslan prodded the fire, feeding it till it burned high and bright. "I am not astonishing," he said. "Your mother, however . . . ."

"I haven't seen anyone stand up to her like that since Father died."

"Not even you?"

"I merely annoy her. You made her laugh. That's a gift, you know. Women love you."

"They seem exceptionally fond of you," Arslan said.

"Oh, no," said John. "I love women. They love my rank and station. You they love for yourself."

Arslan shrugged uncomfortably. "Shall I see that your belongings are moved back into the castle?"

"No," said John. "We're sailing to Normandy."

But when he went to leave the hall, his way was barred. Men who had bowed to him in his mother's absence were now obedient to the Queen of the English. His own loyal troops were separated; the castle was full of her men, or men who had been John's while it was understood that he was the royal heir of England, but now they belonged to the royal lady of England.

He had not bargained on that, although in retrospect it was inevitable. She had moved without the slightest hesitation, had taken all the power into her hands, and left him shut in these walls.

He kept his temper, which did him great credit. He requested an audience. The lady at the door of the royal apartments—which had, until this morning, been his—said courteously, "Her majesty is weary and needs to rest. When she wakes, I'll give her your message."

There was nothing for it but to retreat in as good order as possible, and try to gather what few rags of either dignity or authority were left. His belongings came back while he did that, and were set in one of the lesser apartments. Petit the valet came with them, and one of his squires, and the Turk Kalila looking somewhat ruffled.

"They've taken the ship and sent it away," she said, "with the Flemings still on board. The harbor's full of the queen's men. She's disbanding the garrisons."

"She's blind and a fool," John gritted. "She doesn't have the faintest suspicion of the truth."

"Will you tell her?" Arslan asked him.

John's breath hissed between his teeth. "How? Tell her I'm crowned king of ghosts and shadows? Convince her that I'm no threat to her favorite son? She'll laugh me out of the castle."

"You can try," said Arslan.

"You do it," John said. "She likes you."

That was not mere temper. He meant it. Arslan opened his mouth, then shut it again. He had got himself into this. He could, he supposed, get himself out.

\*     \*     \*

When Arslan went back to the queen's door, he found it open for him, and her majesty wide awake and in excellent temper, sitting in her chamber while a maid combed out her hair. It was thick, and the color of snow; it fell below her waist. Without wimple and veil, wrapped in a robe of midnight wool lined with sable, she was splendid.

He said so as he kissed her hand. She waved off the compliment, but she did not call him a liar, either. "Beauty is what you make it," she said. "I am old; I feel it in every bone. But I will not submit to it."

"Are you wise, majesty, to confess such a thing to me?" Arslan asked.

She smiled and patted his cheek, letting her hand linger for a moment. "You won't tell anyone who shouldn't know."

He bowed.

She sat back and stretched, a little stiffly, but there was grace in her yet. "Before we waste any more time, tell John my answer: No."

"He's not asking a question, majesty," Arslan said.

Her brow arched. "No? He's making demands, then? It's still the same answer. He's not Richard's heir, and he's not going to be, if Berengaria does her duty."

It would be more to the point, Arslan thought, if Richard did his, but he was wiser than to say such a thing to Richard's mother. "John is a practical man," Arslan said. "He knows where he stands in the order of things. He's not demanding anything. He does ask that you understand certain things, things which the world doesn't know, nor should it. This is not a rebellion, majesty. He is not colluding with Philip to seize the throne of England. What he is doing—"

"Please," said Eleanor. "I don't fault you for being an innocent; you're a child, you have a pure heart. You don't understand the Devil's brood. Of course John wants the throne of England. He's a Plantagenet. He was born, bred to want it, and any other worldly power that he can get his hands on. But he can't have it. It belongs to his brother, and there it will stay. When his brother dies, which God forbid be soon, it will go to his brother's son. John is an afterthought, a tactical error. He is not a king."

"But, majesty," Arslan said, "he is."

"He's deluded you as far as that? Why, child, I thought better of you."

"Majesty," Arslan said as firmly as he dared. "Please, listen to me.

I do know what my lord is. Certainly he wants to be King of the English; just as certainly, he will not make cause with Philip of France to seize that office. He's not that much a fool. He'll take it if he can, in his own right, unbound by any alliance with a king who is known for his hatred of all your line."

"Oh?" said Eleanor. "He may not be a fool, but he is a prince of schemers. He's reckoning to take Alais and the Vexin, swear fealty to Philip and so gain Normandy, then come round with that weight of worldly power behind him, and seize England. His oath will last just as long as it serves him, and no longer—but he will swear it. So would I, if I were in his position."

"Lady," said Arslan, "in another world, that might well be so. But in this one, it is not. Philip has mounted an invasion of Britain. That is why my lord has fortified the coast. That is why he has raised the levies. And that, lady, is why he is sailing to Normandy. He's letting Philip believe that what you say is true—and if you believe it, lady, who are his own mother, how can it fail with Philip? He is defender, not rebel. He is protecting this realm, not seizing it from its rightful king."

"Of you I would believe such a thing," said Eleanor. "Of John? Never."

"Lady," said Arslan, "John is not king of England, not yet, but he is a king, trueborn and consecrated. He is king of Britain, of the old realm, the realm that has endured since the making of the world. That realm has chosen him and crowned him. Now it is in danger. Your actions lay it open to invasion from the sea. Lady, we beg you, leave the troops in place, and let John play out his game with Philip. Richard's crown is not in danger. Britain's realm is. And if Britain falls, so will England—and England's king with her."

"Now that," said Eleanor, "is a furious fancy. John is king of nothing. While Richard lives—and before God, child, that will continue, whatever John may do—John will never be king of anything."

"John is king of all Britain," Arslan said, "an office which Richard refused, to Britain's cost; but Richard was never meant for it. Will you leave the troops in place, majesty, and let John go? You may go with him if you please, or send guards whom you trust, but let him go. Richard's safety may depend on it. That of Britain certainly does."

"Richard is in the Holy Land," said Eleanor, "and England is safe, because I am here to keep it so. I, child: Eleanor, by the wrath of God Queen of the English. Not John Lackland."

Arslan bent his head, not in submission, though she might think so, but because there was fire in him, and he dared not lash her with it. The gates of her mind were locked and barred. She knew what she knew. She would hear nothing else.

"Remember, lady," he said, "when the time comes. Remember what you said to me, of both your sons." He bowed low over her hand, and set a magic in it, a pearl of white light that would linger for a while and then wink out. Maybe it would give her pause. More likely she would shrug it away.

He had done what he could. There was nothing more to do or say.

# CHAPTER 37

Eleanor reduced the garrisons along the coast, but she did not dismiss them entirely. Maybe she had heard Arslan after all, or more likely she reckoned it a simple and sensible precaution. She had taken every office and prerogative that John had laid claim to, with the title of regent and the powers of a queen, and a more difficult, contentious, complicated task, Arslan could not imagine.

John withdrew to the royal castle of Wallingford—to sulk, people said. It suited him to let them think so. As soon as he was settled there, he summoned the guardians, invoking powers that Eleanor refused to admit existed. That pleased him, Arslan thought, and rather amused him.

They came by the straight tracks from north and east and west. Hugh Neville, who had been in Sherwood, had met Father Hugh on the track, riding down from Lincoln; they rode in together. William the Marshal came from the marches of Wales, where he had been contending with a bit of rebellion among the wild Welshmen. Eschiva came last and latest, riding from Dover. She had been standing guard on the rampart of Britain, on the white cliffs where the head of Bran was buried, looking out forever across the sea.

Arslan was with the guardians when she came. Kalila led her in, having taken on the office of door-guard. It was near dark, and a steady rain was falling. Her cloak was wet, her boots and the hem of her gown plastered with mud. She looked, nonetheless, as if she knew nothing of cold or damp; she refused a bath and rest, accepted wine and bread and cheese, and settled by the fire.

She had not acknowledged Arslan's presence. He saw Father Hugh's brows raised, and John's shrug and shake of the head. No one said anything, for which he was grateful.

He kept his gaze averted from her, though he yearned to dwell on her, to fill his eyes with her face. This was a gathering of great import, the king and the guardians of Britain; he and Kalila were there on sufference.

They came round to it quickly, as soon as Eschiva had got her breath. "This is serving me better than I thought at first," John said. "Philip thinks that I've been put a stop to by my mother, and that I'm powerfully resentful of it and her. He's biding his time now, waiting for me to escape and come to join him."

"That won't last long," the Marshal said. "This is too rich a prize, and time is flying. The Crusade won't go on much longer. If he's going to move against Britain, he'll do it sooner rather than later."

"Before summer, I'll wager," said Neville, "unless he's distracted yet again."

"I've been thinking on that," John said. "The walls of air are as high as they can be, and you guardians are laboring mightily to maintain them. But what if we find another way—a vessel, as it were, to contain the power that is in all of you? If we can focus it, gather it, maybe we can strengthen it beyond anything that the four of you alone can do."

"A vessel?" asked Neville. He rubbed his jaw, fingers rasping on stubble. "What, like a mirror? A cauldron? A holy well?"

"A living vessel," John said. "One so empty that magic can't help but fill it full."

"You're mad," said Neville as they all began to understand. "You can't bring *him* back."

"Why not?" said John. "He's a great weapon."

"He is a great plague on Britain, and a great enemy to the barons. If you bring him back, you'll cast the whole kingdom into disarray."

"Only the mortal kingdom," John said, "and my royal mother is well capable of managing that. We need this talent he has, or this utter lack of talent if you prefer. The Wild Magic showed us how best to use it—maybe this was what it meant us to do all along?"

"Such a weapon can turn and lop off the hand that wields it," the Marshal said. "He's thoroughly hated in England, thanks in part to your efforts. We'll be lucky if his return doesn't bring about a war."

"Mother won't let that happen," John said. "It will keep her busy, too, which is all to the good. Shall we do it, my lords, my lady? Shall we take this weapon for ourselves?"

"If we say no," said Neville, "will that stop you?"

"No," said John.

"Then you didn't need us at all."

"I do," John said. "Someone has to go to Normandy and find him, and bring him back to Britain. He'll need the straight tracks, and a ship, and passage through the walls of air."

"I'll go," said Kalila before Arslan could open his mouth.

It was as if the walls had spoken. She never spoke in councils; she was the perfect servant, silent, invisible, and discreet. Since her brother died, she had become even more silent; without him to liven the days with squabbles, she was a quiet creature—too quiet, Arslan realized with a small and potent shock. He had been so caught up in his own troubles that he had thought no more of her than of the knife he wore at his belt: always there, always useful, but little regarded except when he needed it.

John spoke for them all. "We do thank you, sir Saracen, but we need someone inconspicuous—someone who not only won't be missed, but who can travel unnoticed. One of my couriers, maybe, or if one of you guardians has a servant whom you trust—"

"No one will miss me," Kalila said. "As for my being noticeable . . ." She took up the mantle that Eschiva had laid aside, and pulling off the turban, wrapped herself in the heavy dark wool. She did not do anything remarkable, that Arslan could see, but he caught his breath. Where a moment before had stood a Seljuk youth, now was a slender dark-eyed woman. She looked no more foreign than some of the darker ladies of France, or the black-eyed beauties of Provence or the Italies. Another subtle shift, and even that was dulled and muted; she could have been a tavernkeeper's daughter or a merchant's wife, with a round, ordinary, brown-eyed face.

Eschiva applauded her. "Oh, splendid! This is wonderful."

The Marshal and Hugh Neville were gaping like fools. John, Arslan was interested to notice, was not surprised at all, nor Father Hugh, either; but Arslan would have expected it of him. Father Hugh knew everything.

"Yes, this is splendid," John said, "and very, very clever. Madam, how well can you play a Gascon widow, say, on pilgrimage through the shrines of France?"

"How well do I need to feign the accent?" she asked.

His lips twitched. "Is there an accent you can feign better?"

"Provençal," she said. "I can be a respectable lady from Toulouse. I'll need a maid—that may be a difficulty. No lady of rank will travel without one, even on a journey of severe penance."

"I'll go."

Yet again the walls had spoken. Arslan had known that Susanna was there in shadows, listening, but he would never have expected her to betray her presence. She came into the light, meeting John's startlement with a bland stare. "Think. She needs someone versed in the Arts, but we can't spare Eschiva, even if she could escape notice: people do remember a woman as tall as a man, with hair the color of a beacon fire. Whereas I'm a little brown dumpling, and no one troubles me with a second glance. I'll make a fine maidservant, don't you think? So plain and so reassuringly nondescript, in the shadow of my beautiful lady."

"Are you that eager to escape me?" John asked a little too quietly.

"You know I'm not," she said, "but who else can go? All the rest of you are needed here. Yes, even you, lion's cub! You're the cord that holds the rest of them together. If you go, too much will unravel."

She was not speaking to John, not just then. Arslan considered any number of words, but in the end he said none of them. The truth cut close to the bone. A time would come when he could leave, but not now.

It was an almost physical pain to think of Kalila going away. She had been divided from him by the width of Britain as often as not, that winter, but France was across the sea and under Philip's power. He had lost her brother to Britain's cause. He could not bear to lose her.

Maybe he already had. She was looking to John and not to Arslan, and Susanna was beside her. They were convincing, he granted them that: the demure young widow from Toulouse and her somewhat older and somewhat plainer maid, waiting on the prince's pleasure.

John nodded. "Yes. Yes, it's the best way—maybe the only one. My lords, my lady—can a ship be readied for them as soon as they can reach the sea?"

"There is one at Dover," Eschiva said. "It might be worth recalling that the castellan's wife there is this man's sister. If we send a message from her to bolster ours, he might be more easily persuaded."

"Excellent," said John. "Yes, that is very good indeed. We'll do it, then. Ladies, can you be ready to go by morning?"

"Easily," said Susanna. Kalila nodded without speaking.

"Good," John said. "See to whatever you need. My lady Eschiva, I'll not ask that you leave again so soon, but—"

"They need a guide," she said, "and someone to speak for them in Dover. I'll go. Only let me have that bath and that bed, and I'll be grateful."

"Anything you wish," said John, "and my thanks with it."

That was unusually gracious of him. She bowed to it, and rose, swaying a little. She was not as strong as she pretended. Even so, she shook off Arslan's hand when he would have supported her, and withdrew unescorted to the bath and the bed.

Her message had been abundantly clear. Arslan elected to ignore it. He gave her time for the bath, during which Kalila also retreated, but she went with Susanna; they were arm in arm, plotting Kalila's wardrobe for the journey.

The men stayed behind, exchanging glances, until Hugh Neville burst out laughing. "What a mob of mooncalves we are! Lion cub, don't tell me you've known all along."

"It was my order," Arslan said. "She hid herself on the ship coming out of Acre, after both I and her brother had commanded her to stay in the city. It was all I could think of at the time, to keep her safe and explain what she was doing in my company. She played the part well, didn't she?"

"Admirably," John said. "I might not have suspected, either, if you hadn't left her behind when we went into the north."

Arslan stiffened. That memory had softened only a little with time's passing.

John did not press the subject too much further. "After that I watched her, and it was obvious. Are all Turkish women like her?"

"Sometimes," said Arslan, "in the tribes, the young women ride and fight and shoot with their brothers. In the cities, no. They live in veils and do as ladies do."

"Remarkable," said John. The others were pleased to agree.

Arslan escaped after that, without particular pretext, though if anyone had asked, he would have indicated the garderobe. He tracked Eschiva by her memory and the faint scent of her in the air, following it to the ladies' chambers. Servants were bringing out the basin when he came, carrying away the makings of the bath. He slipped in past them.

She was in her chemise, wrapped in a blanket, plaiting her red-gold hair. Firelight gleamed in the coils of it, and cast a rosy sheen on her milk-white skin. Her beauty stabbed his heart.

If he had hoped to surprise her into warmth, he was disappointed. She greeted him coolly, as if she had been expecting him; she did not invite him to sit.

He sat in spite of her, on the bed—which made her lips tighten. Good, he thought nastily. Let her reflect that a husband had rights which he could claim, and the law would support him if she refused.

"Good evening, my lady," he said civilly.

She did not answer. He had not expected her to.

"It's not Easter," he said, "nor London, but it will do, don't you think? Isn't it time we settled this quarrel?"

"Are we quarreling?"

"It may be that in Britain there is another name for two months of determined silence and dedicated avoidance. Was it that unforgivable, what I did?"

There was no yielding in her face at all, not even by the slightest fraction. "Did you lie with her?"

He gritted his teeth before he said something he would forever regret. He chose the words carefully and spoke them with care. "You know that I did not."

"Did you want to?"

"I wanted to lie with you," he said, "and only you, then as now."

"I wish I could believe you."

He could not answer that, not without making it all immeasurably worse.

She finished her plait and bound it with a bit of ribbon the same color as her eyes. For a moment his heart leaped, but then it stilled again. Green ribbon was common enough. This could not be the gift he had bought for her in Canterbury.

Her eyes were green glass, flat, hard, and empty of expression. He found nothing there to touch, no hope for any words he might say. She was implacably turned against him.

And all because he had shown courtesy to her mother. It was absurd; outrageous. It was utterly unjust.

He rose with stiff dignity. "Good night, lady. May you have a safe journey."

She was a little nonplussed. What, had she expected a fight? Should he have seized her and flung her down and had his will of her?

That was not in him, however angry he might be. If that made him weak, so be it. Better weak than dishonorable, even to his own wife.

# CHAPTER 38

Eschiva did not know what had got into her. She had watched him, listened to him, and wanted with all her heart to come down from her high pinnacle and take him in her arms and end this long contention. It had been folly when it began, and now it was worse than folly. It was grief to them both.

But when he sat in front of her with his heart in his eyes, some demon of perversity had given her nothing but cruel words to say. She should have leaped into his arms and not driven him off. At the very least, when he was gone, she should have gone after him. She sat by the fire instead, all night long, wide awake and sick at heart.

He was not there in the morning to say farewell, though John was, and the rest of the guardians. She upbraided herself for looking for him, and worse, for caring that he had not come. Coward, to hide himself away from her, even after her cruelty.

That fired her temper, and carried her out of the castle, through the town, and past the gate. He was there, mounted on the brown cob that had followed him from Windsor, dressed as a poor clerk. She rebuked her heart for leaping up and singing.

Susanna spoke for them all. "You can't come with us," she said. "Didn't you hear what the guardians were saying? You have to stay in Britain."

"Did anyone say I was leaving the kingdom?" he asked. "I have messages to carry to Dover. It's only sensible that we should travel together."

Susanna pursed her lips but forebore to argue. Kalila shrugged and almost smiled. Eschiva hid behind her mask of irritability, but her heart was beating hard. Coward, was he? After all, maybe not.

The straight track ran close by the city for those who knew how to find it. Arslan and Kalila rode on it side by side, the others behind, casually alert as one always should be on such a track. It was strange to see the Turk in woman's dress, and so unmistakably a woman, too, with her hair bound up under a veil and her body hidden in gown and mantle. Certain elements of her baggage, however, made Eschiva suppress a smile. From the shape and heft of them, she had kept the Turkish horseman's bow and the sword of fine eastern steel.

They began to slow. Arslan's back tensed. Kalila slid the bow from its wrappings and strung it in a smooth deft motion. She kept the arrow in her free hand, ready to nock.

A shape stirred among the trees. It was coming toward them, moving without haste. They halted. Eschiva felt out the wards; her brows went up.

Hugh Neville rode out of the Worldwood, as casual as if it had been a mortal forest. He was dressed for a journey, and he was smiling. "It seems," he said, "that I have errands to run in the east. Can you bear my company?"

"You need to ask?" Susanna smiled and let him kiss her hand.

But he was not watching her, once greetings were done and they had ridden on again. He was watching Kalila. She never knew: her eyes were on Arslan. Eschiva, watching all of them, caught herself smiling wryly. Arslan was as oblivious to Kalila as she was to Neville. Eschiva should have been a troubadour: she could have sung it, and made herself immortal.

They were two days on the straight track to Dover. The first night they paused near Windsor, in an inn like the plain folk they were pretending to be: a clerk, a forester, and three women who had enlisted their protection. There were few travelers on the road that night; they had the sleeping-room to themselves, with a fire and clean beds, and the innkeeper's good brown ale.

Arslan turned up his nose at that, and Kalila, being a Muslim, did not drink such things. Susanna and Neville twitted them for it, amiably. Eschiva drank the ale and ate the stew that came with it, with barley bread and strong cheese, and came to a decision.

While the others prepared to sleep, she went out into frosty starlight and secured wards about the inn, not for great need but because it was a useful pretext. As she had hoped, when she went back in, the lights were dimmed. Kalila and Susanna shared a bed. Neville was about to slide in beside Arslan, leaving Eschiva the third and last for herself. She stopped him and tilted her head. He grinned and retreated.

Arslan had his face to the wall. She slipped under the coverlets. His shoulder was a wall, broad and impenetrable. With beating heart she laid herself along the length of him.

He went rigid. She slid arms about his middle. If he cast her off, she would hold on.

He turned in her embrace, with quickness which was startling in so big a man. And he was a man now, not a gawky boy: the strength of him was a man's, and the face looking down at her in the dim light, the eyes too dark to read. She reached up and drew his head down, and kissed him long and slow. At first he did not respond, but suddenly he caught fire.

She laughed and wept, covering him with kisses. "Ah, God, I've missed you!"

He mercifully did not point out that it had been entirely her fault. He did say, "So I'm forgiven?"

"Am I?"

"I'll think about it," he said.

She bridled, but he was laughing at her. Cruel—but she deserved it. She burrowed into the warmth of him, the familiar scent, the body she had come to know better even than her own. They moved together, as long and slow as that first kiss had been, and deliberately so; they wanted to savor each other, to make it last all night if they could, if flesh could endure it.

"Never," she whispered in his ear. "Never again."

He sighed, which was his only answer. When she traced his face again in kisses, she tasted salt. He had been weeping.

How strange; she had never thought of him as a man who wept. Even for Yusuf he had mourned dry-eyed, the fire in him burning the tears away.

For her he shed tears—of joy, she could hope. She rode him slowly to the summit, and lingered there until he gasped and let go. She cried out. He had filled her with living fire, too strong even for pain.

She fell into a sleep like unconsciousness, but full of dreams and visions. Most of what she saw then, she would remember when she woke, though she would not understand it until its moment was come.

But one thing she understood. She sat up in the dawn, and said, "He's there. He's come to Dover."

They woke one by one in their various ways, Arslan first as always, blinking at her, fogged with sleep.

"The bishop is in Dover," she said. "He's come over without us."

"John will laugh," said Susanna. "He'll laugh loud and long."

"What will you wager he already knew?" Neville said.

Susanna yawned and stretched. "I'll be sorry not to risk the roads of Normandy. I hear they're beset with brigands."

"We could all do with a little mayhem." Neville rose from his solitary bed and pulled on his shirt. "Shall I go looking for a pack of robbers?"

"His grace of Ely will provide us with plenty of that," Susanna said dryly.

"Maybe it would be best if—" he began.

"We'll go on," she said. "We still have an errand."

He bowed to her will. In the mortal world he was one of the great lords of England and she hardly more than a commoner, but in this world they lived in, this Britain, she was the king's chosen lady. He was her knight and her servant, and well he remembered it.

Dover was a sea-city, a city washed in salt and wetted with spray. It played host to the trade from Calais, and was one of the great gates of Britain. From its snow-white cliffs, the head of Bran, whose scepter John carried, kept ceaseless guard over the kingdom.

William Longchamp had come in with rather more dignity than he had gone out, dressed as a lord of the Church and not a serving-woman. He had taken lodging in the castle with his sister and his brother-in-law the castellan, in their own chambers of course; he would hardly settle for anything less.

Eschiva was known here as the Bishop of Lincoln's ward, a pious lady and sometime pilgrim who lodged respectably in the town. In that semblance she went calling on the castellan's wife, taking with her a pair of her kinswomen and their clerk and their guardsman.

The Lady Jeannette had not inherited the arrogance of her brothers. She was a little brown wren of a woman, bright-eyed and sharp-nosed and quick. She loved a good gossip, and she was wonderfully hospitable; she was never happier than when she had a castleful of guests and more on the way.

She was delighted to see Eschiva; she welcomed Susanna and Kalila with open arms and the two men with admiring glances. When they had been settled in a room as comfortable as a castle could offer, plied with dainties from the kitchens, and greeted as thoroughly as guests could be, she said to Eschiva, "Well then, tell me all the news. Have you heard from that young husband of yours? Have you mended the quarrel, and made yourself happy again?"

Arslan twitched but held still. Eschiva meant her smile to be mysterious, but Jeannette clapped her hands in delight. "So you did hear! Was it wonderful? Is he coming here? Will he take you away to his castle and ply you with endless delights?"

Arslan must be biting his lips till they bled. There was the faint but discernible sign of a blush on his cheeks. Eschiva wrenched her eyes away from him before she betrayed them both. "He may," she said, "when his duties allow."

"May that be soon," said Jeannette. She smiled at them all. "So then, are you here for the sea air? Will you be going to Normandy?"

"We had thought of it," Susanna said, "but the one we came to find is here." Eschiva opened her mouth, but Susanna forestalled her. "No, cousin. No more pretenses. Lady, we've been sent to your brother, to speak to him regarding a matter of importance. Will he see us?"

Jeannette frowned. For an instant Eschiva could see her brother in her, in the sudden darkening of her mood, but she was not by nature a dour woman. "How did you know he was here?"

"We had word of it yesterday," Susanna said. "We were going to Normandy to find him; it's God's good grace that he's come to England."

"He's come for justice," said Jeannette. "Not that I'd expect it of you, lady, but if you've come to arrest him, my husband and I will do all we can to prevent you."

"We don't wish him harm," said Susanna. "Quite the opposite, in fact. May we speak with him?"

"I can ask," Jeannette said, "but he'll want to know who you are."

"We come from the Count of Mortain," Susanna said.

Jeannette sucked in a breath.

"And since we are speaking the truth," said Eschiva, "this gentleman is the King's Forester, and this is my young husband whose castle is waiting for us to be free of all our duties to liege and kingdom, and this lady is his kinswoman from beyond the sea. We do come from John, and we bring a message that he may be eager to hear."

Jeannette looked hard at each one in turn, Arslan in particular. Something about him seemed to reassure her. "This is true?" she said to him.

He nodded. "We're sorry we deceived you. Suspicion is a habit, I'm afraid. Sometimes it's too strong."

Eschiva felt the hot flush in her skin. Surely he was not speaking to her, or of her, but the guilt was none the less for that.

"I do forgive you," Jeannette said. "These aren't easy times. It's hard to know whom to trust."

He bowed over her hand, which made her giggle like a girl. Eschiva could well understand that; he made her feel much the same.

Jeannette recovered her dignity with commendable swiftness, smoothed her skirts and straightened her wimple and said, "I had better take this message to him myself. Will you pardon me?"

"Gladly," Eschiva said, though Jeannette's eyes were on Arslan.

Not until Jeannette was gone did it strike Eschiva: she was amused. But she was not twisting her gut with jealousy. If nothing else came of this journey, that alone made it worth the doing.

# CHAPTER 39

Welliam Longchamp agreed to see John's messengers, but not, from the time it took and the expression Jeannette wore when she came back, entirely willingly. "It might be best," she said, "if as few of you went as possible. He's not in the most cheerful mood."

They all exchanged glances. Susanna said, "Two of us were sent in the beginning. Let us go. If we fail, we'll bring in the rest."

That was not entirely to everyone's liking, but Jeannette nodded briskly. "Come, then, while he's still inclined to let you in at all. He has been downright cantankerous since he came back."

Kalila could hardly blame him: he was well hated in this kingdom, and he had left it in great haste. She followed Susanna in silence, like the guard she had been for so long. It was still strange to feel the swirl of skirts about her knees, and to be looked at as a woman. In a way it was simpler than being a turbaned infidel in a Christian country, but even so, it was terribly complicated.

The bishop had laired himself in the best and warmest room in the castle. He had a pair of monks with him, burly silent men who looked more like guardsmen than men of God, and a young novice who was reading to him from the lives of the saints. He kept the women waiting through the lives of Saints Felicity and Perpetua, but stopped the boy before he had well begun with Saint Munditia. Kalila would have liked to hear the rest of that, but it was hardly her place to ask such a thing.

"Brother," Jeannette said with strained patience, "here are the messengers I told you of. I'll leave you with them if you don't mind; I have guests in the hall."

The bishop waved her away. He was glaring at Susanna. "John sent me *you?*"

"He trusts me," Susanna said placidly. She knelt to kiss his ring, and as Kalila rather uncomfortably followed suit, she sat without invitation, arranged her skirts, and regarded the bishop with a calm dark gaze. "So, your grace. What brings you back to England?"

"Justice," he said. "I was cast out like a criminal, who had been the king's own justiciar and the Pope's legate. I am still the latter, by order of Pope Celestine, may God bless and keep him. I wish a fair and formal trial without interference from the mob, and if possible, reinstatement to the office from which I was driven."

Susanna's brow arched. "Indeed," she said. "Somewhat might be done to help your cause."

"And why," he demanded, "does John of all people want to help me now, after he led the forces that drove me out?"

"Times change," Susanna said. "The queen is in England now, and ruling with a heavy hand. John has a thing to ask of you, a favor if you will, for which he can pay in kind."

The bishop's eyes narrowed in suspicion. "John does favors for no one. What does he want of me?"

"Your presence in England," she said, "and the pleasure of your company."

"And?"

"Isn't it enough?"

"No," he said. "I'm not an idiot. Your leman despises me. What use is he going to make of me? Will he be flaunting me in his mother's face?"

"Would you mind if he did?"

"I would mind if it got me killed."

"We can promise you," said Susanna, "that your life and body will be safe while you remain under John's protection."

She did not, Kalila noticed, mention his immortal soul. He appeared not to notice the omission. "That's all I'm to do? Be a defiance to the queen?"

"And, one hopes, be properly tried and acquitted of wrongdoing in the conduct of your office."

"He will see to that?"

"He will do his best," said Susanna.

She had him. He was suspicious still, but not of anything that should have concerned him. He had no magic; he did not know he lacked it, nor know what gift it gave him. Nor was Susanna about to tell him. His innocence, Kalila suspected, was a great part of his strength.

"My lord will send an escort for you," Susanna said, "of size and rank as befits your station. We'll remain with you here until it comes—hostages, if you wish, for his goodwill."

"Good," said the bishop. "That will satisfy me."

Arslan went back to John by the straight track, and Eschiva with him, bearing word that would please John very much indeed. Kalila stayed with Susanna in Dover, and Hugh Neville stayed with them, to Kalila's surprise. She would have thought that he would be eager to go on about his business, whatever it was that the chief of the king's foresters did. Allah knew, there were no forests here; only grassy downs and white sea-cliffs.

They were not prisoners in the castle. Jeannette's husband the castellan was as hospitable a man as his wife, and he loved to go hunting with hawks. Susanna was not overly fond of the sport, but Kalila had grown up with falcons. The first time the lord went out hawking, she yearned so visibly that Neville said, "Well, lady! Would you come, too?"

He did not say it as men often did to a woman, half amused, half in disbelief. He was asking honestly. "I should be glad to come," she said. Belatedly she remembered her duty to Susanna, but that lady said, "Oh, go, go! You don't have to ask my leave."

Kalila was so delighted that she forgot herself and kissed the prince's lady on both cheeks. Susanna laughed, returned the kiss, and pushed her away. "Go on, before they leave without you."

She danced ahead of Neville down to the mews, which she had already investigated thoroughly when no one was about. The hawk that she had had her eye on, a merlin, was young but well started, and no one had claimed it. The falconer was dubious until he saw how she took it on her fist, gentled it with a feather, and fed it a bit of meat to assure it that she was, for this day, its master.

"You know falcons," Neville said as they rode out in a company: the castellan, Neville and Kalila, and a handful of young nobles from holdings in or near Dover. She was the only woman, but with Neville beside her, that was not a difficulty.

"We used to hunt with hawks," she said, "in the hills near Beausoleil where I was born. I rode with my brothers, and with my lord Arslan; whatever they learned, I learned with them."

"You learned it well," he said.

She shrugged. "Would you have thought so if I were still in trousers?"

He flushed slightly. He was a fair-skinned man as so many were here, where the sun was weak and often veiled in rain; any hint of color was clear to see. "I thought that you were a fine hunter and a master archer," he said, "and no novice with a sword. I still think all of that—and that you are also a falconer."

"In my country," she said, "now as in ancient days, we learn to ride and shoot and abhor the Lie; and we learn to hunt and fight."

"Women, too?"

"Sometimes," she said. "I'm a Seljuk, a Turk—not a creature of the cities."

"This country must be impossibly strange."

"Strange, yes," she said, "but not impossible."

"You never yearn for your own land and your own people?"

"I do," she said, "but not so much that I'm like to die of it. I could have gone back, after all. I chose to come here."

"Because of your lord?"

She nodded, and managed not to blush, too, which she was proud of. "And because I wanted to see what it was like."

"Do you like it?"

She studied his face. He grew his beard, as men often did not here; she liked that. It made him familiar, somehow, and handsome, too, in the way of the long lean men of England. His hair was the color of oak-leaves in autumn, his eyes the clear blue of a summer sky. They were beautiful eyes, and warm as they rested on her, waiting for her answer.

She gave it at last, after proper thought. "I do like it. It's wet and cold, but the green is wonderful. And flowers—so many flowers. Your roses are as sweet as the roses of Damascus, and those are the sweetest in the world."

"You've seen Damascus?"

"Oh, yes," she said. "Jerusalem, too, of course, and Acre, and Antioch."

He reached impulsively and took her hand. It was brown and strong, callused with bowstring and swordhilt, not a lady's slender white hand at all, but he seemed to find it pleasing enough. "You've walked in all those places? Have you crossed the Jordan?"

"Many times," she said.

"Ah," he sighed. "I do regret it, you know: the duty that keeps me here, that binds me to Britain. I'd have liked to go Crusading."

"Maybe someday you will," she said.

"Maybe." He did not sound as if he believed it. He shook his head, let go her hand. She was sorry that he had done it, but not so bold that she would go seeking his clasp again. "I'm bound here. I chose that duty as much as it chose me. Whatever regrets I have, I won't give up my office for them."

"Nor I," she said, "even to be in my own country again. Here is where God requires me to be. I can't refuse the fate that's written for me."

He nodded. "Our faiths aren't so very different, are they? Or our fates, either."

It would seem not, she thought as they hunted with falcons over the green rolling hills within sound of the sea. Her merlin was a fierce hunter, eager for the kill, but willing to come back to her hand. Something about it made her think of Neville, the way he looked at her, the ease with which they conversed. He was a free creature, too, freely choosing to ride beside her.

It dawned on her belatedly that he was courting her. She had been courted by women while she was Karim, and now and then by men who liked a beautiful boy, but she had never been courted as herself before: in Beausoleil she had been too young, and after she left there, the world had known her as Karim. She rather thought she liked it.

Did she like him? She rather thought she did. They had hunted together before he knew what she was, run messages for John, ridden in his train. He was amusing, lighthearted but not light-minded, a good teller of tales, a fair-to-middling singer, and, though he hid this from nearly everyone, a powerful enchanter. The forests were his, the power of wood and water, and the wards of England were partly in his hands.

Now he looked at her as if he thought her beautiful, and listened to her prattle as if he thought it interesting. He was here, she understood, because of her. He had followed her.

He was not Arslan. But that, just then, was no ill thing.

After their hunt was done, when they had ridden back to the castle and eaten the day's meal and gone to whatever diversions the lengthening evening offered, Kalila left the women gossiping over their embroidery, put on tunic and hose and bound up her hair under a cap, and went hunting.

She found him in the third tavern she entered. He was with some of the young men from the day's hunt, passing round flagons of ale and playing desultorily at dice. She slid in beside him, caught the dice cup as it went past, and won the round. They all roared, except Neville. He stared.

He did not pick her up by the scruff of her neck and toss her out—she had gambled on that when she began. But he ended the game somewhat more abruptly than the others might have wished, flung a handful of coins on the table, and hauled her out into the street.

The shadows were long, the sun touching the horizon. She grinned at him from under the hat, which had fallen over her eyes in the hasty exit. "You are a very poor loser," she said.

"Is this a game?" he demanded of her. "Are you trying to get yourself killed or worse?"

"What, you think I'm a stranger to taverns?" She laughed. "I'll wager I've been in more than you have, sir forester—and won more fights in them, too."

She had been in some of them with him, taverns and fights both. She watched him remember, and confront the memory with what he knew now, and be hopelessly confused. He was not angry: she was glad to see that.

What she did then, she did with careful calculation, and full understanding of what would come of it. She reached up, for he was nearly as tall as Arslan, and took his face in her hands. She drew it unresisting down and kissed him, there in the street, and no matter who saw.

He swept her up and carried her off. The place to which he took her was an inn, and in the inn a room, well appointed and somewhat more pleasant than a lord's chamber in a castle. No drafts; no reek of the garderobe. No dogs tumbling on the floor. And no servants to stare and whisper and spread scandal, only an innkeeper who, once amply paid, was both silent and discreet.

Kalila had heard enough guardroom gossip to know what to do. This must be what it was to be drunk on wine: dizzy, happy, and warm all over. She dropped her garments wherever they fell, and delighted in his expression as he saw the whole of her. She was beautiful, if slender—too slender, the canons of the love-poets would declare, but in this country the canons must surely be different.

He was as dizzy as she, but he had had a flagon or three of ale. He was beautiful, too, long and lean like a hunting wolf. His skin where the sun did not touch it was milky white. Hers was greenish dark, like olives. She let down her hair, all the heavy masses of it, rippling below her waist.

He breathed the scent of it. Enchanter though he was, he was all under her spell. She was under one herself, and she knew it; she embraced it. She embraced him, and did things that she had heard of but never done. He murmured with pleasure. His hands began to move, to touch her in ways, in places, that she had never known could be so delightful.

They tumbled together onto the bed. Her legs parted of their own accord. She gasped at the sudden pain.

He recoiled. She held on, so that he pulled them both to their feet. "You—you are not—" he stammered.

Poor thing, he was shocked. She could be angry: he had thought her a wanton. But she had been acting like one. "I've never taken a man to bed before," she said.

He freed himself from her, scrambled up his garments, covered himself as modestly as if he had been a woman. "I never meant to dishonor you. Lady—"

"My lord," she said, "I want to be dishonored."

"I don't make a sport of taking maidenheads," he said stiffly.

"Good," she said, "because I would not give mine to a man who did."

"You are a respectable woman. I can't—"

"If my brother challenges you to a duel over this, he'll have to fight me first. No one else will care."

He blinked at the thought of her fighting as his champion. It made him laugh, incredulously but with honest mirth. But when he spoke, it was to say soberly, "I know my reputation, and it's carefully cultivated, but I'm not in the habit of debauching virgins."

"You sound so prim," she said. "You came hunting me. What did you think would come of it?"

"I . . . didn't think," he confessed, and not too loudly, either.

"I did," she said. "I considered the rumors—and the truth. I decided. Come here."

She spoke so imperiously that he had obeyed her before he knew it. She took his hands in hers. "I will be your leman," she said, "and you mine. I will not give up my Faith even to please you, but neither will I ask that you profess Islam. I will go my way as I need and am needed, and I will ride where I am sent, as you will, for the kingdom and its king. I do find you pleasing, my lord, and I accept your suit, though maybe you began it in a misunderstanding."

He shook his head in wonder. "You are like no woman I have ever known."

"That's because you've never known a Turk before." She kissed his hands that rested in hers. "Do I please you, my lord?"

"You astonish me."

"But am I pleasing?"

"Very . . . much so," he said, taking a breath in the middle, as if she had pummeled the wind out of him. "I suppose if I ever touch another woman, you'll sweep off her head with your sword."

"Of course not," she said. "But do tell me, and not hide her from me, or I'll sweep off something of yours with my sword, and it won't be your head."

"God's feet," he said, "I went hunting a doe and found myself a tigress."

"There are does enough in the world," she said, "but tigresses are a rarer prey."

"Yes—they turn the hunter into the hunted." He did not seem greatly dismayed by that: he was smiling. He stooped to kiss her hands, and lightly, almost shyly, brushed her lips with his. "You are a marvel," he said.

"Love me," she said.

This time he did not shrink from it. He was careful, and tender; the pain was as little as he could make it. After that he gave her pleasure, more than she had expected of a Frank; but was he not an enchanter? They were not as other Franks were.

She held him in her arms when it was done, and smiled. She had chosen well. Yes: well indeed.

And no guilt. No regrets, that this was Hugh Neville and not another. It was a victory of sorts, and an ending, too: a farewell to childhood, and to hopes that had never been more than illusion. This was real and true and strong. This would endure.

# CHAPTER 40

John roared with laughter when he heard the message that Arslan and Eschiva had brought. "God's teeth! All the sorcery in the world, and the man calmly ups and takes ship and lands himself in our laps. Are we blessed? Are we born lucky? Shall we exploit this for all it's worth?"

He was not asking to be answered. In public he had to pretend to be sulking, for the benefit of his mother's spies, but in this secret council, he got up from his chair and danced with glee.

Arslan had learned never to be surprised by what John chose to do. In this instance he sent the escort he had promised, but stayed in Wallingford, ostentatiously refusing to involve himself with his mother's rule of England. That did not prevent a riding of barons from coming to beg audience with him. He received them in a bare hall with a small escort of armed men, one of whom was Arslan. His clothes were as plain as he could bear to be seen in, his jewels nonexistent. He cradled a small heavy bag in his lap.

The barons did obeisance as was proper to the son of a king, which made his lip curl. The one who spoke for them, Arslan knew only slightly; he was from somewhere in the south of England, and he had a sonorous voice of which he was very proud. He let it roll forth in splendid cadences. "Your highness, we bring news that dismays us all. The Bishop of Ely has returned—he is in Dover. He threatens to call us all to justice."

John sat half-smiling, toying with the fastening of the bag. "He is? He does?"

"Of course, your highness," said the baron, "he will be dealt with. We will cast him out again."

"Will you?" John let his gaze wander across their faces. "Tell me, is he as afraid of you as you seem to be of him? I'm wagering he's not. You see, messires, not only is your news old news, his grace of Ely has promised me seven hundred pounds of silver within the week, if only I will speak for him. He's sent me this in earnest of his promise, and kindly, too, since I'm in such need of it."

He poured a stream of silver from the bag into his lap, smiling at them. They blanched.

"You see," said John sweetly, "what need will do to a man. I grieve that I can't offer you wine—we drank the last of it yesterday. There should be fish for dinner; I did order the boys to see what can be pulled out of the river. You won't mind if they bring home the commoner sort of fish, surely, messires? It will be a proper Lenten sacrifice, with prayer and penance to wash it down."

They retreated so hastily that they barely remembered to say their farewells. John gathered up his pieces of silver, poured them back into their bag, and tossed it at Arslan. His grin was all sharp teeth. "Now see where they scurry," he said.

"What will you do when they catch you in the lie?" Arslan wanted to know. "The bishop never offered you anything."

"No," said John with utter lack of remorse, "but they might—and I do need money. They cut me off short, before I could hide away all that I had—and good troops don't come cheap."

"You made sure your mother paid them off," Arslan pointed out.

"It still wasn't cheap to hire them in the first place," John said, "and I'll be hiring them again soon enough. I'll need full coffers for that."

Arslan sighed, but held his peace.

John had gambled and won: within the week the barons were back with a laden pack train and an offering of silver surpassing that which Ely supposedly had promised him. Better yet, it came from the king's exchequer—and with it they offered him homage as the king's heir.

Hardly had he sent the barons out again, this time having regaled them with a moderate feast and a decent supply of middling bad wine, before the escort came in with William Longchamp in their midst. He was dressed as a clerk—Arslan's own expedient, which he seemed to have reckoned equally useful—and his arrogance was considerably muted.

John had Susanna to thank for that. Her expression reminded Arslan vividly of a mother put out of patience with her child: lips pressed together, brows knit. When Ely was brought to the hall, he looked ready to burst out in a rant, but her stern glance reduced him to a sputter or two, and then silence.

"Well, sir," said John. "I did what I could, but it seems there's no justice in England. They'll not give you your trial, nor your justiciarship, either."

"Did you even try?" Ely demanded.

"I did let it be known that I would take your part," John said, "and they seemed suitably appalled—but they made it clear that they will not have you back."

Ely spat on the floor. "They bought you."

"They did try," John admitted. "I do have somewhat to offer you. A retreat; a place of safety until the hunt dies down. They'll drive you out with armed force if they can, or keep you imprisoned if you stay. My people are instructed to let it seem that you've returned to Normandy."

"While I skulk about in your shadow? What use is there in that?"

"Safety," John said. "Breathing space. Service to the king, if under another name and office than the one you hoped for. You do want to serve the king, yes? Isn't that where your heart is?"

"You are an evil man," Ely said, but he bent his head. "I'll stay while I must. What choice do I have?"

John spread his hands. "Maybe none," he said. "You are welcome here. It's a bit ascetic at the moment, but we'll see to that. Be at ease, rest in comfort. When you're ready, there's plenty to do."

"For you?"

"For Britain," said John.

"We should tell him," Arslan said. The guardians were gathered again, in haste and in secret, to consider this weapon that had come straight to their hands. "He should know what he is, and what use we'll make of him."

John shook his head. "Not that man. The blinder he is, the better. If he knows how badly we need him, he'll use it against us."

"I have to agree," Father Hugh said, not willingly. "As little as I love a lie, he's best left innocent."

"He has a gift for minutiae," John said. "They say God is in the details. Let him find God among the clerks. Who knows, it might even make him happy."

"You could be more charitable," Eschiva said, but not as if she expected him to listen.

"Charity is a saint's virtue," John said. "Kings can't afford it. Nor can you, since you'll be using him to strengthen the wards. Is there new word from France? Is it beginning to move?"

"Not yet," Hugh Neville said. He was propped in a corner, long legs stretched out, hands folded over his middle, looking as if he had fallen asleep. He opened one eye now, and it was brightly alert. "It's biding its time. I think it's up to something."

William the Marshal nodded. "There's magic being worked, but it's deep—almost too deep to sense. It will be slow to work its way to the light, but it will be all the stronger for that."

"It may not be as hidden as you think," said Neville. "I kept my ear to the ground while I was in Dover. Everybody who came across from France was spreading the same rumor: that Richard made attempts on Philip's life on the Crusade, and Philip left because of them. Philip is sworn to exact a price, and is determined to seize as many of Richard's lands as he can."

"We knew that," John said. "My mother was contending with it before my alleged rebellion brought her flying across the sea. Did you forget? Philip was in Normandy—he even tried to seize Rouen."

"Yes, we knew it," Neville said, "but there's a difference in the rumors now. They're more hostile. People are saying that maybe someone should make sure that Richard never comes back to England alive. And," he said, "they're saying that you, my lord, will reward anyone who makes the attempt."

"Are they?" John shook his head. "They're fools, then. I don't love my brother, but I'm hardly inclined to kill him."

"Still," said the Marshal, "it's alarming that this should be said of you. It can be turned against you."

"Can't everything?" John pushed himself out of the chair and prowled the room, a rare nervous gesture, or maybe he had only been mewed in this castle too long. "Do you think it's aimed at me? To weaken me?"

"It could be," Neville said. "They don't know who the true king is, I'm sure of that, but it seems they perceive you as the heir—however unwilling Richard may be to give you the title. They'll destroy him if they can, and discredit you; if they can see that you're imprisoned or stripped of your titles, so much the better."

"I should think they'd be happy now," John said. "I've been play-ing Achilles sulking in his tent for so long it's tedious. As far as they can know, I am in prison, and precious little silver to keep me com-fortable there, either."

"That won't last," Eschiva said, "now that you've won yourself a thousand pounds from the king's treasury—and barons bowing to you as your brother's successor, too. Are you trying to draw attention to yourself?"

"Would it hurt if I did? I've got you, lady and lords, and the crown and the scepter, and the power of Britain—as little good as it does me where any mortal can see. What does Richard have that magic would shrink from? His crown is mortal gold. His army is rid-dled with fever. He's won no friends among the kings. England is paying for that, and will go on paying, unless I can draw away the kings' hostility."

They all shivered as if a chill wind had blown through the room. But the fire burned steadily, and the hangings never moved. The moment passed without clear foreseeing, or none that any would admit to.

Eschiva went away with the guardians to work the magic that would transform a magicless man into a weapon against the enemies of Britain. Arslan could and perhaps should have gone with them, but although he had been part of the embassy that brought the man here, he had no stomach for this particular working. He left John, too, to his webs and his plots, and sought refuge in the open air.

On his way down to the gate, he found Kalila in a corner out of the way, kneeling and bowing in prayer as she still tried to do five times a day, every day, as every good Muslim did. She had gone back to turban and trousers, wisely enough in his estimation, though any-one who knew she was a woman would hardly be deceived.

He waited for her. He had hardly seen her since she came back to Wallingford; it seemed she was always out on errands. He was hun-gry, just then, for the company of kin, for a face he had known for as long as he could remember.

She finished her prayers and rose, still rapt, a little, in the memory. When she saw Arslan, she started. Her expression was not welcoming at all. If he had been minded to call it anything, he would have called it guilt.

It passed quickly; she smiled and spoke his name, and the amity between them was as it had always been. But there was a faint, false ring to it.

He had been meaning to ask if she would go for a gallop outside the walls with him, but he greeted her instead, said words that he forgot as soon as he had spoken them, and left her, he hoped, less puzzled than he himself was.

She did not follow him. That too was strange; so strange that he spun about, opening his mouth to demand an explanation. She looked as if she expected to be flogged at the very least: stiff, straight, set-faced.

Instead of the sharp words that had come leaping to his tongue, he said, "You may as well tell me. It will come out sooner or later."

She had been ready with defiance, but he had caught her off guard. She could only sputter and stammer, "What? What can I—"

His steady stare silenced her. She scrambled herself together and began again. "I don't know what you mean."

"You're a terrible liar," he said. "You always were. What have you done? What makes you think I'll have your hide for it?"

"I don't think you'll have my hide! I don't know why I'm being such an idiot. It shouldn't matter to you. You did it yourself. Except I'm not going to marry him. I don't want to, and I don't intend to. So don't try to make me."

"You—him?" She had startled Arslan after all. "You and a man?"

She lifted her chin. "Of course a man! You expected a woman?"

"*You* and—" He was making no sense at all. He struggled to say it without tripping over his tongue. "I think I thought of you as some sort of warrior saint."

"Like Saint Perpetua?"

He was speechless. If he was not careful, he would burst into wild laughter.

"I am not a saint," she said. "But you—if you lay a finger on my lover, you will die a martyr."

He flung up his hands. "There now! What would I want to do that for?"

"To protect my virtue."

"You can't do that yourself?"

Now she was at a loss for words. "You don't even care?"

"Of course I care! You're more a sister to me than my sisters.

Would it do any good if I raged and ramped and threatened to hack off his ballocks? Is that what you want of me?"

"No!" She leveled her glare on him. "Don't you think of it, either."

Arslan drew a breath and gathered his wits. "Is he honorable?"

"Completely."

"Does he cherish you?"

"Utterly."

"Do you love him?"

"Yes." She said it in a little surprise, as if she had not thought of it before. "Yes, I do."

"Well then," he said. "That's no more or less than I have to offer my lady, and I had the gall to marry her."

She sighed. The tension left her so suddenly that her knees gave way. He caught her before she fell, and held her up while she found her feet again.

She held on to his arm even after she was standing steady, and looked hard into his face. "You're all the brother I have," she said. "I don't want to lose that. Promise I never will."

"I promise," he said.

"No matter what I do?"

"No matter at all," said Arslan.

He had cause to remember that promise, come evening. Father Hugh and the Marshal had left as enchanters could, but Hugh Neville lingered in Wallingford. He came to Arslan after the revelry in hall began to die down, as Arslan waited for Eschiva to come to bed. He had brought a jar of wine and a pair of cups, and his expression made Arslan sit bolt upright. "She's risked her honor with *you*?"

Neville's shock gave way quickly to laughter. He filled one of the cups and held it out. "Appalling, isn't it?" He did not mean the wine. "There's no accounting for the will of a woman."

Arslan surged out of bed, past the cup which remained hovering in the air, and bore Neville back against the wall. Neville was smaller and slighter and a fair number of years older, but he was still a strong man, with powers beyond the mortal. Arslan struck aside the lash of them. "If you don't love her, truly love her—if she is no more than a few nights' diversion—by the seal of Solomon that bound my mother, I swear—"

"There now," said Neville. "Don't go swearing great oaths that could damn you for everlasting. I love her dearly, and I love her more, the more I know of her. She's splendid—wonderful. There never was such a woman."

Arslan closed his hand about Neville's throat and searched his face. He looked an easy, idle, handsome trifle of a man, but Arslan knew what a deception that was. If his protestations were lies, too . . .

It seemed they were not. His eyes were clear, no flicker of falsehood. He was not afraid, though Arslan could crush his throat in an instant.

Arslan let him go. "Love and honor her, and you live; we'll be brothers. Dishonor her in any way, and I become your bitter enemy. Do you understand?"

"Perfectly," Neville said. He was smiling. "I'm a happy man: I'm walking away alive and entire. You're alarming when you're in a temper, do you know that?"

"I've been told," said Arslan. He looked down at himself and understood part of Neville's smile. He was naked, and the other was both clothed and armed. "Alarming?" he said.

"Very," said Neville. He reached past Arslan and retrieved the cup where it still hung in the air. "Wine?"

Arslan eased abruptly, smiled, and took the cup. "To the ladies," he said.

"To the ladies," said Hugh Neville, with an audible sigh of relief.

# PART FOUR

# RANSOM

Advent 1192–Easter 1193

# CHAPTER 41

R ichard had disappeared.

The Crusade ended in the summer, dribbling away to nothing in a long round of fever and foolishness and endless wrangling. The Infidel still held Jerusalem. The Holy Sepulcher was still lost to Christendom. Little by little the army began to come home, until at the end of Advent nearly all who had survived that pestilential war were safe by their own firesides.

But no one had seen Richard since he left the harbor at Acre. He had let everyone know that he would be keeping Christmas court in his own lands. Then he had sailed away, and vanished from the earth.

"He's alive," Arslan said.

The queen held Christmas court at Windsor that year, and she had let it be known that her youngest son was expected to appear. John would happily have continued to conduct his affairs well outside of her orbit, but a royal command was difficult to refuse. He was at Windsor therefore in the heart of royal Britain, and the king's seat was very obviously unoccupied.

They had endured an evening of court, which consisted chiefly of sitting stiffly in the queen's presence, eating roast goose, and listening to a succession of singers and poets, some of whom claimed to have come direct from the Holy Land. Kalila, turbaned and trousered and playing squire to Arslan, had addressed the most flamboyant of those in the Arabic of which he claimed a native's knowledge, and sent him into babbling retreat.

It was not the splendor of revelry that any of them had expected of one of Eleanor's courts. Richard's absence cast a pall on them all.

Some of them had escaped after that: Arslan and Eschiva, John and the guardians, Susanna from a place among the ladies-in-waiting, and Kalila still shaking her head at the gibberish that the singer had tried to pass off as the language of the Prophet. When they were settled in John's chamber, which was barely big enough for all of them, they turned inevitably to the question that burned in every mind in England: what had become of Richard.

Arslan was unwontedly sleepy with wine and warmth. While the others spoke, he had slid into a drowse, a dream wrought of the words they were speaking and sealed with Richard's name. Out of that half dream, he roused to a sudden certainty.

"He's not dead," Arslan said. He had cut across a meander of conversation, abrupt and sharp as a blade. As they all stared at him, he said, "The spirits tell me—he's alive. But they can't tell me where."

"Can you guess?" William the Marshal asked him.

"By the Virgin's teat," John said, "I can do that. Pick an emperor, a king, a duke, a lord of any degree, anywhere in Europe—you can wager gold that Richard has made an enemy of him. I'll guess that Philip had something to do with it, though whether he did the actual deed . . . well, my lords and ladies, I'm but a king of ghosts and shadows. You're the great enchanters. Where is my brother?"

"We don't know," Father Hugh said for them all. "Tell us, young lion. What do your kinsfolk say of him?"

"Walls," he said slowly, from memory and from the whisper of bloodless voices in his ear. "Walls of stone. And walls—walls of air. *Ja nus hons pris ne dira sa reson . . .*"

He had sung that last, softly, in a voice that seemed hardly his own: *No captive will ever speak his mind . . .*

John shivered. "God! You sound just like Richard."

Arslan blinked, opening his eyes, coming to himself. "What? Did I say something strange?"

"Always," Eschiva said with gentle raillery, but she sobered quickly. "Could you see where he was?"

"You weren't with me? But I felt—"

"The walls of air," she said. "I can't see past them. Can you?"

"Darkness," he said. "The light of a lamp. A high tower, and a room in it. A man sitting—sitting on a stool. He has a lute. He's making a song.

> *"Ja nus hons pris ne dira sa reson*
> *Adroitement, s'ensi com dolans non. . . ."*

"Leave it to Richard," John said, "to whine in rhyme. Can you tell who's got him?"

Arslan shook his head in frustration. "It's no one I know. Not Philip. He's not in France. But France has something to do with the walls about him. I keep seeing a hedge of lilies, and a leopard caught in them."

"A hedge of lilies . . ." John mused. "France, of course. Anything else?"

"Only walls," Arslan said. He pressed his fist to his brow, which must be pounding with pain. "He does look well, if bored. He's not been harmed that I can see."

"Too bad," said John. "I always did think a flogging would do him good." He tugged at the beard he had grown that summer, to look older, he said, but Eschiva suspected that he had done it to look more like a king. It did suit him. It also made him look less like his mother, which in his estimation would be an advantage. "So then: can your spirits do anything? Can they set him free?"

Arslan shook his head. "They have no power over things of flesh. They can only watch."

"Whoever has him is going to want something," John said: "if not his life, then his kingdom."

"Or the revenues of his kingdom," Eschiva said. She felt the prickle in her skin that came with a true seeing. "Watch, my lord, and wait. If he's being held for ransom, you'll be approached—because you might be thought to wish him held prisoner till he dies. What would you pay for that?"

"Not enough to keep Philip happy," John said, "or whoever is holding him with Philip's blessing. But if I pretend—"

"Yes," Father Hugh said. "If you keep up a pretense of conspiring against your brother, you'll learn much."

"Maybe it won't be a pretense," John said. He yawned and stretched. "God's bones, I'm tired. That woman wears me out more, the older we both get."

"Would you let him be killed?" Eschiva asked him.

A shudder ran through him. His teeth clacked together; he said, "Not for this. But keep him locked up? I might. He'll be a bloody nuisance when he comes back. If he finds out that I've got a crown even prettier than his, he's going to want it. Then what do I do, O my guardians? Smile and grovel and give it to him?"

"It is not his to take," Father Hugh said. His expression was amiable, but his words were completely unyielding. "What is his is his. What is yours remains yours. He can take from you, my lord, but only if you let him."

John considered that, narrow-eyed, smoothing his beard in long slow strokes. At length he said, "I think it's time I stopped putting Philip off. Can you help me escape to Normandy?"

They glanced at one another. The Marshal frowned; Neville shrugged. Eschiva sighed. Father Hugh said, "Yes, we can help you. But not till after you're out of the queen's sight."

"That goes without saying," John said dryly. "I can be patient for a while longer. Just do what you can to get me across the sea."

At the end of the year, the queen received word of what John had known for a week and more. Richard was a captive. Eleanor's spies brought a copy of a letter that, they swore on holy relics, had been delivered to Philip of France three days after Christmas—a year and a day after Philip had come back from Outremer.

Within the day, everyone in Windsor knew what was in that letter. This was not a secret that could be kept. John got hold of the very copy, after he had heard half a dozen different versions of its contents.

Richard's ship had run into a storm off the coast of Italy, and come broken to shore not far from Venice. The king and a few of his people had escaped alive, but found themselves in a land full of enemies. Richard escaped one noble count of that region with vengeance in mind, but left eight of his knights in that gentleman's hands. Six more fell to another and equally vengeful lord near Salzburg, but again Richard broke free.

"They got him near Vienna," John said as he read the letter in his chamber. "He'd made his way through a net so fine you'd think a mouse wouldn't escape, but in the end they caught him. Archduke Leopold has him—do you remember, the one who got in such a snit over some slight or other at the capture of Acre? He's holding my brother with the full blessing of the Holy Roman Emperor, who writes to Philip with such royal affection. I'm sure they're dancing in the streets from Paris to Prague."

"Surely they are," Arslan said. "Just as surely, I doubt that Philip is as ignorant of this as the letter pretends. Was it meant to fall into your mother's hands?"

"I'd hardly be surprised," John said. He turned the copy in his fingers, reading to himself the orotund phrases of its beginning. *"Henry, by the grace of God ever-august Emperor of the Romans, to his dearest and most particular friend Philip, mighty and splendid King of the Franks, greetings and sincerest salutations."* He snorted. "John, by the grace of the pagan gods never-revealed king of all Britain, says to this: The rooster may crow, but it's not he who makes the sun come up."

"You think Henry's innocent of Philip's sleights and plots?" Neville asked him.

"Not in this life," John said, "but I'm thinking Philip might not have told him everything that a good jailer should know. I'll play Philip; he's my chosen instrument. Which of you would like to play Henry?"

"On what pretext?" the Marshal asked.

"He'll be wanting a ransom," John said. "If one of your people— or one of you, if your office will allow—is with the embassy that goes to bargain with him, won't Britain be well served?"

"When the time comes," Father Hugh said, "we'll decide on it."

"But first," John said, "I'm for Normandy."

"Let me go," William Longchamp said.

He had come to John from the clerks' workroom, threadbare and ink-stained and nondescript, but in John's presence he took back a little of his old haughty bearing.

"Let me find the king," he said. "Bishop Savary of Bath is going—he'll need a clerk. I'll unmask when I'm out of England. Just let me go."

"Why?" said John. "So that you can turn on me?"

"No," said the Bishop of Ely, for he was that still, even discredited and supposedly exiled. "If I find the king and bring him back, I can do what I may to prevail on him to name you his heir."

"You'd do that willingly?"

Ely looked him in the face, as honest as ever. "Who else is there? Richard is somewhere in Germany, God knows where. His queen is in Rome. There's no sign of a child. The one in Brittany is much too young to be of use in this turbulent age. You're all there is—and I'll do my best to persuade Richard of that."

"First find him," John said, "then get him home, preferably without bankrupting the kingdom. I'm for Normandy myself, as soon as my mother lets me out of here. We'll travel together. You'll be safer with me than with Savary, as long as you're on this side of the water. I'm not likely to be shocked when I recognize your face."

"Nobody recognizes me," Ely said, but he did not press the point. He had won as much as he needed, and he knew it.

John escaped from Windsor in the first week of the new year. His mother was thoroughly distracted by the news from Europe; she forgot for a little while to keep a hawk's eye on her youngest son. He took advantage of her lack of attention, gathered the diminished train that he had brought to Christmas court, and broke for the sea. By the time Eleanor knew what he had done, he was on shipboard, sailing to Normandy.

Arslan and Kalila went with him. Eschiva and Neville did not.

The night before John sailed, the true king's council met once more, gathering in the castle at Dover. It was a clear and moonlit night, the sea dashing strong against the cliffs, and the power of Bran thrumming softly in the earth beneath them. William of Ely lay in the center of their circle, lost in enchanted sleep. He was smiling, his expression gentler and more peaceful than it could ever be while he was awake.

The four guardians knelt at the four quarters, hands outstretched over the man's body. Neville was at the head, Father Hugh at the feet; the Marshal had the hands, and Eschiva the heart. Ely was full of magic, a deep well of it, perfect in his innocent strength.

As little as she could ever like the man, Eschiva could honestly marvel at this unwitting power of his. "Are you sure?" she asked John, who stood beyond the circle. "Can you—dare you let him go?"

"Can you?" John asked.

She nodded. "He's freed us to bolster our strength elsewhere than in maintaining wards. We're ready to take what he's kept for us. We'll seal him when we're done, so that no ill thing can enter."

"Will I still be able to use him? I have plans for him, lady, and I need that beautiful void of his."

"What will you do?" the Marshal asked. "If Philip gets his hands on it, he'll reckon it a splendid gift."

"Philip won't get near him," said John. "I'm sending him after Richard. If he finds my brother first, and keeps a good solid eye on him, don't you think it will be better for us all?"

"Yes," said Father Hugh. "Yes, that's very well thought of—very clever, in fact. We can take what is ours, set in him what he'll need for the hunt, then seal him so that no one else can touch him. He'll be our hunting hound, and our watchdog after that. My lord, that is brilliant!"

John did not acknowledge the praise, but it had found its mark: Eschiva caught the flicker of a smile. "Can you do it now, tonight? I don't dare delay, or it will be Southampton all over again. This time my mother won't stop at letting me sulk in peace. She'll see that I'm locked up under guard."

"We can do it," Eschiva said. She had already brought to mind the spells, the words and wardings. She called the Powers to her, the forces of earth and air.

The other three joined in the note she sang. Together they raised the magic out of this man and contained it in chains of water and of fire. The power of Bran aided them, and the walls of air that were so close, rising up above the breast of the sea, and the moon to which Eschiva was bound, that ruled the tides of magic about the isle of Britain.

Ely was empty, a vessel from which all the wine had been poured out. Eschiva laid on him the powers that he would need to hunt a king, then drew back to work the wards. She was struggling now, for she was weary and his emptiness was so very, very tempting. She wanted to fill it, not close it off; to pour herself into it and become a part of it.

A strong presence rose behind her. Its essence was fire. It caught her and held her before she fell, and made her strong. She sealed the vessel with a Word, limning it on the sleeping brow in letters of air and fire.

Then at last she could open her eyes on the mortal world, and breathe air into mortal lungs, and let her magic fold itself within her and go gratefully to sleep. Arslan's arms were about her, his breath ruffling her hair. He did not speak. She lay back against him and sighed.

Her heart ached that she must part from him. And yet she had to stay, to sustain the wards, and he had to go. He had to be John's guardian, since Britain's guardians could not. They had settled it long since, in full agreement—in grief, too, but this they must do.

There was still this night. They would take all of it that they could, and make it last, until he should come back again.

# CHAPTER 42

John came to Normandy in a rare winter gift of quiet seas and muted cold. The gates of France were open for him, her arms spread wide to welcome him into a deadly embrace.

He played the rake to her whore with enormous relish. From the moment he set foot on land, he insisted—loudly—that he be accorded the rank and honor of the king's heir. In a little while he overtopped even that excess, and demanded the title of Duke, which was Richard's own. "Richard is locked in a dungeon somewhere, who knows where?" he declared wherever he could be heard. "What with the army of enemies he's made, he'll be lucky ever to see the light of day, let alone come back to his lands. Whereas I am here, my lords, and alive and well, and perfectly capable of ruling as you deserve to be ruled."

Normandy was a harsh land, and its people were as hard as the stones under their booted feet. They were old Viking stock, old sea-reivers; now they raided the nations of the world, and conquered them as William the Bastard had conquered England. They regarded John in suspicion, and for the most part reserved judgment.

That suited his purpose very well. He circled for a long while around Rouen as if afraid to venture its famously impregnable walls, in which Philip's sister Alais had long been kept under strict guard. No one need know of the messengers he sent from Alençon, where he had gathered as many of the barons as would come, to the castellan of Rouen.

For this errand Kalila was dressed as Arslan was, as a young nobleman of the Franks. The cotte and hose were easy enough to manage, but no man of this country wore heavy plaits below the waist. If she would play out this game, she must make a sacrifice.

Once she had made up her mind, it stayed made up. Arslan grieved a great deal more than she, as Petit the manservant cut off the long locks one by one. He refused point-blank to crop it short so that she matched Arslan. He cut it to her shoulders and across her brows, and would have curled it if she had let him; but she would not sit still for that.

When it was done to his satisfaction, he let her see herself in the polished silver of John's mirror. "I look like a Frank," she said, astonished. "Arslan! Did you put a wishing on me?"

"Not at all," he said, sounding bemused himself.

"This is real magic," said Petit. "Servants' magic. You're the height of young men's fashion in Paris now, demoiselle. Make sure you put on all the clothes properly—don't ask this one, he'll dress himself upside down and backward if he's left to himself. I've provided several changes, and plenty of spare linen. And," he added before she could protest, "a sturdy sumpter mule that can also carry armor and weapons, which I'm sure you'll be wanting."

They were almost too well equipped when they left Alençon, but neither Kalila nor Arslan dared offend Petit by refusing his gift. It was useful, they conceded, particularly since Petit had provided clothes and linen for both of them—a wealth of worldly possessions such as neither of them had had since they left Beausoleil. It made them feel remarkably wealthy, and rather sinful.

The third member of their party was waiting for them, and none too patiently either. William Longchamp rode an evil-eyed brown mule, wrapped in a monk's habit and sniffing loudly at the excess of their baggage. Kalila found him more amusing than anything else; she was looking forward to his expression when he learned what they had planned for him.

For the moment he knew only that he was being escorted to Rouen, where he had allegedly been since his second flight from England. He would take back his name and rank there, and begin the hunt for the king.

Rouen was a fortress city, all dour stone and echoing passages. Kalila found it strangely familiar, like the castles of Outremer: a house of war in a warlike country. It was a grim place in winter, under a mantle of new snow.

The castellan was waiting for them. He was one of the twice-titled:

lord of Rouen in Normandy and Earl of Leicester in England. There was Saxon blood in him, in the length of his bones and the clear pallor of his eyes. He looked nothing like Hugh Neville, but the sight of his long English face made Kalila's heart clench. She was missing her lover, and badly. Even Arslan's presence barely consoled her.

She kept her foolishness to herself. What she had to do required a clear head. She could not cloud it with memories of long lazy nights and warm wanton mornings.

William Longchamp greeted the earl with a perfunctory bow and a sharp, "Where are my things? Have they come yet?"

"Some while since, your grace," the earl said politely. "Edgar, show the lord bishop to his rooms. Unless his grace has more to say?"

Ely shrugged him off. The page bowed him through the door.

Arslan turned to follow, but the earl stopped him. "There are guards outside whom I trust. One will accompany him wherever he goes."

Slowly Arslan sank into the chair that waited for him. Kalila was already seated, alert but at ease. John trusted this man, and John did not trust easily at all. She would hope that the bishop could be safe here.

The earl looked them over at his leisure. He seemed to take Kalila as what she pretended to be: there was no sudden pause or widening of eyes. Arslan attracted more of his attention; she fostered that, she hoped, by making herself smaller and putting on a bland expression.

"So," he said at last. "Tell me—is he well, my lord John?"

"Very well, my lord," Arslan said. "You've had his dispatches?"

"I've even read them," said Leicester with a flash of quick humor: "both the ones that he'd want known and the ones that he most certainly would not. This is a complicated game he's playing. He must be aware that he could be charged with treason if he missteps by even a little."

"You know why he has to do this," said Arslan.

Leicester nodded slowly. "I had dispatches from the Marshal as well. We of Britain, we knew a king had come, but I admit it was a shock to learn his name. It was not the one I would have expected."

"It was offered to Richard," Arslan said. "He refused it."

"It's not his sort of kingship," the earl said. "But maybe, after all . . . yes, I can see it might be John's. He's a secret man, and this is a secret thing."

"So you'll do it?" Arslan asked.

The earl inclined his head. "I'll see them safe on the road, with a suitable escort. The other thing . . . I'll play the part. It's only my duty to the king whom the world knows."

"Your duty is all you need do," said Arslan, "and all my lord asks of you."

Kalila's duty had been decided on the cliffs of Dover, but Arslan had had no part in it. As far as he knew, she had simply accompanied him here, and would follow him, and therefore John, to Paris after John had played out his game in Normandy.

She dreaded the moment when he discovered what she was to do. It would have been wise to warn him, but it was simpler to wait until the bishop's escort was gathered and ready to ride. When she came out in riding clothes, Arslan did not blink: he was to ride out after Ely was safely on his way. But when he saw her horse among the bishop's escort, he began to understand.

She had still hoped, rather desperately, to escape before he could catch her. But the escort dallied for this and that; the bishop insisted that he must have some necessity of travel that had been packed away and must be found after long and hectic search; and Arslan planted himself in front of Kalila and said, "What do you think you are doing?"

"My duty," she said.

"In Germany?"

"The hound needs a huntsman," said Kalila.

"But you are not—"

She swallowed. Her throat was aching. The dread of this moment had been worse than the moment itself was proving to be, but she could still feel the hot blast of his temper, barely held in check. "I was given the means to do what must be done." She drew out the thing that she had been wearing since Dover, concealing it from everyone, and most of all him. It seemed a pretty bauble, a golden apple on a chain; it rang softly when she shook it, for it was a bell.

He started so violently that she recoiled. "Where did you get that? Who gave it to you?"

"Your lady gave it to me," she said, not without misgivings.

"Eschiva?" He looked as if he had been struck with the flat of a sword. "Eschiva!"

"It's like the bishop," Kalila said. "It's a vessel for magic. I'm to carry it always and never let it go, and when the time comes, I'll do what I was taught to do."

He was not listening. "This is Eschiva's?"

"She took it from her belt," Kalila said. "It's all strung with them."

"But I've never seen—"

"She said it's not something men are supposed to see. We did women's magic, old magic. She also said you would be in a right rage, and if you had to blame anybody, blame her. But it's not her fault. There isn't anyone else. She has to stay in England; you have to go with John. I was the only one they all could trust to do this thing."

"They all knew? All of them?"

"She said I should tell you," said Kalila. "I made her swear not to say anything. It was my cowardice. Don't fault her for it."

He shook his head from side to side. "This is revenge. I can't even rage at her—she'll tax me with it forever after."

"I thought it was mercy," Kalila said. "I knew you'd fret. You're fretting now. Bid me farewell, brother, and if you have any blessing to give me, I'll be glad of it."

He came back to himself with a blink, a shudder, a sudden hard stare. "Don't get yourself killed," he said. But before the words could quite cut to the bone, he took her hands, pulled her in, hugged the breath out of her. "Go with God."

"As Allah wills," she murmured in his ear.

# CHAPTER 43

Kalila rode off to Germany in the company of a man who, if he had known the truth of what she was and why she was there, would have been appalled. Arslan, watching her go, was more alone than he had ever been. Even after Yusuf died, Kalila had still been within his reach. Now she rode away to God knew what outcome, and there was no one to stand at his right hand.

As she said, it was duty. It was destiny, too, for both of them. Once he opened his eyes, he had seen what Eschiva and the rest of the guardians had roused in her. She was wrapped in a mantle of magic, deeply warded and protected, but gifted with a power that astonished him. She was as mortal as woman could be. He had never even guessed what was inside her, waiting to be unlocked.

Yet he should have guessed. Eschiva obviously had. The Powers had known when they chose Yusuf for John's champion in the greenwood.

Eschiva . . .

Eschiva had secrets. She who he thought had given him everything, lived a life he had never even known—except in dreams. In a dream of the otherworld, after the horned king told him his duty, he had seen her robed in white, with a girdle of golden bells. One of those bells lay deep in his baggage, all but forgotten. Another hung about Kalila's neck, imbued with magic that would protect her in the German forests.

He had laid a further ward on her in that last embrace, and put in it all the strength that he could spare. He would know, too, if she had any need of help, and she could draw his strength if her own was not enough. To seal it, he had slipped his mother's blood-red stone into her purse. She would find it, he hoped not too soon, and understand.

It was a dangerous thing he had done, but he did not regret it. He would not lose her as he had lost her brother. He had sworn that oath to himself, and he would keep it.

As Arslan prepared for his own solitary journey back to Alençon, saddling his mare and Petit's mule with his own hands, a soft voice said behind him, "Messire?"

He turned. He had heard her step in the stable aisle, and known when and where she paused. She was a plain woman in a plain gown, not in the first flush of youth but not old, either, with a doe's soft eye and a dove's voice. In spite of the almost monastic simplicity of her dress, Arslan did not mistake her for a serving-woman. She had the sweet humility of a lady who could well afford the indulgence.

He bowed over her slender white hand. "Lady," he said. "You honor me."

Her brows rose. "You know who I am?"

"I know there is a princess in this castle."

She smiled faintly. "Princess? Or pawn?"

"Aren't they the same?"

Her smile widened. She was lovely when there was light in her face. "They said that you were different," she said.

"More than anyone knows," he said.

She gathered her mantle about her. It was chill in the stable, the chill of stone, even amid the warmth of the beasts. "I came to ask a thing," she said.

He waited.

"Will you tell me—truthfully—what your lord intends? I know what my brother is offering him. Does he have any intention of taking it?"

"My lord will do what serves him best," Arslan said.

"He doesn't, does he?" She did not seem remarkably cast down. "All my life I've been a pawn in the game of kings. Henry kept me close, promised everything, did nothing, and so kept my brother perpetually out of play. Richard, I think, forgot me. Richard's soul is burned clean of women, except for his mother. Now John enters the game. Women like him. Would he be a good husband, do you think?"

"With a wife he doesn't despise? I should think so."

"He'd despise me," she said dispassionately. "Will you give him a message?"

Arslan bowed.

"Tell him that he may play as he pleases, but I come at a price. I've been a pawn long enough. When he takes me, he takes me as a queen."

Arslan bowed again, lower yet. He hoped she could not see his pity, but only his admiration. "I shall tell him, my lady," he said. "You have my word on it."

Arslan, who had thought to return as he had gone, with Kalila at his side, rode alone to Alençon. It was a painfully solitary ride. He was even glad to meet the pack of John's squires outside the town, playing at battle in a fallow field. The farmer looked on, thanking God perhaps that it was winter and he had not yet plowed or planted the field, and knowing better than to come between the gentlefolk and their play.

Arslan's former peers, now his inferiors in the way of the world, were even less fond of him now than they had been before. Still, they were familiar faces, and they were hacking at one another even more ineptly than usual. He swept through the lot of them, disarmed every one, and bore their swords and lances to the castle and the prince.

"Pray, what is this for?" John demanded as Arslan let the armload of weapons fall with a clatter at his feet.

"Tribute," said Arslan.

"From robbing children?"

"Those children are older than I am," Arslan said.

"Only in body," said John. "I should put you in charge of them. You can teach them to fight like knights of Outremer."

"God help me!" Arslan said in honest horror. "They hate me enough as it is. If you set me over them, I'll be dead in a week."

John did not, thank God, press the point. He came down from his chair, spread his arms, and pulled Arslan into a bruising embrace. In the midst of it he whispered in Arslan's ear, "Is it done?"

"All of it," Arslan whispered back.

John let him go. "Welcome back, lion's cub," he said. "Welcome back indeed."

Just as John had asked and expected, when he sent official word to the castellan of Rouen, demanding surrender of that castle and the lady held captive in it, the castellan refused either to receive his mes-

sengers or admit him to the castle. At the same time his council at
Alençon broke against the rock of the Norman barons' intransigence.
John might become their duke, and they would swear fealty to him
when he came to it; they were not unwilling to accept him as the ex-
isting duke's heir. But they would not give him that title while
Richard lived to claim it.

It was all very satisfactory, and very damning on the face of it. John
greatly enjoyed a new fit of the sulks, packing up his train and de-
parting from Alençon in high dudgeon, and declaring for all to hear,
"Very well. If my inferiors won't acknowledge the living truth, I'll see
what my liege lord has to say." That lord, of course, was Philip, to
whom the Duke of Normandy must swear fealty.

He took the road to Paris with a scowling face and a light heart.
Philip's men were waiting for him at the border, a company of men
who wore the garb and the armor of Flemish mercenaries, but Arslan,
at the sight of them, felt his hackles go up.

To the eye there was nothing suspicious about them. They were
big men, fair-haired for the most part, with strong blunt faces. They
could have been Arslan's kin, in fact. But when he looked at them
with the inner eye, he found nothing of kinship in them. He was fire
and earth. They were heavy clay, deep earth and stone. Only their captain showed sign of human blood. He seemed to be a Fleming indeed: he had the face, the manner, the accent. But Arslan doubted
that he was a simple hired soldier by trade.

Arslan effaced himself as much as he could. John did not seem uneasy; he greeted the captain and willingly accepted the escort as a gift
from the King of the Franks to, as the captain put it, "the Duke of the
Normans."

These were guards, but Arslan did not think they were meant to
protect John, but rather to keep him in their sight. Arslan was sure
that messages were sent to the king, and that whatever these guardsmen did, they did at Philip's command.

The first night, when they paused to rest, camping in a hayfield
rather than taking lodging in town or castle, Arslan kept watch. John
was well guarded, and not by false Flemings. Arslan had set wards
round his tent, and made bold to double the guard of Englishmen
outside it. He walked the camp after that in the starless night, breathing scents of earth and the promise of rain. Winter's grip was loosen-
ing; he caught the first elusive hint of new green.

Through this living sweetness crept the heaviness that he had sensed before, like cold clay and the breath of tombs. Tall stones ringed the field. They had not been there in daylight. A heavy figure moved among them, like a stone itself, but walking on legs like a man.

It was tending the stones, banking them in earth, bowing before each one and whispering a word. Arslan, wrapped in shadows, listened for the word, but it was too soft even for his ears. He dared not sharpen them with magic. This was sorcery, deep-rooted in earth, and it was meant, all too clearly, to keep John contained.

He could not break it down. It would be too suspicious. He had to guard John, keep watch over Philip's gift, and pretend to be one of the many innocents in John's train.

He studied them as best he might in the dark and from conceal-ment. They seemed but stone, blind and deaf, no life in them. And yet when the skeletal shape of a dog crept between them, following a rabbit's scent, there was a soft sound like a breath of wind. The dog vanished in a puff of dust.

This was more deadly than he had thought. There was no living thing that he dared send outward, to see what came of that. He went back to John's tent in more trouble of mind than before, and some lit-tle desperation, too. The guardians should be here: great enchanters, learned and wise. Not he who was still little more than a child.

John was safe, sleeping soundly. Nothing had tried to pass the pro-tections that Arslan had raised. Arslan wrapped himself in his cloak and sat in the corner of the tent, knees drawn up, still as one of those deadly stones.

John was unperturbed when, in the morning before they rode out, Arslan told him what marched with him. "Didn't you expect some-thing of the sort?" he asked.

"We did," said Arslan. "But this is powerful magic."

"Dark magic?"

"Earth magic," Arslan said. "It's neither dark nor light. That makes it more dangerous, because it makes no distinction. If you touch it, you die. It's perfectly simple."

"So we don't touch it," John said.

"Easy," said Arslan, snapping off the word. "And when we come to Paris, to the heart of France, how simple do you think it will be to escape?"

"Does Philip suspect, then? Does he know what I am?"

"I don't think so," Arslan said. "But if he acknowledges you as your brother's heir, and your brother is under his power in Germany, he'll be looking to keep you close. Through you he can seize the whole of France, and England, too."

"I do know that," said John, "but I also know that as long as I play this game, Britain is safe."

"Until he decides that you're so safe in his power, he can begin his invasion."

"I'll play that round when it comes," John said. "Here now, up with your chin. I'm a bold bad rebel, I'm grabbing anything that's to be grabbed, and I'm Philip's dearest, most loyal vassal. You, my friend, are my tame lion. No skulking and hiding in Paris, messire. No cloak of shadows. I'm going to flaunt you. If Philip looks for magic and mystery, he'll never expect to find it in my latest and most exotic favorite."

"I'm not sure—" Arslan began.

"Pretend," said John.

It was a royal command. Arslan had no choice but to obey.

# CHAPTER 44

❧

Paris fancied herself the queen of the world. She sneered at Rome, sniffed at Constantinople. Of Damascus and Baghdad and Aleppo she knew nothing, and Jerusalem was a dream and an empty tomb.

She was a crowded, noisy, turbulent, filthy city, and in the heart of her, on the Ile de la Cité that sailed like a ship on the breast of the Seine, her king ruled the only domain that was truly, incontestably his. Everything else was held in fief by variously obstreperous vassals, of whom John was but one—but it was generally conceded that he was one of the worst.

That was a distinction, and enviable. It attracted a great crowd for his entry into the city, and he played his part to the hilt. He was dressed in more of Philip's gifts—but these treasures of silk and ermine and gold were safely mortal and nothing magical. Arslan made sure of that before he would let John approach them. He rode in royal splendor, in a ducal coronet of heavy gold, and a crimson mantle lined with ermine, and a cotte thickly embroidered in gold thread with the leopards of his lineage. He was mounted on a milk-white horse, a heavy and docile thing and no pleasure to ride, as John muttered to Arslan, but the creature was certainly splendid, with a mane that rippled to its knees and a tail that trailed out behind.

Arslan rode close beside him, unveiled as a favorite, eye-searingly glorious in scarlet and gold. Petit had been beside himself with delight at the opportunity at last to transform a recalcitrant boy into a work of art. For the sake of the game, Arslan endured it. He was clipped, shaved, scrubbed and polished to a metallic sheen, then dressed like a king in a plethora of garments, each more extravagant than the last, and hung with jewels and gold till he clanked like a bellwether on market day. When Petit was done he could barely move, but that was seen to: he was lifted onto the close kin of John's milky cart horse, this one a gleaming black bay, in trappings as gaudily be-silked and bejeweled as Arslan's own.

The effect, as John avowed, was magnificent. "Ah, that your lady could see you now," he said. "She'd drag you into the nearest corner and strip it off and have her will of you."

Arslan laughed in spite of himself. He felt gross and oversized in this city of little dark quick people, and this fancy-dress made it no-tably worse, but he did try, for a moment, to see himself as a woman might. Women did love a gaudy show—even Eschiva, who was wise enough to know better.

Paris loved him. It loved them all, reckoning them a sure sign of England's defeat, but Arslan roused the throng to vociferous delight. He smiled and waved and flung pennies from a bag that someone thrust into his hand. They cheered John, who flung silver, but to Ar-slan they sang love songs. They had a name for him well before he came to the Ile de France: Bohemond, like the princely giant of the first Crusade.

The king awaited them at the bridge to the Ile de la Cité, glorious in blue and silver, and everywhere the lilies of France. Arslan shivered inside himself. A hedge of lilies indeed, and England's leopard caught in it, riding toward the King of the Franks with his arms outstretched and a brilliant smile on his face.

Philip's smile was less extravagant. Like John he was not a tall man, but where John was sturdy and strong, he was slender, ele-gant, with a finely carved face and long delicate hands. His welcome was as elegant as his person, framed in gracious phrases. He opened the Ile to them, and made them his guests therein—and, so that all could hear, he greeted John as "My lord duke." John dismounted from the white horse and knelt on the crimson carpet that had been spread for him, and before the eyes of all Paris, swore fealty to Philip as his liege lord.

They were all taken into the royal house of France, and given lodg-ings that were of the best, and an army of servants. Not London it-self had made John more welcome. He was the most honored of guests, and his every whim was his host's command.

The grand show of greeting went on and on. The court seemed determined that it should never end. In a dizzy whirl of feasts and hunts, dances and jousts, games and entertainments, France opened its heart to Henry Plantagenet's youngest son.

It was all pretense. Arslan, caught in the thick of it, felt as if he had bitten into an apple, ripe and seeming sweet, and swallowed a mouthful of ashes. He was an honest favorite, that much he would grant these courtiers, but all their smiles and expressions of love for John were false. John was a thorn in the royal side, and however brightly gilded he might be, he was still a treacherous ally.

John was in his element. He played the game with inborn skill. He trusted no one, and the king least of all. Every embrace, every smile that he had from Philip had meaning, and friendship was no part of it.

In the dizzy whirl of a court that never seemed to sleep, quiet moments were precious few and far between. Arslan could not even find them in church or chapel. Wherever he went, he had a following. If he went to Mass, he was surrounded by devoutly praying oglers. If he rode hunting, every one of Philip's squires and young knights seemed determined to win a place at his side. If he crept out in the early morning to practice his swordplay or his archery, several dozen spectators appeared as if from air.

It all seemed intended to confuse the mind and blur the senses. John kept a clear head; Arslan struggled to do the same. As much as he could, he searched among the innumerable courtiers, hunting for any who might have made the false Flemings that still, at Philip's insistence, stood guard over John. A spell of that magnitude needed a powerful sorcerer, or circle of sorcerers.

All he saw about him were bright birds and gilded blossoms. The great lords walked apart, lions amid the butterflies, but all of them appeared to be mortal. Surely one or more of them was well masked, as John was; as the Marshal and the Forester were, and Father Hugh. Guardians did not proclaim themselves; that would make them targets.

And yet there were two who betrayed themselves—intentionally? Or did they not care? The day after John's arrival, the king celebrated it with a solemn Mass in the cathedral that ornamented the prow of the Ile. The Archbishop of Rheims was there, and the Abbot of Saint-Denis, and half the prelates of France, an army of churchmen thanking God for this gift that had fallen into their king's hands.

As Arslan watched from John's side in the half-built splendor of the cathedral, he saw more than the light of the sun shining through jeweled glass on the tonsured heads of the bishops. It glowed upon the archbishop, clothing him in a soft radiance, which deepened as he entered the Canon of the Mass. The others were mortally devout and lit by earthly light, all but the good abbot at the archbishop's right hand. As he lifted up his hands in prayer, they filled with the same soft light that illumined the archbishop.

Either it was so common a sight as to be unremarkable, or no one else could see as Arslan saw. The spirits in this city held aloof—to his relief, for he had labored hard and long to perfect the mask that would make him seem altogether human. They still followed him, but no more than they followed any mortal.

None of them flocked about the two enchanters, not in the cathedral, not outside of it—none at all, not even one. There were crowds of them on the slowly growing towers, amid the masons' scaffolding; they crouched along the edge of the roof, peering down at the city, some leaning out so far that they mimicked the waterspouts. But they conducted themselves as if the abbot and the archbishop did not exist.

The abbot went back to his abbey, unescorted by spirits. The archbishop went with the king and his guest to the palace, likewise free of insubstantial admirers. The light had left him; he seemed altogether mortal and altogether unmagical.

And that was a magic in itself, not at all unlike that which distinguished the Bishop of Ely; but this, Arslan suspected, was art and not nature. Arslan tracked it by its absence, and so found the third mage of the circle: the Duke of Burgundy, back from Crusade. There might be no more; or there might be an army of them. That much he had learned from Britain's guardians.

He kept watch on them. They were watching John, he could be sure, but John was doing nothing to arouse sorcerous suspicion. To every sense both mortal and otherwise, he was the ambitious youngest son who had taken advantage of his brother's captivity and seized the most convenient of his titles.

And that was a truth, if not the only or the deepest one. John reveled in it—even knowing what the consequences would be.

She saw Arslan first as he wandered somewhat dazed through the myriad splendors of the court. She was one of the greater beauties, since in that court they were ranked like jousters: greater, middle, lesser. She was kin to the deposed King of Jerusalem, and she did resemble him, tall and golden-fair. But Guy was a handsome fool, and this lady was not. Not at all, though she had the wide blue eyes and the serene oval face of an angel in a cathedral.

Her name was Melusine. She begged for an introduction to the young Lord Bohemond, and when she was named to him, she smiled at the widening of his eyes. "Oh yes, my mother did name me that. It is our ancestor, after all."

"Melusine de Lusignan," he said. It had the cadence of a song. He bowed over her slender white hand, and found himself smiling into her eyes. She was very beautiful, all ivory and gold.

She was not so innocent to look at, either, as her eyes went smoky; her lips seemed fuller, the curve of her breast deeper, a sweet swell that rose delightfully as she drew in a breath.

He gasped. She was very, very strong; so strong she made him dizzy, like a draft of pure wine. She heard the gasp, saw the expression that must have come with it, and purred like a cat. "Beautiful man," she said. "Dance with me."

He should not. He knew beyond doubt what she was, what she could do. Yet the scent of her, the beauty that seemed richer, riper, the longer he looked on it, the honey sweetness of her voice, captivated him. Even the clear memory of skin like milk and hair like fire could not undo her spell.

Did she know what he was—all of it? The spirits did not seem to, but she was more than a spirit. She was a sorceress of such power that even through the mask that made him seem human, he felt the force of it.

*The game,* he thought. *Play the game.* John played it in layers of truth. Arslan could do the same. Truth: this woman aroused him as none other had, not even Eschiva. He wanted her with the sheer mindless heat of the body. He ached, burned with wanting.

There was nothing of the heart in it. It was all the flesh—the mortal flesh that, itself, was only half the truth.

She danced with a serpent's suppleness, swaying to the music. He was heavy beside her, clay-footed, huge and lumbering, like a thing made of earth and animated with sorcery. He danced because she willed it, and not for simple joy in the body's movement. He was her creature, the slave of her spell.

Truth; but his heart, she could never touch.

# CHAPTER 45

❧

"Come home with me," said Melusine. Arslan stared blankly at her. They had been dancing since the world began. All the lamps burned low, and the stars turned past midnight to the dawn.

Her body was wound with his; her head was thrown back, her eyes so deep that he could drown. "Come home," she said, "and comfort me."

"Comfort?" His voice was thick, his tongue unwieldy. "Lady, you don't seem sorrowful."

"I smile through my grief," she said. "I have no beautiful man, no enchanting creature to love me. The knights of France, they're boors or butterflies. The knights of Germany . . ." She shuddered delicately. "The knights of the English, they are almost bearable. But the glorious knights of Outremer . . . now there are men to set my heart to singing."

"Then you should find one," he said, "or many, if your heart needs more. Since I'm only almost bearable."

She laughed like a cascade of bells. It was perfect artifice, and like all perfection, perfectly marvelous. "Beautiful man! Come with me."

"Bohemond! Bohemond!" It was a roar like a bull's, and a jeering chorus: "O shining hero, O light of France—your lord is calling."

Arslan nearly collapsed in relief. Three of John's squires came carousing toward him, well laden with wine, holding one another up as they trumpeted their message. They had saved his life and perhaps his soul, though they could hardly have cared less for that.

Melusine's grip tightened, but Arslan slid out of it, stumbling into the midst of the squires. Their mockery was a cold wind blowing her spell away; their too-firm assistance, even as it left bruises, brought him somewhat to his senses. They carried him off, dropped him in front of John's door, and went roistering back down the passage.

Arslan pulled himself to his feet. His knees wobbled abominably. Somehow he steadied them. False Flemings stood on either side of the door, motionless as stone. They offered no interference as he opened the door. Nor, and for that he was grateful, did they blast him into dust.

John was awake, alone, and sardonically pleased to see Arslan. "Were my bullies in time?" he inquired.

"Barely," Arslan said. As feeble as he had been outside that door, now that he was within, he could not contain his restlessness. He paced while John watched. If he could have flung himself into a hard ride across cruel country or a battle against blood enemies, he would have done it.

After a while John said, "The others are no more than mortally sinful, but that one is evil. She wants your soul."

Arslan stopped just before he collided with the far wall, spun. "You've found them, too?"

"Saint-Denis and Rheims and Burgundy," John said. "It's fascinating—as soon as I saw each one, I knew, just looking at his face. Am I as easy for them to see, I wonder?"

"I don't think they know," said Arslan, "or that they've found me out, either. But she . . ."

"She's the worst of them all," said John.

"Worse than the king?"

John dismissed Philip with a flick of the hand. "Under all that silk and silver and that pretty face, he has the soul of a clerk. He'll order a thing done because it's expedient, but he'll never dirty his hands with it. There's no grandeur in him—only a niggling sort of petty evil."

"You think he commanded her to seduce me?"

The corner of John's mouth tilted up. "I doubt he needed to say a word."

"It's your fault," Arslan muttered. "You dressed me like a poppet on a pole and set me up for all the world to gawp at."

"And it did, didn't it? It gawped magnificently. Do you think you can resist her, if you have time to prepare?"

Arslan shivered. "She's terribly strong," he said.

"So are you."

"And if I fall? What then? I know all your secrets, my lord."

"Don't fall," said John. "Pretend. Let her seduce you. She'd get a rise out of a dead man, let alone a strapping young one who hasn't bedded his wife since Christmas."

Arslan's teeth ached with grinding together. "The wife might have something to say of that," he said with careful control.

"Yes—that any sacrifice is worth the safety of Britain."

"She's not that magnanimous," Arslan muttered, but not loud enough for John to hear, nor did he ask to hear it. John was not interested in Arslan's delusions of honor and fidelity. He loved Susanna, Arslan would lay wagers on it, but when she was not in his bed, someone else was. John could no more imagine devoting himself to one woman than could a ram, or a bull in his herd.

"Tomorrow," John said, "you can let her find you again. Use the night to prepare. I'll make sure you're watched whenever and wherever the two of you are. She won't harm you if I can help it."

Arslan did not respond. It was not wise or reasonable, but he was angry. Angry enough to turn his back on his lord and strip without care for the richness of the garments he was casting off, pull his pallet across the door, and fling himself onto it.

John's snort had a gust of mirth in it. "Believe me, boy, if I could take this burden on myself, I would. But it's not me she wants—and that's well, because if I fall, so falls Britain. Think of yourself as the king's bodyguard. You take the blows that should come to him. You have to admit, there are few more pleasant than this."

Arslan gritted his teeth, stuffed the blanket in his ears, and refused to hear any more. Even so, he heard John's laughter. John had no sympathy at all for his trouble.

Come morning, Arslan would have put on his plainest clothes and gone hunting for as long as he could possibly escape—lifelong, if he could have done it. But Petit was waiting for him, barring his way, with a bath and razors and yet another extravagance of the tailor's art. This one was bronze and gold, and the jewels were amber and garnet and topaz.

Petit clucked contentedly as he worked. "You," he said to Arslan, "are God's gift to manservants. No, not that sulky face of yours! But that body . . . ah! Just like an image in bronze. You should cherish your beauty, messire. It's a rare thing."

"That would be the sin of vanity," Arslan said.

"Acknowledging the truth is a sin? Here, turn a bit to the left—yes, stop, there. Now don't move." Petit tugged and fussed at the jeweled cotte till it hung exactly as he wished it. "Good, you can breathe now. If you're so afraid of being thought vain, why haven't you gone into a monastery? Because it would be a waste, and you know it. You belong in the world."

"I'm an imperfect spirit," Arslan said. "I have no call to God."

"God calls everyone to the vocation that's best for him. You would have been a wretched monk." Petit stood back to admire his work. "Beautiful! Remember, keep those laces tied until she unties them, and don't lose the collar—it's a treasure of our lord's house."

Arslan set hands to the heavy golden thing, to take it off, but Petit slapped them down. "No, no, no! You let that be. Just don't leave it beside her bed. Milord John will be wanting it back."

"I am not going to bed her!" Arslan burst out.

Petit ignored them. "Go—go. Her ladyship is waiting."

This must be how it was to be a whore. Prinked, primped, and prettified to catch the eye of the lubricious customer; set out on display; and sold to the highest bidder. Melusine had bought him as surely as if she had paid in gold.

He was the sweet cake that John fed to the guardian of hell—the blissful distraction, the tender sacrifice. Had Eschiva known when she joined in sending him away? Was this her last revenge for the quarrel that had so divided them?

Or was this why she had quarreled with him—not because he had been friendly with her mother, but because she foresaw what would come?

He was going to go mad. He would welcome it. When he had imagined sacrifices, he had imagined dying as Yusuf had, or submitting to imprisonment such as Richard suffered somewhere in Germany. He had never thought that he would be a lamb upon this altar.

The memory of John's laughter stayed with him like a breath of cold wind as he made his way through the idle chatter and relentless intrigue of the court. People followed him, babbling at him, plucking at his mantle, doing battle for his attention. He glanced at those whose need was as simple as that, smiled at those who insisted on more, but never stopped or slowed.

She was waiting, and making no secret of it. He had to pass Philip to come to her; even under her spell he could hardly ignore the king. Philip smiled as Arslan made obeisance, and caught his hand as he rose to retreat, saying, "Sir Bohemond! There's hardly been a moment to become acquainted. Will you walk with me?"

This was not a rescue. The fine dark eyes were opaque, too blank even to be called cold. The smile had the edge of a sword. And yet, with that, Philip conveyed a sense of cordial interest and even benevolence. He, like John, was not a man to begrudge another man his height; his look was long and openly admiring. So it was true, Arslan thought. Philip, like Richard, had an eye for a handsome man— though considerably less reluctance to perform his royal duties in the marriage chamber.

At the moment it was both comforting and excruciating to be compelled to walk beside the King of the Franks, past Melusine in state with a flock of admirers, and round the whole of that hall in stately procession. Philip had a trained mastery of conversation, an art for which Arslan had never had a great gift. So adept was Philip that Arslan never needed to say a word; he smiled, nodded, and let Philip speak for them both.

Their perambulations took them at length to an alcove shielded from the rest by the heavy fall of a tapestry. Arslan stiffened, searching the shadows for signs of treachery, but there was no one there— neither man nor spirit. Except for a haughty and very handsome young squire, they were alone.

"Now, messire," said Philip, dropping his façade of elegant ennui. "Tell me. Is it true, your father is dead?"

Arslan had never expected this. The eyes that had been so impenetrable were alive now, fixed on him, willing him to deny the truth. But he could not do that. "At Hattin, majesty," said Arslan.

"You look," said Philip, "exactly like him. Exactly. You could be his fetch, or his living image."

"You knew him, sire?"

"When I was small," said Philip, "for a while he was at court, attending my father on his liege lord's behalf. He used to carry me on his shoulders. It was like riding on top of the world."

"Yes," said Arslan. "Children in Beausoleil used to fight for that honor. I always won, but my father made me share. Generosity is a greater virtue than always being first, he told me."

"He told me," said Philip, "that a king is not measured by the count of his coin or the number of his battles, but by the state of his country. If the nation is safe, its borders protected, its people content, the king has done his duty."

"Did you agree with him?" Arslan asked.

Philip smiled. "At the time," he said, "I declared that I would rather win my name with my sword. Now? Oh, yes. He was a wise man. The king belongs to the land, messire, even more than the land to him. He holds it in trust to a higher power. If he fails that trust, he pays in a manner greater or lesser according to the nature of his failure."

"You think a king should stay home, then?"

"I committed an error," Philip said. "I left my country to pursue a war that could not be won. I was swept up in the tide of it: so many kings, so many nobles and common people, all taking the cross and vowing to take back the Holy Sepulcher. I should have been remembering my own country, my own people, the earth to which I was born." He paused. "Do you reckon me a coward, messire? I left the Crusade. Am I less in your eyes for that?"

Arslan shook his head slowly. "No, majesty. You are a strong king. I don't doubt your courage."

That pleased the king, although he made no great show of it. "It's strange," he said, "to see you in the service of such a man as John. Mind you, your father served his father, who was worse in all ways: more treacherous, more ambitious, more impervious to moral law. But you are a child of light. What do you see in the Devil's get?"

"England is as dear to him as France is to you," Arslan said. "He wants its crown—how not? But he loved it long before he undertook to rule it."

"You serve him because he loves a country you were never born to?"

Arslan drew a careful breath. This was treacherous ground. Philip was a subtle man, and dangerously keen of wit. Arslan must be utterly, perfectly mortal, not a glimmer of the otherworld in him; and so too must his answer be. He said, "I serve him because the Saracens took my patrimony, and my brothers in Anjou were not at all inclined to share theirs. He understands the heart of a landless man."

"He gave you a wife, I hear: an heiress of some little wealth."

Arslan lowered his eyes before they betrayed him. "Yes, she is wealthy, is my lady. Her hand was generously given."

"And generosity is a lord's great virtue." Philip smiled again. "If I were to be more generous still, would you swear fealty to me?"

"Have you a wife to offer?" said Arslan.

"I might. Though lands would suit you better, yes? What would you say to the whole of your father's old demesne, and the rank of count?"

"I would say, majesty," said Arslan, "that my eldest brother might object, even if the Count of Anjou would agree."

"If Richard never comes back," Philip said, "John will hold that office. As for your brother, the man is a dullard. I'll fob him off with an estate somewhere."

"La Forêt was never my heart's home, majesty," Arlsan said, "and as generous as your offer is, I would rather not be lord of a demesne that belongs to my brother."

"Something else, then," Philip said. "I'll recompense you well, and match loyalty with loyalty."

"How loyal is it, sire, to desert my lord?"

"You are a difficult man," Philip said, "just as your father was. He was stubborn, too, and that pride of his—nothing could shake it."

"You remember him so clearly," Arslan said. "Yet you must have been an infant when you knew him."

"I was four and five summers old," Philip said. "Not so young as that. The lessons he taught me, I never forgot."

"He would have been glad to know that," Arslan said.

Philip smiled. For an instant Arslan saw the child he must have been: haughty even then, and painfully aware of his position, but open still to the wisdom of an honorable man.

The smile died. Philip returned to himself; he glanced about, and seemed to remember the press of a multitude of duties. "Go on, messire," he said, still courteous but clearly distracted. "Be welcome; be at ease. Ask for whatever you desire, and it shall be given you."

It was a dismissal. Arslan bowed as a good knight should, and took his leave.

# CHAPTER 46

❧

A rslan had hoped that Melusine would have grown bored and found herself another plaything. But when he came out from his audience with the king, she was there, lying in wait, all but unattended, in her gown of shimmering blue silk and her veil of cloth of silver. The gown was cut close to her body, like a serpent's skin, gleaming and supple; the mantle over it barely sufficed to conceal the shape of her. She had cast a glamour, so that his sight shifted between an angel of innocence in Our Lady's own colors, and the ancient spirit of the Lusignans, the undine Melusine.

How odd that his heart's lady should be half a river-god, and this demon of temptation was a water-spirit. Fire and water—they were opposites, forever opposed and yet forever bound.

She held out her hands to him. "Beautiful man! Have you taken pity on me after all? Your kings and lords—a pox on them! They persist in taking you away from me."

"Lady," Arslan said, bowing over those white hands.

Hardly a scintillating retort, but it was not intelligence she wanted of him. He could be large, gleaming, and brainlessly beautiful—it was the simplest thing in the world, while he stood in her presence. All night he had prayed and pondered and gathered his magic. His mask of humanity was as strong as he could make it. His defenses were raised to their fullest strength. His heart and soul were warded behind high walls, and his outer self, the image of the man that he might have been without his mother's blood and power, was free to fall under her spell.

And fall it had, headlong, dizzy and half-blind. Some new scent was on her today, intoxicating in its sweetness. There was no chemise beneath her gown of silk; he could see every curve of her, the jut of nipples as she roused to his presence, even the cleft between her thighs. She swayed toward him. Her lips were red and full. Her kiss was as sweet as her perfume.

She slipped hands beneath his cotte, quick and sly as little serpents. He gasped and nearly spent himself at her touch, but he had a little strength left. She closed fingers about the hot and fiercely aching thing.

Every part of him but that gibbered at him to escape, to run, to hide. But she held him fast. "Come home with me," she purred in his ear.

She had a house on the left bank of the Seine, near the university and the crowded warren of the students' lodgings. It was not in the most respectable quarter, by far, nor was it a likely place for a lady's bower, and yet once he was inside, it seemed leagues away from the noise and bustle of the city. Within its wall was a rare delight, a remnant of old Lutetia: a villa in the Roman style, with an atrium and a pool, and a garden that ran down to the river.

She had baths—proper baths—and a hypocaust that still heated the floor after a thousand years. He could walk barefoot there if he chose, reveling in the warmth of those tiled floors.

The undine he could resist, but for real Roman baths and a hypocaust he would have bartered his immortal soul. She, water-spirit that she was, led him straight to them, past servants who obviously had seen such a thing before, and spirits tamed and broken to harness, laboring over the furnaces and in the baths. They kept the hot pool hot and the cold pool clear and chill as melted snow, and flitted about their mistress and her prey, relieving them of their garments and their ornaments. Arslan snatched at his trews, but they vanished in a puff of air.

She was even more beautiful naked than clothed. Her skin was as smooth as cream. Her hair, loosed from its veil and its elaborate plaits, rippled to her knees. She plucked or shaved the rest as eastern women did, or perhaps grew none: as she slipped into the water, her skin took on a faint blue tinge and a shimmer of nigh-invisible scales.

She floated in the water amid a drift of lilies. Her hair undulated and coiled as if it had a life of its own. Her nether lips were as red as those of her mouth, like coral set in blue-white marble.

Arslan hesitated on the pool's rim. The water steamed gently. His body was rampant with lust for her. He felt as if his skin were heated bronze, but inside of it, within the walls and the wards, his spirit was a cool, quiet thing, like deep water. Somewhere between the palace and this house, he had found the strength that John insisted he had. Whether it would be enough, he did not know. But it was more than he had expected to find.

He stepped down into the pool. The spirits watched him dully—none of the bright interest that their free kin had toward anything human. The edge of anger at that gave him the rest of the strength he needed. He hid it deep, smiled at the undine drifting in the water, and kissed the waiting mouth. It was the lightest touch, the merest tease.

She folded dripping arms about him, drawing him down. He could feel the snake's strength in her, however soft it might choose to be. But he had no intention of resisting her. He kissed her again, more deeply, but again drawing back before she was satisfied.

The third kiss was hers, long and white-hot. In his heart he laughed. She was a Frankish spirit, bred among a blunt and uncultured people. He would wager that she had never had converse with the jinni and afarit of the east, nor even with the incubi and succubi who haunted convents and abbeys across the breadth of Christendom. She had no patience, and little art, either, except to allure with her witchy beauty, capture the victim as he fell into her hands, and have her will of him.

Arslan had taught Eschiva the eastern arts of love and delight. Melusine was prey. He brought her to the thin edge of frustration and held her there until she gasped and moaned, thrashing in the water.

He lifted her up out of it and onto the heated tiles, and stretched out beside her, tracing every inch of her in the flutter of lips and tongue. He could feel the scales, taste them, along her sides and her flanks and up to the joining of her thighs. Her breasts were firmer than a woman's, the nipples small, hard, and sensitive to the least brush of his breath across them. She cried out as he closed his teeth upon them, gently, nibbling ever so softly.

He dared not grow complacent. She was an ancient creature, and powerful. He might have deceived her for the moment, but the slightest failing of vigilance could betray them all. And yet, as she gave herself up to her body's pleasure, he began to smile. Was it possible she had never been seduced before?

She was all but blind with it, her face blank, empty of wit or will. He played her like a lute, note by note and then in a ripple of delirious chords. When her whole body thrummed like a taut string, when her breath came fast and hard and her eyes rolled back in her head, he brought an end to it. Her cry was piercing, and it went on and on.

No servants came running. The captive spirits watched as dully as ever. She lay slack on the tiles, every muscle loosed. He lay beside her, propped on his elbow.

She opened her eyes. They were smoke-blue, sated. Her lips curved in a slow smile. "Beautiful man. What treasure have I found here?"

He shrugged a little. "I lived a year in Damascus."

"Is that Venus' castle in the east?"

"Some would say it is."

She stroked a finger down his arm. "You're all bronze," she said. "And gold. And ah, so gifted! No man ever took such thought for me. Crude kisses, pawing hands—your touch is silk. What a wonder you are!"

Flattery was her dearest weapon. Arslan wriggled uncomfortably, which only charmed her the more.

"Again!" she commanded him. "Take me again to Paradise."

He was willing. The heat had left him, to which she seemed oblivious, but he was truly glad. He taught her the second of the dances that the Star of India had taught him, the one that was even longer and even more intricate and even more deeply devoted to the finding of every spark of pleasure that a living body could hold. In the full movement of the dance, she would have matched him step for step, but she knew nothing of that, nor did he intend to teach her.

His pleasure was to blind her and deafen her and befuddle her until she could not even find the door of consciousness. She was limp as he lifted her, breathing shallowly, but the heart beat strong in her breast. There was a door opposite the one through which he had entered; as he had hoped, it led to a chamber the use of which was unmistakable. He laid her in the billows of the bed and covered her with silk.

When he went back through the door, it no longer opened on the bath, but on an antechamber in which stood a new company of captive spirits. There was no garment there, nor anywhere in the bedchamber; his own clothes—and the golden collar that Petit had warned him not to lose—were gone.

He went looking for the collar as much as for anything else, walking on the warm floors, through halls and chambers that could not have been contained within the walls that he had seen from outside. He found the atrium and its pool full of flame-colored fish, but its doors opened on rooms even stranger than before. Some had windows looking out on a sky full of stars, although in the atrium it had been barely midafternoon. Others were full of spirits in chains, laboring over forges or ovens or looms on which seemed spread the warp of the world.

Here was power that could raise men of earth and give them life and breath. He found his way to the heart of it by turning left whenever his feet tugged him to turn right, by going down when impulse would have sent him up, and by turning toward darkness against the beckoning of light. There he found a door, an ordinary wooden door, but it was not bound with iron. Its fastenings were bronze.

He set hand to it. There were wards on it, which stung a little, but they did nothing more to him. Maybe it was that he was wearing mortal flesh, and nothing else.

He had expected a sorcerer's cave: darkness, gibberings, a flutter of bats. He blinked, dazzled. It was a wide airy room with high windows that let in a flood of light. It most resembled a scriptorium in a monastery, with its lecterns and shelves and book-chests. But scriptoria were not served by winged spirits or shambling shapes wrought of earth, and that surely was a wyvern suspended from the vaulting. It was dead, or so he hoped; the glitter of its eye must simply be the light striking a jewel set in the empty skull.

Two men in black sat together under one of the windows. One was reading from a book nigh as tall as he was. The other passed the time as he listened, weaving a net out of light and shadow.

As Arslan paused in the doorway, the Archbishop of Rheims plucked a passing spirit from the air, bound it in the net, and sent it stumbling, earthbound, toward the rest of its kin.

"Ah," said the Abbot of the Saint-Denis, pausing in his reading. "A cacodemon. Those are a rarity."

The archbishop smiled and began a new net. "I should like someday to find and secure an abraxas. She has one, I'm told, but I've not seen it."

The abbot's brows lowered. "That, my lord, is because she keeps it in her bedchamber."

The archbishop flushed slightly. The abbot's expression lightened a very little. "Well then, that reflects well on your virtue, my lord."

"And yours, my lord?"

"She told me of it. She keeps it, she says, to admire when her nets are empty."

The archbishop's net was taking shape with preternatural speed. His fingers were deft, his weaving and knotting as tight as if he had been a fisherman and not a fisher of souls.

Arslan was not even aware that he had moved, until the net was shredding in his hands, and he was standing over the two great prelates of France, stark naked and too furious to care. There were few magics more cruel than this, to bind the free spirits of air; and few that could have enraged him more perfectly.

Abbot and archbishop gaped up at him, until he saw them understand what and who he was; then their faces settled into expressions of kindly contempt. "Messire," the abbot said. "Have you lost your way?"

Arslan drew a shuddering breath. If he said the words that crowded to his lips, he would betray himself, and therefore John. It was bitterly painful to bite those words back, to put on an expression of baffled innocence, and to say, "I went out of the room, and it wasn't where it was before."

"My poor boy," said the archbishop. "Come, we'll call a servant to take you back where you belong."

"Is there a privy?" Arslan asked, he hoped not too plaintively.

They seemed to believe that he was what he seemed. He bumbled about while he waited for the servant, colliding with spirits, unbinding their nets under cover of simple human restlessness. They were watching him. He must have been shocking to their sensibilities, shameless innocent that he was.

Then he heard the archbishop murmur, "Does he not put you in mind of Adam before the Fall?"

"Was she the Serpent, do you think?" the abbot asked.

"One would hope not," said the archbishop, "in view of what that would make us."

"No, no," said the abbot. "*Mea culpa*; it was a poor jest. She is one of the children of God from before the Flood—preserved from it by her watery nature, and granted the right of salvation."

"Which she has yet to take," the archbishop said, "but hope is eternal. She's useful as she is, however we may deplore her methods."

"This one will gain us nothing," said the abbot. "Look at him! Not a brain in his head."

"He's a fine fighter, they say, and a great favorite with the ladies. As how not, if any of them has seen what we see."

"He was born an infidel, I've heard," the abbot said, "and converted by an act of God."

"But not before the act of the knife," said the archbishop. "Was he Richard's boy, do you think, before he was John's? And now he's hers. If anyone can find the truth in that pretty skull, it will be our lady of the waters."

"What truth do you hope to find?" the abbot asked.

The archbishop tilted his head, spread his hands. "Who knows? John was born untrustworthy, and frankly, my lord, I'm amazed that he'd be so taken with this empty-headed ox. That's Richard's taste in favorites, not milord John's."

"John loves the exotic," said the abbot. "He'll hire Flemings instead of his own English to fight for him, because they're foreigners."

"Now that is true," said the archbishop. "And speaking of that—"

They leaned together and lowered their voices. Arslan was almost done freeing the spirits in the room, a fact of which they seemed unaware. The spirits brushed him as they flew past, each bestowing a gift or blessing. He hoarded them, quickly, before these guardians of France understood what he was doing.

They were not fools or weaklings. It took power to snare spirits as the archbishop did so casually, and the wards in this place were as strong as ever Eschiva could raise. Arslan was here because the undine had brought him here. His body was his safety: the beauty that everyone insisted on, and the befuddlement that they would expect of a man under Melusine's thrall.

He strained to hear what they said of the false Flemings, but he caught only snatches, and nothing that strung together into sense. All too soon, the servant was there, hulking and human and silent, to take him back to his cage.

# CHAPTER 47

Arslan had succeeded too well. He had seduced Melusine, and she was besotted. She would not let him go.

The more obsessed she was with him, the less desire he had for her. It must have been the way of the spell, that only one could be caught in it. He did not need desire for the arts that he practiced, arts that never came near the consummation of the body.

Did she even know that he had not touched her with more than lips or hands? She did nothing to offer him pleasure; she was entirely caught up in her own body's delight. And that was exactly as he would have it—if only she would let him out of her house.

He had hoped for another rescue from John, but no squires came bellowing at the gate, nor did a more discreet messenger appear to demand the young lord's attendance. He had been abandoned in this house of magic.

During the time when she slept a blissful, sated sleep, he wandered the maze of rooms. Wherever he could, he set spirits free. He had lost count of the days, except that it must be more than seven, because the human servants were eating Lenten fare. He would expect Melusine to live on fish, but the men and women in her employ had more mortal appetites. They had gone from mutton and fowl, when they could get it, to fish and lentils and cheese.

There came a day, at long last, when she was not in the house. That morning, if morning it was, she had risen from her bed, summoned the maids, and had herself dressed in clothes too plain for court but sturdy enough for a journey. He had clutched at her and pretended to plead, but she kissed his hands and pushed them coyly away, and ran her fingers through his tousled hair. "My beautiful one," she said. "I hate it, too, but I have to go. I'll be back as soon as I can."

"Where?" he demanded. "Where are you going? What is more important than me?"

"Nothing in the world," she said, "but I still must go. The king is calling me. Be good, my love, while I'm away. If the boredom is too great, ask Bruno to take you to the garden. There are pells there, and targets for shooting. Bruno will provide you with what you need."

"I don't want to hack at pells," Arslan said. "I want to lie with you."

She stroked his rod, which had risen to her touch, and for a breathless moment she wavered. But duty was strong. She tore herself away. "Soon," she promised him. She left him with a last, lingering glance.

As soon as she was truly and safely away, Arslan rose out of the bed that was his prison, and strode through the house until he met a servant. "Bring me clothes," he said. "Bring them now."

The servant ducked her head and bolted. Arslan could only hope she would obey. He sat in the passage to wait for her. If she did not come back, he would find a servant who would. Or he would find his clothes—somewhere. He had not found them yet, but that did not mean he never would.

The third servant he caught came back with a bundle clutched to his chest. It was not the golden splendor of court dress, but there was gold in it. He hugged the servant tightly, to the man's vast discomfiture. "How did you know? Tell me!"

The man's answer was so soft that he could barely hear it. "I heard you talking to yourself, my lord. And saw you freeing the little wild ones. I didn't bring your beautiful silk, my lord. It would be too easily noticed."

Arslan shook out the garments that he had brought. They were plain wool and linen, as nondescript as a clerk's gown. "I thank you," he said to the giver, "and bless you for your forethought."

The man clasped his hands, startling him, and kissed them. "All of us are freer since you came. Whatever you've done, however you've done it, we are grateful. Only remember us when you come with your army to kill her, and let us go. None of us serves her of our own will."

"Won't you go now?" Arslan asked.

"She'll know," said the servant.

Arslan smiled. "Not if you leave now."

He watched understanding dawn. "Oh," said the servant. "Oh, my lord!"

"Go now," said Arslan, "all of you, and quickly. Take only what you find to hand. You must be out of Paris by nightfall. I don't know if I can cover your tracks longer than that."

"That will be more than long enough," the servant said. But he paused. "Are you mortal, my lord?"

It would have been a strange question in any house but this. "My father was," Arslan said.

The servant smiled in something very like bliss. "Blessed be your mother, my lord," he said, "and the spirit that is in you."

He went then, before Arslan could thrust him out bodily. Arslan wasted no time in watching him go. The clothes fit remarkably well considering how much larger he was than the run of men in Paris. The golden collar he coiled and laid in the purse that hung from the belt.

He knew the mazes of this place now, the tricks and deceptions of each door and stair. He took the straight way to the gate.

There he paused. This was the weakness in his plan: if she had worked it against him, he would have to reveal himself in order to break the ban, or continue to be trapped here.

But there were no wards that had not been there before, and all of those were set to recognize him. There was a slight strain as he passed through them, as if they were not certain of his right to do so, but he pressed forward, and they gave way.

A mortal could not have left this place; he would have been bound by her spell. On impulse Arslan touched the wards with a flicker of the flame that lay hidden deep inside him—the power of a spirit of fire, unsullied by human flesh. If she read it as he hoped, she would believe that some other spirit had stolen him, but never that he had stolen himself.

Arslan was asleep when John came back to his rooms. He had not slept since he first saw Melusine, and even he needed to rest once in a great while. He woke in a heap on the floor, staring up at John's face. It was suffused with rage, the ruddy beard bristling, the black eyes glaring murder. From the count of his bruises, he had been flung from his pallet and kicked across the floor.

"You were gone," said John with icy precision, "for eleven days. Not one word came from you. Nobody knew where you were or even when you had gone. You were last seen with the king; it was assumed that the king had taken you with him to Normandy, where he is now, seizing the Vexin for the crown of France. But you had vanished from the earth."

"You knew where I was," Arslan said. "You ordered me to go there."

"I didn't order you to disappear without a trace!"

Arslan sat up gingerly. Nothing was broken, but he thought a rib or two might be cracked. "I'm sorry, my lord. She kept me close; I couldn't escape until she left. Unless you wanted her to know what I am?"

John spat, but not at Arslan. "Get up. Is anything broken? Good. Sit down. Here's wine. Drink it."

Arslan was glad of the wine, and the chair, too. His head was still fuzzy with sleep. "She has a house," he said, "on the Left Bank, or at least the part of it that is in this world is there. The guardians meet there, and do their magics in one of its rooms. They enslave spirits, my lord, and force some to labor in chains, and others to inhabit earthen images. Your false Flemings are theirs."

"I knew that," said John testily, but his rage was gone. "Philip's giving me an army of them, to help me take back England. He's been most insistent that I accept the gift."

Arslan smiled a broad slow smile. "Has he? That may be delayed a little. I freed all the spirits I could find, and the human servants, too. They'll have to capture themselves another army of spirits before they can animate the bodies."

"You did *what*? They'll come straight to you!"

"They won't," said Arslan. "They're convinced I have no brain at all. I hardly said a word, and the use she was making of me hardly requires a higher intellect."

"So you were strong enough," John said.

"You were wiser than I," Arslan said. "And I never broke my vows to my lady."

"How on earth did you manage that?"

"I practiced the arts I learned from a Damascene whore."

John snorted, choked, laughed aloud. "God's ballocks, boy! Do you mean to say that *you* seduced *her*?"

Arslan nodded. Somewhere in those endless days, he had forgotten how to blush. "No one had ever done such a thing before. Can you believe that?"

"Easily," John said. He paused. "Arts, you said? I don't suppose . . . ?"

"Are you commanding me?"

"Later," said John. He shook his head, lips twitching. "And I thought I'd seen all the ways you could surprise me. Do you have any more gifts or talents that I haven't been apprised of?"

"I don't know of any, my lord," Arslan said.

"Be sure to tell me if one suddenly comes to mind," said John.

During his captivity, Arslan had thought that the whole court knew where he was and what he had done there. But as John had said, he had last been seen walking with the king. When he reappeared, he was greeted with somewhat less than delirious joy—they had a new darling, a jouster who claimed to have won all the tournaments on the Crusade—but he was still a great favorite. He never even needed to invent a reason for his leaving the king in Normandy; the court found several, which hardened into rumor and then into fact. He was particularly fond of that which declared that he had been promised the Princess Alais and the duchy of Normandy if he would dispose of John.

Melusine was nowhere in evidence, nor were the rest of the guardians of France. As much as Arslan dared, he hunted for signs of rents in the fabric of the kingdom. There were no more than there had been before, even with Philip in Normandy, and even though he contemplated invasion of England. He had sworn to take back all the realms that Charlemagne had ruled, and that was all of the Plantagenets' domain on this side of the sea. He had cast his eye on England because it belonged to the house he hated, and because if he could take it, he would severely discomfit both Eleanor, who had been his father's wife long before he was born, and Eleanor's elder son, whom he hated above all.

"They were lovers a long time ago," one of the old ladies of the court said a day or two after Arslan came back. She was a great gossip, and although she had grown a little deaf, she was as sharp of eye and wit as ever. "So pretty they were together, the dark and the fair, the big golden boy and the little black-haired one with the handsome face. Then one day they quarreled, I doubt even they remember what for, and ever since, they've been at one another's throats." She sighed. "Lovers make the worst enemies of all."

Arslan sighed with her. He knew—and if word reached his lady of what he had done on John's orders, if she saw it as she had seen his amity with her mother, this time there would be no forgiveness.

It was as it must be. The comtesse patted his hand in sympathy. "You know, yes? And you so young. But they were no older. Young love hurts worst."

"Does it ever hurt less?" he asked.

She could always hear him, even when the rest of the world met with a blank stare. "No," she said, "but you learn to bear the pain more easily."

She was wise, and wicked, too; she caught his face in her gnarled old hands and kissed him more thoroughly than he had ever been kissed, even by the she-demon of the Lusignans. He was dizzy when she let him go, and dazzled. "Allah!" he said, falling into the Arabic of his childhood. He had to struggle to remember the French. "You must have been splendid when you were young."

"I still am," the comtesse said, but she was pleased: her eyes were sparkling as they must have done when she was a girl.

Not long after that, John had word from Rouen that made him laugh in delight—but very, very privately, because in the way of the game, he should be royally indignant. Philip had seized the Vexin, which was the gateway to Normandy and the sea, and had taken Gisors; then he had marched on to Rouen in the full expectation that it would open its gates before him.

He had found the gates shut and barred, armed men on the walls, and a cold-eyed castellan who said to him, "I care nothing for any bargain you may have struck with my liege lord's brother. My fealty is sworn to Richard, duly crowned king of England and rightful duke of the Normans. Until he comes in his own person and tells me otherwise, I will not surrender this castle to the crown of France.

"However," he had added with some softening of the stony façade, "if your majesty would wish to enter as a guest of my lord duke, albeit in his absence, your majesty is most welcome."

Philip had been flat astonished—speechless, John's spy said. "You mean," he said when he found his tongue, "that I can be a guest as my royal sister is, and as your beloved duke is a guest of the German emperor. Thank you, but no."

"Pest," John said when he heard that, but he was not excessively angry. "I did hope he'd take the bait. It would have been convenient."

"Not so convenient for Rouen, if the outraged armies of France laid siege to it," Arslan said.

"You think they'd do that, with the edge of Leicester's sword at their king's throat?" John shook his head. "It really is a pity. We could have traded kings, and saved the trouble of a ransom."

For that was the other news which had come that cold Lenten morning. Richard had not yet been found, that anyone knew, but the emperor and the archduke had finished a lengthy spate of bickering and settled on a ransom.

"A hundred thousand marks of silver," John said after both messengers had gone, "and tenscore noble hostages. Mother will be appalled."

"They're out to break you," Arslan said.

"They very nearly will, too," said John. "If it were my choice to make, I'd fling the demand in their faces. He got himself into it, let him get himself out, the bloody idiot. But I'm only a king of shadows. Mother will pay. Mother will do anything for her golden darling."

"Will you try to stop her?"

John laughed, so bitter he nearly choked on it. "Will I try to stop the tides of the sea? I'm the rebel, messire. I'm the traitor to my brother. She'd sooner listen to Richard's jailers than to me."

"My lord," said Arslan, not without a moment's misgiving, "that's a game you're playing, to weaken and distract France. You know that; I do. Isn't it time she did, too?"

"Messire," said John with a twist of scorn, "wasn't it you who tried as best you could to tell her the truth of me? How well did you succeed?"

"She ran over me like an armored charge," Arslan said ruefully. "But what if we all tell her—the guardians, you, I? What if we prove it? If she's on our side, my lord, playing the game as the castellan of Rouen has been playing it, she'll be a truly formidable ally."

"Formidable, yes," John muttered. "Suppose you tell me how you intend to accomplish that, seeing as how I'm here, she's there, and the King of the Franks is mounting an invasion in my name."

"Are you a prisoner?" Arslan asked. "Have you tried to leave? You could join Philip in Gisors—properly outraged at the debacle of Rouen, and prepared to help in any way you can. If England is taken, after all, what will Rouen matter? He'll have the whole of the rest of Normandy, and the whole of England, too. Convince him of that, and he'll all but carry you across the sea."

"You," said John, "are a clever man."

"You would have thought of it yourself, my lord," Arslan said, "once you had time to think."

"Don't console me," John snapped. "Get the escort ready. We're going."

Arslan bowed. John looked disappointed. He would have wanted at least a show of dismay. That was a pity, but Arslan had been expecting this command. John, for all his appearance of ease, was as restless as his men had begun to be. It was time to begin the next round of the game, in Normandy and in England, and, God willing, in Germany as well.

# CHAPTER 48

~~~

A rslan would have hated Germany. Not only was it dark, wet, and closed in with forest from one end to the other, its proudest boast was the quality of its beer.

William Longchamp astonished Kalila by taking to this hunt as if he had been born for it. He was still a remarkably choleric man with no gift of tact, but he proved to be gifted in the hunting down of captive kings. Nor was it only the magic that had been laid on him. This was part of him, born in him.

The guardians had chosen perhaps better than they knew, though it was an article of Kalila's faith, as of the high magic, that there was no such creature as chance. The bishop sought out the most remote and inaccessible of fortresses, grim stony piles tangled in the branches of forests or perched on crags above swift-running rivers. He was indefatigable, pressing on through snow, ice, sleet, and the lash of rain, following a track of rumor and whisper and, if he had known it, inquisitive spirits.

She could see them. She had always known of them because of Arslan, but at best she had never seen more than a flicker on the edge of vision. Then she was given magic. Maybe it was the magic itself, or maybe it was the red stone that she had found in her purse long after it was too late to give it back to Arslan. The world had become a notably more populated place. It did not alarm her; as strange, even grotesque as many spirits were, they meant no harm. The great ones, the dark and powerful things, kept to the deeps of the earth and the upper reaches of the air.

Ely's track had taken him deep into Franconia, and into the threshold of spring. It was not the soft English spring nor yet the startling beauty of Syria after the winter rains, but a forest spring: melting snow, first shimmer of green in the clearings and on the branches of the trees. The bishop's escort was making slow headway down a muddy road beside a river swollen with snowmelt. His patience, never considerable, was sorely taxed. He was as close to profanity as a man of his calling could be.

Kalila escaped as she had done often before, taking to the forest on her surefooted Arab mare. According to the maps that Ely carried, corroborated by hangers-on in the last town, there was a castle ahead, held in fief to the German emperor. Already she could see the swirls of spirits that in this country surrounded human habitation. She even thought she could tell by the patterns of their aerial dance whether they heralded city, town, village, forester's hut or hermit's hovel, or the stony confinement of a castle.

There were a great number of spirits of air in this region. They flew in flocks like birds, even sang to one another; and they leaped and gathered and wheeled over a jut of rock that rose out of the trees. Something was echoing them from below, a clear and eerie singing.

Kalila's mare tensed. Her ears pricked; she slowed, picking her way down the narrow and somewhat overgrown track. It ended on the riverbank, so close to the foot of the castle's crag that Kalila gasped. The tangled trees had deceived her; she had thought it much farther away than it was.

There was a veritable whirlwind of spirits over the tower, and the water was full of them. Kalila had not been daring to hope; there had been endless disappointments on this journey, some of them bitter. But she had never seen so many spirits in so desolate a place. The stone about her neck, always warm with the magic that filled it, was burning hot.

> *"Ja nus hons pris ne dira sa reson*
> *adroitement, s'ensi com dolans non. . . ."*

Kalila clutched at her mare's mane. Arslan—Arslan's voice—

No. This was harsher, deeper, and its accent was different. But she had heard Arslan sing in that selfsame voice, with those selfsame words. He had said—John had said—

"*Ya Allah*," she breathed. And in that breath, words took shape, matching the mode and the tone of the song that floated down from the tower.

*"Mes par confort puet il fere chancon."*

The wheel of spirits slowed. The wind paused. In the tower was silence.

Just as Kalila was about to lift her voice again, the singer above sang:

*"Mout se feist  bon tenir de chanter,*
*quar en chantant  ne set l'on maiz que dire. . . ."*

That was not the same song at all. It was a lament of sorts: "Best to stop singing, since when one sings, one never knows what to say." Nor did she, for she did not know this song. But a spirit spiraled down out of the flock above her, perched on her shoulder, and sang in her ear. She sang it as she heard it:

*"Ne mot ne chant  ne puet l'on maiz trouver,*
*tant i sache hom  esgarder ne eslire,*
*que maintes foiz  ne soit estez redis. . . ."*

Thereby she, or the spirit on her shoulder, agreed with him: there was no word or song to be found in the world that had not been said and said again.

He finished the verse with a slightly defiant flourish:

*"S'en est chanters  plus maz et desconfis,*
*ne ja pour ce  ne sera l'amours pire."*

But though there was no good left in singing, sang the man in the tower, love would not be lessened, not for that.

That made her smile. She left her mare grazing hobbled on the bit of grass by the riverbank, measured the trees that closed the tower in, and set herself to climb the one that rose closest to the window from which the singing had come. This was not an art they often practiced in Outremer, but she had scaled enough crags and towers to have some sense of handholds and footholds. Crags did not sway and towers did not bend under one's weight, but with prayer and grim determination, she came up level with the slit of window. It was very deep, no more than an arrow slit.

She eyed the gap between her precarious perch and the window, carefully not considering the long, long drop below. It was too far to jump, and she had no wings. But she had a voice. "Malik!" she called. "Malik Ric!"

The man within burst out in an exclamation. "By God! Am I going mad?"

"I don't think so, sire," she said. "Can you get to the top of the tower and drop a rope? I think I can get up from here."

"God's feet!" was the only reply. She waited, swaying, clinging to the branch and to hope, for so long that she knew he had failed in what she asked. But she had succeeded. She had found the King of the English.

Just as she was about to begin the long descent, a rope slithered down from the battlements. It was still an ungodly distance from the branch to the rope, but she clutched Arslan's red stone where it hung at her breast, though it seared her hand, and leaped with blind faith. Her free hand caught the rope, or maybe it caught her hand, or a spirit guided it there. The other snapped free of the stone and secured her weight. She struck the wall with bruising force and clung, winded, for a stretching moment.

The rope began to ascend in jerks, as the man above hauled it up hand over hand. She whispered a word that Eschiva had taught her, to make herself light. From the sound of the exclamation and the sudden speed of her ascent, the spell had succeeded.

She let it go as she caught hold of the battlement. Strong hands hauled her up and over, depositing her more or less upright on the tower's summit.

"Hell and damnation," said the King of the English. "What's a Turk doing here, singing that of all songs?"

"Looking for you, sire," Kalila said. "How did you know—"

The big hand slapped her cheek lightly. "I'm not blind, boy. Who sent you? My sister? Nobody else would have a Turk ready to hand, not even Mother."

Kalila had to pause to get her breath. Plantagenets, one and all, were overwhelming on first acquaintance; and this one was the largest, the reddest, and the most headlong of them all. He was not any taller than Arslan, nor much broader either, but Arslan was a quiet man except when he was fighting. Richard was born boisterous.

"William Longchamp is on his way here, sire," she said. "Others are searching, too, but he's the closest."

"*Longchamp* has himself a Turk?" Richard's astonishment nigh blew her over. "No, no, tell me you belong to someone else—that's a worthy man, as worthy as a man can be, but I simply can't imagine—"

"I belong to myself," she said, "and of course to God. Are you well, sire? Have they treated you with proper respect?"

Richard shrugged off the question. "They've been decent enough. Now tell me how you know that song. Is Blondel nearby? Is it he you belong to? Is he hunting for me?"

"I'm sure I don't know, sire," Kalila said.

Richard's ruddy face grew a few shades ruddier. "That song," he said, "I composed with Blondel de Nesle during the siege of Acre, one long dull afternoon while the engines hammered the walls. No one knows it but the two of us. How do you know it? Did he teach it to you?"

"No, sire," Kalila said. "When you sang the first verses, the rest came to me."

"What, out of the air?"

"Yes, sire," she said.

She thought he might strike her, but he kept his fists at his sides. "No matter. You've found me. Go back down now and tell my lord of Ely that I'll be glad to see him. This has been a longer and duller slog than the whole siege of Acre."

"Sire," she said, bowing to the stones of the roof as if he had been a king of her own people. That pleased him: his scowl lightened. He was smiling as he lowered her down from the tower.

The rope ended twice her height from the ground. She let it go and slid the rest of the way down the wall, knees loose, so that she crumpled and rolled when she struck the ground; but she came up lightly, reaching for the mare's bridle, slipping loose the hobbles, swinging into the saddle. Richard was watching from the battlements. She bade him farewell with a lift of the hand, and turned back down the tree-choked track.

The Bishop of Ely did not thank Kalila for the news that she had brought, but his dour face lightened visibly. He could not quicken the pace—not with wagons and mud—but now that he knew his hunt had ended, the mood of his whole escort transformed from grim endurance to a kind of dizzy excitement. For months they had hunted the wastes and wilds of Germany, and here was Richard at last.

Or so Kalila hoped. She had seen no one in the castle but Richard. Arslan's ruby had burned all the while she was with him, but now as she rode with Ely's train, it was no warmer than her skin. He must be guarded, and not only by stone and steel.

She had been prepared for that in ways that she would not be fully aware of until the time came. So too had Ely. She rode as near to him as she could, which happened to be just behind him, at his right hand.

The road was not so muddy nearer the castle. Logs had been laid down across the track, to give wagon wheels purchase; the oxen groaned a little less piteously, and the horses seemed grateful for the respite.

From the road, the castle was visible for some time before they came to it, rising out of its thicket of trees. The way up to it was narrow and punishingly steep. Ely, eyeing that goat track, hissed in annoyance and ordered his wagons to be put up at the base of the crag, and their most critical contents loaded on the backs of already protesting sumpter mules. As mule train and horse train, they ascended to the frown of the gate.

Kalila was directly behind Ely. He, no fool in the ways of the world, had sent a dozen armed guards ahead. They reached the gate without mishap, but also without sign of life from the castle.

As the others came up behind, the captain of the guard hammered on the gate with the haft of his mace. "What ho within!" he bellowed. "Open up! You've guests, messires, hungry and cold and slathered in mud. Open up, for Christian charity!"

Kalila's hackles rose. Something was listening, but it was not a human presence. It crouched inside this lair of stone, watching, waiting for Allah knew what. She murmured a prayer of protection, and added to it one of Eschiva's words.

The thing inside the castle seemed to rouse at that, pricking ears, searching for the tiny tingle of magic. Kalila regretted it, but it was too late; the spell was spoken.

Just as Ely's men were about to break down the gate, someone inside shot the bolt. The gate opened ponderously. A man in mail stood inside it, armed with a spear. He seemed mortal enough, a burly fair-haired German with a narrow measuring stare. "*Meine Herren*," he said. And then in gutturally accented French: "I welcome you to the Mädchensburg."

Ely's men-at-arms glanced at one another; a grin ran down the ranks. The Maiden's Castle, was this? That was a pleasant omen—although, Kalila thought, it was not the most pleasant of places. More likely it had been built as a prison than as a lady's bower.

The German knight admitted them with decent courtesy. It was not so small a castle now that they were in it, and it was not at all empty of inhabitants. There was a strong force within those walls, and a margrave in command of them, attended by a dozen knights and a small army of squires. Not a maiden was to be seen, only men, and every one of them in mail.

The bishop's company was not made up of soft men: they had traveled the length and breadth of Germany, and fought where they had to fight, and suffered cold and wet and hardship enough. Yet beside these mailed warriors they shrank to insignificance. These men had been on Crusade: the marks of the sun were on them still, and the scars of war and of fever.

None of them appeared to recognize Kalila as Richard had. She kept her head down and hid among Ely's clerks, and hoped that she escaped notice.

Whatever she had sensed inside the castle, here in the hall were only mortal men. The margrave received them with the same stiff politeness as his gate-guard, and offered them the hospitality of the castle. Ely was hardly fool enough to refuse it. Here as he had in countless other towns and castles, he said nothing of his errand until the ceremonies of greeting were all advanced. Then he circled round to it, little by little, while his men waited with schooled patience.

Kalila did not need to be patient. She was a scout, a spy if she chose to think of it so, and she had already marked the tower in which she had found Richard. It was guarded at the foot by giants in mail. What guarded it above was not human.

She passed the mortal guards without difficulty, but the thing in the shadows was keenly aware of her. She had a vision of teeth, many and sharp, and serpentine length, and a mind as ancient and cold as the river that flowed far below the castle.

She ascended the stairs with beating heart. She was protected by every power that the guardians of Britain could bring to bear, but she was still very small and alone, armed with a scrap of steel against the child of Iblis.

It did not take shape in form that she could see. It was formless, a deepening of shadow, a suggestion of eyes. Even without shape, it breathed. The whole of the tower swayed in the rhythm of that breath.

She ascended into the belly of the creature, wrapped tightly in her little web of spells. Richard was on the other side. The top of the tower was free, she knew that already. She had only to remember him, and the sky.

She made the sky happen, made light in the dark place. The darkness resisted. It buried her, drowned her, overwhelmed her. She fought it without thought or reason, for pure visceral terror—of nothingness; of not-being.

She stumbled and fell to her knees. The pain saved her. It was a spark of blood-red light in the center of the darkness. She gathered it into the searing coal of Arslan's red stone, and wrought the splendor of simple daylight.

She stood in front of a door. It was barred, but there was no lock on it. She slid the bolt and opened the door.

Richard was sitting in what light the slit of window afforded, plucking idly at the strings of a lute. One of the strings snapped. He cursed, and looked up into Kalila's face.

"What, no rope up the wall this time?" he asked her.

"The bishop is here, sire," she said. "Shall I take you down to him?"

He rose with alacrity. "Not, mind," he said, "that I'm shut up here without relief. I'm let out to play."

"If the lord bishop has anything to say of it," said Kalila, "you'll be let out for more than that."

"Freed?"

"There is a ransom," she said.

"Ah," he said. "Well. Silver's like grass: mow it down, it grows back."

He was like a child, headlong and heedless. Kalila, no stranger to kings, sighed for his fecklessness but bowed to his rank, and led him out of the tower.

The darkness was gone from the stairs, but she sensed it deep in the castle's heart. It was still there, still on guard, but it threatened neither Kalila nor the English king. It was set to keep strangers from approaching Richard, not to keep Richard from leaving the tower.

She understood something as she descended the long spiral of steps. Richard captive was no threat to any power here. Richard free was another matter altogether. If they could keep him, the mortals and spirits of this country, they would do it. He was far from free, and a very long way from England.

# CHAPTER 49

"They found him."

John had had no messenger, not here in Gisors, in the train of the French king. Yet he woke in the middle of March with none of his usual atrocious morning temper, sat bolt upright in bed, and said, "He's in a castle near Würtzburg. They're taking him to the city. The bishop is with him. Your Turk, too."

Arslan had been up for a long while, doing squire-service, although he had no need to do such a thing. He nodded as John spoke. "Yes. I had the same dream."

John glowered. "You're not even surprised. You should be astonished—awed. I, messire—I had a dream, and it's a true dream."

"Very true," Arslan said, "and suitably awe-inspiring. You have great power, my lord, if you trouble to admit it."

"Here? Off my native soil?"

"Aren't you heir to Normandy, too?"

"Normandy isn't mine," John said, "except in the game. It's not home. I'll take it when the time comes, and keep it as best I can, but all the kings of England before me . . . they thought of England as a conquered country. I think of it as mine. Normandy is the wealth I keep for the use I can make of it. England holds my heart."

Arslan bowed to that. John appreciated the irony, and the sincerity of the sentiment, too.

"It's going to be some days before word gets here," John said. "I have to be present, to be suitably amazed and appalled—to play the game to its conclusion. You will put on your plain face and ride for the sea. You'll find a boat, I'm sure. Go over the water and make my mother believe what I am. I'll follow as quickly as I can, with Philip's invasion as hard on my heels as I can tempt it to be. With luck it will suffer all the sins of excessive haste and overweening arrogance. You'll just have time to slam the gate shut on my backside. We'll break the army of monsters that he sends, but it's going to be close. How fast can you ride?"

"As fast as the straight track will take me," said Arslan. "May I have your leave to go now?"

John peered at him. "You're already dressed like a clerk. You knew!"

"I know you, my lord," Arslan said.

John's growl was his only answer.

Arslan's errand was urgent, and his danger not inconsiderable, but his heart was light. He felt as if he had been set free from a prison, as if he could spread wings and fly.

He rode the grey mare out of Gisors. It was a risk; she was far too well bred for a poor clerk. But he needed her strength and her swiftness. He was fortunate that he attracted no undue notice. The wards here were set to keep enemies out, not to keep stray clerks in.

The guardians were not here. He had been startled when he came to find them absent; he had thought that Melusine had gone with the rest to console Philip for his failure at Rouen. They were nowhere in evidence, and no one knew where they were, even the court gossips.

They were preparing the invasion, Arslan suspected—which meant that they would be somewhere along the coast. That in turn meant that while he might be safe enough on the track through Normandy, when he came to the sea, he would run afoul of them or of the wards that they had set.

It was similar in its way to the warding that had kept Arslan in Melusine's house. All magics came down to a simple few kinds of working—Father Hugh had taught him that, and Eschiva and Bertrada had shown him how to use the knowledge.

He needed it now. The Worldwood was stranger even than he remembered. It was as quiet as ever, but that quiet was too deep. It was waiting like a cat on its prey.

This time the cold-drake would not be illusion. He armed himself as he rode, stripping off the mortal mask, the better to do battle. Without knowing quite why he did it, he searched in his bag and found the golden bell. He made a cord of hair from his horse's tail, plaiting it tightly, and hung the bell about his neck. It sang softly as he rode.

If he touched it he could see Kalila. She was riding through a wood even darker than this one, beside a big redheaded man on a big bay horse. Arslan smiled to see her. Richard seemed delighted with the company. She looked well; so did the English king, though he was obviously a prisoner: there were armed men on all sides, and a glimmering cord of honor and knightly oath binding him to this captivity.

The track narrowed. Trees closed in on it, weaving branches thickly overhead. The mare shied. That was utterly unlike her; Arslan, astonished, came as close to losing his seat as he had in a long while. She snorted and jibbed as he found his balance, veering toward the edge of the track.

There was nothing at all ahead. Not a single thing. Yet it took all of his skill to get the mare past that narrowing of the track. He had to dismount in the midst of her whirling and plunging, calm her as much as he could, and lead her on foot.

The track felt strange, insubstantial. The trees seemed no more than shadows. If he set a foot awry, he could tear through the fabric of this world, and appear—where? In hell? Limbo? Purgatory?

He moved as carefully but as quickly as he could. The mare was rigid with tension, but quiet; she clung close, snorting softly to herself.

He had not thought to come to the sea so soon, but the track was near its end. He braced himself as always before a battle, breathing lightly, stepping soft, alert to every shift and flicker of the air. Even with that, when the track vanished, he fell headlong into emptiness. There was no thought in his mind. His body leaped, twisted, caught hold of the mare's saddle and scrambled onto her back. They fell together through a roar of wind and darkness.

The mare lurched and staggered, then by some miracle found her feet. She stood on a shingle beside the sea. The air was full of salt and spray. Stars wheeled overhead, and yet the sun shone behind a veil of mist.

The guardian stood between him and the sea. She was dressed in black; she looked remarkably ordinary, a fair-haired woman standing on the shore, staring as if he were a prodigy.

He supposed he would be to her, now that his mask was laid aside. He watched astonishment give way to understanding, and then to a deep and abiding anger. Yet she laughed. "Beautiful man! You made a fool of me."

"I gave you pleasure," he said.

She nodded, eyelids growing heavy, lips growing fuller as she remembered. "You gave me great pleasure. You shall give even more when I take vengeance for the thing that you did to me. What are you? Ifrit?"

He bent his head. Her words were a distraction. He could feel the gathering of power, the trembling of earth underfoot, the restlessness of the sea. The wards of France were up. The ship he had come to meet was on the other side of them, wallowing in a sudden swell.

"It was you," she said. "You set my servants free. That was not wise, beautiful man. You made it terribly difficult for us to obey our king's command. We had to raise spirits from the earth, at excessive cost; our army is still rather less than we would wish."

"Good," said Arslan.

"So," said Melusine. "Whose are you? Richard's? You're perfectly to his taste."

Arslan searched through the veil of her words, testing the walls with his magic, seeking a weakness, a gap, any escape. He found it in the barrage of power that she flung at him, the white heat of lust commingled with the cold chill of revenge. It was deep in the heart, and it wore his face, but never as he saw it in a mirror. This was temptation unalloyed, and beauty bare.

He would lose it if he blushed, if he recoiled from it. He flung himself toward it, horse and gear and all, and vanished into it.

This was not the Worldwood, but kin to it. It was like the shore he had left, but empty of living presence. The sea that crashed on it was clean, the air free, unwarded, unwalled. He breathed deep of the sharp salt scent.

He was utterly, irretrievably lost. There was nothing within sight or sense that he knew; no track, no sign of where he could go. Only the shingle, the spray, the silver vault of sky. No bird nor spirit hovered in that sky; no fish swam in the sea. This was a world without living thing.

He turned about, wheeling the mare on her haunches. Emptiness met his eyes wherever he looked.

The golden bell chimed with the movement. Such a sound had

never been heard in this lifeless place. It was soft, sweet, yet it echoed and reechoed above, beneath, and about the roar of the sea. He closed his hand over it to still it, and gasped.

It was not Kalila whom he saw this time, but Eschiva clad all in white with her bright hair unbound, and about her waist a girdle hung with tiny golden apples. She was standing on a promontory above a restless sea; her arms were spread, her face blank, ecstatic. She was as full of magic as the sun is with light.

All the hatred, all the revulsion he had felt toward Melusine, transmuted into love and longing. There was no power in it, nor any magic but what any human creature could raise; only the pure desire. Heart called to heart, spirit to spirit. He touched leg to the grey mare's side. She stepped delicately from the lifeless shingle to the living soil of Britain.

She sighed a mighty sigh, shook herself, and lowered her head to graze. Arslan slid bonelessly from her back. His knees collapsed beneath him; he sprawled in the grass. There was nothing left in him but a shred of consciousness, and relief as profound as the mare's.

He could not let go, not yet. He had to speak. "John," he said. "John sent—the French—"

Eschiva was kneeling beside him. Her face was frightened. That was not like her at all. He tried to lift his hand, to touch her pale cheek, but his body would not obey his will.

He forced his lips to move, his tongue to shape the words. "John sent me. France will invade—armies of earth; captive spirits. They still believe that John belongs to them. I betrayed myself. But they won't know—the way I ran—they won't—"

"Hush," she said. "Save your strength."

She said it briskly, returned to herself again, though the effort showed in the pallor of her face and the tremor in her hands. She lifted him with more strength than he would have believed she had, and heaved him onto the mare's back. "Can you hold on?" she asked him.

For answer he clung to the high pommel of the saddle and set his teeth. She led the mare down off the headland.

# CHAPTER 50

He would not stop trying to talk. Eschiva gave up trying to silence him, but long before he was done, and long before they had come to Dover Castle, she had heard all that she needed to hear. She sent a call through the inner realm of Britain, a summons that shook the secret ways.

Jeannette was in the castle, thank the gods; she had been talking of going to visit her husband's sister in Canterbury. She took Eschiva in without demur, and exclaimed over the one whom Eschiva brought. "The poor thing! Is he wounded? He looks bled out."

Eschiva shook her head, but Jeannette was paying her no attention, calling for servants, having a room prepared and a bed made up, and sending word to the kitchens to fetch a posset. "Tell Cook to use the herbs in the red bag—he knows which I mean. Just a pinch, mind! And sweeten the lot with honey."

There was no stopping her once she had begun. In any event it would be a while before an answer came to Eschiva's summons. She let Jeannette fuss over Arslan and a little over her, let herself be tucked in bed beside him and fed her own share of the posset. It was surprisingly good: there was wine in it, and honey, and sweet spices, and a pungent undertone of herbs. If she had been less distracted, she would have paused to discover what they were. Valerian root, perhaps; lavender; a dash of feverfew.

Arslan had fallen asleep. The grey cast was fading from his cheeks. She laid her hand against one, welcoming the nearness of him, the warmth of living flesh. She had forgotten how beautiful he was. She had not even known how much strength he had. To do as he had done, to walk from shore to shore across the sea, through walls of air on either side—that was very great magic.

He had drained himself dry. If he had been mortal, if he had not been the ifritah's child, he would have died. Her strength in him, the fire of her spirit, had saved him.

Eschiva laid her body against his, clasping him close. She wept a little, for weakness, but dried her tears before she woke him. Her arms that had been empty were filled again. Her heart's ache was eased. She did not, just then, choose to think of anything else; of any strangeness, any scent on him that should not have been there. Scent of woman most particularly, clinging to him like sweet and cloying smoke.

He was clean of sin against her—the small charm that she cast was clear enough as to that. She would accept it, for the moment, and simply be glad that he had come back to her.

The Marshal of Britain brought the one whom Eschiva had summoned, riding on the straight track from London. They entered the castle as a noble lady and her guard, asking lodging for the night. Even if the day had not ended in storm, with sheets of rain lashing the walls, Jeannette's open hospitality would have received them.

Arslan was still asleep. Eschiva left him under the watchful eyes of a flock of spirits, dressed herself and plaited her hair, and went decorously down to Jeannette's bower.

Jeanette was in hall with her husband, finishing the daymeal. The Marshal had dined with his charge in the bower: the remnants of their dinner lay heaped on a table. He had a cup of wine; his companion sat with hands folded, waiting in conspicuous patience for the world to make sense.

Eschiva bowed low over the queen's hand. Eleanor fixed her with a cold stare. "Are you responsible for this?"

"Majesty," Eschiva said, "I beg your pardon, but there was no choice. The need is urgent; time is short. There's no space for delay."

"Madam," said Eleanor, "there will be space for explanations. Either this is a remarkably vivid dream, or I've ridden from London to Dover in less than half a day."

"No dream, majesty," said Eschiva. "You are in the true Britain now. I am one of its guardians. This lord of warriors is another."

"Nonsense," said Eleanor. "Dreams and foolishness."

"Nonsense never brought you here, majesty," Eschiva said. "Now I beg you, listen. Richard is found. John has had word before any other; he'll come as quickly as he can. Philip is mounting an invasion, an army of what will appear to be Flemings in John's pay. You must raise Britain, majesty, to drive them back."

Eleanor sat still under what must have been blow after blow. She seized on the one that must matter most to her. "Richard? Richard is found?"

"Safe and well, majesty," said Eschiva, "in a castle in Germany. They're moving him to Würzburg; the Bishop of Ely is with him, and an abbot or two."

Eleanor crossed herself. "Thanks be to God," she said fervently. "John is coming? Leading an invasion?"

"Running ahead of it, majesty," Eschiva said. "He played it as a diversion until his brother should be found. He's forcing it now to be set in motion before it's fully ready. He begs you to fortify the coast; to be ready for whatever comes."

"My son the rebel," Eleanor said, "my son the traitor says these things? My son who seized the duchy of Normandy and surrendered the Vexin, which his father and his brother both labored long to keep? That son? The one who, if he comes, will do his best to usurp the throne of England?"

"Your son needs to usurp nothing, majesty," Eschiva said more sharply than perhaps she should. "He has done what he has done in order to keep France occupied while a man under his command searched for and found his brother. Yes, it was he who sent the bishop! Are you so blind to him, majesty? Do you see so little of what he is?"

"I see him clearly," said Eleanor. "He's as treacherous a creature as ever drew breath. He craves kingship; it twists in his gut that he can't have it."

"But, majesty," said William the Marshal, "he does have it."

His calm deep voice startled Eleanor into speechlessness. He set down the cup from which he had been drinking, and leaned toward her. "Lady, have I ever been aught but loyal to the crown?"

"Never," she said with conviction. John she did not trust. This man she did—or she would never have come to this place, nor laid her life and safety in his hands.

"I am loyal also to another crown," he said, "and another king. Your elder son is King of the English. Your youngest son, lady, is king of all Britain."

Eleanor laughed aloud. "Oh, yes! In his dreams he is."

"In all realms of dream and waking," said the Marshal, "John is the true king. He wears the crown of Arthur, and wields the scepter of Bran."

"No," said Eleanor, stubborn in disbelief. "John was never meant to be king of anything. Richard is king, born and bred and raised by my own hand. To him I gave all; to the other nothing. Nor does he deserve more than I've given him."

"Britain chose him," said Eschiva. "He was sealed and consecrated by powers of which you, with all due respect, your majesty, know nothing. Do you understand? John has no need to seize a throne. He already has one. All of this that he does is a game, a ruse, a diversion. He's saving this realm, majesty, not betraying it. Now will you open your eyes and see, and help us as only you can do?"

"I don't believe you," Eleanor said.

"Then believe this."

They all started, even Eschiva who had heard his step outside the door. Arslan was standing in it, swaying slightly, but he was up and dressed and managing to keep his feet. He raised his hands. They were full of fire, streaming out of him, wreathing him in flames that neither burned nor consumed him.

"This is magic, lady," he said. "This is power such as your youngest son possesses, which he wields for the defense of Britain."

He approached her, walking slowly. Eschiva could feel the heat of him even across the room. Eleanor sat stiff, stone-faced, with glittering eyes. He knelt in front of her, clothed and mantled in fire, and said, "Lady, he needs you. They both do. Try to see as we see. Your elder son has been captured by the allied powers of Europe. Your younger son is struggling to hold back the invasion of Britain."

"My younger son is causing that invasion."

Arslan shook his head. "No, my lady. Why would Philip leave the Crusade under a pretext so thin it makes him look a coward, unless he reckoned to exploit your son's absence? He's succeeded magnificently in drawing Richard's fangs. John lets him think that the inevitable heir—for he is that, lady, regardless of what anyone may wish—is safe in his hand. Now he thinks that he has Normandy, and that England is ripe to fall into his hand.

"But look, lady. If John lures him out in haste, and breaks his invasion—which he can only do with your help—then England will be safe, and you can see to freeing Richard and taking back Normandy."

"That," said Eleanor slowly, "is the very voice and mind of my youngest son. Yet why would he do anything for Richard? Why not simply take it all?"

"He has made a bargain," Arslan said. "Britain is his now. England will be his in the end. He can wait. But letting the world think that he can't—that's strategy. I said before and I say to you again: If even you believe it, how can his enemies fail to be deceived?"

"Because it's true to his spirit." Eleanor was frowning, deep in thought. They all waited for her to speak again. When she did, it was with the swift decision that had marked her since she was a girl. "Very well. I hold you hostage for the truth of what you say. If it proves false, you die a traitor."

Arslan smiled. "That's a fair bargain, your majesty."

"I'm glad you think so," said Eleanor.

When Eleanor moved, she moved with irresistible speed. She used her instruments ruthlessly. Arslan was given a night to rest, no more, and no matter how strenuously his lady might object. Then he was sent along the coast of England, mustering every man or boy who could wield some semblance of a weapon. Anything that they could lift would do: scythes and pruning hooks, pitchforks and threshing flails, as well as ancient swords and spears that had come down from Roman days.

Word came from John through the walls of air: Philip had agreed to keep the Peace of God and not mount the invasion until the days of Lent had ended. Fast upon this message came John himself, strutting down the plank of a French ship at Southampton and riding up to London as the heir of England. England, which hardly knew Richard but knew John well, was delighted to welcome him home again.

John came with a company of guards—false Flemings as Arslan had said. Their semblance was more convincing than she had thought; the magic that made them had been strengthened, and the spirits within them even more deeply subdued, so that they walked and spoke almost exactly like men.

Only in their eyes could she see the truth. They were dull earth over a roil of trapped panic. Most of them were mad, twisted and tortured by the spell that was laid on them. It was, as Arslan had said, pure callous cruelty to enslave what was never meant to be held within the bonds of earthly substance.

The Archbishop of Rheims and the Abbot of Saint-Denis must be supple of mind even for churchmen, not only to suffer this ugliness but to take part in its working. This was a dark art, not the darkest but black enough. England's guardians did not practice it.

The creatures were warded against dissolution. Eschiva nearly destroyed herself with her own spell of loosing, which lashed back at her from the surface of the wards.

She was in London then, lodged in the Tower, bound as waiting woman to the queen. Eleanor was using her as ruthlessly as anyone else, keeping her close and demanding to be taught everything that Eschiva knew. Fortunately for Eschiva's peace of mind, Eleanor was far too busy with the cares of the kingdom to spare much time for the high art.

Eschiva was not about to let anyone see how badly her spell had failed. Arslan, who would not have been deceived, was somewhere near Harfleur, the last she had heard, mustering farmers and fishermen for the defense of Britain. The exhaustion, the weakness, passed for the onset of her courses; she pretended to drink the potions that Eleanor's physician brewed for her, and let herself be confined to bed for a day. She could do her duty as well from a featherbed as from a corner of the bower, pretending to stitch at a tapestry while her magic roamed the whole broad loom of Britain.

She had not meant to fall asleep between Corfe and Arundel. Waking was delicious: a long slow kiss and his arms lifting her, clasping her close.

Too late she remembered what she was wiser to hide. He held her not inconsiderable weight as if it had been no more than a child's, and searched her face with eyes that saw everything she had done, and everything she had failed to do. "Lady! You could have died."

"I'm a little stronger than that," she said tightly. "Put me down."

Of course he ignored her. He must have come straight from the stables: he was in damp riding gear, and he smelled of rain and mud and horses. There was a chair by the bed; he lowered himself into it with her in his lap. Her hands laced behind his neck. That was not what she had asked them to do, but they would not thrust her away from him. She was still damnably weak.

"This is my fault," he said. "I showed them how easy it was to undo their spirit-bindings. I should have left well enough alone."

"How did you—"

He flushed. "I couldn't stand it. There was a whole house in Paris, full of them. When she went away, I went through the house and freed them all."

Eschiva's brows went up. "She?"

"Melusine."

In that name was a great burden of things: hatred; pity. Guilt.

"What," Eschiva asked him perfectly calmly, "were you doing in her house?"

He drew a breath. He was shaking. She regretted, deeply, that she had ever begun this conversation. They had been avoiding it since he came back to Britain—successfully, she had thought. Weakness had betrayed her. Now there was no escape.

"What does any man do in the house of Melusine?"

There. He had said it. And yet . . . "You didn't. I can tell. You didn't break your vows to me."

The splendor of his relief dazzled her. "No! No, I didn't. But," he said after a pause, "she thinks I did. Do you remember the arts of India?"

A wave of heat ran through her. She remembered them very well indeed. "The conquest of kisses?"

He nodded.

She threw her head back and laughed. She was too weak for that; it made her dizzy, and nearly made her lose consciousness. But it was a magnificent jest.

He waited patiently for her to finish. "John laughed, too," he said. "I was afraid you'd kill me."

"Geld you, maybe," she said. "Kill you?" She smiled slowly. "Not while you know *those* arts."

"You're not too angry?" he asked her.

"I'm furious," she said. "But I'm going to let you live. I'll even let you live entire. Because, my lord, the thought of Melusine, the one and true and only Melusine, conquered by the arts of a Damascene whore, is so delicious that I want to savor it for a long, long time. But you, my lord," she said, holding him fast, glaring into his wide grey eyes, "will pay for this until the day you die."

He did not seem too terribly appalled by the prospect. And she, she realized, was feeling much stronger. His presence was healing her. She curled more comfortably in his lap and laid her head on his shoulder and said, "I'm going to find a way to set those spirits free."

"I know how," he said.

She started upright. "But you said—"

"It's not as easy as it was before," he said. "We can't just unbind the spirits; we have to break the vessels that hold them—the bodies they wear."

"How do we do that? Kill them?"

He shook his head. "This is like one of the Jewish magics, the spell of the golem. In that spell, the name of God binds the creature's brow. If that seal is broken, the spell breaks."

"This has nothing to do with God," she said grimly.

"There is a warding on them," he said, "and a seal, set where a man's heart would be. It's dreadfully obvious, but that seems to be the rule of the magic. Stab them to the heart, and their vessel turns to dust. There's a heap of foreign earth behind the stables, that was a false Fleming not an hour ago, and a spirit spinning over it, mad with joy instead of captivity. That's proof enough for me."

She kissed him long and hard. "You are a wonder and a marvel," she said.

"I told the queen," he said, "before I came here. She'll send picked men to dispose of them—quietly, to prevent an uproar."

"Good," said Eschiva. She searched his face. "This spell troubles you."

He shrugged, uncomfortable. "They're kin. Distant, odd, and not particularly intelligent, but to see them bound in slavery . . . I can't bear it. Nor can I forgive the sorcerers who did it to them."

"It is unforgivable," she said.

"I want to unmake them—destroy them. But that would make me even worse than they." He shuddered. "Life was very much simpler when the only killing I did or could do was with my hands, in a fight."

"Do you want to be simple again? To pretend to be mortal?"

"No," he said, but slowly. "I can't go back. I'd never want to, if it would cost me you. But . . ."

He never did finish. She clasped him tight and let the silence stretch, and listened for sounds that mortal ears would never hear: the cries of spirits released from bondage.

# CHAPTER 51

The false Flemings were dead. Eleanor's men were fast and ruthless. Some of them died doing their duty; the ensorceled things could fight, and they were deadly. But there were many of Eleanor's men and few, as yet, of the French king's magical slaves. By the third day there were no false Flemings left in England.

As for those who waited for Lent to end and the invasion to begin, England was ready. On Good Friday her armies took their places wherever a force would be likely to come to land. The guardians had buttressed the walls of air with stronger spells than ever, calling on the Wild Magic and the high magic and every power in Britain. By Easter day it would be over, one way or another.

More than mortal armies stood waiting along the beaches and on the headlands. While Eleanor called up the plain folk of England, the guardians had summoned the wildfolk and the fair folk and the spirits of earth and water and air. In the hush of the holy days, in the slow stretch of time between the Crucifixion and the triumph of the risen God, they waited, patient as armies learned to be.

John was camped at Hastings, where William the Bastard had led an army of Norman reivers and fierce warrior spirits to overwhelm the Saxon hosts, and where the kingship of all Britain had passed from feckless Harold to the victorious Duke of Normandy. Battle Abbey had offered John the hospitality of its walls, but he had elected to camp with his troops on the windswept ridge where, as everyone there knew, Harold had drawn up his army. It was not the best-omened of places, but it was the best place to camp, and the best vantage over the shore. John, being John, was not about to surrender an advantage simply because a predecessor had made poor use of it.

"God grant me better fortune than Harold had," he said as darkness fell on the eve of Easter.

Arslan had been walking among the troops both mortal and otherwise. Few of the men were warriors by trade. Those who were, John had deployed as best he might, each veteran in command of a company of fishermen and farmers. He had few knights in evidence—most of the chivalry of Britain were elsewhere in the long line of defenders from Truro to Dover.

Here, John had sensed and Arslan agreed, the brunt of the attack would come. Philip had a fine sense of symbol, and John had done nothing to disabuse him of the notion that he had a loyal ally in England. As far as Philip knew, John lodged innocently in Southampton, waiting for his hired troops to sail into the harbor. So they would, one could suppose—once they had taken the rest of the English coast.

"He'll know where you stand, once he tries to attack," Arslan said.

"I don't think he will," said John. "How was I to know that Mother would raise *farmers* to fight off my Flemings?"

"Your mother is a terrible woman," Arslan said gravely.

"Horrifying," said John, not entirely in jest. He peered out over the starlit shore and the gleam of waves rolling in from France. Nothing rode on them yet. The walls of air were intact.

"Come to my tent," John said abruptly. "I need you for something."

They walked down the hill in the dusk, through the ranks of the camp. The men were in good spirits. They greeted John as he passed, some shyly, some with the rough equality of men who had seldom troubled themselves with the protocols of princes. John was at ease with them, more so than with men of his own rank. He knew their language, their jests, and seemed to know the things that concerned them.

He was different with the common folk: lighter-hearted, less difficult, less twisted with suspicion. Arslan did not mind that it took so long to cross the little distance to John's tent. It was a calm evening, starlit, warm for spring in Britain. He was happy as he always had been before a battle, the happiness of completion. His life was full. If he died tomorrow, he would have lived enough. And if he lived, it would be a victory.

John's tent was all but empty—surprising, even as thinly as his forces were spread. A boy was sitting in it, perched on a heavy wooden chest.

Arslan grinned broadly at the sight of Bertrada's third youngest. "Edwy! What are you doing here? Do you have a message from your mother?"

"Dozens," said Edwy. "And this. It's partly Lady Susanna's gift, too. But mostly his." He tilted his wild red head at John, who was visibly amused at such lack of respect. He hopped off the chest and heaved up its lid, and hauled out its contents, grunting with effort.

It was armor: coat and chausses of mail so finely made that it shimmered like silver, padded gambeson to wear beneath the coat, fine leather leggings beneath the chausses, great gleaming helm, and scarlet shield blazoned with a lion rampant. Arslan laughed in wonder: the lion wore a collar of golden apples, each painted painstakingly by a skilled hand.

"I did those," said Edwy. "Do you like them?"

"They're wonderful," Arslan said. He lifted the thing that had wrapped the mail: a surcoat such as knights wore in Outremer, scarlet silk embroidered with the collared lion. Beneath it lay a belt and a scabbard, and a sword with a hilt of bronze and gold, the quillons in the shape of pacing lions. He drew the sword a palm's breadth from the scabbard, to see the shimmer of the damask steel, and to mark its quality. "This is worth a king's ransom," he said.

"Not quite," said John dryly. "It didn't bankrupt England. It barely bankrupted me. That wife of yours wouldn't rest until she made sure the blade was made in India—not Damascus, she was insistent on that."

"The best blades come from India," Arslan said. "I told her that once. She remembered it."

"This is her gift, too," said Edwy. "She measured you while you were asleep—and that wasn't easy, she said. It is true you never sleep?"

"Not as much as she thinks I should," Arslan said.

"There's room to grow, she said, but you had better not get much taller. You can get wider—but not too much. This is supposed to last you."

Arslan's throat was tight. It was a father's duty to arm and equip his son when he was knighted. Arslan had no father; he had expected to equip himself, once he came to his demesne at last, and meanwhile to make do with the gleanings of the royal armory. The mail-coat that fit him best, the armorer told him, had belonged to Richard in his youth.

This was all new. It had all been made for him. It had room to grow as Edwy had said, but when it was on, the lacings drawn snug, the helm resting on his shoulders, it fit splendidly.

The world was a different place through the slit of a helm. Arslan drew the sword and tested its balance, moving carefully within the small space of the tent. John, when Arslan caught a glimpse of him, looked almost indulgent. Edwy was grinning all over his freckled face. He clambered up on the chest, unfastened the helm, and heaved it off, nearly flinging himself head over heels.

Arslan caught him and set him on his feet, helm and all. He was a big lad for twelve summers, and would be a substantial man, but Arslan in armor outweighed him by a goodly fraction. "You can tell your mother," Arslan said, "and your cousins, and this king of Britain, that I thank them all most profoundly. This is a gift beyond my deserving."

"Certainly it is," John said, "but the women insisted, and I thought it would be interesting to see you in something other than Richard's hand-me-downs."

"Are you going to sleep in it?" Edwy asked in bright curiosity.

"Why, would you?" asked Arslan.

"I don't think I'd ever take it off," Edwy said.

"That would get uncomfortable," said John. "Not to mention rank, after a while. Help him off with it, boy, and tell him the rest."

Edwy waited until Arslan was helpless, bent over, halfway out of the coat and wriggling free of its stifling confines. "They sent me, too. They said you needed a squire, and I was old enough, and Mother was tired of all the trouble I kept getting into. She said you'd whip me into submission. You won't do that, will you? I don't mind whippings, but submission is an awful thing."

"Muslims submit to Allah," Arslan said. "They say it's sublime."

"I don't want to be an infidel," Edwy said. "Mother said to tell you that if you want to send me home, so be it, but if you don't want me, she'd rather you passed me on to someone brutal. With cudgels."

"When we have a day or two to spare," said Arslan, "you had better tell me what you did to earn your exile. Tonight we all need to rest. You, too, puppy—after you've readied my armor and weapons, seen to the horses and their gear, and wheedled the cooks into giving you whatever they have left from dinner."

"I'm not hungry," Edwy said. "My lord."

Why, thought Arslan, a title. For that child, that was groveling respect. "It's not for you," he said. "It's for me. Now go. Move!"

The boy bolted. As soon as he was safely gone, Arslan's grin broke out. John's mirrored it. "You'll have your hands full," he said.

"So will he," said Arslan. He eyed the chest and its contents, calculating its weight. "I had better move this before someone falls over it."

"I'll have it brought to your tent," John said. "You have one, you know. It came with the rest. If there's anything lacking in it, tell Petit. He saw to its appointments."

"If Petit had anything to do with it, it's been outfitted for a king."

"He has a completely inexplicable fondness for you," John said. "Go on. I, unlike you, require sleep every night, and I feel it creeping up on me."

Arslan bowed, not because John expected it but because, just then, he felt inclined to offer respect. Even before he had retreated, Petit had emerged from some recess known only to servants and begun to prepare his master for bed.

When this was over, Arslan was going to discover whether Petit had a son or a brother or a cousin. Not that he felt a pressing need for a manservant, but Petit had spoiled him terribly. He was growing accustomed to perfect service.

The tent was pitched not far from John's, a little nearer the sea. It was rather ordinary on the outside: a knight's war-tent, neither large nor excessively small. Inside, it was as wonderful as he had expected. Its fittings were plain but of excellent quality, its bed long enough—which was always a difficulty—and its floor warmed with an eastern carpet. The chest at the bed's foot was full of clothes that he did not recognize, finely woven wool and new linen and a shimmer of silk.

John's men brought his armor while he was still discovering the hidden wealth of the tent, and Edwy came back not along after that, bearing the cooks' largesse. There was enough for two, as Arslan had expected, and the boy had the appetite of his age. He chattered as he ate, regaling Arslan with all the gossip of his family, and every message with which his mother had charged him.

He would have talked all night, but Arslan had laid a wishing on his wine. He was Bertrada's child: he caught the taste of it even as it set him to swaying where he sat. "My lord! That's not fair."

"I don't need to be," Arslan said as he tipped the boy onto the pallet that was spread near the tentflap. "I'm your lord and master, and I command that you sleep."

Edwy was as strong as he was contrary. He tried to cast a counterspell from the very edge of sleep. Arslan batted it aside, not entirely without effort. As it went chittering off into the night, he began to wonder what he had done to deserve this particular gift—what dereliction of duty Bertrada happened to be punishing him for.

He shook his head at his own foolishness. Bertrada had given him the unsung favorite of her sons. That he was also the worst scapegrace of them all would have weighed in her estimation, but she must reckon Arslan capable of dealing with it. The boy was as gifted in magic as in mischief, and he was not too inept with sword or bow, either. He would make a good squire, once he learned to discipline his wilder impulses.

Arslan lay on the bed, which was just as he liked it: not too hard, not too soft. He would not sleep tonight; he was on guard over the walls of air. But he could do that in comfort, soothed by the soft rasp of Edwy's snore. He rested his body while his spirit did its part for the kingdom's defense.

# CHAPTER 52

They came out of the sunrise, riding on the swell from France: a fleet of ships with lilies blazoned on the sails. They found all the ports closed against them, and John waiting on the shore at Hastings. He stood with his army on the ridge over the sea, under the banner of the English king.

Arslan came to stand beside him, having walked the lines since dawn. They went on much farther than he had expected. The fishermen and farmers, the few knights, the men-at-arms, stood in the center; to right and left of them stood armed men with pale intent faces, and perhaps a hint of transparency about them as the day brightened. They wore armor of antique fashion: Norman mail and helmets of the last century, or Saxon byrnies, side by side as if their ancient enmity had been forgotten. Saxons too had come as invaders; and Romans before them, and Celts before that, driving back the little painted people. All of these stood in silent ranks, the last of them hardly larger than children, painted in blue swirls and spirals. Their eyes had gleamed through tangles of black hair, fascinated by him as spirits always were.

All the old warriors of Britain were waiting in this place. This earth was blessed with blood, and sown with bones. It would meet this invasion as it had every other: to drive it back if it could, or to make the invaders part of it if they won the victory.

The walls of air had begun to shimmer. The enemy beat on them, battering them with spells. That was expected: Arslan held within himself the guardians' conjoined power, ready and waiting for the moment when the walls went down. It was close now.

He glanced at John. John, like him, was in armor, but had not yet put on the helm. His face was calm as he watched the fleet come in.

The commanders must be suspicious: it was clear that they had been herded here. Yet they came on, arrogant in their numbers. There were sorcerers on those ships, casting spell after spell, unsparing of the cost.

Arslan was the only enchanter here, except for Edwy, who was very young, very quiet, and struggling not to wet his breeches. The rest were as thinly scattered as John's knights, sustaining walls across the whole southern shore of Britain. He felt the burden on his shoulders, weighing him down even more than the beautiful mail.

He straightened under it, drew a breath, and willed himself to be strong. Mortal battle did not frighten him. This was a new thing, a thing he had never done before. He felt oddly naked in all his panoply. Even cold iron was poor protection against the power that came against him.

The walls of air bent down as the fleet came near to land. The guardianship of Bran, the protection of Arthur, faded and withdrew. Arslan raised the shield that he had been given, lifting it over all that army, living and dead. The enemy's spells fell on it like a hail of arrows. He felt the sting of them, the force of the blows as if through armor.

Prows grated on sand. Men and things like men swarmed over the sides.

John rode down from the ridge. Only Arslan followed, and a company of his personal guard under Longsword's command. Edwy stayed on the ridge—a concession Arslan had fought for.

Halfway between the ridge and the shore, John halted. He reached inside the casque of his helm and lifted out the crown of Arthur, and set it on his head. It gleamed in the paling light: for the day that had dawned bright and clear was swiftly clouding over and darkening with mist.

The four guardians of France stood on the sand. They were all in mail, even Melusine. Hers was like a coat of fishes' scales, molded tight to the curves of her body. She carried no weapon, not even a knife, but her whole body was a weapon.

She looked much less human on the soil of Britain than she had in France. The eyes with which she scanned the army were flat and cold, snake's eyes. They came to rest on John, but not before they had taken in Arslan and gone colder than ever. "So," she said. Her voice was a hiss. "All the masks are gone."

John smiled. "Clever, weren't we? Did you ever guess?"

"I blush to say that we did not. You play the fool very well, John Lackland. Too well, some might say. Don't you worry that you might become the thing you pretend to be?"

"Not these days," John said. He leaned on his saddlebow and bared his teeth. It was not a smile. "If you leave now, no harm will come to you. Take your boats and go back to France. This is no land of yours."

Her answer was a blast of magic so strong that it nearly flung Arslan from the saddle. His shield held, but just. John swayed as if buffeted by wind. He raised his arms.

That was the signal they had all been waiting for. The earth boiled beneath the invaders' feet. Spirits rose up out of it, Norman and Saxon, Roman and Briton, Celt and Pict. In the same moment, the army poured down off the hill. In a blaring of horns and a shrilling of war-cries, they fell on the French.

"Remember!" Arslan bellowed as they came. "Aim for the heart!"

She aimed direct for his heart, battering and battering at him. Her hatred stung the back of his throat. The rest of the guardians had drawn away: the churchmen toward the boats and the raising of stronger spells, the Burgundian duke into the battle.

A swirl of spirits converged upon them, shrieking in rage. They knew what had been done to their kin. They beat upon the guardians' heads like enraged birds, baffled and befuddled their spells, and blinded them with swirls of sand and sudden mist.

But none of them approached Melusine. She was Arslan's task, and his doom, too. He saw his death in her eyes. She knew what he was, and therefore how to destroy him. The body could die, and easily, as a mortal body could; but she would scatter the fiery spirit to the winds of heaven.

He was very young, and she was ancient. For every spell that he knew, she knew a counterspell. He could not defeat her in a plain duel of magic.

The battle was raging: clash of swords and spears, shrieks of spirits winging overhead. The false Flemings fought like men of bronze, tireless, relentless, feeling no wound not a stroke to the heart. Even headless they would fight on, driven by the spirit within them and the compulsion upon them.

Arslan could not let them distract him. His shields were wavering.

Were her spells losing the fiercest of their edge? Her hatred dimmed her vision and clouded her judgment. But she would have spells to spare, long after his shields were broken and his spirit destroyed.

He drew the sword that had been made for his hand. She laughed at it. Well she might, though it was cold iron; she was not mortal, she was warded in spells, and he was nearly overcome. He was desperate, and well she knew it.

He raised the shimmering blade, kissed the cross-hilts, and held it up across his body. Then he dropped his shields, every one.

She blasted him with bolts of living rage. He caught them as if they had been strokes of a sword. The steel began to hum; his nose caught the sharp scent of hot metal.

She hissed in anger. Her hands swept about, gathering power out of the air, from the mist that now closed them in, and from the water that lapped her feet. She sang death into it and hurled it, whirling high, then plummeting for the stroke.

He swept up the sword, even seeing the spell that she cast beneath, aimed at his heart. The blade's cold steel clove the great spell and burst it into flaming shards. In the same wild sweep, the flat of the sword smote the death-spell. Metal and spell shrieked together. The spell leaped back, winging like an arrow for the undine's heart.

She writhed, twisting away from it, but it had a mind and enslaved spirit of its own. It veered, aimed again, and struck.

She went up like a torch. She did not scream. Her eyes fixed on Arslan. They were flat with hate, yet she smiled, a little wry, acknowledging the victor. That smile lingered in his mind long after her body had withered to ash and blown away in a sudden strong gust of wind. Spirits scattered the last of it, and danced on the remnants of her bones.

Arslan's body wanted nothing more than to slide limply from the back of his mare and lie unconscious in the sand. But that would have been madness. The battle was still raging. The rest of France's guardians were very much alive, and all the more determined to win this fight. John's English yeomen were brave but unskilled; they were falling before the ensorcereled soldiers.

He found strength somewhere, and lifted rein. The mare started as if she had been asleep or enspelled, shook herself so hard that his mail rang, and plunged gladly into the thick of the fight. This they both understood. This they could win or lose without fear for their souls.

The sword was alive in his hand. It sang as it whirled and flashed and slew. It seemed to know where the heart was, and to seek it with insatiable thirst.

John was in the thick of the fight. He had a crazy courage that was startling in so careful a man. Yet he kept his core of cold calculation: aware of all the fronts of the battle, and wielding his forces against new assaults even as he beat back the forces that came against him.

Most of his mortal guard were down or separated from him. All the men about him were the risen dead. Saxon and Norman fought side by side in supernatural amity; Roman and Briton joined together to destroy the earthborn giant that came on John with whirling mace.

The French forces had gained a furlong of ground. Still boats came to shore, bringing fresh fighters. Months of labor, thousands of spirits, had wrought this army. Britain, with all its land to protect, was spread too thin. Reinforcements were coming; the straight tracks were full of marching men and spirits. But they could not come fast enough to save those who fought here, suffering defeat as the Saxons had so long ago.

It would not matter if the rest of Britain could drive the invaders back into the sea, but there was John in the golden crown, taking the brunt of the attack. If he was killed or taken, Britain's straits would be desperate: one king captive in Germany, another dead or captive here, and the kingdom's heart cut out of it.

John had known the risk when he took it. He meant to hold on until new forces came. But he might not have reckoned on being a target. The fullest force of the assault drove against him. The dead could not be killed, but they could be banished from the land of the living. They were falling more slowly than the mortal soldiers had, but just as surely.

The thought that came into Arslan's mind, even as he beat back a stabbing blade, was so preposterous, so outrageous, that he discarded it even as it took shape in his awareness. Yet it clung, persistent. John's forces had fallen back another furlong. The sand was swarming with invaders. Sorcerers on the ships kept the spells strong, granting life to shaped clay.

John was terribly beset. Arslan had been driven inexorably away from him. He redoubled his efforts, although his arm burned with fatigue, and his breath was an ache in his lungs, and his mare grunted with effort. They were both bleeding.

If he was going to do it, he must do it soon, if in fact it was not too late. It could cost him everything. His body was weakening. His magic was still strong, fed with the power of Britain, but the flesh that contained it could not bear much more.

He called on it all, every bit of it. As it flooded into him, he let go his will. He became the magic. No mortal could have done it, no creature whose flesh was all of earth and none of fire, not though he were the greatest of sorcerers.

He raised the sea from its depths to high heaven. He brought down the sky with wind and torrents of rain. The fleet was crushed between them. The sorcerers, rapt in sustaining their army, had no time to defend themselves. Those that did not drown in the first wall of water were pulled under by the spirits below and held down by those above.

The spirits saved him. They rode on the tide of power and made it immensely stronger. The last of them, ever so gently, eased him free from the great spell and battered the fleet to shards. For a moment he saw a horn-crowned head against the sky, and eyes like a stag's, darkly luminous, resting on him with immortal calm.

On the shore, the army began to falter. Without the sorcerers to bolster the spell that held spirit to clay, the golems were easier to kill; they had lost somewhat of volition, grown slower, less skilled with their weapons.

They were still deadly, and John's army was a sadly depleted thing. He had begun to let them drive him back, step by step, in as ordered a retreat as the press of battle would allow. Arslan was fighting like one of the false Flemings, because he was here and it was a battle and there was nothing else he could do. His body was a leaden thing. His mind had drained into his sword arm, which by now was mostly ruled by the sword.

They were almost to the ridge. The enemy pressed hard. A long gap of sand had opened between them and the sea. They would not care: those that had the wits would know that there was no ship to carry them home. They must win or die here.

The sea boiled. Warriors rose up out of it in armor of fishes' scales, blowing on trumpets made of great curved shells. They fell on the enemy from the rear, even as a horn rang on the ridge above the battle. The first of the armies of Britain had come, bedazzled by their swift march on the straight track. William the Marshal led them, and with him a hundred knights, fresh and eager for the fight.

John was still strong enough to call out to him: "About bloody time, man! What took you so long?"

There was no simple answer to that. The Marshal chose to reply in action: sweeping his army up over the ridge and down upon the enemy.

They drove the invaders back into the sea, where the creatures of the deep devoured them. When the sun hovered on the horizon, setting in blood, there was nothing left of the battle but the wounded and the dead.

John insisted that he was not the former. Arslan hoped that he was not among the latter. He went looking for Edwy, and found him in the surgeons' tent, stitching up a sword cut. He looked up at Arslan out of a face that had acquired a magnificent set of bruises, and said somewhat thickly, "Just let me finish, my lord, and I'll get you out of that armor."

Arslan ignored that. "What happened to you?"

Edwy had the grace to look guilty. "I just went to see if I could help. I got a fist in the face. But," he said with a touch of smugness, "I got the thing in the heart. It really did puff into dust. The spirit inside it put a blessing on me before it went. I'll never have boils as long as I live."

"That's not an ill gift," Arslan said.

"I thought so," said Edwy as he bound off the last stitch. The wounded man grinned at him; he could not grin back, but he thumped the man on his unwounded shoulder. "You'll live. Make sure you use the salve I gave you—and don't pull the stitches till the Sunday after next. Go to Mass, thank God for saving you, and then pull."

"You could be a physician," Arslan said.

"Or a tailor," said Edwy. "You look half-dead. If I get you out of your armor, will you promise to sleep?"

"I'll sleep when I can," Arslan said. "I'm looking for John. I heard he was here."

"He was," Edwy said, "until he had a summons from his mother."

"Eleanor?" Arslan wondered if his ears were playing tricks on him. "The queen is here?"

"Here and taking charge. She can't help herself, I suppose."

"I had better go to the rescue," said Arslan. He staggered as he turned, but kept his feet. Edwy tried to head him off, but he was as heavy as stone. He dragged the boy for a little distance before Edwy grunted and let go. The boy followed him, but he did not care about that.

John must have dragged his feet heroically: he was just coming to the queen's pavilion when Arslan reached it. Eleanor was within, with the Marshal and William Longsword and a handful of barons, and a bishop or two. They all rose at John's coming, all but the queen.

He paused just within the circle of light. He was still wearing the crown, whether because he had forgotten it or, knowing John, because he wished his mother to see it.

She saw it. Her brows rose. "So this is what you look like in a crown," she said. "Does it make you happy?"

"It makes my head ache," he said. "I didn't expect to see you here. Weren't you going to receive the fruits of victory from some suitably secure castle?"

"This one I needed to see," she said. "It was . . . illuminating. And convincing. Richard could never be the kind of king this calls for."

"He'd probably have fought a better battle," said John.

"Probably," she agreed, "but he couldn't have mustered the troops that you raised. You surprise me—and I'm not easily surprised. There's more to you than I thought."

"Yes," he said. "There's a crown on my head that belongs to no one but me."

"Henry would have been pleased," she said. "You were his favorite—the one he hoped would be most like himself."

"Why, Mother, you sound almost like a mother. Don't strain yourself; I don't need you to be proud of me. Just do your part in all of this as I do mine. It will get your Richard home again as you so dearly desire."

"Will it?"

He took the crown from his head and held it up between them. "On this I swear: whatever I can do to free the King of England, I, who am King of Britain, will do."

She rested her eyes on the gleaming golden thing. "Why?" she asked him. "You could have it all."

"Britain, unlike England, cares how a king comes to his crown. I'm bound to be honorable while I have this."

She laughed long and deep, the kind of laughter that aches in the belly and brings tears to the eyes. When at last she could speak, though still wiping her eyes, she said, "Great are the wonders of God! The slipperiest of all my sons, forced into honor by a golden crown. Who would have believed that kingship would make a man more honest rather than less?"

"It's a lovely irony, isn't it?" said John. "And very useful, I'm sure. France won't be invading again for a while; we've made certain of that. Philip will turn eastward now, and try to use Richard as a weapon against us."

"And you," she said. "He'll use you. He never forgives a slight, and you've made a fool of him in ways he won't forgive."

"No, Mother," said John. "You made a fool of him. As far as he knows, since he didn't come on this expedition, I'm still his loyal ally, and you raised the whole of Britain to stop me."

"His guardians saw you," she said. "They're captives, but we'll have to send them back. Then he'll know."

"Demand a ransom," he said, "and set it so he'll have to struggle to pay it, then drag your feet until all this is over. You'll need to set guards on them who are impervious to magic, but I'm sure our own guardians will know how to go about that."

"Better yet," said Arslan, speaking far out of turn, but his tongue had a mind of its own, "ask the spirits of Britain to watch them. Only be careful that the spirits understand: they aren't to kill or maim the men who enslaved their kin."

"You see to it, then," Eleanor said, running ahead of John with royal arrogance. "We'll set the ransom. A hundred thousand marks of silver for the lot of them, do you think, my lords?"

"I think," said John, "that that is their precise worth. He'll never bring himself to confess to the world that he paid Richard's ransom." He smiled in deep contentment. "Oh, that will gnaw at his liver! But we should take care, Mother. Let the world think England suffers in the gathering of ransom—or Henry will double it, and leave us no better off than before."

She nodded. "Yes. Yes, that's very clever. Be it done, then, and done with all deliberate speed."

"I'll go," said Arslan. "I'll go to France."

"No, you will not," John said. "We'll send Father Hugh—he's a churchman, he has immunity. You they'll hold hostage, and we need you here. Have you forgotten? You're a jailer now. You have three noble prisoners to see to."

Arslan had not forgotten, but neither had he taken thought for what it meant. It was a heavy burden, but he had brought it on himself. He bowed to his king, and to his king's mother, too, and set about doing the duty they had given him.

# PART FIVE

# KING OF ALL BRITAIN

### Spring 1193–Spring 1194

# CHAPTER 53

Something was wrong.

Richard had been enduring his captivity with remarkable patience. It had lightened since William Longchamp found him in the stronghold outside of Würzburg: he had been brought to more civilized places, allowed to move about under guard, and even permitted to ride and tilt at the quintain in the castle yards of Würzburg and Speyer and Hagenau.

Yet as the months stretched on and on and every report had England draining itself dry to gather the ransom that the emperor demanded, Kalila began to see a difference in the king. She could not remember exactly when it began. After Easter, certainly. Word had reached the bishop then of the invasion of Britain; France was driven back, John's supposed rebellion defeated. The messenger had brought Kalila a second letter, written in Arabic by Arslan's hand, that told the truth of the matter: the destruction of France's magical assault, the killing or capture of its guardians, and the ransom that Philip must pay for the return of his kingdom's strongest sorcerers. John had won a clear victory.

But the tale that was told in the world was that John had rebelled, and his rebellion had failed. That was the tale Richard heard. Kalila tried to tell him the truth, but he would not hear it. "My brother is a traitor," he said the more stubbornly, the harder she tried to dissuade him. "He seized my dukedom and tried to take my kingdom. But for Mother, he'd have won it, and England would be paying tribute to the French crown. I'll kill him for that. By God's right arm, I'll gut him with a blunt pike."

Richard had the family temper, and the family obstinacy to go with it. At first she was not at all surprised to see how angry he was at his

brother, and how unwilling to hear any good of John. He was a prisoner, powerless, and John was free to do as he pleased. Small wonder
Richard was furious.

But as spring blurred into summer, Richard's anger did not abate,
even by a little. That was not like him. His temper was hot but quick.
Once he had had his fit of rage, he always grew calmer and began to
see reason. About John, he would not. It was as if something fed that
outrage, some demon that yammered in his ear and would give him
no peace.

Toward Midsummer Richard was moved again, to Worms, where
the imperial court was gathering. By the time they came there, Kalila
was sure that a spell had been laid on the king. Messengers had come
to the emperor from the King of France: their presence was a crawling in her skin. She was not admitted to their council, but she had
made friends with the servants, and one of them arranged to be present, invisible as only a servant could be.

Kalila met him afterward in a tavern in the town, a discreet establishment where one of the king's servants could meet a handsome boy
in peace. She had not known what sort of place it was until she was
in it; then it was too late to bolt.

She made the best of it. She was not the only black-haired person
in the room, but she was the darkest by far; in this country of fair-
haired ruddy men, she was exotic enough to be unusually desirable.
She had fended off half a dozen drunken advances before Dieter appeared, wind-ruffled and damp with rain, and heaved the seventh admirer bodily up off the stool and seated himself on it.

He was a big man, going to fat as he grew older, but he had the
bull's strength that often resided in such men. He grinned at her. She
grinned back. "Thank you," she said in her stiff new German. "That
was getting inconvenient."

"I'll kill him for you later," Dieter said. He had said nothing to the
serving boy, but a flagon of beer appeared on the table in front of
him, brimming with foam. Kalila toyed with a second, from which she
had surreptitiously poured most of the contents into the straw of the
floor, and managed to elude the boy who came to fill it up again.

Dieter drank half of his flagon in a gulp, blew the foam from his
mustache, and bellowed for sausages. Sausages came, with a bowl of
the appalling sour cabbage of this country, and a loaf of hard black
bread. He tilted a brow at her, offering a share. She twisted off a

chunk of the bread and nibbled on it. This was a difficult country to be a Muslim in: everything edible was either pork or beer. If Richard had not had a manifest passion for mutton and beef, she might have starved.

It was a while before Dieter was ready to speak. At length he sat back, belched nobly, and said, "Win a wager for me. Otto says you've got to be a Provençal. I say you're a Spaniard. You've got the Moorish look—there's no mistaking it once you've seen it."

She smiled at him. "I'm not either of them," she said. "I'm a Seljuk Turk."

"That's a kind of Moor, yes?"

"It is a kind of infidel."

He grunted. "Well! Who'd have guessed? I see you in church with the English king. You don't catch fire or run out screaming from the Mass."

"I'm immune to the curse," she said. "I grew up with Christians."

"Well," said Dieter, still amazed to be sitting across a table from a live and breathing infidel. "We were right in this much: you're no Norman. Followed your lord from the Crusade, did you? You're loyal—more than most. I like that in a man. Even if he's not baptized."

"I thank you for that," she said, and she meant it.

He shrugged. In the pause, a beery voice sang in finely accented Latin,

*"O admirabile Veneris ydolum,*
*cuius materie nihil est frivolum. . . ."*

The image of Love incarnate was a boy so fair his hair was almost white. A black-clad arm was draped over his shoulders; the singer, a monk at least twice the boy's age, was well gone in beer.

Dieter leaned toward her. She stiffened, bracing for a proposition that she had no intention of accepting. He said, "You have good instincts, sir Turk. That was a most interesting council. Did you know the French king is to meet with our emperor on St. John's Day? It seems Philip isn't satisfied with the terms Henry laid on the English. He wants a share of the profits. They're going to raise the ransom—double it if they can."

Kalila's breath hissed between her teeth. This was exactly what

John had been afraid of, and had tried to prevent. "Did any of them give a reason for this change, aside from sheer naked greed?"

"Nothing worth remembering," said Dieter. "Philip's in some kind of trouble, from the way his men were hawking and shuffling. Henry couldn't get it out of them. I'll see what their servants are saying."

"I'd be grateful if you'd do that," Kalila said.

He smiled. She thought he might touch her hand, but he refrained. "I'll do anything for beauty," he said.

She was almost sorry to have to disappoint those wide yearning eyes. Even if she had wanted any man in the world but Hugh Neville, this one would have been deeply shocked to discover the truth of her sex.

As if like a mage he could read her thoughts, he said, "You're a eunuch, aren't you? That's why you relieve yourself where no one else can see. You don't want them staring."

She half rose. Indignation was not difficult to feign; she simply had to choke on laughter. "Sir! I could call you out for that."

He blanched. She had acquired somewhat of a reputation with a sword; her lighter, stronger Indian blade had notched no few of the German knights' broadswords in practice matches. "No, no, sir Turk, I never meant—I was only supposing—"

"Don't," she said. "We are modest people, sir. Do you fault us for that?"

"Not I, sir Turk," he hastened to say.

She nodded sharply. "Good. It's forgotten. When you've spoken with the French servants, send me word. I'll see that my lord is suitably appreciative."

"Your goodwill is enough, sir Turk," Dieter said. He was yearning again, even more than before. She eluded him with a face of blandest innocence and a protestation of duties that she dared not shirk.

As it happened, she did have duties, attending Richard in his daily practice at the pells. He wanted a bath afterward, and her in attendance, which had become a habit—though he did not yearn as Dieter had. He never demanded that she strip for him, either. He understood Muslim modesty, did the one whom the people of Syria had called Malik Ric.

He let her go after that, saying that he wanted to rest and work on the song he was composing with the emperor. Often she stayed for that; Richard was a fine poet. But today she was too restless even for singing.

The French messengers were housed near the emperor. She wandered not exactly aimlessly, on a track that happened to bring her past the rooms where they lodged. There seemed to be no one within, and there were wards on the doors, a faint blue glimmer that she had learned to see.

Allah showed his favor most clearly when she had passed those doors and gone down toward the servants' quarters. A murmur of voices came to her, carried on the odd currents that sometimes ran through castles. She paused, straining to hear. It might be nothing but servants' gossip, but the prickle between her shoulderblades promised more.

They were speaking Greek, of all things—to avoid being understood, surely. It was a pity for their secrecy that she had learned the language as a child, from Greek travelers who tarried in Beausoleil.

There were two voices. One was softer than the other, and had a distinct French accent. That one spoke first, barely above a whisper. "You've made the preparations?"

"Almost," said the other. "By morning it will all be ready."

"You can't move faster?"

"No," said the second man with a snap of impatience. "This is not some village love charm. It is a great magic—and great magics take time."

"Enough, enough! Save your curses for the enemy. This is a great magic, as you say. It has to work, or we're dead men."

"It will work," the harsher voice said. "Be sure the boat is ready by sunrise. He will be on it. The emperor promised to see to that."

"Getting him on the boat doesn't concern me. Getting *her* to him does. What's to stop her from wrecking us or sinking us, once she's done what we ask of her?"

"One thing," said the harsh voice. "We must bring him back to the emperor, and the emperor will be most angry with her if that fails to happen. He has a binding on her; I have the Word that seals it. If I need it, I will use it."

The first man sighed like a gust of wind in the stairwell. "I hope that will be enough. The king was insistent that we succeed. We're dead if we don't."

"We succeed," the other said, "or we run. The true Emperor of the Romans is always in need of skilled masters of the Art."

"If we get that far," the first man said, but he gave up the argument after that.

Kalila heard their footsteps retreating. They said nothing more that she could hear, but she had heard enough. She had no doubt that they had been speaking of Richard, of laying some spell on him, which required that they take him somewhere on the river. And who was this *she* that they had spoken of? It must be some witch or sorceress, of whom there were a startling number along the Rhine. It was a river of magic, steeped in it, but rather more of it was dark than light.

Richard was asleep with his lute in his lap. His head had fallen back; he was snoring loudly. It was a profoundly undignified posture, but that did not disturb Kalila. She sat in a corner and tucked up her feet and watched him. There was no one else in the room. Richard's following of churchmen was elsewhere, either at Mass or in council; she did not greatly care which.

The Frenchmen who spoke Greek had talked as if a spell would be laid on Richard tomorrow, but had said nothing of any other or earlier spell. Yet something was on him. She had to work hard to see it; it was only visible from the corner of the eye. It looked like a veil of gauze laid over him, clinging close to his body. It pressed tightly to his eyes and ears, nose and mouth, as if to blur his senses.

She wished desperately then for a real mage; for Arslan, or for Hugh Neville, either of whom would know what this shadow was. She could only see it and sense it, and know that it was doing something to Richard, but what, she could not tell. He seemed dulled, muted. He was sleeping a great deal. But he was a prisoner, and although with Ely's coming he had been treated more like a royal guest, he was still more closely confined than a man of action could easily bear.

Tomorrow he was going to be taken away, and something would be done to him that might be irrevocable. If these people still believed that Richard and not John was the mystical king of Britain, they might be planning a thing that would destroy the whole kingdom. They were not going to kill him, that much she had gathered, but there were many things worse than death.

She was not enough for this. Everyone who would be was far away in England. Ely . . .

He had magic in him. They had explained it, how he was like a cup full of wine, and they had given him what he might need to find Richard. They had done somewhat the same to her, except that she had proved to have a great deal of magic in her. Both Arslan's ruby and the golden bell had been feeding it, making it stronger.

Could she use the bishop like a weapon? Could she discover how to do that before it was too late? And more to the point, would he allow it? She would have to tell him things that the guardians had kept from him. Most likely he would not believe her. Even if he did, he might hinder more than he helped.

She had no choice. She left Richard sleeping, passed the pair of burly Germans who stood guard at his door, and sought out the Bishop of Ely.

William Longchamp was indisposed, his clerk said. That, Kalila discovered, meant that he was napping over his breviary. She tensed at the sight, in fear of an epidemic of spells, but he was no more or less laden with magic than he had ever been. It was an honest nap, and an equally honest start into wakefulness when she had been standing over him for some little while.

He crossed himself swiftly. When she did not burst into a shower of sparks, he eased enough to sit up and scowl at her. "You are not my favorite nightmare," he said.

"Nor are you mine," said Kalila. She backed a step so that he could rise if he chose. "When the sun comes up tomorrow, two servants of the French king are going to take a boat down the Rhine. They will be taking your king with them."

Ely stiffened but did not move. "Where did you hear that?"

"On a stair," she said, "near the emperor's rooms. They were speaking Greek. God guided me; who else of Richard's servants here would have understood them?"

Ely's eyes narrowed. He liked her little and her race and religion less, but she thought that maybe he trusted her. "Where are they taking him? What will they do?"

"Nothing good," she said. "Will you come with me and help me do whatever is necessary to keep him safe?"

"He hasn't even left yet," Ely pointed out. "I'll put a guard on him and order them to keep him there."

"I don't think that will help," she said. "The emperor is behind this. He can overwhelm any force we'll bring to bear."

"What good am I, then?" he demanded. "I'm old, weak, lame, and short-tempered. I have no training in weapons. I know nothing but God and chancery."

"You found the king when no one else could," she said, carefully not mentioning the fact that she had done the finding. She had been following the road he had chosen, after all. "You serve him more loyally than anyone else. I need loyalty; I need you. Leave the swordplay to me, if there's to be any."

"I still don't see—"

"God told me," she said. "It has to be you. Can you arrange to be ill for a day or two, so that no one knows you've gone?"

"I'm ill just thinking about this madness," he said irritably. "Very well. I'll do it. If I get killed, I'll haunt you for the rest of your days."

"That's a fair price," she said. She bowed to him, for respect, and because in spite of all appearances, he was a brave man.

# CHAPTER 54

~~~

It was summer in Germany, but the dawn air was cold. A mist rose up off the river, twining about the pilings of the quay. Ely in a monk's habit and Kalila in the plainest cotte she had, with mail under it, made themselves invisible amid a heap of boxes and bales and kept watch over the boat that her bones told her would carry Richard down the river. It was quite an ordinary boat to look at, such as plied the Rhine from end to end, with a cabin amidships, and oars drawn up along the hull. There was a mast, but it had not been stepped; the sail was stowed nearby. The only odd thing about it was its prow: eyes were painted on it as on the ships of Greece and the east, the better to see its way over the water.

Kalila's plan was desperate, and of course mad: to slip aboard and hide, wrapped in shadows. If she had been a mage, she would have considered making a fetch, an image of the king, and setting it on the boat in Richard's place. But she did not know how to do that. It had to be Richard in the flesh, and she had to pray that when the time came, she would know what to do and how to go about it.

They brought him near sunrise, when Kalila and a conspicuously silent Ely had been on the boat for what seemed a very long time. They were tucked in amid the cargo, hidden under a canvas, but from beneath it they could see how the crew began to board the boat as daylight came. There was an older man with the look of a seaman, and two or three sturdy younger men, and a company of men in boat-men's smocks that fit oddly over mail.

Richard came with the last of these. He was not bound, but he walked like a man in his sleep, open-eyed but blank. He went where he was directed but said nothing, nor showed by glance or expression that he was aware of the world about him.

He stank of magic. Two men came last, wrapped in cloaks and hoods; the same stink was on them. They disappeared into the cabin with Richard. The men in mail took stations about the cabin, not even pretending to lend a hand with the boat.

The second mage, in coming aboard, had set wards on the boat. Kalila almost smiled. It was too late, if he had but known it.

The boat cast off from the quay in remarkable silence. The river it sailed on was not the river that mortals knew: it followed the track of the mist. The city vanished behind. There were no banks to be seen, no cities or towns, no castles, only the swift current of the river, the veil of mist, and the boat with its painted eyes. The captain manned the steering oar; he needed nothing else on this current.

Kalila loved maps and studied them whenever she could; she loved the shapes of land on the earth, the tracks of rivers, the names that men gave to them. She knew that this river ran broad and steady enough from Worms to Mainz, then narrowed into steep gorges and treacherous eddies. Yet the boat, although it sailed from the quay of Worms, never passed through Mainz at all. Toward midmorning, as the mist drew back, she saw the shadow of crags, and felt the sharper tug of the current on the boat's hull. They had come far downstream on the tide of magic, into the great gorge of the Rhine.

The river was a living thing, but its heart and spirit were here. In this black water, under these crags, the strongest magic of this country had its dwelling place.

In all that time, not one voice had spoken on that boat. The boatmen and the guards were so silent that she wondered if they were creatures like John's false Flemings. No sound came from the cabin, which was proof that Richard was under a spell: if he was not talking or laughing or singing, he was composing poetry. Silence and Richard were not close kin.

Ely seemed asleep beside her: his eyes were shut as if to close out the strangeness of this boat and this voyage, and he made no more sound than anyone else aboard. She began to wonder if she was the only living soul on this boat.

Her legs were cramped and her back was stiff, but she dared not move from her hiding place. When the helmsman's eye roamed idly over his boat, she ducked down lower and prayed he did not see the gleam of eyes under the canvas. He was not human: the farther the boat sailed, the more like a water-creature he looked, a river otter with round brown eyes and grey-brown hair sleeked close to his head. His crew were of his kind; they let go even more of human semblance than the helmsman had, except for the hands, which they needed to sail the boat. They ran bonelessly on all fours, tumbling over one another, turning work into play. If Kalila had been less in fear of her life and Richard's soul, she would have smiled to see them.

However charming they might seem, they were enemies. They were taking the King of England into the secret realm of Germany. In Britain it was forest; here, it was river, and lofty crags, and far voices singing amid the swirling of waves.

The place to which they came had a presence in the living world as well; Kalila had passed it on the search for the king. She knew that sheer crag rising high above the river, facing a steep green ridge that dropped down to the broad expanse of water, and somewhat upstream of those, the rock on which lay the bones of myriad travelers, lured to their death by the creature called the Lorelei.

Kalila was aware of that long before they passed its rock. It was a red throb of power, a wave of pure female heat. The guardsmen stirred for the first time, fixing on it. The half-inhuman boatmen ruffled their fur and bared teeth at it. Ely, beside Kalila, clutched her arm till she feared the bones would break. Even if he willed himself to see nothing, hear nothing, perceive nothing that was not of simple earth, this power burned through all his barriers, direct to the heart of him.

Kalila felt nothing but the heat on the skin. She had known more true desire from one of Neville's glances than from this enchanted rock, which had every man on the boat panting like a dog.

Mercifully they went on past it, though not far: only to the little town under the crag of Rheinfels, where the towers of a castle rose against the sky. They were not quite in the world: the town was deserted but for a flitter of shades and spirits.

They disembarked from the boat, the mages leading the blind and stumbling Richard, the men-at-arms surrounding them, and Kalila with a firm grip on the bishop, creeping behind. She was last off the boat; as she set foot on land, the captain's round brown eye caught hers. He saw her perfectly clearly.

She froze, but he did not cry the alarm. He turned back calmly to the task of mooring his boat.

It was a long while before her heart stopped racing. The way was steep, the houses built at odd angles, some reached by steps up and some by steps down, and those that were of wood were thickly carved and painted and gilded. It was a profoundly German town: robust, self-satisfied, vivid and lively but with a core of dark beneath.

The place to which Richard was taken would be a church in that other world. Here it was a shrine, but not to any Christian god. There was no crucifix within. The wide circular window above the altar was the wheel of the world. The one image in all that place seemed at first to be of the Virgin, and yet something about it was strange. It was carved in wood, black with age, in a stiff and ancient 'style. The Mother nursed her Child, offering him her bare breast; he opened his arms to her in infant joy. He wore a crown like the sun. She wore the crescent moon on her brow. The orb of the world turned beneath her feet. Only slowly did the oddity strike Kalila: there were serpents wound about the Mother's arms, and her belt was a serpent biting its own tail. No Christian would ever carve such a thing, serpent as friend and ally, even servant, rather than implacable enemy.

King Philip's mages bowed before the image. In this place they had let fall their hoods. One was a Frenchman, but the other was not what she had expected: he was not Greek but Egyptian, and he was of the old blood of that country. His eyes were long and dark in his red-brown face; they were lined with kohl, as if he could not bear to let go of that ancient fashion.

Kalila shrank into her bit of shadow. The Egyptian mages were the oldest order of all—some said they had invented magic. If there was one here, a single Seljuk with a cobbled bit of magic had no more hope of opposing him than an infant against an armored knight.

She had to do what she could. There was no one else. Ely had gone into a state that she recognized from old battles: numb, staring, blank with shock. He could not believe anything that he saw, therefore he chose to see none of it.

He would do as she bade him, which was enough. They crouched together behind a pillar and watched as Richard was made to kneel in front of the carven image. He was deeply enspelled, but she thought she could see signs of resistance: beads of sweat on his brow, a knot of tension in his jaw beneath the ruddy beard.

That gave her hope. She sought inside herself for the bits of magic that she had been given. On her breast beneath shirt and cotte, the red stone burned with familiar fire.

Her hand sought Ely's and clasped it. His fingers were thin and cold. He made no effort to pull away, even when magic began to flow out of him and into her. Perhaps he could not feel it; perhaps he was too deep in shock to care what she did.

A wind rose in that airless place. It blew out all the candles, leaving only the light of the jeweled windows and the shaft of sun streaming through the door. A shadow stood in it.

Kalila's hackles rose. The same raw heat that had come off the rock of the Lorelei was here, flooding into the shrine. Even the Egyptian quivered at the touch of it. Richard alone seemed unmoved.

And that was the second glimmer of hope that she had had. Richard felt nothing for women, not even the stirring of instinct that, it was said, served Philip well in doing his royal duty. If this spirit had been male, he would have been its captive. But it was not, and he was no deeper in the enchanter's power than before.

That was still deep enough. The spirit glided toward the altar. It wore a woman's shape, and walked on delicate white feet, but the suppleness of its movements was not truly human.

This must be kin to that Melusine whom Arslan had destroyed: a water-spirit, wrought to allure and destroy mortal men. It was wrapped in a mantle of green shot with silver; the hair that flowed free over its shoulders was more green than gold. Its eyes were green, and its teeth were white and sharp.

It halted before the altar and let fall its mantle. It wore nothing beneath. It must know what the sight of it was doing even to the mages, but it was as careless of itself as an animal.

When it spoke, it spoke in a voice of almost unbearable sweetness. "Is this the sacrifice that you would make to me?"

The Egyptian bowed low. "Lady, we bring a charge from the Emperor of the Germans. He bids you remember the oath you swore to him and to his ancestors, and the duty you owe to the land and its people."

The green eyes narrowed. A spark had kindled in them. "He commands me?"

"He asks, lady," said the Egyptian.

"He is mortal," said the Lorelei. It lifted fingers on which the nails were pearl-white claws, and combed them through its hair. The tendrils of it curled of their own accord, tangling the shimmering claws, capturing the light of the rose window. It was weaving a spell, and making no secret of it.

The Egyptian freed himself with a counterspell incanted half in a gasp. "Lady, you are bound."

"Not by you," the creature said.

He spoke a Word that rang like a gong. The wooden image swayed on its pedestal; the light from the rose window dimmed. The Lorelei shrieked in pure rage, but even as the sound of that outcry died away, it said flatly, "I am bound. What does the emperor bid me do?"

"Bind this one," the Egyptian said, tilting his head toward Richard, "as you are bound. Take his spirit and keep it in your care, and bind one in this body that will do as the emperor wills."

"Ah," said the Lorelei. "A simple thing. Must I keep his spirit whole?"

"Whole and unharmed," the Egyptian said, "but bound beyond hope of escape."

"It would be even simpler to kill it," the Lorelei said.

"The emperor does not wish it dead," said the Egyptian.

The Lorelei inclined its head. With no more warning than that, it reached for Richard.

He surged up even as Kalila bolted out of hiding. His hands closed about the white throat. Tendrils of weed-green hair whipped about his wrists.

Kalila flung fire. The French king's mages whipped about. The men-at-arms came alive, drawing swords, converging on her.

The magic inside the fiery stone caught all the armed men and sent them away. The mages stood in flat astonishment. In that instant, the power turned upon them. Kalila had nothing to do with it. It was as if she were a weapon to be wielded; her will stood aside, and the magic did as it would.

She was still the master of her body. The mages were at war. The Lorelei grappled with Richard on the stone-paved floor.

Kalila drew her dagger from its sheath, a thin sharp blade such as Assassins carried, sharp enough and long enough to thrust up through ribs into a beating heart. She struck almost blindly, not even certain that the Lorelei had a heart, or that its flesh was mortal enough to be wounded.

The cold steel caught a glancing blow as the creature writhed in Richard's grip. He seemed as deep in the spell as ever, his eyes as blank, his face as empty of expression, but he was fighting with deadly skill. Kalila stabbed again. The creature shrieked; its skin withered and charred where the blade had cut.

Richard wrenched the knife out of her hand and turned it against his adversary. Kalila's body jerked about. The French mage was down. The Egyptian seemed unruffled. He was chanting softly, weaving a fabric of magic in the air of that place. It was eerily beautiful: an army of tiny bright spirits in the shapes of beasts and birds, strange not-quite-letters and bits of human bodies—a hand, a foot, a rampant phallus.

The magic took Kalila's hand and swept it across that tapestry of spells. It caught in her fingers, wrenched and tore. The Egyptian chanted louder, faster. She could feel the magic in her, bleeding through myriad small wounds. The chant pierced each one with blinding pain.

Kalila stumbled toward the Egyptian. He was wrapped in wards, impenetrable, and her knife was in Richard's hand, tormenting the Lorelei. Yet he was still small enough to encompass with her arms. She heaved him up, finding him no great weight, and flung him toward the image on the altar. He cried out and twisted, but his shoulder struck full in the Mother's face.

The image toppled to the floor and shattered. The Egyptian's scream was completely silent: a shard of wood had pierced his neck, nigh cleaving it in two.

The magic left Kalila, dropped her half-lifeless to the floor. Some last remnant of warrior instinct brought her scrambling about, clutching at anything that could pass for a weapon. Richard was still locked in combat with the Lorelei. Its fingers clamped about his throat; his face was dusky crimson.

Kalila seized it by the hair, braced her feet, and did her best to fling it over her head. It turned on her as she had hoped, and let Richard go. It was hideously strong, and its teeth were sharp, snapping at her throat. It bore her down, crushing her with its leaden weight. Her ribs creaked and began to crack. The breath stabbed in her lungs.

Richard reared up over them both. Stretched between his hands was a length of iron chain. He caught the Lorelei by the throat and snapped the chain tight. Kalila's nostrils wrinkled at the stink of burning flesh.

Richard flung the creature flat, still gripping the chain, and braced his knee on its breast. It arched its back, but not to struggle. The same heat that had come from it when it entered the shrine had risen again. Long white fingers crept up his thigh.

He batted them aside. "That doesn't work with me," he said, "nor with my friend, either. What would it take to rid us of you? We're not giving you blood or souls. What else will satisfy you?"

"You," the creature gasped through the pressure on its throat.

"Oh, no," Richard said. "I'm for ransom, but not by you. Suppose I give you your life. That should be enough, don't you think?"

"I am bound," said the Lorelei. "I must—"

Once again he kicked its hand aside. "You are bound to protect the realm of Germany. Yes? Then I'll swear you an oath. I will do nothing to harm this realm or its emperor. As soon as my ransom is paid, I'll be gone, and never return. I am no threat to you or yours."

The Lorelei lay still. Richard did not let down his guard, but he waited while it pondered what he had said.

At length it said, "The one who spoke the Word is dead. I am no longer bound. Yet the emperor—"

"As far as the emperor need know, you've done his will," Kalila said. "Give me the Egyptian's face; let yonder bishop take the other. Let us wear them only long enough to save us all."

"That won't be enough," Richard said. "Show me what I would have been like—what to do, how to look. I'll play the fool for as long as it takes."

"Mages will know," said the Lorelei. "The faces I can give. The rest, no. The spell fades at dawn. Be sure to be in a safe place, or you will be betrayed."

It would not be moved to do more, even by threat of the chain. Richard bound it to the altar amid the shards of the pagan image. When he turned, he started.

Kalila looked down at herself. She looked the same as always, and yet . . .

A shadow lay over her, a shimmer of strangeness. It made her walk differently, hold her head differently. If she opened her eyes just a little wider, she saw as an Egyptian would see, a mage of an order that was older than the world. And there beside her, coming slowly out of hiding, was one who to all senses appeared to be the French mage— but that man's body lay dead at the false mage's feet.

She bowed to the Lorelei. It did not seem unduly discommoded to be bound with chains to an altar. "You," it said, "wear masks upon masks. Beware lest they become the truth."

Kalila bowed lower yet. Richard hissed at her, impatient to be gone. She let him drag her into the long light of evening.

# CHAPTER 55

The boat was still at the quay, the otter-boatmen waiting, lying about in attitudes of boneless ease. They came awake gratifyingly quickly, nor seemed startled to see only three when a dozen had gone out.

Richard did his best to seem ensorcelled: he walked slowly, and his eyes were blank. It was the same mask he had worn in the shrine, and it seemed to be enough. Kalila led him into the cabin as the Egyptian had done, pushing Ely ahead of her, but unobtrusively, she hoped.

The cabin was dim and close. Ely crawled onto the bunk and turned his back on the others, drawing into a tight knot of rejection. He was not well, but there was little anyone could do for him here. Kalila let him be. If all of them were fortunate, he would ascribe this journey to a fever-dream, and never remember that it had been real at all.

Richard folded himself onto a low stool and peered hard at Kalila for a moment before he shook his head. "Remarkable," he said. "The likeness is perfect."

"I do hope so," Kalila said.

There was a long silence. In it, the boat cast off from the quay. For this journey, up the river against the current, it needed all its crew at the oars, and mast and sail, too.

When Richard spoke at last, Kalila started. "This was really magic, wasn't it? I didn't dream it. That really was a demon of the river, and I really did overcome it with cold iron."

"Really," said Kalila. "And, sire, that you had iron with you—how did you do it?"

"I was chained when I was first captured," he said. "I kept the chain as a remembrance. When they tried to drug me, I hid it."

"That wasn't a drug, sire," she said. "That was a spell. You had cold iron on your body and resistance in your heart; that's why the spell couldn't take hold." She paused. "I must admit I'm surprised. I had heard that you had no use for these misty fancies."

He grimaced. "No use at all, but they keep coming after me. I'm not quite the fool that some may think I am. I can defend myself if I have to, even against mist and dreams."

"They want your soul enslaved," she said. "You heard the Lorelei—mages will know that the spell failed. I'll play this semblance as far as I can, but—"

"How will they know?" Richard asked.

"They can see," she said.

"Did the French king's mages see that I wasn't enspelled?"

"No," she said, "but—"

"Then how will anyone else be able to tell? I'll play the game, messire Turk, and I'll play it to win."

Kalila grinned, which must have been disconcerting on the somber Egyptian face: Richard looked startled. "Obviously you're a better player than I am, sire. But what if you're asked to do something that will harm England? What then?"

"I'll play it out when it comes," he said. "Just convince Henry that his plot succeeded. I'll do the rest."

Kalila bowed. Her heart was not altogether at ease, but the sharp edge of fear was gone. She had been thinking of Richard as a burden; a mortal who must be carried, as Ely was, from place to magical place. She had forgotten that he too, like John, was of other than mortal blood. And he was a very good general. She had an ally here, not simple baggage. That was a great comfort.

The boat brought them to Worms in the dark before dawn. Richard had to carry Ely off it, with Kalila pretending to compel him, but once the bishop's feet were set on living earth, he revived enough to stumble between them. He could even manage a murmur of protest: "Majesty, you shouldn't—it's not fitting—"

Richard took no notice, and after a while Ely fell silent. Kalila hoped they passed for a group of drunken revelers, coming home very late indeed from their round of the taverns.

They returned to the castle by the same way from which Richard had come. Yet when they reached the place in the wall in which the postern gate had been, there was nothing. The stones were un-marked, the moss on them both ancient and undisturbed.

Kalila's heart sank. There were other gates, but her bones told her that none was safe, only this one. Except that there was no gate to be seen.

She approached the wall and closed her eyes. Her hands ran along the stone. As they drew near the corner, they began to tingle. A moment later, she felt the interruption of the courses of stone, the shape of a frame and, abruptly, the warmth of wood under her fingers. Still with her eyes shut, she found the ring that she remembered having seen. As soon as her fingers closed about it, the spell of concealment melted. She opened her eyes on a perfectly ordinary postern gate.

It was not warded. She drew a sigh of relief at that. Carefully still, and watchful for guardians who might be more deadly than simple wards, she led the two men into the castle.

Henry Hohenstaufen was unmistakably the son of Barbarossa: a big ruddy man with a luxuriant red beard of which he was justly proud. He was not, for all of that, either a fool or a dandy. He had a considerable personal liking for the English king; they were men of the same mettle, warrior-poets alike, and in a different world would have been loyal allies.

In this world, in which Richard was a prisoner and Henry was his keeper, they were cordial enemies. Each would destroy the other if he could, nor would Kalila have put it past Richard, if their positions were reversed, to have commanded that Henry be soul-bound and enslaved. Kings did what was best for themselves and their kingdoms. That was the way of it in every world that she had heard of.

She must remember, here in front of Henry, that she was a mage in service to the French king, and therefore Richard's bitter enemy. Ely, blank still with the shock of all this magic, stood like a stone—enough like a mage deep in the working of his art that, she hoped, he seemed to be holding Richard enspelled while Kalila addressed the emperor. It was still barely sunrise, but Henry was up, fully dressed, and on his way to Mass in the chapel.

Richard stood like a stone knight, stiff and expressionless. Kalila, speaking in the Egyptian's harsh-sweet voice, said, "Majesty, it is done as you commanded."

"Indeed," said Henry, walking in a circle round Richard, examining him minutely. Kalila held her breath. "I hope it's not too well done," he said at length. "I do want him bound, but not so that anyone can tell. A subtle binding, sir sorcerer, not a mass of clanking chains."

"Surely, majesty," Kalila said, "and that is most wise. This we laid on him as a precaution; we reckoned it safer on such a journey. If your majesty will allow, we will take him back to his rooms, and slowly bring him out of this deep dream. Thereafter, majesty, only the greatest of all mages will be able to determine that this man lives under a spell."

"That will do," Henry said. "Only see that he remains bound to my will."

"Of course, majesty," said Kalila.

She was dismissed, and none too soon. It was all she could do to walk steadily out that door, and not double up on herself in sudden, piercing agony. The Lorelei's spell had been effortless in the casting, but in its undoing it was pitiless.

Henry's guards took Richard away. She dragged Ely with her, it did not greatly matter where, if only it was away from curious eyes. If it seemed that the French mages had vanished into air, that was well.

The chapel was full of people, waiting for the emperor to come to Mass. The bishop's room was beyond it, deserted now, by Allah's mercy. She had to carry Ely the last of the way, and lay him in his bed. He was feverish, groaning with the same pain that twisted in her vitals. She settled him as best she might, and laid on him what protection she could.

As she drew back from him, he caught her hands. His grip surprised her with its strength. "Tell me it was a dream. Whether it was or not—say it was!"

"It was a dream," she said. "Rest. You did your king great service—in your dream. Rest and be content."

The king's name calmed him. He let her go. She had meant to go back to Richard, but her legs would not carry her. She sat for a while beside the bishop, who seemed to have fallen asleep, and devoted herself to the simple task of drawing breath.

The pain passed none too quickly. Ely had worn his own face since shortly after they left the emperor. She supposed that she was the same. Her hands when she lifted them were her own, without the shadow of that other semblance.

After what seemed a long while, she managed to get to her feet. Richard's rooms were not terribly far away. She would walk that distance, even keep her head up and pretend to be her wonted self.

She passed Richard's guards as she often had before, nor did they seem to find anything odd in her expression. She had thought that Richard would be abed, but he was sitting with his lute, picking out a slow tune in a minor key. He looked up with the beginning of a smile, but it blurred strangely.

She had not seen him move, and yet he was holding her up. Her knees had completely given way. He swooped her up and laid her in his bed, and set hand to the lacings of her cotte. She tried to fight him off, but he was too strong. A distant part of her, beneath the part that gibbered incoherently, observed that once he saw the truth, he would recoil in horror; therefore she was safe. Unless of course he throttled her.

He took off cotte and hose and boots and pried her out of her mail, but he left the shirt and trews, as if like a Muslim he were a modest man. He made no move to touch her past what was needed for her comfort. When she was undressed, he spread the coverlet over her and left her, returning to his stool and his lute.

Even as exhausted as she was, she knew the bite of shame. This man was honorable—she knew that. No one had ever accused him of taking a lover against his will.

She could let go then, while he made his song beside her, and the day rose beyond the walls of the emperor's palace. At last, and blessedly, she could sleep.

She had been dreaming of Hugh Neville, of his voice murmuring in her ear and his kisses wandering across her skin. The dream was vivid: she could feel his arms about her, the warmth of his body beside her, snoring softly.

Hugh Neville did not snore. She drew herself together, very carefully, and eased out of those heavy arms. It was Richard, of course, sound asleep. From the slant of the light, it was nearly sunset.

He had done her no violence, and most likely, when he went to bed, he had been as far from her as the bed's expanse allowed. It was not his fault that sleep had brought him to her—or her to him, in her dream of her lover.

The door burst open. She sprang up, blinking, stumbling, hunting desperately for anything that would serve as a weapon.

The glance that Henry's captain of guards shot her was pure contempt. Richard's snoring stopped, but he seemed even more deeply
asleep.

The captain's men scattered through the room, looking for Allah
knew what. It seemed they did not find it. They did not approach
Kalila or offer her any insolence—perhaps because she had found her
sword and was balancing it lightly in her hand. Some of them had
good reason to know why they should not venture within reach of
that blade.

"Nothing," said the captain at length. "Not a thing. He's not the
one who did it."

"Did what?"

The captain would not look at Kalila past that first devastating
glance, but he did answer. "Nothing that concerns you."

"Now it does."

She was smiling. Her sword's point rested gently against the vein
of his throat. His men stood helpless. Their captain would be dead
before any of them could move.

"What is my lord supposed to have done?"

"Nothing I can tell you," he said, and that was insanely brave of
him. It was probably also the truth.

"Tell me anyway," she said. There was magic in her still, after all.
She met his eyes and willed him to speak, and the words came tumbling out of him.

Nine imperial men-at-arms had appeared in the Odenwald, with
no memory of how they had come there, and no tale to tell but that
some mighty enchanter had cast them out of his fortress on the
Rhine. Two French sorcerers had vanished without a trace. And the
Lorelei had been found in chains, stonily silent as to how it had come
there.

"It was the Egyptian," the captain said under the compulsion of
her spell. "Who else could it have been? He did as he was bidden, and
brought the English king back as he was bound to do—but he serves
the French king, after all. Why shouldn't he dispose of the emperor's
men and steal the power of the greatest guardian of this kingdom,
then fly home to France?"

"Why not indeed?" said Kalila in deep gratitude to the power of
Allah and, however reluctantly, to the Lorelei's silence. "Yes, look to
France; there's nothing here to trouble you. The spell is secure. The

prisoner is bound. And you," she said, "will remember nothing but that you found him abed with his Turkish boy."

"Abed," said the captain, "with—"

She lowered her sword and turned him about, toward the door. "With his Turkish boy."

They all followed him, caught in the same spell. Kalila sank down where they had left her, shivering convulsively. Magic was—so—easy. So simple. Like leaping off a crag. But the ground, when it struck, could shatter every bone.

She did not want to be a mage. She wanted to be a simple Seljuk soldier, loyal to her lord, fighting in his battles, and serving his family until she died a simple and virtuous death.

Except that she could not even be that, because she was not a man. She had no desire to marry some good Muslim and live in his harem and bear his sons. Her lover was a Christian and a Frank, and a mage. He had told her, swearing it as his God's own truth, that he would love a daughter as much as a son, if not even more; because in the inner realm of Britain women were the greater mages and the stronger powers.

Such a strange world she had found herself in. She listened with other than ears, and heard the emperor's men hunting the French sorcerers. She prayed for forgiveness for the lie, but she did not ask to take it back. It served Britain, and Britain's king, that Germany and France should be at odds. It might even protect Richard, if Henry was sufficiently distracted to refrain from testing the Lorelei's spell.

# CHAPTER 56

Saint Michael's Mount hung in the pellucid air between the sky and the sea. John had sailed to it on the sun's track, and would sail back on the track of the moon. In between, he enjoyed the hospitality of the abbey, which did secret homage to him as king of Britain.

He had come for a council that was somewhat considerably delayed, but he was not at all angered to be kept waiting about. The news, in fact, gave him enormous pleasure.

Philip had not enjoyed the best of seasons. His council with the Emperor of the Germans had not come to pass. It seemed that he had conspired with the emperor in some matter respecting Richard's captivity, but the sorcerers whom he had sent had been discovered in acts of treachery—one report had it that they had beaten and bound one of the guardians of the realm, and slain a company of the emperor's personal guard. The emperor's outrage had been so great that he had all but broken off negotiations with Philip over his share of Richard's ransom. Then, to Philip's manifest dismay, the emperor had sworn alliance with his former enemy, another Henry, Henry the Lion of Saxony—and Richard had been full in the center of this new accord. Word was that Richard and the emperor had become fast friends, and Philip was close to being declared their mutual enemy.

That was reason enough to delay this council—that and the difficulty of acquiring, completely in secret, a hundred thousand marks of silver.

"We do need the silver," John said, standing with Arslan on the north tower of the abbey. The tower and the crag fell away sheer; the sea dashed the shore far below, sending up a mist of spray. The wind whipped their faces and sent their cloaks booming out behind them. John laughed as it buffeted him nearly off his feet; Arslan caught him, bracing him until he got a grip on the parapet. He grinned into the gale. "Otherwise, this bloody ransom will strip us bare. And now the German wants another fifty thousand—is that Philip's cut, do you think?"

"I think Philip may not get any, if your brother carries on as he's been doing." Arslan leaned on the parapet, shielding John somewhat from the wind. It barely swayed him: he had made himself part of it, so that it blew through him rather than against him. It was a strange and splendid sensation, as if he had become one of the cloud of spirits that swirled joyously about this place.

"Do you find it suspicious?" John asked. "That Richard and Henry are suddenly such devoted friends?"

"Why not?" said Arslan. "By all accounts they're cast in the same mold. Is it surprising that they'd like each other?"

"Not at all," John said, "but all this conspicuous amity—it smells wrong. And why did the ransom go up, if they're such great friends? Richard's an idiot about money, but not as much of an idiot as that."

Arslan had his doubts, but he held his tongue. In any event they were about to gain a companion: Eschiva had tracked them down. She slid into Arslan's arms under the shelter of his cloak, and held on tightly for a moment before she greeted John. Then: "Messages have come. Philip is on his way. And there are letters from Germany."

John was already halfway to the door that led downward to the abbey. Arslan was inclined to linger, but Eschiva tugged at him. "One of the letters is in Arabic," she said.

That put him to flight. He swept her up in his arms and carried her, laughing, down the stair.

The others were in the hall of the guesthouse: Hugh Neville, Edwy the squire, Susanna stitching serenely at a bit of embroidery. Neville was pacing like a tiger in a cage, snarling at the folded parchment in his hand. He could not read Arabic, a gap in his education which he was feeling far too keenly these days. He fairly flung the letter at Arslan. "Read it!" he snapped.

"The man needs a woman," John opined, perching on the arm of Susanna's chair, "or a good long season in a monastery, with cold baths and floggings. And a hair shirt. A hair shirt most definitely."

Neville bared his teeth at him. Arslan unfolded the parchment and began to read. It was written in Arabic letters in Kalila's fast, fluid hand, but the words were Turkish, the dialect of her clan, which Henry's spies, or Philip's, would be unlikely to understand.

"Well?" said Neville. "What does she say?"

"A great deal in a small space," Arslan said. "Richard is well, but has been forced to play a dangerous game. His dear friend the emperor has tried to enslave his will. The effort failed, but the emperor doesn't know it; he blames French sorcerers for some of the consequences. It seems that one of the guardians of the realm was left chained to an altar, among other delights. That's a tale for a winter's night, she says; what matters is that whatever is said of Richard, or whatever he seems to have done, don't believe it—his will is his own, and he's playing the same game you are, my lord. He wasn't able to keep the emperor from increasing the ransom, but he did convince Henry not to double it. It's better than nothing, she says."

"That's all?" Neville said. "That's all she says?"

"Not quite," said Arslan. "She says that she's well, and she's been a small scandal: it seems she's been declared to be the English king's boy. It's convenient in some ways; nobody questions her, or troubles to ask her what she's up to when she goes out spying. She adds that the Bishop of Ely will be coming to England before the year is out, to collect the ransom and the hostages."

"And she? Will she come?"

"She says," said Arslan, " 'Tell my beloved that I must stay behind; though it aches my heart, I can't in duty or honor do otherwise. Tell him too that when the ransom comes, if he can come with it, but not as a hostage, I will thank God—for before heaven, my arms are empty, and magic is poor comfort in the long nights.' "

"Richard can't be much better," John said dryly. "Do you think he knows what she is yet?"

"I rather suspect not," said Arslan, "or he'd have sent her home."

"Would to God he had," muttered Neville. He flung himself into a chair, glowering at them all. "Duty! Honor! A plague on them both."

"Amen," said John. "Let's hope Philip shows his face soon, and his silver, too; you'll be off to Germany that much quicker."

"I'll go sooner," Neville said. "I'll go tomorrow. I've had enough of this. She needs me; I can feel it. But she's too proud to beg."

"You have duties of your own," Eschiva said.

"Damn duty! Give it to him." He jabbed his chin at Arslan. "He's a better mage than I am, and prettier, too."

"When the ransom goes," John said, "you go with it. Until then, you grit your teeth and endure, along with the rest of us."

Neville's teeth were gritted for a fact. He looked ready to kill something.

"God's ballocks," John said. "You're far gone. You'd best marry her when you find her, and get it over."

"I can't," said Neville in a strangled voice. "She won't convert, and she won't let me petition the Pope."

"Who said you needed Christian marriage?" said John. "Marry her by the old laws. They're just as binding."

"I don't think—" Neville began.

"You don't," said John. "That's obvious. Stop that now and get your horse, and see what's keeping Philip."

It was rough, but it was kindness. Arslan went with him for company, and for protection, too, for he was sorely distracted.

The sea had retreated from the causeway; it was gleaming wet, but they rode across on land and not on water. The wind had died down a little; the air was sharp with autumn chill, but the sun was almost warm. They rode in silence. Neville had brought a goshawk; he loosed it to hunt amid the myriad flocks of birds that dwelt along this coast.

As it circled high above them, choosing its prey from among so many, Neville said, "I did mean it, you know. You should be guardian in my place. I'm the least of the four, and you're stronger than any of them, except maybe your lady."

"I'm also horribly young and rather backward in my studies," Arslan said, "or so Aunt Bertrada told me the last time I was in Gloucester."

"As far as that lady is concerned, every male alive is in dire need of managing. Merlin himself could appear before her, and she'd tell him to wipe his feet; then she'd give him a piece of her mind."

Arslan grinned. "She would, wouldn't she? But, Hugh—"

"But, Arslan," Neville mocked him, but gently. "You're bound to Britain as it is. Why not take my place? You can give it back after all this is over."

"I don't think it works that way," Arslan said.

"It can if we want it to. There's a rite, an oathtaking. We can do it tonight, just the two of us, and I'll be gone in the morning."

"But the king said—"

"The king doesn't know or care what's in my heart. I should have gone months ago—before Midsummer. She needed me then, and I was too much a coward to go to her."

"What will you do?" Arslan asked him. "What can you do? You'll betray her if you go now; everyone will know what she is. That could be dangerous for her."

Neville did not want to hear that, but Arslan would not let him be. "You heard the king. When the ransom goes, you go with it. Then you'll have a purpose and an office, and reason to be where she is. Maybe it will even be safe then for her to be a woman."

"I hate you," Neville said calmly.

"Yes," said Arslan.

The grey goshawk found its prey at last, and struck in an explosion of feathers. A company was riding below it, knights and men-at-arms under the lily banner of France. But more to the point was what they guarded: a train of wagons and laden mules. Philip had come after all, with the ransom for his guardians.

The King of the Franks and the king of all Britain met inside the walls of Mont-Saint-Michel. Philip was as haughty as ever, and his expression as he saw what crown John wore and what scepter he carried was as appalled as anyone could wish. John smiled at him and said, "Good day, brother. I trust you had a pleasant journey."

"It was no more pleasant than it should have been," Philip said though set teeth. "So that's how you did it. The true king isn't in Germany at all."

"He's still a king," John said, "and he's still my brother."

"You swore oaths to me," said Philip.

"Invalid oaths," John said, "as long as he lives to contest them. Do you remember, dear cousin, when we were children, how you would lord it over me because you were God's gift to France, the one and true and only heir, and I was no more than an afterthought? I never forgot, cousin. Not even for an instant."

"So this is revenge. How petty."

"Isn't it? And it's, oh, so sweet. You need your guardians back. I need your silver. A simple bargain, don't you think? Simplicity is such a lovely thing."

"You," said Philip with pure venom, "are a sneering little toad. Give me back my people and let me go."

"Oh, no," said John. "They're still in England. You don't think I'd risk them on the sea, do you? Especially in these troubled times. They'll be sent back to you, safe and well, once your silver is secure in our coffers."

"Henry's coffers, you mean."

"Maybe not," said John. "It's no business of yours in any event, is it? We have the silver. You'll have your sorcerers. All's well with the world."

"No silver," said Philip, "unless you return my people."

"No, no, no," John said. "This is a German sort of transaction. Or is it a French one? You pay us, we give you your property. No silver, no hostages. Maybe we should dock a finger or toe here and there, to make up your mind for you?"

"Give me one of them," Philip said, "and I'll give you half the ransom—the rest to be paid when the others are sent back."

"Why? Which would you like?"

Philip was not such a fool as to dare hope, but his eyes brightened a very little. "Give us the Archbishop of Rheims."

"Ah," said John, "the primate of France. And you're under Interdict, yes? The Pope is not amused, cousin. We'll give you Burgundy—not that you need a marshal of troops, particularly, but he is a decent opponent at chess. I've found him amusing on long dull evenings. The others are too much given to reading Scripture and praying."

"Do you have any conception of what it costs me to conceal their absence?" Philip demanded.

"I can guess," said John. "You should find less prominent guardians, cousin. It's less difficult to explain when something odd happens, and much easier to spare them if they happen to be lost."

"Indeed," Philip said. "Britain always has made a virtue of mediocrity. We in France prefer to choose the best."

"Oh, yes," John purred. "We the mediocre killed one of your best and hold the rest for ransom. That must rankle, cousin."

"That reminds me," Philip said. "Three ransoms—but one blood-price. That was never discussed."

"It was never at issue," said John. "That was a just execution, for unspeakable crimes of sorcery."

"She was murdered," Philip said. "We felt her death in the very fabric of France."

"Good," John said. "Then we're well repaid for the things that she did. Foul things, dark things. You call yourself a Christian king, cousin; a just king. Yet you permitted *that*."

"We will have recompense," Philip said. "Believe it. You will pay for this—for all of it."

"I'm sure I will," said John.

"Every oath that you swore me," Philip said. "Every promise that you made with lying tongue and crooked heart, I will call to account. You will lose it all, John Lackland. Normandy, Anjou, Aquitaine—all of it. Even your miserable little Britain, if I can encompass it."

That was a curse, and a great oath. John sat unmoved, as if he did not understand what Philip had done; but Arslan thought that he understood very well. He nodded to Edwy, who stood waiting, trembling with the importance of his office. Edwy ducked his head in a ragged bow and ran to do his duty.

The Duke of Burgundy was in good health, if somewhat discommoded by chains of iron and wards that prevented him from wielding his power. He greeted the kings with proper courtesy, and bowed low to the ladies.

"This one you may have," John said, "when we take the silver. The others we'll keep until the ransom is safe."

"I will not—" Philip began.

"This is not a negotiation," said John. "This is what I give you, and what I take."

Philip's eyes had gone blank. He was beyond anger. "Everything you do, King of Britain. Every insult, every injury—I will remember. There shall be an accounting."

"So you said," said John. "Will you dine with us, cousin, to seal the bargain? It's simple fare, as abbeys go, but the wine is rather decent."

"I will not break bread with you," Philip said, biting off each word. "Take your silver, little king. Give me my vassal and let me be gone."

"What, so soon? I'm desolate."

Philip hissed at him. He laughed, which stung Philip to even greater rage, but he cared not at all. John was not magnanimous in victory.

# CHAPTER 57

Before the year's end, at last, all the ransom was gathered, the hostages chosen, and Queen Eleanor and the Archbishop of Rouen had mounted their expedition into Germany. Word of it ran far ahead, even to Richard in Speyer.

Richard was playing the game of deception too well. It was not only his bosom friendship with the emperor; that could have been explained by the likeness in their temperaments. It seemed that he had no words to say but what Henry willed him to say; and that was most strongly evident when he spoke of his brother.

The anger was old, and had begun in Richard's own heart, but Kalila was convinced that Henry had been feeding it. He needed no spell or sorcery; the steady murmur of his voice was enough, and the tales that he told of rebellion and treachery. Richard was direly set against John. Kalila could say nothing to dissuade him. When she tried, he either met her with a blank wall of resistance or lashed her with sudden temper.

Ely had left in the autumn, taking the long way overland and by sea to England, to bring the ransom and the hostages back to the emperor. Kalila surprised herself by missing him. He was irritable, unpleasant, and profoundly difficult to like, but he had been, in his way, a cord that bound her to those she loved. Once he was gone, no one knew who in truth she was, and no one but Richard cared that she existed. She was more alone than she had ever been, and so lonely that she was sick with it.

She should have gone with the bishop and ignored the niggle in her bones that bade her stay near Richard. She would have come back; and she would not have endured this long grey autumn and this bleak winter in a country so very far from anywhere that she could call home.

Yusuf would have thumped her for wallowing in self-pity. She made herself live from day to day, doing squire-service for Richard, running his errands, practicing with weapons, riding, hunting, whatever Richard was permitted to do. Henry kept him by now on a pleasantly long leash, with a constant complement of guards, but they had been instructed to let him go wherever he pleased.

Christmas passed with its more than half-pagan revelry. Word came in the new year that the ransom was making its slow and laden way across Germany; the queen and her train would meet Henry at Speyer on the date he had appointed. The list of hostages that came with the message was lengthy and illustrious, but when Kalila stole a look at it, she did not see one name that she had been searching for. She told herself that she had bidden him not to come as a hostage, and yet she was all contrary; she was near to tears of anger because his name was nowhere to be seen.

Three days before the ransom would arrive, Henry summoned Richard to him. It was late in the evening, long after the daymeal had been cleared away. The court was still dancing in the hall, keeping winter's cold at bay with wine and beer and song. Henry received Richard in the solar beyond the hall, a smaller room warmed by a great log burning in the hearth.

The emperor was nearly as alone as a man of his rank could be. A silent squire attended him, and a man whom Kalila recognized: the captain of the guards who had taken Richard to the Lorelei.

Henry's expression was as affable as ever; he was smiling. Yet her hackles rose. She moved a little closer to Richard, and braced herself for whatever might come.

The preliminaries were not particularly lengthy. There was wine, heated and spiced, and conversation regarding the hunting, the weather, the outcome of the tournament at the New Year. Kalila slid into a light doze, standing at attention by the door.

A word brought her fully awake. "So, cousin," Henry said. "You'll be free soon, if all goes well, and twice crowned a king, too. King of Provence—there's a title to delight a man's heart."

"It surely delights mine," said Richard. "You're generous beyond my deserts, sire."

Henry's smile took on a slight, dangerous edge. "Yes, I am, aren't I? I've heard a very strange story, cousin; one that I would call disturbing, if it were true. This man here tells a tale of a spirit of the realm and two servants of the French king, and certain deceptions that, in all honesty, would appall me—if they were true."

Kalila glanced at the captain of guards. He stood rigidly to attention, his face set in stone. He was afraid. And well he might be, if Richard managed to convince the emperor that his tale was a lie.

Richard's brows had raised. "That sounds like a very interesting story. I had a dream like it once, was it last year? Or was it while my father was alive? I dreamed that the King of France was dead, and his dukes were dancing on his grave. Did you have the same dream, cousin?"

"I've had one quite like it," said Henry, "but mine was of the King of England. No; this is another tale. In it, the King of England disposes rather cleverly of the French king's men, chains a powerful spirit to a stone, and puts on a cloak of deception that conceals the truth from the whole world—until a witness comes forth to uncover the lie."

"That is an odd dream," Richard said. "Was it something you ate? I'll be sure to avoid it."

"No dream," said Henry. "Stand up, cousin."

Kalila caught her breath at the lash of magic. She could not tell if Richard felt it. He rose, but that could have been a move in the game.

Henry was watching him with veiled intensity. "Now, cousin," he said, still in that cool and conversational tone, "put your hand in the fire."

Richard stiffened. Kalila poised to leap, but his glance froze her where she stood. "Which hand?" he asked, his voice flat.

"Your left hand," said Henry. "We'll let your sword hand be. The other you can spare, surely. Put it in the fire."

Kalila could not breathe. Richard stretched out his hand. The fire roared. She could feel its heat even by the door. Beads of sweat swelled on Richard's brow and ran down his cheeks. It could have passed for inward resistance to the compulsion of a spell. She felt the force of it, the heavy weight of the emperor's will, so strong that she jerked forward a step before she caught herself.

Richard set his hand in the fire—for a moment, before he cursed and spun away. "Why? What use am I to you if I'm maimed?"

"Why, none," said Henry. "But if the binding had been true, you would have obeyed me—and I would have preserved your precious skin. You're a good liar, cousin, far better than I ever imagined, but in the end you fail the test."

"My word is good," Richard said. "I swore that once freed, I would do nothing to harm your realm. I'll abide by that oath."

"I'm sure you will—until it's more expedient to break it."

"I will not break it," said Richard, with a growl in his throat.

"Maybe," Henry said. "You almost got away with it, cousin. If Philip hadn't sent a message inquiring as to the whereabouts of his servants, and if my captain here hadn't told us where to find the bodies, I might never have suspected—at least until you were safely out of my hands. There is a price for this, cousin. The sentence for murder is death; since you are a king, it can be commuted to lengthy imprisonment."

"You can't do that," Richard said. "My ransom is about to be paid. My people are coming to take me home. We've done all that we can to satisfy your terms. If I refused to have my soul taken out of my body and held in slavery, and my body used as a weapon against my people, can you blame me?"

"Not at all," said Henry. "I'm not letting you go, either. You're too dangerous. If I have to keep you here until you die, I well may."

"How many days will that be?"

"Cousin," said Henry, "you wound my heart. What makes you think I'll have you killed? Bound, yes, and in chains if need be, but your life is safe from me."

"Such as it will be, locked in a dungeon for the rest of my natural life." Richard turned, rubbing his hand where the skin was reddened and beginning to blister. "Just tell me. What were you going to make me do, once I was back in England?"

"Nothing that you wouldn't have done of your own will, if you'd thought of it," Henry said. "Your brother—but there, that's no matter now, since you'll be bound here. He'll have the crown after all, or as close to it as makes no matter."

Richard glared. "John? What were you going to do to him?"

"Muzzle him, of course," said Henry. "Did you know he's wearing a crown when he's at home? The crown of Arthur, he calls it. I doubt he means the child in Brittany."

"There is no such—"

"It's pure gold," Henry said, "or so I'm told. He wears it as a king, holds audience, presides over high courts in the cities and castles of Britain. People bow to him and call him king."

That was not news; Kalila had told Richard of John's secret kingship. Either he had forgotten it, or he was playing the game again after all. His face suffused with rage; he heaved up a chair and flung it with a crash against the wall. Even Henry retreated from that grand Angevin wrath. "God damn him to eternal perdition! And damn you, too. Who told you this? Are you back in Philip's claws again? How much was the bribe this time?"

"A hundred thousand marks of silver," Henry said, "and your brother's head on a salver, but I declined to agree to that. I offered you instead, nicely trussed and with an apple in your mouth."

"Ah," said Richard, almost purring. "Ah, Philip. He was my bum-boy once; he never did forgive me for growing tired of him. And he was tiresome, cousin. His face is pretty enough, but he whines incessantly."

"His silver makes a sweet sound," Henry said.

"Have you actually heard it?" Richard inquired. "Because, dear cousin, he may have omitted to inform you, but that was the exact amount of the ransom he paid to my brother for three of his servants who had been captured under somewhat compromising circumstances. It seems they were invading England. Astonishing, isn't it? And now he's got another hundred thousand to buy my perpetual imprisonment. It is perpetual, yes?"

"In strict point of fact," said Henry, "it is not. He wants you kept here until Michaelmas, after which we may negotiate another payment, or you may be sent home."

"How very profitable for you," Richard said.

"Indeed," said Henry, "and as for Philip's wealth or lack of it, half is to come from him. The other half, he has sworn by the bones of Saint Denis, will come from none other than your royal brother."

"That is not possible," Richard said flatly.

"One would think so, yes? But he did swear to it."

Richard turned slowly about. His eyes were blind. He was completely under Henry's spell, bound by the name of his brother and trapped in uncontrollable rage. It was masterfully done. Kalila could applaud it even as she hunted wildly for a way, any way, to undo it.

There was none. It was no more magical than before. Henry

should have trusted in the power of his tongue, and not in the French king's sorcerers. But then, thought Kalila, the French king was filling Henry's coffers at a remarkable rate. Between France and England, the Holy Roman Emperor was making himself gloriously rich.

# CHAPTER 58

The Queen of the English rode into Speyer with a grand display. She had brought the whole of the royal household, a great company of bishops and barons, and a small army to guard the coffers of the ransom; and with them two hundred heirs and kin of wealthy houses to stand hostage for the return of England's king. She herself, with her ladies, carried the regalia that would adorn the King of Provence, and led the retinue that would accompany him to his crowning. They were bright with banners, glorious in silk and gold, riding to the music of shawms and sackbuts, trumpets and drums, pipes and bells and a clangor of cymbals, and a choir of monks singing the *Te Deum* as they came.

Richard awaited them in the emperor's company, standing in the gate of the castle. He was dressed in a cotte of crimson silk and a mantle of cloth of gold, both Henry's gift. The amity between them was sorely strained. Henry's expression was cold. There had been no banners, no roar of welcome as the English entered his city.

They came on bravely, but when they halted, Eleanor's face was as chill as the emperor's. She had aged in the year since Kalila saw her: she was gaunt, pale, worn to the bone. She dismounted from her snow-white jennet with her ladies' assistance, and leaned on the arm of a stalwart Saxon maid. "This is a cold welcome," she said in her clear and uncompromising voice, "for a kingdom's worth of silver and an army of hostages."

"It is a brave show," Henry said. "I greet you, lady of the English, and commend you on your promptness."

She inclined her head as queen to vassal. From anyone else it would have been an insolence, but it was purely Eleanor. She turned her dark gaze on her son. He seemed to shake himself out of a dream.

Without a glance at the emperor, he left the gate and went down to her, enveloping her in a glad embrace.

That was all the gladness the queen had in Speyer. Even the German lords and bishops labored to warm the chill in the emperor's heart. Richard, who knew whence it came, was powerless against it— and his rage at his brother was so great that he was reduced to simmering silence.

Kalila cared much less for all of that than she should have. She had searched the crowding faces as the English embassy streamed through the castle gate, but none was that which she had prayed to see. There seemed an endless number of tall, lanky, brown-haired men in that company, but not one was Hugh Neville. He had not come.

She ran as far as she could run, which was not remarkably far: only to the top of a tower. She refused to indulge in tears. For all she knew, he had another woman now, even a wife. He was a Frank and a nobleman. What would he care for a Turkish hoyden whom everyone was calling Richard's catamite?

Was that why he had not come? Did he think she had thrown him over for the English king? Could he even believe that it was possible?

She had worked herself to a fine pitch of fury when the air shifted behind her. She whipped about, sword in hand.

Hugh Neville looked down the length of the Damascene blade. His brows were up. He was not afraid, not even slightly. And he should be.

"What are you doing here?" she snapped at him. "You're supposed to be shut up in some dank English castle with some plump English partridge on your knee."

"I was never fond of partridge," he said, "and it's dank enough here to keep even an Englishman happy."

"You have a wife by now," she said. "Don't you?"

"Not yet," he said.

Her throat was tight. She forced her voice through it. "But soon. Yes?"

"If she'll agree to it," he said.

She dropped the sword and flung herself at him. They went down in a tangle of limbs; he grunted as he struck the stones, and wheezed as she fell on top of him. She wanted to scream at him, to pound him to a pulp, but he was so helpless, lying there winded, that she could only sit on him and glare.

Slowly he got his breath back. He knew better than to try to escape her. Unlike Eleanor, he had not changed. He was still young, still strong. His beard was a little shorter, his hair a little longer. He had a new scar at the corner of his eye.

Her finger brushed it. "That could have blinded you," she said.

"It was a glancing blow," he said. "I never noticed it till after."

"After what?"

"After the French king invaded Britain. You knew of that. I saw your brother write the letter. In Turkish. Which I am going to learn, and Arabic, too, because you are going to teach me."

"Am I?"

"From the look of things," he said, "there will be plenty of time."

"Why would you care to learn the language of the Prophet? It's difficult, complicated, and will take you years. Won't your wife object?"

"Do you?"

She reared back. "You're not marrying me!"

"I would like to."

"You can't. Your Pope—"

"We'll be handfasted in Britain," he said, "by a priestess of the old way. No Pope, no *qadi*. No strictures against commingling of faiths."

"What about my strictures? I told you I didn't want to marry."

"You told me you didn't want the Christian rite. This isn't Christian. I'll say Muslim words if it will make you happy. I'll even say them in Arabic, if you'll teach me."

"I go away for a year," she said. "You come to find me. Do you greet me? Do you ask after my health? Not at all. You inform me that I'm about to become a wife."

He opened his mouth, shut it again. When he did speak, it was to say, "You cut your hair."

She dropped beside him, half ready to scream in rage, half inclined to burst into laughter. He drew a breath carefully, testing bruised ribs. Equally carefully, he slid a finger down her cheek. "God," he said. "God, I've missed you."

"I didn't think you'd come," she said.

"I wanted to come months ago," he said. "The king wouldn't let me. Sometimes I thought I'd go mad. You needed me—you needed me so much—and I was bound. But for that, I would have taken wing and flown to you, and be damned to honor or duty or any other thing that would have kept me from you."

She stared at him. She knew what passion was in him: he was an ardent lover, skilled and indefatigable. But he had the Saxon reluctance to trap his heart in words. That was her province, to babble in tongues, pouring out her every thought. Now she could find no words to say. She did as he always had: she answered him with her body, stooping over him, dragging him up, kissing him till his eyes rolled up in his head.

She let him go. She was dizzy and reeling. He was grinning like a fool. "Don't," she said, "become complacent. Don't ever take me for granted."

"Not in this world," he said, "or any other that we inhabit."

That was a mage: careful to the last. "I would have hated you if you'd come sooner," she said, "and myself even more, for taking you away. And yes to what you asked. Yes."

"Yes?"

"I'll marry you. The old way. When this is over, when Britain is safe and both its kings are on their thrones—we'll set hand in hand."

He took her hands in his and kissed them, palm and palm, and pressed them to his heart. The world was back in its orbit. She was saying all the words, and he was speaking with his silence.

Henry's recalcitrance took the lot of them from Speyer to Mainz. There at Candlemas, with all the candles lit against the winter dark, in the chanting of the monks and canons in the cathedral city, he clung to his refusal. He would take the French king's silver. He would not let Richard go.

"Why Michaelmas?" Richard demanded as he sat with his allies of an evening. "Is it some mystical feast?"

"Michael is the great archangel, the warrior chieftain of heaven," Neville said, "and his feast is near the equinox. Summer and winter shift the balance then, and winter conquers for a while."

"What, are they plotting to invade England again?"

"Not this time," Kalila said. She did not know where the words were coming from. They spoke themselves, out of the magic inside her. "It's a pretext. The emperor sees a river of silver flowing into his realm, year after year. He also sees the weakening of Britain. The crown of Britain and that of England are bound together. If both of you are free and ruling as allies, the realm is strong. But if you are at odds, you weaken it; you offer entry to whatever forces your enemies bring to bear. If you stay here, sire, Philip will seize all of your lands within the bounds of France, and extract Henry's tribute from them."

Richard growled at the mention of his brother, but he did not let himself be distracted from the rest. "I've got to get loose. Henry's bad enough, but if Philip is making another move on Normandy, I have to be there—I have to stop him."

Eleanor seemed to be asleep, but her voice was wide awake. "Henry is crowing like a cock on a midden, but however rich Philip's promises may be, our silver is here, it's solid, and he can get his hands on it. I'll talk to him again in the morning."

"What makes you think you'll shake him now?" said Richard. "He hasn't budged in a fortnight."

Eleanor opened her eyes. They gleamed under the hooded lids. "For this, he may budge. Neville, fetch the commander of the treasure-guard. We have preparations to make."

The emperor woke in the morning two days after Candlemas to find a company of servants in his chamber, and the copper basin of his bath set in its accustomed place. But instead of cauldrons of water heated exactly to his taste, he found them pouring in bucket after bucket of silver pieces, ringing and chiming as they filled the basin.

The Queen of the English sat in a chair beside the basin, robed in cloth of silver and crowned with gold. Her hands were folded in her lap, her expression serene. The maid who attended her was as dark as a Moor, and oddly uncomfortable in gown and veil after so long in cotte and hose.

Henry looked like a startled bear: sitting up in his high bed, his body thick with ruddy hair, and his beard in plaits to keep it orderly. His blue eyes stared out of all that hair, bulging with astonishment. "What in the name of the saints—"

"Good morning, your majesty," Eleanor said. "Your bath is ready."

Even as she spoke, the last bucket of coin filled the basin to overflowing. The servants, wearing Henry's livery but the faces of English noblemen, drew back and bowed low.

"This is not all of the silver that came with us, majesty," said Eleanor. "We'll gladly fill a second basin if you wish. Or would you rather we lined your fishponds?"

"Why?" Henry demanded. "What are you doing?"

"Proving a point," she said. "This coin is yours, to do with as you will. What else is offered you is still in France, if it exists at all—for I assure you, your majesty, if half is to come from my younger son, that half will never reach your hands. Set my elder son free, majesty, and we leave with firmest assurances of alliance and goodwill. Keep him imprisoned, and who knows what will come of it? Certainly not our silver."

Henry rose from his bed, wrapping himself in a blanket. He walked round the basin of silver and inspected the feigned servants, too. He would have seen them foremost among the hostages, the heirs of the great earls of England. They held themselves with proper respect, but they did not flinch from his presence.

He returned to the basin and plunged his hand into it, running the silver coins through his fingers. Eleanor waited, letting him understand fully the distinction between promise and reality. He was a man of wit and intelligence, and his greed, it seemed, was not immeasurable. "After Mass today," he said, "send your son to me."

Kalila helped Eleanor to her feet. She was steadier than she looked; she played a game, too, a game of ancient frailty. She did obeisance slowly but with dignity, and let herself be guided from the room.

Once out of Henry's sight, she stood straighter and walked on her own feet. "That will do it," she said with satisfaction. "Go, child. Fetch Richard, and warn him. He's to be on his best behavior, or by God I will leave him here until Doomsday."

"Lady—" Kalila began.

"I can find my own way," said the queen. "I'm not so sure Richard can. Go with him to Henry. Do whatever you must; only be sure that he wins the battle."

Richard was waiting, pacing like a lion in a cage. He stopped and spun at sight of Kalila. His eyes narrowed; he peered, baffled, before he said, "Well? Did she do it?"

"He wants to see you after Mass, sire," Kalila said. It dawned on her as she spoke, and as Richard frowned at her, that he had not seen her in women's clothes before, nor had she ever quite got round to telling him that she was Kalila and not Karim.

"After Mass," Richard echoed her. "She failed?"

"I think she succeeded, sire," said Kalila, "but you're to set the seal on it."

"Yes," said Richard. "He would insist on that." He paused. "You have a brother."

"Two, sire," said Kalila, "but one is dead."

"You look—just—like—"

She had mercy on him. She took off the wimple and the veil, and did her best to look contrite. "I'm sorry, sire. I forgot you didn't know."

"All this time," he said. "*All* this time. And you never—"

"Truly, sire," she said. "I grovel in shame. I never meant to deceive you. But there just never seemed to be time to explain."

"Explain?" he said on a rising note. "*Explain!* God's *feet!*"

She braced against the blast of his wrath. She did deserve it, and he had not killed her yet; she did not expect that he would. When he began to cool down, she said, "I really am a Turk, sire, and I really am trained to weapons."

"Damn it, I know that!" he snapped, but his temper was much milder than it had been a few moments before. "I should have suspected, too, the way you faced that she-monster. It didn't tempt you at all. I thought you were a eunuch, even after you tried to make me think you weren't."

"But, sire," she said, "I'm not."

His lips drew back from his teeth. "You must have laughed till your sides ached."

"Not at you, sire," she said, "though I did find it amusing to be called your boy."

"They say you're in Neville's bed now," he said. "Do you even care what that does to his reputation?"

"No more than he does," she said.

He looked her up and down, and shook his head. "God's ballocks. You play the game better than any of us."

She lowered her eyes. "Sire, I don't think—"

"Stop pretending to be modest. I suppose you'll play my squire in front of Henry. Does he know?"

She shook her head.

"Good," he said. "Don't let him find out, either, or he'll never let me go."

Richard dressed with care for his meeting with the emperor. He put on good clothes, but not too royal; rich enough for his rank, but not ostentatious. He took only one attendant, the dark young squire who had been his constant companion. She caught him sliding glances at her, until he caught himself and kept his eyes fixed firmly ahead.

Henry took his time coming back from Mass. Richard waited in an antechamber, where he amused himself in composing a duet between a clerk and a tavern wench. Kalila took the wench's part, with relish once she saw that Richard had decided to be amused.

The song had grown outrageous by the time the emperor deigned to appear. Kalila broke off her verse, but Richard picked it up and brought it to a rousing finish before he turned and bowed, and said, "Majesty."

"Cousin," said Henry. "You're in excellent spirits."

"Should I be cast down, cousin?" Richard inquired.

"That depends," Henry said. "Are you expecting to be set free?"

"I do hope for it," Richard said.

"I will do it," said Henry, "but in return, you must do one thing." Richard arched a brow.

"I ask you, as king and vassal, to take an oath that you will do no harm to me or to my realm."

"I've already sworn to that," Richard said, a little deeper than he might have done, and with a little less calm.

"This is a great oath," Henry said, "a binding oath, an oath that will destroy you if you break it."

"In short," said Richard, "an insult?"

"Call it a surety," Henry said, "and a tribute to the quickness of your wits."

"I will swear your oath," Richard said.

"Come, then," said Henry.

The way that he led them should have taken them to his chapel, but when the door opened, both Richard and Kalila caught their breaths.

They stood in the door of the Lorelei's shrine. The image of the Mother and Child was gone. The altar was bare, but its stone seemed filled with a golden light. The light brightened as Henry approached it, and blazed as he bowed before it. The stone turned to glass. Within the glass was a blue-green shimmer of water and a glitter of gold.

There was a ring within the altar like a relic inside a Christian shrine, a golden ring suspended in the water. Henry reached into the stone or glass or water or whatever it was, and brought it forth. It was a simple thing, without stone or engraving: a round of pure yellow gold, gleaming in the big ruddy hand.

Kalila swayed with the force of the power that radiated from that glittering bauble. The altar had concealed the greater part of it. Here was the power that had fed the Lorelei, the soul of this realm, its heart and center.

"Is—" Richard's voice died in his throat. He tried again, with more success. "Is that what I think it is?"

"The Ring of the Nibelung," Henry said, but softly, as if the spirits of air could hear and trumpet it to the skies. "Tell me you didn't know what you did, binding that spirit to this rock, with this ring within it."

"It was convenient," Richard said. "If I'd known—God! I could have had the ring."

"It would have blasted you where you stood," said Henry. "This is a curse made substance, cousin. It gives me power, but in the end it will consume me. You think my father drowned in that river before he came to the Crusade? This is river gold, cousin. It binds us all, and keeps us within our borders. Barbarossa thought that he could escape; that the cross would protect him. He paid the price for his presumption."

"Are you sure you can trust me?" Richard asked with a twist of irony. "This is a mighty secret. I could use it to destroy you."

"The ring would destroy you first," Henry said. "You are suffered to look on it because I give you leave. Swear on it, cousin. Swear the oath. And if you break that oath, the curse of the Nibelung will fall upon you: death and worse than death; damnation everlasting. Every river shall rise up against you; every spirit of air shall be your enemy. The earth will not shelter your bones, nor will fire devour them. You will hang forever between earth and heaven. Now will you swear the oath?"

"I do swear," Richard said steadily.

The ring flashed blinding bright. Even Henry flinched a little, though the golden thing was clearly part of him. He recovered himself, drew a breath, laid the ring back in its shrine. His hands were shaking just visibly. But he was content. "You are free," he said to Richard. "Your ransom is accepted. You may return to your kingdom. But have a care! If you set foot in my realms again, not only I will call you to account. The ring will try and sentence you. Remember your oath—and remember to what you are bound."

"I'll not forget," Richard said. His eyes were on the ring, but there was no covetousness there. When he glanced at the emperor, he let slip a glimmer of pity. His crown was mortal and bound to no secret powers. He was fortunate, Kalila thought, and well he knew it. He had been this man's prisoner for a while, but Henry was bound forever, nor could he ever be set free.

# CHAPTER 59

❧

*The Devil is loose. Look to yourself.*

That, rumor declared, had been all the warning Philip of France sent to John, the rebel of England, when at last the Emperor of the Germans let Richard go. It was a most persistent rumor, and heavily laden with flights of fancy—"Just like Philip," John said.

He was settled rather comfortably in Nottingham Castle. Rumor had it that he, having heard the dire news, had packed up and fled into Philip's arms. "As if I'd hide behind *those* skirts," he said. He was amused; he had been amused since the spate of rumor began. "Philip's desperate, if he's resorted to all these fancies."

"Not so fanciful," said William the Marshal, "if the right people believe them. Your brother, for example. Henry did get at him—that much we're sure of. He convinced Richard that you really are what Philip says you are."

"I hear he's in a right rage," said John.

They were in the castle yard, watching one or two of the young knights and some of the squires tilt at the quintain. As they paused, Edwy the squire caught the wooden Saracen a glancing blow with his lance. The thing whipped about as he cantered past on Arslan's brown cob, and knocked him flat. The cob gave up any pretense of being a destrier and trotted off toward the stables.

Edwy was up before the others reached him, reeling but hale enough. Their mockery was good-natured: Edwy was popular among the young men. They dusted him off, determined that nothing was broken, and ran to retrieve his mount before it passed the stable door; but the cob had met its master there, and submitted to capture.

Eschiva smiled as Arslan led the cob back to the bruised and grinning squire. No one knew yet that she was there: she had come out while John and the Marshal were speaking, and stood silent, making herself invisible. Even Arslan had not seen her; he was preoccupied with Edwy, and with a challenge from all the rest, to take revenge on the wooden Saracen for the insult to his squire.

He was no longer the enemy and favored target of John's young men. He offered no foothold for jealousy; he would not quarrel over his place in John's following, and he never made a boast of his lord's favor. Even the most stubborn had given up in the end, and come to a grudging acceptance; then Edwy had gone a fair way toward banishing the reluctance. Edwy worshipped Arslan with complete and uncompromising devotion, and whipped soundly any squire who spoke ill of him.

Arslan had mounted the cob. He was not in armor, having been in the stable with his mare, who was near to foaling. Someone lent him a helmet; someone else handed him a lance. Under him the cob was almost sprightly: it picked up its feet a fraction higher, and even snorted. Arslan cantered him in a circle, settling in the saddle, firming his grip on the lance. Eschiva sighed a little. He was beautiful always, but she did love to see him on a horse.

In the warmth under her heart, their child rolled and kicked. She winced as it caught a rib, but her smile deepened. She rested a hand over the swelling curve of her middle, half a gesture of protection and half a caress.

Arslan completed his circle and checked the cob, gathering its hindlegs under it. It sprang into a sudden gallop.

His lance caught the wooden Saracen full in the center of its shield. The lance splintered. The shield flew high and wide. The grimacing bearded head broke off and rolled, tumbling up against Eschiva's foot.

The young men roared. *"Revenge!"* The cob wheeled, pawing the air. Arslan swooped, caught Eschiva, and whirled her, dizzy and laughing, into his arms.

The cob settled sensibly under that substantial and doubled weight. Eschiva wriggled until she was as comfortable as she could be, and took the kiss that hovered irresistibly. That won a cheer, at which she barely blushed. She loved being scandalous—a wife who lusted after her husband; shocking.

Arslan lowered her gently to the ground and sprang down beside her, tossing the cob's rein to Edwy. They were all begging for another round, but he shook his head. "I've killed my share of infidels today."

"Kissed your share of beautiful women, too," someone muttered. Arslan laughed, but Edwy's expression boded ill for whoever had spoken.

John and the Marshal beckoned. Arslan linked arms with Eschiva and went to stand with them on the gallery above the yard. "News?" John asked Arslan.

"She'll not foal tonight," Arslan said, "or tomorrow night, either, from the look of her."

The Marshal rolled his eyes. "Mares. They live to make fools of us men."

"Rather like their human sisters," John said, with a bow to Eschiva that exempted her from the charge. He leaned on the rail as the game below turned from the quintain to the pells. "Richard's in a rage," he said. "He's crossing France like the wrath of God."

"No interference from Philip?" Arslan asked.

John's smile was nothing short of smug. "Not as long as I've got his kingdom by the short hairs. I trust the good abbot and the lord archbishop are still safe and sound?"

"They are, my lord," Eschiva said. "The abbot did try to escape through a rathole a few days ago, my aunt tells me, but he's safe in a cage now; she's keeping the cats out of the room."

John blinked once, frowned, shook his head. "You surely can't mean—"

"Yes, my lord," she said. "He tried a transformation, with admirable success, but my aunt had her eye on him, and a cage ready. She did consider returning him to his proper form, but he's certainly easier to keep in this one, and cheaper to feed, too. She asked the archbishop if he'd care to join his colleague, but he respectfully declined. He hasn't been as rebellious as the abbot; in fact, my aunt says, he's quite remorseful about his sorceries, and he's vowed to retreat to a monastery once he's released, and spend a year in penance. He's a good man, she says, if somewhat misguided."

"And I thought you were fools or mad to keep those two sorcerers together in a simple manor, under a woman's care. I see I underestimated you all."

"Aunt Bertrada has been raising infant mages for years," said Arslan. "A pair of French sorcerers are nothing to that. She bids us tell you that your guards are all well, and she's finding them useful for getting the fields plowed and planted."

"I'm glad she can put them to some use," John said.

"No one is ever idle in my aunt's house," said Eschiva.

"She won't have much longer to entertain them," said John. "Once my brother is safe in England, off they can go. I hope he learns to appreciate the things we've done for him, because God knows, it's been a bloody nuisance from beginning to end."

"They say he's sworn to strip you of all your lands," Eschiva said, though the Marshal frowned at her for saying it, "and pull every claw, until you submit to him as your liege lord."

"I had heard that," John said blandly. "Pity Philip won't believe it. It might have been amusing to see how far we could carry that old deception."

"He might believe it after all," Arslan said. "You have been wearing a crown, and I don't think he ever truly believed that you were your brother's ally. Richard certainly doesn't—and he ought to know you better than Philip does."

"That is the trouble," said John. "They all know me. Even Mother is never entirely sure that I'm to be trusted." He straightened, and shook himself. "Well. We'll be ready for him when he comes. The rest is in God's hands—or the gods', if you prefer."

Eschiva did not know how she survived dinner that evening, sitting decorously and making conversation and eating, it was true, with splendid appetite—but watching her husband throughout, and counting the moments until they could in courtesy excuse themselves and retreat to their chamber.

He would have lingered, drinking wine and chewing over bits of policy, but after she had slipped her hand beneath the table and sent it wandering up his thigh, he had the wits to excuse himself. "My lady," he said to the others, without too quick a catch of breath, she thought. "She's a little indisposed. If you'll excuse . . ."

Of course they would, with Eschiva trying visibly not to faint in his arms. Once they were out of sight of the hall, she recovered remarkably, and all but dragged him up the stair and through the door. She was stripped and had his clothes half off him before he began to get his breath.

He was by no means unwilling, but he was wonderfully startled. "What in the world—"

She kissed the words out of him, bore him down, and gave him back some of the more delicious lessons that he had learned from his preceptress in Damascus. Her body was on fire. He was too beautiful to bear—the height of him, the breadth, the strength and swiftness; the smooth flow of muscles under the fine bronze skin. His hands fit him now, and his feet; he had become what for so long he had promised to be, a big tawny lion of a man.

And he was hers, every glorious inch of him. She measured him in kisses. From foot to head, threescore and twelve and two; from shoulder to shoulder, three dozen and one; from root to tip of his rod—

"My lord! My lord, your mare! She's down—she's—"

Eschiva would kill Edwy—after she killed her rival, that four-legged hussy. Arslan was on his feet, pulling on tunic and hose, ready to run out barefoot if Edwy had not flung his boots at him. Eschiva followed a little more decorously, putting on her shift and the plainest gown she had, and finding her shoes cast away in a corner. She snatched up her bag of medicaments, wrapped her hair in a kerchief, and ran as swiftly as her thickening body would allow, down to the stable with the rest of them.

Her body's heat had cooled enough to permit her to think, which was not altogether an ill thing. The sight of him kneeling in straw, guiding a small caul-wrapped hoof out of the heaving body of the mare and into the world of the living, weakened her knees, but she mastered herself. Edwy did not dare enter the stall; Eschiva had no such compunction. Arslan had reached inside to find the other hoof, which should have been visible long since.

She knelt beside the mare and laid her hand on the swollen side. She could see the foal, caught and somewhat twisted. She rested her free hand on Arslan's shoulder, so that he too could see. His jaw set. "My hands are too big. Edwy! Come here."

Edwy came at the run and dropped to the straw. Eschiva gave him the vision that she had given Arslan. His smaller hands, so guided, found the foal and straightened it, just as the mare's spasm thrust it outward.

Two hooves, one wet dark nose, and a pair of ears unfurling as Arslan folded back the caul. The rest came as it should, scrambling already, struggling to lift its head, to rise.

"A daughter," Arslan said to the mare, as tenderly as he had ever spoken to his lady. "You have a daughter, beloved."

The child in Eschiva's belly leaped, so that she gasped. Arslan forgot the foal, instantly, completely. "Lady! Are you—"

"I'm well," she said somewhat breathlessly. "No, truly, I am! But it seems that someone else wants to be heard. We have a daughter, too, my love. Are you terribly disappointed?"

"Not ever in this world," he said with heartfelt sincerity. "But if she would be so kind, I would prefer not to see her until Midsummer. Now is much too early."

"She will come in her good time," Eschiva said.

It was long and very late before they could finish what they had begun. Eschiva did not try to persuade Arslan to retreat to the bedchamber. Edwy had fallen asleep outside the mare's stall. The foal, having stood and nursed and taught itself to gallop in circles round its weary mother, lay flat beside her as she restored her strength with a manger of cut fodder. The stall across the way was untenanted, the straw clean and sweet.

Arslan let her have her will of him, nothing unwilling himself, but his desire was a pale thing beside the white heat of hers. She drained him dry, and still she could have gone on, insatiable. She could have eaten him alive.

He lay spent, sprawled in the straw, regarding her with wide grey eyes. She kissed the brows above them and the lips below, and drew back, the better to drink him in.

"Is this—" he gathered himself to say. "Is this something magical? Or—"

"It's as natural as anything in the world," she said, trailing her hand over his breast. His heart was not beating as hard as it had been; the sweat was drying slowly. "Do I appall you? Are you scandalized?"

"I'm startled. I never expected—"

"When is a woman more completely a woman than when she's carrying a child?"

"She is never more beautiful," he said. He stroked the rounding of her belly and cupped her breasts, gently, for they had grown tender. "I should like our child to be born at home. Can we do that, do you think?"

"What? Go to Outremer?"

"No," he said. "To Ynys Witrin. Where I've never gone, because there's never time, my lord can't spare me, the kingdom needs me.

I've never even seen it. And yet in my heart I know she should be born there. The light of that place should be the first light she sees."

He had surprised her. He did not do that often these days; not that he had grown predictable, but she knew now what a marvel he could be. "Daughters of my line have always been born on the Isle," she said. "How did you know? Did someone tell you? Bertrada?" And a little coolly yet: "Mother?"

He shook his head. "I just knew."

"Spirit of fire," she said. "When this is ended, but before she is born, we will go to the Isle. I promise you."

"Both of us," he said.

"All three of us," said Eschiva.

# CHAPTER 60

Richard returned to England completely without fanfare. There were no banners, no cheering crowds, no royal processional. England, stripped of its silver and its noble heirs, thinned to the bone by a hard winter and a wet, cold spring, had nothing left to give its king.

That mattered little to Richard. He had kicked the dust of Germany from his feet, and left Normandy with a heartfelt promise to return. Just now, and most urgently, he wanted John.

He sent forces to seize his brother's lands, all of them, as he had sworn to do. He himself rode headlong for Nottingham, more headlong perhaps than he would have done if he had not been a prisoner for nigh on two years: he was dizzy with freedom. No army encumbered with baggage and siege-engines could keep pace.

He left the army to follow as it would, and took a small company of his own troops, picked men on good horses. Hugh Neville rode with him, and Kalila in her Norman squire's guise. Neither of them wasted breath in trying to dissuade him, past assuring him that yes, John was last known to be in Nottingham, and no, he was not in France as rumor insisted.

Nottingham Castle was deserted. Not a soul stirred inside it, though the town was as busy as always. Richard sent his men through the castle, but they found nothing, not so much as a stray dog. That whole castle was as empty as a shell from which the bird had hatched.

When they gathered again at the gate, they found a living thing at last: a redheaded, freckled imp of a boy perched on the corbel of the arch. He was as mortal as any of them, dressed in cotte and hose of good quality, with a lord's badge on his shoulder: scarlet shield, golden lion rampant. Kalila thought she remembered him among the pack of wizardlings in Bertrada's house, which meant that however human his origins, he was not so mortal after all.

He grinned down at them, as insouciant a young creature as ever drew breath, and said, "Good day, King of the English. Are you looking for someone?"

Richard's temper by then was hanging by a thread, but that grin was impossible to resist. "Good day, imp on the arch. Have you seen my brother?"

"Not since yesterday," the boy said.

Richard's fists clenched on the reins; his horse jibbed, protesting. "Indeed? And where was he then?"

"Right here, sire," said the boy.

"Well," said Richard as his temper began to slip, "where is he now?"

"He told me to tell you," said the boy, "that he's not in the mood to be murdered, and he doesn't fancy being hauled out in chains and made an example of, either. He says that if you can calm down and be a reasonable being, he'll welcome you to his kingdom; but if you persist in being a bullheaded ass, you won't find him before Doomsday."

"He can't be far, sire," said the captain of guards in Richard's thunderous silence. "Not if he only left yesterday, and if he's got his whole household with him."

"He's as close as your shadow," said the boy on the arch, "and as far as the back of the moon."

"You're moon-mad," Richard said.

The boy laughed and poised on the arch, and leaped. The men gasped; a few cried out. But the boy floated down as light as a feather and stood by Richard's horse, hand resting on the rein. "If you will swear a truce," he said, "I can guide you. Will you do that, King of the English?"

"Does he swear in turn?" demanded Richard.

"By earth and sea and sky," the boy said, "and the hidden realm of Britain, of which he is king."

Richard snarled at his willing obedience. "Very well. I swear. A truce until tomorrow's sunset. Then, unless he does homage to me as king, we'll be at war."

A brown cob trotted out of the stable that, all the men swore, had been empty. It was saddled, bridled, and equipped for a journey. Kalila knew that horse—it had been Arslan's. The warmth that rose in her at that, the smile that came of it, made the whole world brighter.

She had not felt until then that she was in her own country. Wherever Hugh Neville was, she was home; that went without saying. But this land, this particular earth and sky, had belonged to her no more than any other, until she had this reminder that her brother was somewhere in it.

The redheaded boy led them out of the castle and down through the town. The forest was waiting for them, the deep wood of Britain. Her first brother, her brother of the same womb, was buried there. This was the heart of the realm, as the shrine of the Ring was to Germany.

When they rode under the first of the trees, Kalila saw that the guards were no longer with them. Richard seemed not to notice; his eyes were fixed on the guide. Behind him only Kalila rode, and Hugh Neville. The men were nowhere to be seen.

The wood was full of whispers. Spirits flitted among the trees. A ring of them swirled briefly about Richard's head, crowning him with faery gold. It melted into air as soon as they left him.

She did not try to measure time within the wood. After what might have been an hour or a hundred years, they met a man on the forest track. He was a sturdy man, gnarled like a tree, dressed all in green and with a bow slung behind him. He bowed extravagantly as they approached, and said, "Welcome, King of the English! Welcome to Sherwood."

Richard came to himself a little. He peered at the green man; he frowned. "I know you," he said. "Robin—your name is Robin. We met in Nottingham once. You told me I'd gain a crown, but the kingdom would go elsewhere. I thought you were a madman. But—"

"Oh, I'm quite mad," said the spirit of the wood. "And wasn't I right, too? You have a crown. The kingdom has gone where it has gone."

"I have all of it that I could want," Richard said.

"So you do," said Robin, "O king of men." He bowed to the others, with a glint and a grin at the boy and a low reverence to Neville, and for Kalila a long, long stare. Somewhat after she had begun to twitch, he said, "Such honor! Lady, your blood, your presence, graces all this realm."

She hardly knew where to look. The others were staring, too, which only made it worse.

He was a mercurial spirit, and he had an errand that would not wait. He freed her from the weight of his regard and sprang up on the brown cob's rump. The cob twitched its tail but suffered his presence.

John was waiting close by, she thought, but it suited Robin's humor to take them by a long and circular way, tracking sunwise round the center of the wood. It was a rite of sorts, and a magical working, as if they must walk the round of a wall before they entered the gate.

Richard's patience was not infinite, and he could reckon the sun's track as easily as any other traveler. When they had nearly come full circle, he reined his horse to a halt and would not go on. "Enough," he said. "Take me to my brother now, or this game is over."

Robin danced on the cob's rump, whooping with laughter. He whirled, spun, vanished.

The track had shifted. It was subtle, but the sun struck it at a different angle. The trees came together in an arch there, and light shone through, like sun through the high window of a cathedral.

Kalila did not mean to put herself forward, but the light was so beautiful, so clear and so pure, that she could not resist it. She rode beneath the arch into a wide green bowl, a grassy hollow full of sunlight. The grass was starred with flowers, purple and gold and white; there was a stream running through it, tumbling into a pool.

John was kneeling by the pool. There were people with him, some mortal, many not, but in that moment only he mattered. He was dressed for hunting, but the crown of Arthur was on his head. He was intent on something in the water, a flash and gleam of silver. As Richard and the others approached, he asked the thing in the pool, "Is this a willing sacrifice?"

The pool boiled. A huge fish leaped out of it, a fish nigh as tall as a man, with sides that shimmered silver and rose. It fell on the grass, twisted and convulsed, and died in the pitiless air.

Green men gathered in a circle about it, lifted it up and laid it on a bier like a slain king, and bore it away toward a house of wood that Kalila could have sworn had not been there a moment before. Yet it seemed ancient, that house, sunk into the grass, with ivy twining up the walls, and a goat grazing in the thatch of its roof.

John rose from his knees. Then at last he seemed to see his

brother, and his brother's companions. He was not a man for effusions of greeting; he bent his head to them, and said, "I welcome you to Britain."

Richard swung his leg over the high pommel of his saddle and slid to the ground, taking no notice of the odd pointy-eared creature that took his horse's rein. His whole heart and soul were fixed on John. Kalila's nose twitched. The air smelled of hot metal: the scent of wrath.

John stooped and cupped water in his hands. It streamed through his fingers, but the cup of his palms never emptied. "Do you know," he said, "we're two sides of a coin. In any other realm, the king accepts all the burdens that are laid on him. You, brother, never would. You refused this; you put on the mortal crown, took your taxes and tribute, and went sailing off to Jerusalem. But Britain needed a king— more than it had in many a long year. What could it do but go looking for some expedient? And there was I, the afterthought, the Devil's child. It chose me for lack of a better, crowned me and used me, and will continue to use me for as long as I draw breath. All because you, brother, would not take this thing when it was offered."

Richard's response was swift and shockingly profane. "Codswallop! You took that crown with both hands. You danced with glee when it came to you. Don't try to tell me you did anything else—because I know you, little brother. I know you much too well."

"You don't know me at all." John turned his back on Richard. A throne of green turves had appeared in front of the house. He sat on it. His palms still cupped the water of the pool. A spirit offered a chalice of clear glass; the water filled it as if with light. Spirits of air and men clad in green lifted a great mantle of green and laid it on John's shoulders; a tall man in a crown of antlers laid a scepter in his hand.

John sat as king, looking down upon his brother. Richard was speechless, staring up at a sight he would have thought never to have to see.

Yet it was true. It was ordained. Even before the day of his crowning, when he had refused this thing, it had been meant to be.

He began to laugh. It was born deep in his belly, rising up through the bellows of his lungs, bursting out of him in a long roar of pure and painful mirth.

John waited him out. The flocks of spirits, the creatures of wood and water, the living soul of Britain stood astonished.

After quite some time, Richard's laughter faded. He stood hic-coughing, tears streaming down his face, and said in a strangled voice, "Oh. Oh, God. I never wanted England except to pay for my Cru-sade. You did want it. I knew it then. It's no different now. And you have it—the deep part of it, the part that never mattered to me. I still don't want it. Why did I think I did? I got enough of mists and mag-ics in Germany. God forbid I suffer them here."

"You always were a philistine," John said.

"I'm a man of the world," Richard said. "The real world, the world men live in. You can keep your airy fancies."

"I do intend to," John said. "I'll have England, too, in time."

"I'll have to die first," Richard pointed out.

"So you will," said his brother. "Another Crusade, another fever, another harebrained battle—something will get you, brother. And I'll be alive; I'll outlast you. I'll take everything that was yours."

"As long as you don't make any move to speed my passing," Richard said, "I don't honestly care. Life's for the living, brother. I won't fret over what happens when I'm dead."

"You may not," John said, "but your kingdom will. Name me your heir, brother. Give me the promise: England, Normandy, Anjou."

"What, you don't have Normandy already?"

"I lied," said John, "to keep Philip out of England. It worked, didn't it? He'll never set foot on this island while I wear this crown. He paid a good part of your ransom, brother. Did you know that?"

"There will be a price for that," Richard said. "Philip can hold a grudge longer than God. He'll make you pay."

"I'll worry about that when the time comes," John said. "Don't you admire me? I'm thinking like you, for a change."

"You're thinking like a fool," Richard said. "But a canny fool. Say I name you my heir. What's to keep you from playing the rebel in earnest, or deciding that you want to dance to Philip's tune after all? It is tempting, and his coffers appear to be bottomless."

"Faery silver," said John. "Hollow promises. I'd rather extract concessions from you, and be sure of them."

"Was that supposed to be a compliment?"

John shrugged. "If you like." He rose and came down from the grassy throne. "Dine with me. I'll taste everything first, if you're suspicious."

"No," said Richard. "I think I can trust you that far. We don't murder each other, do we? War, rebellion, quarrels in the grand mode—we do all of that. But we keep each other alive."

"The better to torture one another," said John. He led Richard into the house, with the others following.

Richard stopped short just within the door; the rest halted behind him. From outside, the house seemed a simple cottage, nothing noble or grand about it, but beyond its door was a splendid hall. Its vaulting arched overhead, tall as trees. Its floor lay far below, a broad circle about a hearth; the hearth was deep enough to roast a herd of oxen.

They stood in the middle, between earth and heaven as it were, on a long gallery that opened to a stair on either side. All of the people in the hall—and there was a great throng of them—could see who came in.

Richard's eyes were starting from his head, not at the hall, not at the hidden court of Britain, but at one who sat at the high table. Two thrones were set in the center of the dais. Both were empty. Each was hung with the leopards of the Plantagenets; over one was suspended a crown of gold, and over the other, one of green oak leaves wound with leaves of ash and the spiny boughs and soft white blossoms of the thorn. To the right of the thrones was a smaller seat, and in it sat the Queen of the English.

She did not seem near as frail here as in the lesser world. Her eyes were clear, her beauty carved clean. She did not stoop or tremble, but sat proudly upright, head high, watching serenely as her elder son vaulted the rail of the gallery and dropped three man-heights to the woven rushes of the floor. In the silence, the grunt of his landing was distinct, but he barely limped down the aisle that had opened for him. The others, following more sedately by way of the stairs, came up behind him as he stood in front of the queen.

"You, too, Mother?" he said.

She looked down at him from her high seat, eyelids lowered over the dark eyes, face as still as an effigy on a tomb. "I would have told you," she said, "if you had been in any condition to listen. Are you telling me that you trust Philip's word over that of your brother? Are you still fool enough to trust Henry, even after all he did to you?"

Richard's cheeks, always ruddy, were darkly crimson now. "Oh, come, Mother! You know what your lastborn is."

"I do," she said. "He surprises me, too; it seems there is a grain of honest goodwill in him after all. And of course, he can afford to show it." Her glance took in the hall, the court, all the royal show of a kingdom that few men even knew existed. "That convinced me in the end. John is not a generous soul—but he can grant concessions, if he must. Particularly if they cost him little."

"Thank you, Mother," John said dryly. He ascended the dais and took the left-hand throne under the crown of oak and ash and thorn. "Come on up, brother. See these cushions? Swansdown. Your posterior will be delighted."

Richard was breathing hard. His fists clenched and unclenched. All who knew him braced for a blast of royal rage.

It never came. He looked from his mother to John. He searched the faces of the others at the high table: the Marshal and the Bishop of Lincoln and the Lady Eschiva all in white and silver, Arslan beside her in bronze and gold, Susanna in green and gold like a woodland queen, and a company of personages who wore human semblance as a mask, playing at being mortal kings and queens. Richard turned slowly, taking in all who sat in that hall, faces he would recognize, faces he would not, mortal and otherwise, human and inhuman, side by side in the hidden court of Britain. Some made his brows go up: lords and powers in his own world, who were powers here as well. High among them were two of his own bastard brothers: William Longsword and Geoffrey Plantagenet side by side, warrior and Christian archbishop. They inclined their heads to him as his glance passed, offering respect to his earthly rank.

He could not resist; he grinned in return, before he turned back to his mother, and to his brother who waited with sardonic patience for him to make up his mind. "Very well. I'll play this game—on one condition."

"And that is?" Eleanor inquired.

"Let him come down," Richard said of John, "and swear to me on whatever he holds dear that he will be my loyal and faithful servant in all the realms to which I am entitled. There will be no rebellion; no resistance. He will do my bidding when and as I bid him, and be the perfect image of a royal brother. Let him do that, and I will give him his heart's desire. I will name him my successor. But if he breaks that oath, or even strains it, I will find myself another heir."

John left the crown and scepter on the throne with the royal mantle, came down again from the dais, knelt, and set his hands in

Richard's. "I do swear," he said, "to all you wish of me, in the very words you spoke. I'll astonish the world: I'll be a loyal servant, and no longer even pretend to be a rebel."

Richard glared at him. "Do you swear by the crown of Arthur that this is the truth?"

"By the crown of Arthur," John said without hesitation, "I do swear."

Richard's glance was still mistrustful; that would not change easily or quickly. But there was no denying that John had sworn as Richard demanded. "I call our mother to witness," he said, "and the nobles of both kingdoms, and whatever God or gods you worship, that this oath is sworn and sealed."

"Sworn and sealed," said John, "and if while you live I break it, may the earth gape and swallow me, may the sky fall and crush me, and may the sea rise to devour my bones."

With each division of that greatest of oaths, the earth shook. Thunder rumbled. The hall filled with a roaring as of wind, or of the sea crashing on a stony shore.

Arslan descended from the dais with the cup of water from the pool. He bowed to both of them, and offered John the cup. John lifted it to catch both the light of the fire and the shaft of sunlight from the domed roof, and said, "This is the cup of truth. Let us drink it to seal the oath, and to bind us when all else fails."

He drank from the cup, a long draft, as if he had been parched with thirst. When he passed it to Richard, the cup was still full, brimming with clear water.

Richard eyed it warily, but John showed no sign of death by poison. Richard sipped; his eyes widened. "It's good!" he said. He drank it down as if it had been English ale. When he had had his fill, the cup was full again. He grinned at that, giving in a little, at last, to the lure of magic. He bowed as he handed it to Arslan, and turned to his brother. He offered his hand. John took it, clasping it: a contest, and one John could not win, but he put up a valiant fight.

After Richard let him go, John smiled rather tightly, flexing his bruised hand, and said, "Dine with me now, as friend and brother. But first—"

As he spoke, Eschiva had come to stand beside Arslan. In her hands was a shallow bowl of plain and polished silver. In it, steaming gently, lay the sweet pink flesh of a salmon.

# Envoi

## Ynys Witrin
## Midsummer, 1194

The first child of the Lord of Ynys Witrin was born on the eve of Midsummer. It was a daughter and an heir, by the laws of that country; they named her Elen, because she was beautiful, and because Eschiva loved the sound of it.

"My grandmother's name was Helena," Arslan said as he cradled his daughter in his lap. "She was a great lady, and a courtesan, though once she met my grandfather, she lost her desire for anyone else. Do you mind that our child is her namesake?"

"Do you?" asked Eschiva.

"Of course not," Arslan said. "It's an honor to them both."

Eschiva smiled. She was still weary from the birth; it had gone as well as such things did, and all the women said it had been quick—but dusk to dawn was a long labor by his measure. He was glad that she had slid into sleep.

Elen was awake but quiet, taking in this new world with wide wondering eyes. He carried her out of the room in which she had been born, gathering a respectfully silent entourage as he went. He passed through the solar and the hall, across the court and up the stair and onto the battlements of the castle.

It was an old castle, older even than Rome, raised up on a hill in the Summer Country. He had first set eyes on it after the King of England and the king of Britain had come to their accord, when he was freed at last to find his way home. He could have gone east and tried to win back whatever was left of his father's domains, but that had never been more than a passing thought. He went west, with his lady and his squire and the escort that John and Richard both had insisted was proper to his rank and station.

From this, the west tower, he could see the land spread out below,

"This is a royal sacrifice," John said, "a king of his kind, a creature of vast age and ancient wisdom. He gave his life for us, that we may dine on his flesh and all our contentions be healed. Will you eat of it, brother? Will you share it with me?"

Again John tasted first, bowing in reverence, savoring each bite. Richard was less hesitant in this; trust was growing, if slowly. He ate his share with relish, with a kind of bravado. When it was gone—for unlike the water it did not replenish itself—he stood for a long moment as if rapt. "I know," he whispered. "I know what this is. I can hear—I know—"

"Yes," John said. "Adam was forbidden the apple, but no god saw fit to forbid this flesh to those who have need of it. This is wisdom even more than knowledge; a gift of tongues, to understand the speech of beasts and birds; a memory to carry with you into the world."

"You'll never be able to lie to me again," Richard said.

"No," said John.

"You'll have to be trustworthy. You have no choice."

"This is my choice," John said. "I make it freely. It gains me more than it loses, and it will discomfit our enemies rather excessively. That alone makes it worth the cost."

"Doesn't it?" said Richard. He let go his suspicion all at once, and his fit of temper with it; he flung an arm about his brother's shoulders, pulling him into a fierce embrace.

Like their handclasp, it was half war; but it sealed the pact. Arm in arm they ascended the dais. They sat side by side, King of England and King of all Britain, and shared the feast in the manner of kings or of royal brothers: allies and enemies, both at once.

"Leave it to the Devil's brood," Eleanor said. Her expression as she took them in was not quite a smile, but it was clear that she was pleased. "They always knew how to fight a war—and somehow they never quite forgot how to forge a peace."

Richard laughed. John smiled. The queen nodded briskly. "You'll do," she said. "For a moment or two—you'll do."

green and fertile valley and wooded hillside and the silver glimmer of the lake about the tor of Avalon. That was not his land, nor did the inhabitants of the lake and its island shrine pay homage to any man, mortal or otherwise, but it was part of the realm in which he had been made a lord. Eastward, if he turned about, he could see the town which the castle guarded, and the river that ran past it. The olive grove was out of sight to the south, in a valley that could be reached only by certain roads and only at certain times of day. Northward was a long roll of downs and a shadow of forest. Sometimes, when the light fell just so, he could see a city shimmering on the green hills, white walls and shining towers and a gaiety of banners.

"This is your kingdom," he said to the infant in his arms.

Her eyes rested on his face with remarkable steadiness for one so young. His heart filled as he looked down at her, brimmed and over-flowed. He had loved greatly in this world; his kin, his friends, his lady above all, were dear to him beyond words. But this tiny red-faced thing woke in him a feeling so strong, so fierce, that he was not even sure he could call it love. He wanted to guard her, protect her, shield her against all the winds of the worlds.

The wind that blew here was soft, a midsummer wind, full of flower-fragrance. Spirits danced in it, laughing, showering her with blessings. Arslan folded back her swaddlings and held her up so that they could see her. She fit exactly in his two hands, flailing and kicking as infants did, testing the limits of her newborn body.

People were watching from below. The castle was full, for on this day of Midsummer, Hugh Neville the Forester, guardian of Britain, would take to wife Kalila, mamluk's daughter of Beausoleil in the Kingdom of Jerusalem. It was not a marriage the Church would sanction, but here where the worlds met, the Church did not make the laws.

All the guests had been waiting through the night for Elen to be born. Arslan showed her to them as he had to the spirits. They cheered, but softly, so as not to alarm her. She kicked vigorously at the sound.

"Look!" someone said. "She's dancing for us."

Arslan brought her down in a ripple of laughter. She should rest, before her mother woke and came looking for her. He was greatly un-willing to let her out of his sight, but the guests had reminded him: he was lord of the castle; he had a wedding to prepare.

She would be safe in his own bedchamber, with her mother near, and the nurse on whom both Eschiva and Eschiva's mother—O miracle!—had agreed. The woman was quiet, sensible, and possessed of a remarkable gift for magic. She took Elen in her capable arms, reassured Arslan that his child did not need half the castle guard to protect her, and herded him deftly out. He was halfway to the hall before he realized that he had been got rid of—but when he turned to go back, there was Edwy, out of breath, with a crisis among the cooks, and two large parties of noble guests were coming in, and as if that were not enough, the bride had vanished out of even her bridegroom's ken.

Arslan sent his seneschal to settle the war in the kitchens, and Edwy to greet the arrivals. He entrusted Hugh Neville to Father Hugh, who could keep him from flying into shards, and went hunting for Kalila.

She had not gone far. He found her in the olive grove as he had expected, lying on the dry earth under a fiercer sun than had ever shone in England. He turned his own face to it as he walked among the trees, basking in it.

He paused beside her, and sat in the dust. She had put on Turkish coat and trousers, the first time he had seen her in them since she went to Germany. Her arm lay over her eyes; what little of her face he could see was somber. "Regrets?" he asked her.

"No."

"There's a panic in the castle," he said. "Nobody can find you. Your betrothed is half out of his head."

She lowered her arm, squinting in the bright sunlight. "He's what? Idiot. He should know where I am. You did."

"He's not your brother," Arslan said. "He's marrying you today, or hopes he is. That can muddle a man's mind."

"Is there anything that can't? Especially if it has to do with women."

"Not much," he admitted. He studied her carefully. She did not seem in great distress; in fact she looked well. "Are you going to call off the wedding?"

She frowned at him. "What makes you think that?"

"You ran off," he said. "You're not wearing a gown. You haven't said a word to anyone."

"I did need to think," she said. "This is the best place for that. It has real sun. The dust—it catches the lungs, just as it should."

"Do you want to go home?"

She shook her head. "No. No, it's tolerable here. More than that, where he is. He makes even the English sun burn brighter."

"You do love him," Arslan said.

"Did you doubt it?"

"No," he said. "But do you want to marry him?"

"Yes," she said. "I do. That's not what I came here to think about."

"What, then?"

She shrugged a little. "Life. The world—worlds. Birth and death. Children. Things a woman should think of when she gives herself to a husband."

"A man should think of them, too," Arslan said, "or they all come crashing down on his head when his first child is born."

The corner of her mouth curved up. "Difficult night, brother?"

"Beyond belief," he said, "but wonderful—that, too; wonderful beyond imagining."

"Yes," she said. She sat up and clasped her knees. "He's more than twice as old as I am. It doesn't matter at all, except that he's made up his mind; he knows. I think I'm too young to be sure of anything— except him."

"He'd say that was enough."

"Of course he would. He's a man."

Arslan laughed, but painfully. "*Ai!* That hurt. What will you do, then? Wear a turban for the wedding? And armor under your coat?"

"Should I?"

"It would be interesting," he said.

"Uncomfortable, too," she said, "and the very devil to get out of afterward. I think I'll be more decorous after all, even if it leaves the gossips with nothing to say."

"There will always be something to say of Hugh Neville's Turkish wife, whom he married by Druid rite in a sorcerer's castle. Don't ever fear that you'll be dull, sister. You can't be that if you try."

"Nor can you, brother," she said, "or anyone else in this family we've made for ourselves."

There was a silence. It was brief, of necessity, but peaceful. After a while, she said, "I have something of yours, that I'll think you'll be wanting back."

She drew it from her purse, the fiery stone that he had given her before she went to Germany. The sight of it struck him oddly, as if some essential part of him had gone wandering and now had come home.

She laid it in his hand. His fingers closed over it of their own accord. It was warm, full of the memory of her, glowing softly in that fierce eastern light. He slipped the chain about his neck, so that it came to rest over his heart.

Yet he said, "If you want to keep it—"

"It wanted to come home," she said. She sprang to her feet, bold as the boy she so often pretended to be, and held out her hand to pull him up. "Quick, or we'll be late for my wedding."

That was true: the hour was growing late. Yet he paused. "Are you sure?" he asked her. "Because if you're not, no one will force you into anything."

"I am sure," she said. "Really and truly, in Allah's name."

"*Allahu akbar,*" he said: "God is great."

"Hush, you," she said, but she was smiling. They ran back hand in hand, as they had done when they were children. The sound of their laughter ran ahead of them, and reached the castle long before them.

The wedding guests waited in the hall of the castle, dressed in their finery and crowned with garlands. When Hugh Neville came out to stand by the dais where an altar had been raised, a murmur ran through the ranks. He was clad all in green and crowned with green leaves like the woodland lord that he was. Two kings stood at his back, and the Lord Marshal of Britain like a bulwark behind them.

Both Richard and John had come out of the world of the living to stand with this man at his wedding. Richard had some interest in the bride, too, as he professed; for a wedding gift he had given her a manor in Kent, not far from Dover and the sea.

She was so long in coming that Arslan, waiting by the door, began to wonder if she had changed her mind after all. The guests were patient. The celebrants of the rite came out, the Lady Morgana and another lady of the Isle, robed in white, with girdles of golden bells that chimed as they walked; and Eschiva, though Arslan caught his breath at that. She was walking erect, a little more slowly and a little more stiffly than usual, but strong and steady. He would have a word with her afterward. For the moment he would try to trust her, and not fret over her coming so soon from childbed.

The three ladies took their places on the dais. Acolytes followed them, robed in grey and silver. One was Bertrada. Another was Father Hugh, wearing his two faiths with the ease of a philosopher or a saint.

There was always a crowd of spirits in this place. They gave Arslan warning, so that he could turn and greet Kalila. She had Susanna with her, and the Marshal's tall elegant lady, and to his stark astonishment, the Queen of the English. Yet once his eye settled on his sister, there it stayed.

She had not come in a turban after all, nor in armor, either, but her wedding gown was anything but ordinary. It was the full and elaborate finery of her people, tunic and trousers of silk embroidered so thickly that it could have turned a blade, over layer on layer of muslin and linen and silk. She clashed with gold: rings, necklaces, bracelets, armlets, and an extravagant headdress of golden coins strung on chains and ropes of gold, binding the veils about her brows. Her palms were dipped in henna. Her eyes, deep in the veils, were painted with kohl.

It was a proud and defiant thing she did, declaring to this world that she was and would always remain an unrepentant infidel, a Seljuk of the tribe of Alp Arslan the conqueror. Her own Arslan bowed low and offered his hand. She took it, straightened her shoulders, and walked with him into the hall.

She had made her choice, there was no doubt of that. But Arslan eyed her bridegroom narrowly as they paced from the door to the dais. One false move, one flicker of a glance, and Arslan would stop the wedding then and there.

Neville's expression could not have been more reassuring to a brother's heart. He was dazzled; conquered; smitten. When Arslan surrendered that slender hennaed hand into his long strong one, he took it as if it had been the most precious of gifts—which indeed it was, and it was well for him that he knew it.

Arslan barely heard the words that bound them. They were both prayer and spell, invoking powers of earth and heaven, and calling the gods and spirits of this place to witness the vows that these two would take. He was beyond words. This rite in this place, on this day of Midsummer, set the seal on all that he had done since he left La Forêt.

He had been sent to help a king to his throne. He had done that—

and in the doing, been inextricably bound to this kingdom. It was a joyful captivity, nor would he ever wish to be ransomed from it.

The wedding feast went on all the rest of that day and for three days after. If Kalila had been a proper Turkish bride, she would have spent that time in seclusion. But she had never been proper, even as a child. On the first day after the wedding she emerged in Turkish trousers and the turban she had threatened to wear in the rite. On the second day she came out in gown and wimple, which lost a fair few wagers among the guests. But on the third she appeared in tunic and hose, and rode out hunting with her husband and all the guests who were still on their feet after three days of wine and revelry.

Arslan did not go on that hunt. He stayed at home in the sunlit calm of the nursery, singing to Elen, who had had a fretful night. She did not fuss so much when he sang; particularly when he sang the Turkish lullabies that he had learned from his nurse in Beausoleil.

When at last she would consent to sleep, he sat by her cradle, rocking it with his foot. He smiled wearily as Eschiva slid arms about him and leaned against him from behind. "Tell me again that there's nothing wrong with her," he said.

"There's nothing wrong with her," she said, obedient. "Really, my love, there's not. Babies fuss. That's their sacred duty."

"But she's so young," he said, "and so small. A breath of wind could blow out the life in her."

"Not that one," Eschiva said. "She's strong. She was angry, that was all, because she kept herself up watching the spirits dance, and that made her too tired to sleep."

"The spirits? The spirits did it? I'll banish them all."

"Don't," said Eschiva, laughing a little to take the sting out of the word. "They've already been spoken to. They'll be more circumspect after this."

Arslan leaned back against her, sighing as she stroked the ache and the tiredness out of him. "You know what this means," he said.

Her hands paused. "Yes?"

"She's like us. Spirits haunt her."

"You're surprised?"

"No," he said. "I'm pleased, I think. She's going to be formidable. And beautiful."

"Of course. She's our child."

He turned in her arms. "Do you regret it?" he asked. "Any of it?"
"Do you?"

"Not even slightly," he said.

"Nor I," she said. "Not ever, in this world or any other." She stooped and kissed him. "I do love you, O lion of Jerusalem."

"And I you," he said, "O lady of the Isle."

Her smile was almost too bright to bear. But he was half an ifrit; his spirit was fire. He would never be worthy of her, but of this there could be little doubt: he was her match. He swept her into his lap and kissed her until they both were dizzy, and sat with her, deeply content, until the hunters came back from the wood. "No regrets," he murmured. "Not one."